THE BAD WEATHER FRIEND

ALSO BY DEAN KOONTZ

After Death · The House at the End of the World · The Big Dark Sky · Quicksilver · The Other Emily · Elsewhere · Devoted · Ashley Bell · The City · Innocence · 77 Shadow Street · What the Night Knows · Breathless · Relentless · Your Heart Belongs to Me · The Darkest Evening of the Year · The Good Guy · The Husband · Velocity · Life Expectancy · The Taking · The Face · By the Light of the Moon · One Door Away from Heaven · From the Corner of His Eye · False Memory · Seize the Night · Fear Nothing · Mr. Murder · Dragon Tears · Hideaway · Cold Fire · The Bad Place · Midnight · Lightning · Watchers · Strangers · Twilight Eyes · Darkfall · Phantoms · Whispers · The Mask · The Vision · The Face of Fear · Night Chills · Shattered · The Voice of the Night · The Servants of Twilight · The House of Thunder · The Key to Midnight · The Eyes of Darkness · Shadowfires · Winter Moon · The Door to December · Dark Rivers of the Heart · Icebound · Strange Highways · Intensity · Sole Survivor · Ticktock · The Funhouse · Demon Seed

JANE HAWK SERIES

The Silent Corner · The Whispering Room · The Crooked Staircase · The Forbidden Door · The Night Window

ODD THOMAS SERIES

Odd Thomas · Forever Odd · Brother Odd · Odd Hours · Odd Interlude · Odd Apocalypse · Deeply Odd · Saint Odd

FRANKENSTEIN SERIES

Prodigal Son · City of Night · Dead and Alive · Lost Souls · The Dead Town

MEMOIR

A Big Little Life: A Memoir of a Joyful Dog Named Trixie

THE BAD WEATHER FRIEND

DEAN KOONTZ

THOMAS & MERCER

This is a work of fiction. Names, characters, organizations, places, events, and incidents are either products of the author's imagination or are used fictitiously. Any resemblance to actual persons, living or dead, or actual events is purely coincidental.

Published by Thomas & Mercer, Seattle

www.apub.com

ISBN-13: 9781662500497 (hardcover)
ISBN-13: 9781662517778 (paperback)
ISBN-13: 9781662500480 (digital)

Cover design by Damon Freeman

Interior illustrations by Edward Bettison

Cover images: ©Mohamad Itani / ArcAngel; ©Ruben Mario Ramos / ArcAngel; ©Kichigin / Shutterstock; ©Media Bakery13 / Shutterstock

Printed in the United States of America

First edition

This book is dedicated to
Dr. Kim Swanson
for his exceptional kindness.

Man is born unto trouble
as sure as sparks fly upward.

—Job 5:7

Humor is emotional chaos
remembered in tranquility.

—James Thurber

ONE

FLORIDA

Nine feet long, four feet wide, four feet deep, weighing well over a thousand pounds, the crate was a hateful thing, not simply because it was an awkward load that could cause a serious injury to those who had to move it, but also because, well, it gave off what Dooley Peebles called "weird vibes" and what his pal Rosco Moseley described as "bad mojo."

Dooley and Rosco were employees of Mayweather Universal Air Freight. On a humid afternoon in October, in a box truck containing a long-tine forklift rated for four thousand pounds, they arrived at the colonel's warehouse in Boca Raton, Florida.

A flock of red-crowned parrots were busy eating nuts that the colonel had scattered on the pavement for them. As the truck drew near, the birds flurried skyward, a flung Joseph's coat of flashing colors.

Colonel Talmadge Clerkenwell looked older than Florida. His three-piece linen suit glowed as white as his hair, mustache, and goatee. If he hadn't been rail thin and standing as straight as a plumb line, you might have thought he was the fabled founder of the KFC restaurant chain.

The crate, like the colonel, was waiting on the concrete apron outside the warehouse. Rosco Moseley hated the thing on sight and dubbed it "the Beast."

Colonel Clerkenwell was courteous, so affable and at ease that it seemed he must have spent his life loving and being loved through a long smoothness of days. He was also mysterious. No sign suggested what the warehouse might contain. The colonel responded to questions about the place and the shipment with such graceful elusion that it almost sounded as if he had answered them.

The pickup order said the customer was shipping books to one Benjamin Catspaw at an address in California, which made no sense. Not that people in California didn't read books. They probably did. Or used to. But a thousand pounds of books would have been packed in several smaller, more easily handled containers.

The colonel had paid dearly to have his shipment picked up by appointment rather than during the course of Dooley and Rosco's regular schedule. It was to be taken directly to a cargo jet then loading in Miami. Yet the colonel declined to pay extra for more insurance than the standard contract provided, which was two dollars per pound. Dooley was required to offer the enhanced coverage, but Clerkenwell just smiled and said, "Oh, they're nothing but a few hundred old books. The value is purely sentimental."

Although Dooley warmed to most people only after he got to know them well, he liked the colonel within a minute of meeting the old guy. Dooley did not like liars, because he'd come from a family of them who lived by deceit and were as likely to defraud relatives as they were to steal from anyone else. He felt sure that the colonel was lying about the crate being full of books, but Clerkenwell had a quality that suggested he never lied about anything important, neither to obtain an advantage nor to harm another person.

Dooley didn't know what that quality was, couldn't define it, at least not right then, with the gray sky lowering and rain coming soon and the crate needing to be forked into the truck. It was an intuitive perception, almost psychic.

With the crate aboard, on the way to the airport, with Dooley behind the wheel, Rosco Moseley said, "Books, my ass. More like we been made associates to a crime."

"Accessories," Dooley Peebles corrected. "But the colonel isn't a criminal. Just maybe eccentric."

"How you know?" Rosco demanded, and then he answered his own question. "You can't know." He was a hulk with a good heart and a quick mind in which, unfortunately, fantasy and reality were as tightly braided as dreadlocks. His vivid imagination tended toward the flamboyant and the dire. "What if we got ourselves a crate of cocaine?"

"Nobody transports drugs this way," Dooley said.

"So then what if it's a dead body?"

Dooley chuckled. "A one-thousand-pound corpse?"

"Could be four or five stiffs."

"The colonel isn't a serial killer."

"Anyone could be. I could be, you'd never know."

"Oh, I'd know," Dooley assured him.

"How'd you know?"

"You'd tell me. Over and over. Every detail. You're not good with secrets."

The colonel had given each of them a small white envelope. Rosco turned his between thumb and forefinger. "I got me a bad feelin' about this."

"It's a tip," Dooley said. Few people tipped freight handlers no matter how much sweat the load broke out of them, but it happened once in a while. "You suddenly don't like money, give it to me."

"If it's a tip," Rosco said, "why he didn't just fold a bill to each of us?"

"He's old school. Discreet. He's got style."

Rosco tore open the envelope and extracted a pair of hundred-dollar bills. "Double damn! I knew this was trouble."

"Two hundred bucks is your idea of trouble?"

"It was a ten, even a twenty, okay. This shit means he's buyin' our souls."

"*My* soul's priced a lot higher," Dooley said.

A man of many superstitions, Rosco crumpled the bills in his fist and solemnly declared, "I got to find a church, put this in a poor box, clean me of it."

At the airport, the Mayweather jet was taking on cargo. Rosco worked the forklift, while Dooley got the paperwork straight with the guys who would take possession of the crate and get it properly secured aboard the plane.

When he inserted the paperwork—with the recipient's address—in a plastic envelope that was fixed to the crate, Dooley pretended to shudder as if he had received a shock and, in a stage whisper, fearfully declared, *"It's alive!"*

"Asshole," Rosco said.

The funny thing was, when Dooley smoothed his hand across the flap of the packet to seal it, a strange feeling quivered through him, so strange that his pretense of a shudder became a real, icy chill. It passed quickly. He didn't know what the moment meant, so he put it out of mind.

Later, he called Cecelia, his wife, to tell her about the two hundred bucks. "Don't cook tonight. Order in whatever you and the kids want, have Grubhub bring it." On the way home, he stopped at a Baskin-Robbins to buy an ice cream cake.

Dooley was fundamentally a family guy, and not a clueless goof like those on TV. He loved—adored—Cecelia and their two teenage daughters. There was nowhere he would rather be than at home. They shared the news of their day over dinner and then ate too much ice cream cake while playing 500 Rummy.

He was so content in his uncomplicated life that his dreams were always pleasant. That night, the white-suited colonel came to him in sleep, walking out of a dazzling turbulence of hundreds of swooping parrots, escorted by a dozen earthbound flamingos, with a white cockatoo perched on his right shoulder. It was quite unlike any other dream Dooley had experienced. In this dreaming, Dooley realized what quality Talmadge Clerkenwell possessed that he had previously sensed but could not name, which made him so certain the old man never lied about anything important, never to obtain an advantage or to harm someone. The quality was kindness, profound benevolence extended not merely to all men and women and children, but also to animals. Surrounded by bright flamingos that stood in a reverent stillness, the colonel spoke, although his voice came from the cockatoo on his shoulder. He asked Dooley to forget the crate had been unusual in any way, to remember it as just another crate. To forget the chill he'd felt when he sealed the invoice envelope. To forget the name of the recipient, Benjamin Catspaw. To forget the address to which the crate had been sent. And Dooley did forget. As the cargo jet cruised through the night, westering high above the earth, in his bed Dooley erased all—but only—what he'd been asked to delete from his memory.

The cockatoo fell silent, and the voice came from the colonel himself when he said, *"But remember me, Dooley Peebles. Remember me if ever the world goes so wrong that there seems no way to make it right again."*

Then the cockatoo flew off his shoulder, and the flamingos took flight, whirling away with the parrots that had been floating at the perimeter of the dreamscape. Wings bloomed from the old man, and he also flew away. Dooley thought he, too, could fly; he tried, but it wasn't that kind of dream.

A BAD MORNING

Benny Catspaw was twenty-three when he decided that he wasn't paranoid, that in fact someone was out to get him. He didn't think anyone meant to murder him. There were many ways to "get" someone short of shooting him in the head. There were gangs that sometimes merely cut off your legs and ears, while others were satisfied with throwing acid in your face, and still others neutered you and left you with a photo of your package so that you could study it in your old age and wax nostalgic about what might have been. The United States had opened itself to a wide variety of international gangs; the Mafia wasn't the only game in town anymore. The thugs of more recent vintage prided themselves on their flamboyance and on the fact that they were no less psychologically than physically cruel. Nor did Benny believe that anyone was trying to ensure that he would be committed to an asylum; he was not Ingrid Bergman gaslighted by Charles Boyer. For sure, however, someone was trying to thwart him.

Thwart: to hinder, obstruct, frustrate, baffle.

For three years, he'd been a licensed real-estate agent working with Hanson "Handy" Duroc, who founded Surfside Realty, one of the most successful brokerages in Orange County, California. Located in Newport Beach but with listings countywide, Surfside specialized in properties with an ocean view or with a dock on the fabled yacht harbor, as well as focusing on estates in the most prestigious gate-guarded communities. Although Benny had come from nothing and had known more than his share of disappointment, he had big dreams and worked hard. He wasn't among the top five agents at Surfside, but he expected to ascend to that honored realm in two or three years.

Surfside operated out of a quaint, beachy, two-story white-and-yellow building on Pacific Coast Highway in Corona del Mar, which had long ago been annexed by Newport Beach. On the far side of the alleyway behind their offices, a vacant lot was an invaluable asset in this parking-challenged community. On this warm Tuesday morning in October, Benny slotted his Ford Explorer among the gleaming vehicles belonging to his fellow agents—a flotilla of Mercedes and enough Teslas to collapse the power grid.

He used the back entrance, which required a key because even in this monied community, there were drug-addled vagrants who were of the opinion that an unlocked alley door was an invitation to step inside and bunk down or urinate. Before Handy Duroc had ordered that the door must remain locked, an MS-13 enforcer named Santiago—with a shaved head, a second face tattooed on the back of his skull—had paid them a visit in search of a cook with whom he had a score to settle. The cook worked in the trendy restaurant two doors south of the realty offices. The enforcer was so incensed by his error that he wanted to pistol-whip and execute someone working at Surfside—he didn't care whom—to reassure himself that he wasn't losing his edge. He chose Tina Finestra, the firm's number two agent, who weighed one hundred and ten pounds. This was his second mistake. Tina had twelve years of martial-arts training. And attitude. She was determined that no thug from El Salvador would prevent her from conducting a series of showings she had scheduled for a client who was qualified to buy a house in the thirty-million-dollar range. She smashed Santiago's nose, took his gun, breaking two of his fingers in the process, and drove him headfirst into a wall. He fell to the floor, stunned, flat on his back, and Tina dropped on him, using the gun butt to hammer his crotch repeatedly until he passed out. Tina was on time for her first appointment with her clients, and when the police revived the unconscious Santiago, he cried like the child that he was now unlikely ever to father.

This October morning, when Benny Catspaw let himself in by the alley door and locked it behind him, the first person whom he saw was Tina Finestra. Her blond mane looked as if her personal live-in hairdresser micromanaged every strand before she'd left her house. A Botoxed, lip-plumped laser-smoothed blemish-free wonder, she was thirty-two but could pass for twenty even if you didn't squint. She was dressed as though about to film a frivolous cable-TV show titled *Realtors to the Stars*, but she projected the no-nonsense savvy and confidence of a business genius who was also a ninja assassin. There were times when Benny found her desirable, but she scared him so much that he never seriously considered asking her for a date. He suspected that her lovers had a life expectancy approximately that of the mate to a female praying mantis.

She favored him with a smile so warm that he knew he was in some kind of trouble when she said, "Handy wants to see you in his office."

This was the second Tuesday of the month, which always began with a gathering of agents in the second-floor conference room for what Handy called a "dirt review." By the word *"dirt"* he meant *real estate*, properties on the market or soon to be. He would know every listing held by other firms that were coming to an end without a sale having been made, and he would discuss how best the sellers might be cajoled into switching to Surfside. Among other subjects were the ideal price for each new listing and the price reductions needed for "blind, tasteless turkeys," which were houses that drew no interest because they lacked a view and were the creations of architects better suited to designing prisons and pissoirs.

The door to Handy's office stood open, and though it bore no resemblance to the gates of Hell as they were usually depicted, Benny hovered silently in the hallway for a long moment before rapping gingerly on the frame. Handy called out, "Come in, come in," in that affable voice that suggested he was always expecting someone who delighted him. "Ah, it's you, Benny," he said, still buoyant but slightly deflated, as might be a man who needed to tell a friend that a mutual, valued acquaintance had just been shot by his wife, though not mortally. He came to Benny and clapped him on the shoulder and closed the door and said, "Sit down, son, take a load off," as he led him to one of four armchairs arranged in a circle.

At forty-eight, Handy was old enough to be Benny's father, but he'd never before called Benny "son." Between the ages of seventeen and twenty, Hanson Duroc had been a lifeguard on the main beach in Newport, before he had segued into the dirt business. He was six feet three, as fit as a twenty-year-old, as smooth faced as a thirty-year-old, and as perfectly tanned as though God personally airbrushed him with light of a higher quality than mere sunshine. His teeth gleamed whiter than white. His eyes blazed bluer than blue. His hair was waxed into a stiff, stylish, blond flame—yet he didn't look ridiculous, as did most middle-aged men who strove to appear youngish by adopting that coiffure.

By contrast, Benny was five feet ten, with a thatch of unruly brown hair, eyes the color of weak tea, a nose that reminded him of Dustin Hoffman in *The Graduate*, and a tan that would have been a lot sexier if it hadn't caused his smattering of freckles to brighten into flecks of molten copper. When he compared himself to Handy Duroc, which he didn't dare do often, he took comfort in the fact that he was considerably more intelligent than the broker. Benny was confident that intelligence mattered most, and that it guaranteed his eventual ascent to the heights—though when he considered any aspect of contemporary America, from business to politics to the arts to the sciences, he had to admit that flash, filigree, and flimflam defeated substance almost every time. However, he had faith that this triumph of sizzle and sham was a transient condition, a blip, in the noble arc of this great nation that had for centuries mostly rewarded merit and hustle.

Handy's office lacked a desk. In addition to the armchairs and attendant side tables, two straight-backed chairs could be pulled into the circle as needed. Classic surfboards hung on one wall, museum lighted, as if they were the equivalent of David Hockney canvases. The centerpiece of the room was an intricately detailed, exquisitely painted, half-life-size model of a McLaren Speedtail standing on a glossy white plinth as large as a double bed. Among other vehicles, Handy owned a Mercedes-Benz SLS AMG, a Porsche 911 Turbo S Cabriolet, a Bentley Mulsanne, a 1967 Shelby GT500CR, and a Corvette Grand Sport. His dream was to own a Speedtail, which went for about two and a half million dollars, but as yet he could afford only the model he'd commissioned from an artist. He was a car guy.

Benny would have been embarrassed to display a half-life-size model of what he coveted the most—whether a McLaren Speedtail or the actress Riley Keough. Such a bold objectification of desire seemed pitiable, pretentious yet childishly needy at the same time. Handy, of course, saw the model McLaren as a proud statement of his ambition, commitment, and confidence in his business acumen.

As they settled into armchairs, Handy sitting immediately to Benny's left, the broker said, "Son, I believe you have a bright future, a truly astonishing future, in real estate. I think you've got everything it takes. I'm not blowing smoke, not bullshitting you. Hey, you know me, a straight shooter. If I'm not a straight shooter, I'm nothing. And we all know I'm not nothing."

Benny's sense that he was in trouble matured into a conviction that his life was about to be turned upside down. He said, "Uh, well."

Handy made a sweeping gesture toward the wall opposite the array of surfboards, where he had hung a collection of framed photographs of himself with baseball stars, basketball greats, football icons, famous actors, rappers, rock and rollers, gods of golf, and grinning politicians who had gotten away with historic levels of graft, all of whom had used the services of Surfside Realty in multimillion-dollar transactions. "I have so many great friends. I'm connected, wired into the power structure, up with it and down with it, inside where everyone outside wants to be." He began that speech with a smile and spoke with a lilt. But then he scowled, and a darkness came into his voice. "I don't like to be pressured. I don't like to be told what to do."

Benny tried never to rock the proverbial boat because, in his experience, the boat rocked often enough of its own accord. "I would never tell you what to do," he assured the broker.

"Here's the thing, Benny," Handy said. Then he stared at the sun-splashed day beyond a second-floor window and fell silent.

After maybe half a minute, Benny said, "What thing?"

Brow furrowed with anger, Handy leaned sideways in his chair and said, "I'm a big fish. Maybe I'm not a whale, but I'm a great white shark. Am I not a great white shark?"

"At least. At least a great white."

Handy screwed up his face as if he would spit, but he didn't.

He pounded the arm of his chair three times with one fist. "The trouble is, I'll never be Moby Dick."

Benny heard himself saying, "Well, maybe that's not a bad thing, people coming after you with harpoons and all."

Returning his attention to the blue sky beyond the window, Handy Duroc grew silent again. His face settled into a philosophical grimace, or maybe that was how he had looked on his lifeguard tower when he'd searched the ocean for a drowner. Then he shook himself. "Not being Moby Dick—that isn't a reference to my schlong."

"I know."

"I'm plenty big in that department."

"Of course," Benny said and nodded in agreement.

"The thing is, I could one day own a dozen McLaren Speedtails, and I'd for sure *feel* like a whale. But, damn it, I still wouldn't be one. There are already people in this world who could buy like a hundred McLarens and a hundred houses to go with them, and still have a lot more money in the bank than I ever will. They're like the ocean, see, and I'll never be more than a swimmer with nobody who can save me if I start drowning. And you know why, Catspaw?"

Benny thought for a moment, not because he believed he might be able to answer the question—he didn't even fully understand it—but because he had noticed that he'd gone from "son" to "Benny" and now to "Catspaw," which seemed to be a dangerous trajectory. He was in some kind of trouble, knew not why, and needed to guard his words. He said, "No. Why?"

"Because money is power, and a lot of sick people love power even more—a lot more—than they love money."

"I see," Benny said, though he didn't.

Leaning forward in his chair and to his right, reaching out with one hand and clasping Benny's knee as if laying claim to it, Handy said, "There's not much in this world you can trust, Catspaw. But one damn thing you can bet the bank on."

"What's that?" Benny asked.

"I don't give a shit about power over others. I'm just all about money. Give me a mountain of money, and that's all I want, money and all the cool stuff it can buy. I've got my head on straight."

Deciding it was safe to say "you do," Benny said it. Then he added, "I've always said that about you," though he'd never said it until now. He wasn't being obsequious. He was merely confused and worried, saying what he thought might result in getting the hand removed from his knee.

Instead, Handy squeezed his knee and said, "I'm glad that we understand each other."

Benny looked into those bluer-than-blue eyes and considered saying that the point of this conversation eluded him.

Just then Handy let go of the knee and smiled broadly and breathed a sigh of relief and said, "You're aces, Catspaw. I'm glad you understand that all this is beyond my control. That makes it so much easier. No need to attend the monthly dirt review, of course. Just clear out your desk, turn in your door key, and you're free to go. Tina Finestra will take whatever showings you have scheduled, and of course you'll still receive your commissions on any listings you brought in, when they sell and the escrow closes."

Handy Duroc sprang to his feet as if concluding this business had relieved him of a great weight and energized him for the day ahead.

Benny didn't consciously get up from his chair, but seemed rather to be drawn out of it by an updraft created by the taller, bigger, far richer Duroc. "You mean I'm fired?"

Seeming to find that question amusing, Handy issued a brief, husky laugh. "No, no, no. How could you be? You're an independent, licensed agent. The agreement between you and Surfside is an at-will contract. Either of us is free to terminate at any time, as we both just did."

Bewildered, Benny said, "I wasn't aware I terminated."

Handy responded to bewilderment with puzzlement. "Huh? But we just . . . our little chat . . . We understood each other."

"I didn't understand any of it," Benny said.

"I'm not a whale, just a shark," Handy reminded him. "Remember how I said some people love power more than money? How I don't give a shit about power? How all I want is money?"

"Yeah, well, but what does that have to do with me?"

Handy stood there with his mouth hanging open. He looked as if he might dispense a can of cola if Benny put enough quarters in his ear. He blinked, blinked, found words, and said, "You're angry. I was hoping this wouldn't get ugly."

"I'm not angry," Benny assured him.

That was true. Benny never got angry. Not with other people. Not with computers that crashed or pop-up toasters that didn't pop. If people were mean or stupid, he simply avoided them. If a toaster betrayed his trust, he never again bought anything by the company that manufactured it. He believed that life was too short to waste time being enraged or even just peeved; he was aware that this made him an outlier in an age when it seemed a majority of the population was incensed about so many things that enumerating them would result in a list longer than what a greedy child might send to Santa Claus. In fact, even the idea of Santa Claus infuriated some people to the extent that department-store St. Nicks were rarer than they used to be and vulnerable to attack.

"You're angry," Handy insisted.

"No. I just want to understand. What did I do? What happened? What's wrong? Can we straighten this out?"

Handy Duroc's face was taut with anxiety, as Benny had never seen it before. The broker glanced at the phone that stood on the table beside one of the armchairs, at the closed door, at a window, at the other window, as if he might call for security or escape by throwing himself through a pane of glass into the street below. At last he said, "You didn't do anything. Nothing happened. Nothing's wrong. There's nothing to straighten out." He shuddered and wiped one hand over his suddenly damp face. "Now you're going to sue me, aren't you?"

Perplexed, Benny said, "I'm not going to sue you. It's an at-will contract, like you said. I don't have any reason to sue you."

"People sue people all the time for no good reason."

"Well, I don't. I just want to understand. Haven't we done good work together?"

Handy went to a window and stared across the street for a few seconds, and then moved to the other window for a longer period. When he turned to face Benny, he stepped to one side of the glass, as if he'd seen a sniper with a rifle on a rooftop. "I think you're a good guy."

"Well, gee, I think I am, too. I try to be."

"You're a hardworking agent."

"It's my way up, to have something, be something."

Handy wasn't just a broker, he was also a first-rate salesman. He could have sold life insurance to the dead. Benny expected to buy whatever explanation Handy gave for terminating their contract, but he needed to hear it.

Holding his arms out, hands turned up, as though to indicate that he had nothing to offer, Handy said, "I just can't help you understand. How can I when I don't understand it myself?"

"You must understand more than I do," Benny pressed.

"I *know* more than you do, but I don't understand a damn thing."

"So tell me what you know. Maybe it'll make sense to me."

"I can't."

"Why not?"

Handy went to the big scale model of the McLaren Speedtail. He slid one hand over its sleek contours. Lovingly.

Benny waited.

"Son . . ."

They were back to "son," but Benny didn't find that reassuring. After all, his real father had not been either a good husband or a champion of thoughtful parenting.

"Son, I'm not a whale."

"But you're a great white."

"A great white that doesn't want to be reduced to a minnow." He sounded very sad. And afraid. "I wish you well. But that's all I can do. Wish you well. Clear out your office, turn in your key, and have a good life."

Handy had always looked younger than he was. Now he appeared older. He didn't seem to be as tall, either. Shrunken in more ways than his height.

Benny said, "Whatever this is, I'm sorry."

Focused on the Speedtail, Handy Duroc said, "It's nothing you've done."

Benny said, "I mean, this isn't you, and I'm sorry that for whatever reason you've been forced to be something you're not. That's a terrible thing."

When Handy did not respond, Benny left the office. He cleared out his desk. He turned in his key.

(What has happened thus far to Benny is unfair and sad. We've all endured too much unfairness and sadness in our lives; exposing ourselves to more of the same in stories like this could be healing, but it might also risk opening new psychological wounds. Therefore, be assured that while more unfairness will ensue, Benny is too nice and sweet-tempered to be undone by it. The sadness will diminish as the chapters unfold, though some events will require a handkerchief. Also be prepared for shocking developments that overturn everything you thought you knew about the nature of the world as well as for a few moments of almost unendurable terror.)

So Benny Catspaw left Handy Duroc's office, cleared out his desk, turned in his key, and thought, *Some days it doesn't pay to get out of bed.* Nevertheless, he was glad he'd risen and showered and shaved as if he had a job to go to, because now he could join Fat Bob at Papa Bear's and have a to-die-for breakfast.

FAT BOB

Robert Jericho, fifty-nine years old, took no offense at being called fat; he insisted on it. His business card read ROBERT "FAT BOB" JERICHO. His six-foot-two frame carried three hundred ten pounds, but he wasn't sloppy. His flesh was curiously solid. He likened it to the density of ham, which he said was appropriate, considering how much he enjoyed being the center of attention. Every three years, he underwent a CT scan of his arteries to see whether he should start going to church, but in spite of eating everything that his doctor told him not to eat, he never had any plaque. His resting heart rate was sixty, his blood pressure 120/70. His dad, Fat Jim Jericho, had weighed in excess of three hundred pounds all his adult life and lived to be ninety-seven, when he was shot to death by a jealous husband. Fat Bob was of the opinion that he had inherited good genes and that he would outlive his father if he led a more discreet love life.

When Benny Catspaw got to Papa Bear's at 8:48, Fat Bob was ensconced in his favorite booth, at a window table that overlooked Newport Harbor, enjoying a pot of coffee and a double order of cinnamon toast while he perused the menu and decided what to have for breakfast. Bob was a handsome man with thick hair the gray of early Glock plastic and eyes the deep-copper color of certain brands of full-metal-jacket ammunition. He had one tattoo, on the pads of the index finger of his right hand—the word BANG—to emphasize his meaning when, with that finger and adjacent thumb, he made a gun and pointed it at someone. He'd only shot six people with a real gun and only killed two, in every case justifiably; however, with finger and thumb, he'd often expressed his preference for mortal intervention when he had to deal with those to whom he referred as the "squirming vermin of society."

As Benny slid into the booth, across the table from his friend, Fat Bob said, "I know a guy who can do something with your hair."

"It's a thatch," Benny said.

"Only because you don't know how to deal with it."

"I don't want to look slick."

"No danger of that."

"I think the hair, it makes me look like a regular guy, like I'm not on the make. Clients trust me more because of the hair."

"If that's a delusion you need," said Fat Bob, "kiss it on the lips and be happy."

"The way I look worked with you, I think. You bought the first house I showed you and didn't want to haggle with the sellers."

"The price was fair. I didn't buy the place because I trusted your hair."

The ponytailed waitress arrived to take their order, and Fat Bob, being a daily patron, introduced her as Harper. She wore pink sneakers, a lemon-yellow skirt, and a sky-blue blouse. The tiny pink pigs in her necklace were on their hind feet as if dancing across her throat. Her eyes were a reasonable shade of blue, rather than the electric blue of color-enhancing contacts, and she wore no makeup. Efficient, perhaps a little shy, but with a perky quality, Harper seemed to be the kind of girl with whom Benny might have a chance, assuming she had any interest in men.

At the moment, of course, he was in a relationship with Jill Swift, and they really seemed to be going somewhere great together. Therefore, he didn't struggle to say anything charming to Harper, but merely ordered a cheese omelet, bacon, and home fries. And a beer, his first ever with breakfast. He didn't like mimosas, and wine this early in the day seemed to guarantee acid reflux. In his current mood, if he plunged into something as strong as vodka, he would soon be deep in three martinis and need to be Ubered home. Consequently, he said, "Corona. A bottle of Corona, please."

After Fat Bob ordered chicken and waffles to be followed by a stack of blueberry pancakes with a side order of strawberries and cream, he said to Benny, "So did Jill throw you over for a Russian oligarch with a billion dollars and one eyebrow?"

Benny flinched. "Why would you say such a thing?"

"The beer. And there's a new wave of Russian money washing through local real estate. Besides, I never have understood the two of you. She's a steak knife, and you're a dessertspoon."

"I've never been compared to flatware before. And you're being unfair to Jill."

"So if Jill hasn't forked you, what's wrong?"

Harper brought the Corona with a frosted glass. When she departed, Benny said, "I'm . . . taking leave."

"Of what? Your senses?"

"Of Surfside Realty."

"Taking leave. You're going to have a baby?"

Trying not to chug the Corona, too embarrassed to make eye contact, Benny stared out at the harbor as he explained.

Majestic white yachts and smaller pleasure craft plied the sparkling waters under a clear sky in which seagulls performed aerial ballets and squadrons of pelicans floated effortlessly on thermal currents. The window seemed to offer a glimpse of a better world than the dark and confusing one in which Benny now found himself.

"So I haven't been fired exactly," he concluded, "but I've been somethinged, and I don't know why."

As Harper arrived with the detective's waffles and Benny's platter, Fat Bob said to her, "What would you do with his hair?"

Her face puckered in puzzlement. "His hair? Why would I want to do anything with his hair?"

"I'm not offering it to you, dear," said Fat Bob. "I meant, if you were a stylist."

"I like his hair," she said. "He looks so . . . natural."

"Exactly," Benny said as he unfolded his napkin on his lap.

Cocking her head to consider his hair, she said to Benny, "You might comb it, that's all."

"I did comb it. I comb it ten, twenty times a day."

"Oh." She picked up the empty bottle of Corona. "You want another one?"

"If I'm to hold on to my sanity, yes."

"I'll bring you a fresh frosted glass, too."

"You're an angel," Benny said. Then in a spirit of political correctness, he quickly added, "Unless you're offended to be called an angel."

Even as good as it was, her face was transformed for the better by a smile. "I've been called worse."

Harper went away to get the beer, and Fat Bob said, "I'll look into this situation for you."

"Handy Duroc? There's nothing to look into. Whatever's behind this, he's not talking."

Taking a knife and fork to his chicken and waffles, with an expression that suggested he was, with animosity, carving something more terrible, Fat Bob said, "He's not talking to you, but he'll talk to me."

For twenty-seven years, Robert Jericho, a former Los Angeles homicide cop, had been a private investigator with a staff of eight. He refused to accept assignments to gather evidence for divorce proceedings—which he referred to as "mutually assured destruction derbies"—or skip-tracer jobs, or requests to assist anyone trying to obtain a conservatorship over a family member. He worked for class-action attorneys and insurance companies and banks. However, he specialized in serving well-heeled individuals innocent of any illegality, who faced threats of all kinds and who distrusted the authorities, preferring to gather evidence against aggressors privately rather than risk inviting politicized police agencies or corrupt justice-system officials into their lives and, by so doing, be jackknifed from genuine victim into falsely accused criminal by some ideological zealot with a badge. Fat Bob prospered.

"It's no big deal," Benny said. "I'll sign on with another brokerage. Anyway, I can't afford you."

"Hey, hey, I wouldn't charge a friend in need." Fat Bob chose to be offended, thrusting an accusing fork at Benny, a gesture that would have been more impressive if a chunk of chicken and waffle had not been speared on the tines. "Besides, I also do pro bono work for people with disabilities."

"Another crack about my hair."

"Entirely not. Your hair is a burden, not a disability. I'm referring to your niceness."

"Since when is niceness a disability?"

"Since there's been less of it week by week, which is most of my lifetime. Your problem is that you're nice to everyone, even to those who spit on you, like Handy Duroc."

"Handy didn't spit on me."

Still emphasizing his words with the loaded fork, Fat Bob said, "He spit on you, and then he pissed on you."

"Handy was torn up by it. Full of regret." Benny sighed and drank some beer. "Anyway, I'm not so nice. I can be a real bastard."

Fat Bob laughed. He stopped laughing long enough to chew and swallow. Then he laughed again. "If you're going to be nice even to people who spit on you, then you've at least got to acknowledge what swine they are. Otherwise, you'll just put yourself in a position where they can spit on you again."

"What is this obsession with spitting?"

Fat Bob shrugged. "It's a world of spitters. How's the omelet?"

"It's good. Except . . ."

"Too much hot sauce?"

"No. But now I keep wondering if maybe someone in the kitchen spat in it."

DRIVING HOME, BENNY REMEMBERS HIS FATHER

At ten o'clock on a rainy night in May, when Benny was seven years old, his father—Albert, Big Al to some—came home drunk and belligerent, which was the case at least twice a week in those days. His dad was a teacher and a coach who, although young, had held half a dozen positions in public and private schools from which he either quit or was fired before being tenured. The principal or headmaster or district superintendent was reliably an "asshole" or a "control freak" or "as dumb as a brick of shit," and Al hadn't gotten an education just to be bossed around by fools. That year, he had found employment in a public high school so racked by student violence that his formidable size and his inclination to punch people were considered essential qualifications for the position.

They lived in a two-bedroom rented bungalow with occasional cockroaches that moved so slowly you could make a game of stalking them and capturing them with a jar, in which they exhibited no frenzy typical to their species, but instead crouched in resignation for a day or two, until they perished for lack of oxygen or from a cause undetermined. Most often, when a bug appeared on the scene, it was already dead. Benny's mother, Naomi, believed the bungalow—in fact the entire neighborhood—had been built on toxic fill and that every day they lived there took *two* days off their lifespan. She wouldn't allow the dead roaches to be thrown in the trash or flushed down the toilet; she buried them with sympathy in a corner of the backyard.

Naomi, who worked in a vintage clothing store, was a dedicated vegan, although once a month she would fall off the wagon, buy a box of Entenmann's chocolate-covered doughnuts, give one to Benny, and eat the rest in a single sitting, washing them down with a quart of whole milk. Sometimes this descent into sin would so distress her that she would fling herself into an hour-long crying jag. On that night in May, when Big Al came home drunk and bloody, Naomi was lying down in their bedroom, suffering through a migraine.

Benny perched in a chair at the kitchen table, plugging LEGOs into one another. His grandma Dora, Big Al's mother, had sent him a large box of them at Christmas. The kitchen contained a TV and a radio, but they both stood silent. Often the bungalow was full of too much noise, and sometimes Benny needed quiet. He was awake at that hour because he set his own schedule, sleeping in as late as he wished, staying up until he grew bored with being awake. He wouldn't be going to school until September; even then he might not conform to the hours of the education establishment, because his mom hoped to homeschool him.

When Big Al threw open the back door with such force that it slammed into the side of the refrigerator, Benny wasn't frightened or even startled. His father usually came home with a sense of drama from a night of hard drinking. A bruise darkened half Al's forehead, and blood dripped from his split lip, but those details didn't alarm Benny, either, for they were almost as familiar as the crash of the door bouncing off the fridge. His dad was a bar fighter whenever he could find another drunk who was willing to put up his fists.

"*That* sonofabitch got what was coming to him," Big Al declared, raising a fist full of skinned knuckles, grinning broadly. "He'll be crawling home, spitting out teeth all the way, and spend the night puking in the toilet."

His adversary disproved this prediction by stepping through the open door behind Big Al and shooting him once in the back. Benny's father fell facedown on the kitchen floor, and Benny put aside the LEGO block he had been about to snap into his construction.

In truth, the shooter looked like he'd taken quite a beating. His left eye had swelled shut. His nose seemed to be askew. Half his face was dark and swollen. Standing just inside the door, he kicked Big Al twice, seemed to be satisfied, and then turned his attention to the heir of the family misfortune. "So what the hell is that?" he asked, pointing to the curving structure on the table.

"LEGOs," Benny said.

"I know they're goddamn LEGOs," the killer said, words issuing from him with flecks of blood. "What're you making with 'em?"

"Stairs to the moon," Benny said.

"Stairs to the moon?" The idea appeared to anger the stranger. "There aren't any stairs to the moon."

Benny said, "There will be when I make them."

Taking two steps toward the table, the killer raised the pistol so the boy could look down the barrel.

Benny didn't try to run because he knew he wouldn't get far. He was scared, but he wasn't terrified. He'd been witness to more than a little violence before this. You got used to it. He was only four feet tall, weighed maybe sixty pounds. When you were his size, you couldn't do much but wait to see what would happen.

He looked up from the muzzle of the gun and said, "I think it's quiet on the moon. I like when it's quiet."

The stranger stared at him for a long moment, then lowered the gun. "Shit, you're just some kind of dummy. You won't even remember I was here." He returned to the night.

After counting to ten, Benny got off his chair and went around the table and looked down at his father. There was no doubt about Big Al's condition.

Benny went to his parents' bedroom and eased the door open. The knob made a scratchy sound. The hinges creaked. He stepped across the threshold.

The room was mostly dark. One lamp glowed. A towel had been draped over the shade. His mother was lying on her back, on the disheveled bed. It was always disheveled.

When she was deep in a migraine, it was as if she'd stepped out of this world for a while. If she'd heard the gunshot, she probably thought it was just Big Al slamming the door shut after he'd crashed it open.

Naomi moaned softly. The sound had an impatient quality, which meant she wanted Benny to go away without having to speak the words.

He said only, "You won't have to worry about him hitting you anymore," and he quietly closed the door.

LOS ANGELES

The Mayweather Universal Air Freight facility associated with LAX contained hundreds of cardboard cartons and sturdy wooden crates of various sizes and shapes. They were stacked on wheeled pallets, with the north side of the building reserved for outbound freight, the south side for incoming.

The shipment from Boca Raton had arrived during the night—the plane was still being unloaded—and the crate stood now on its own pallet. Judging by the unusual size and shape of the container, Felix Domenico figured it must house a cast-metal part for a large machine, maybe an armature that couldn't be sent in pieces.

When he checked the paperwork in the attached plastic packet, he saw that the sender wasn't a manufacturer and the recipient wasn't an industrial enterprise; both were individuals, and the contents were books. He was suspicious.

Before being loaded on the plane in Florida, the consignment had been cleared by state-of-the-art digital-olfaction robotics that analyzed molecules rising out of the crate. No drugs or explosives had been detected.

However, the cargo could nevertheless be something illegal, anything from ghost guns built by 3-D printing to counterfeit Rolex watches to elephant tusks that had been smuggled into Florida in a previous shipment from Africa. The stated contents—books—seemed unlikely, as they could have been sent more cheaply and conveniently in smaller packages through United Parcel Service.

As manager of the facility, Felix possessed the authority to inspect shipments under certain limited circumstances, a condition to which customers acceded when signing a contract. He wouldn't open the crate unless an initial, less intrusive method of inspection gave him reason for concern.

The big warehouse bustled as incoming shipments were palleted according to local delivery routes, waiting trucks were loaded, and manifests were prepared. In counterpoint, outbound consignments moved to planes on the tarmac, up motorized conveyors to cargo-bay doors. Felix directed a tug cart operator to relocate the wheeled pallet holding the Boca Raton crate to a remote corner of the building, where he could conduct the inspection without distraction.

He began with a fiberscope, a flexible bundle of transparent fibers with a tiny objective lens at the far end and an eyepiece at the near end. This was an industrial tool similar to the medical instrument a gastroenterologist would employ to determine the precise location of a patient's bleeding stomach ulcer.

First, he stood on the pallet, beside the crate, and used a battery-powered drill to make a half-inch-diameter hole in the lid. Then he fed the objective lens and the fiber bundle through the hole, into the crate.

He slipped the spring headband around his brow and adjusted the eyepiece. The handheld control was about the size of a TV remote.

He dialed enough light into the fiber to inspect the shipment, moving the lens slowly over what appeared to be a smooth—perhaps steel—surface, seeking some detail that would identify the object. If the crate contained books, they were evidently packed in a series of metal boxes. Except . . . as far as he could determine, the sleek object lacked divisions and particulars other than bullnose edges. It seemed to be insulated from the sides of the crate by dense foam board to prevent it from shifting.

The fiberscope lost power, and the interior of the crate was lost to view. The light at the high windows and at the open doors rapidly dwindled and vanished as if the sun had been extinguished.

***

A sense of speed alarmed him, as if he were racing through blackness toward a precipice. He became aware of a siren.

Light returned. He was lying on his back, strapped to a gurney in an ambulance. An automated blood-pressure cuff wrapped his left biceps. An oximeter was clipped to one index finger. To his right, a wall-mounted cardiac monitor reported his vital signs.

The EMT, a thirtysomething guy with a shaved head and a red mustache, wore an earpiece with a mic extension. He seemed to be in the middle of a running report to someone, perhaps to the driver or an ER physician at the hospital. "BP coming up fast, ninety over fifty. Pulse coming down, two hundred . . . one ninety." Then he met Felix's eyes. "Hey, the patient just regained consciousness." To Felix, he said, "Abdominal pain?"

"No," Felix croaked. His throat was dry.

"Back pain, chest pain?"

"No. No pain. None."

The EMT continued his report. "BP up to one hundred over fifty-eight." He hesitated. "One zero four over sixty-two. Pulse down to one seventy. Blood oxy up to ninety-three. Does this sound like a ruptured aorta anymore?" A pause. "Yeah, not to me, either. BP one zero six over sixty-seven. Pulse one sixty-two." He regarded Felix as though a miracle must be unfolding. "It's cool. Don't be afraid."

"I'm not," Felix said. "Not much. Just . . . confused."

The driver cut off the siren. They must be near the hospital.

Unwinding the blood-pressure cuff, the EMT said, "You were way out there, way out past the edge, but you're coming back strong. You'll need to undergo tests. What happened, Mr. Domenico?"

Felix had no memory of what happened. He didn't know what he'd been doing when he fell into darkness. The last thing he recalled was coming to work at six o'clock that morning. A plane out of Florida needed to be unloaded. "What time is it?" he asked.

Consulting his watch, the EMT said, "Eight forty-five."

Felix had lost two hours. He strained to remember. Nothing. As his vital signs improved, fear rose in him. But fear of what?

HOME

When Benny arrived home from his late breakfast with Fat Bob Jericho, he parked his Ford Explorer in the three-car garage, two stalls of which were vacant, and he went through the house to the covered patio in back. He walked past the teak tables, chairs, and lounges. He stood where the limestone paving gave way to the lawn, and he stared out at the glimmering Pacific. His house was on a high hill, east of the coastal highway, in a community called Cameo Highlands, at the southern end of Corona del Mar. The sea was in the distance, not up close and dynamic, but it was still there, as real as it was for people who lived west of Pacific Coast Highway and on the low bluff above the shore. The house was 3,120 square feet. The lot measured just three thousand square feet short of a half acre, spacious for this neighborhood. He had done well for a young man of twenty-three, exceedingly well. He had good health, money in the bank, delightful friends, the love of Jill Swift, whom he would soon ask to marry him, and no debts except for a seven-figure mortgage that had not troubled him until now.

He refused to be eaten by worry. Life was always throwing a changeup at him, and he survived all of them. If he worried about every curveball, he would have been sent back to a farm team years ago. Instead, he was still up to bat and confident of his swing.

Right now, the only thing that sort of concerned him was why he was making all these baseball analogies. He wasn't a big fan of the game. He didn't dislike baseball; he simply had no interest in the sport. It seemed something must be *meaningful* about this changeup farm-team up-for-bat stuff, as though he had a psychic premonition that a ninety-mile-an-hour fastball was coming straight at his forehead.

Handy Duroc loved baseball. He was a stone Dodgers fan. But Handy, with his coiffed hair, was the past. Handy had already done all the damage he could do.

Benny went into the house. He stood in the living room, turning slowly in a circle, considering the sleek modern decor. An L-shaped Italian sectional in white mohair. A free-form coffee table of white quartzite and stainless steel. The minimalist Swedish armchairs with sloped backs gave the impression that they were about to be launched at high speed along a track in an amusement park. Everything stood on a pale-gold Tufenkian carpet hardly more colorful than the honed-limestone floor.

If the scene said one thing more than any other, it declared that this was a house in which you would never see a cockroach either quick and skittering or sluggish from breathing industrial toxins. Whether someone might be shot in the back here one night—well, such was life that you never knew.

The doorbell rang.

He wasn't expecting anyone, but he answered it anyway because he continued to believe in opportunity, which could ring the bell as easily as knock.

The FedEx woman was maybe thirty, lean but muscled, wearing a polo shirt with the company logo, khaki shorts, and running shoes.

Her name was Umeko, Japanese for *plum blossom*. She always sprinted from her truck to his door, ran in place while she waited, and then dashed back to her truck, not because FedEx imposed a cruel schedule on her, but because she viewed her job, in part, as preparation for the marathons she ran six times a year. Her mother, Kimiko, had died of a heart attack at the age of forty-one, when her daughter was seventeen, whereafter Umeko had decided to eat a healthy diet and get plenty of exercise.

As he signed for a medium-size FedEx box, and as Umeko jogged without going anywhere, she said, "It's from Boca Raton."

"I don't know anyone in Boca Raton."

"I do," she said. "I was there a few years ago to visit my auntie Hoshi and my uncle Buck. Very lush. Not Auntie Hoshi and Uncle Buck. They don't drink. Boca Raton is very lush."

"Did you run there and back?" Benny asked as he returned the electronic device with the screen that he'd signed using his finger as a pen.

Grinning, she said, "Hey, I might've tried except for Arizona, New Mexico, Texas, Louisiana, Mississippi, and Alabama. Have a nice day, Benny."

"It could still turn out that way," he said, as Umeko sprinted along the front walkway toward the street.

Only then, standing just outside his front door, did he look at the air bill and see that the sender was one Talmadge Clerkenwell.

(While that name makes you uneasy or even inspires a quiet dread, you must remember that Benny has never seen it before and consequently has no clue as to its fateful nature. He might even be smiling as he stands there, charmed by Umeko, bathed in the warmth of the late-morning sun, not yet fully aware of the terrible forces aligned against him. One thing common to all of us in this life, if we are wise enough to understand, is that we live always under one threat or another and must never let our guard all the way down. That is why you, though not Benny, can be thrust into a state of suspense even if the chapter ends not with immediate peril but merely with the name Talmadge Clerkenwell.)

TRASH BARREL

At the Mayweather Universal Air Freight facility at LAX, Tyler Looney used the lavatory and spent the rest of his fifteen-minute midmorning break sitting on his forklift, in the warehouse, drinking a Red Bull and thinking about changing his last name.

He was the piano man and lead singer in a rhythm-and-blues band packing clubs and drawing the attention of some recording-company executives during its periodic weekend gigs in West LA. He worried that the group couldn't go all the way—whatever *all the way* might be for his out-of-fashion music—with a front man named Looney.

Because he loved his parents, Harlan and Lucinda, because his dad was a proud and dignified sous-chef in the main restaurant at a major hotel, Tyler hesitated to make the change. He thought perhaps that if he took his mother's maiden name for performance only, his father, who was crazy in love with her, wouldn't feel disrespected. However, her maiden name was Pinkflower. Maybe Tyler Pinkflower was a contrarian—therefore cool—name for a black musician steeped in the blues and rock and roll . . . or maybe it wasn't. He vacillated on the issue.

As he got off the forklift and went to a nearby trash barrel to throw away the empty Red Bull can, he was softly singing Sam Cooke's classic "Wonderful World," wishing his voice was as creamy as that of the late, great soul man. As he sang, he dropped the can in the barrel—and spotted the fiberscope discarded among the refuse.

He knew this was not a cheap piece of equipment, and he fished it out of the trash. The scope, complete with spring headband and handheld control, appeared to be in good condition.

On that morning shift, only Felix Domenico would have been inspecting a consignment with the device. Felix had staggered past this trash barrel and collapsed unconscious about sixty feet away, in an intersection of two aisles that passed through high palisades of freight awaiting distribution.

Tyler took the fiberscope to the dispatcher, Henry Berger, who was in his office. Henry was a good guy but perpetually harried. At the peak of the morning outrush of delivery trucks, his eyes often seemed to bulge in their sockets. Most of the time, his hair stood on end because he had a habit of nervously running a hand through it. Henry would probably have a stroke before he was fifty.

As the dispatcher accepted the fiberscope, he regarded it as if it were the seventh of the seven signs of the Apocalypse. "What was Felix doing with this? What was he inspecting? He must have been inspecting a shipment. What shipment was he inspecting?"

"I have no idea," Tyler replied. "How's Felix doing?"

"We haven't heard yet. If he pulled a consignment out of the dispatch sequence, where is it?"

"I have no way of knowing," Tyler said. "It's a big building."

"Was it an overnight consignment has to be delivered today, or was it second-day, third-day, maybe an Express Saver shipment?"

"I just fork things around like I'm told," Tyler said, "and try not to hurt my hands."

"Piano hands. I can move you to a tug cart if that's safer."

Tyler shrugged. "Nothing's safe. I just have to make the music career work sooner than later. What do you think of the name Tyler Pinkflower? As a performer's name."

Henry ran his hand through his hair. He looked a little like Art Garfunkel. "Jesus, I don't know. Don't put your career in my hands. What do I know from music? Find out what Felix was scoping."

"I'll ask around," Tyler said.

"And, hey, be cautious with it when you find it. Maybe the consignment had something to do with whatever happened to Felix."

A BENEFACTOR

Benny took the FedEx box into his kitchen and put it on the island and went to the Keurig brewer to make a single serving of coffee. He wasn't accustomed to having beer in the morning; though the two Coronas had been accompanied by a hearty breakfast, he didn't feel grounded. Maybe his vague sense of unsteadiness had nothing to do with alcohol. Maybe it was related to being without a job. He was self-aware enough to know that he was largely defined by work. Nevertheless, a weight of caffeine might anchor him.

As the coffee drizzled from the brewer into the mug and that comforting aroma filled the room, he looked around, trying to decide whether or not the kitchen might be too white. The ceiling was "eggshell white," the cabinetry "glossy snow white." The countertops were white quartzite with minimal gold veining. The bleached-white sycamore breakfast-nook table was surrounded by a U-shaped booth upholstered in white leather. The edges of everything were rounded. All the appliances and drawer pulls were stainless steel. He liked a style that looked not just modern but sort of . . . science-fictional.

He had no interest in the past, either his personal history or the history of the world. He was focused on the future. The past had not been good to him. He'd survived it both mentally and physically, but he had nothing about which to wax nostalgic. Besides, he liked things not only to *be* clean but also to *look* clean, to present an antiseptic impression. He supposed he was only two steps removed from being obsessive about cleanliness, but he could live with that. If sometimes the kitchen looked like a hospital surgery, better that than like Satan's scullery.

He sat on a white stool at the island and blew on the coffee and sipped it and studied the FedEx box with suspicion. A day that began like this one seemed unlikely to bring him good news of any kind from a stranger. Talmadge Clerkenwell. The name sounded like a man out of the long-gone South, so long gone that alligators had not yet found Florida.

With thumb and forefinger, he pulled the tab, and the cardboard zipper stuttered open across the end of the box. He extracted an object coddled in Bubble Wrap.

The thing appeared to be a hardcover book without the jacket, maybe eight inches tall and eleven inches wide, half an inch thick. It bore no title on the front board or spine. When Benny opened it, he found it was a video presentation of a kind occasionally used to market a high-end house. The screen at once brightened to soft blue.

A recorded image appeared: a man standing alone under a silvery fall of light, with darkness gathered all around. He was tall, old, and well tanned. White hair, mustache, and goatee. His shoes, suit, shirt, and string tie were white. His teeth, when he smiled, seemed irradiated. He had a theatrical air, as if he might be the iconic spokesperson for a brand of milk or ice cream, as if he had played an angel in a very old movie when they still regularly made movies that portrayed angels with affection.

"Hello, Benjamin," the old man said. "If your day has been as unsettling as I suspect it has, don't fret. Though worse will surely happen, all will be well in time. No guarantees, of course. But very likely, all will be well." He smiled. "I'm pretty darn sure." His mellifluous voice was that of a younger man than he appeared to be. "My name is Talmadge Clerkenwell. People call me 'Colonel,' though I am not and never have been one. It is, I suppose, an old-fashioned honorific once bestowed upon me out of gratitude, and it stuck. I am your great-uncle, related to you through your maternal grandmother, Cosima Springbok, with whom you once lived for a time."

"She was a batshit crazy witch," Benny blurted at the screen.

"I suspect," Talmadge Clerkenwell continued, "that you have no fond memories of her. She was an unspeakably vile person. After a year of marriage, her first husband, Norbert Banford, committed suicide."

"Cosima probably murdered him," Benny said, as though he and the colonel were engaged in a conversation.

"She probably murdered him," Clerkenwell said, "but that could not be proved. Her second husband was the finest man I ever knew, Beaumont Springbok, your maternal grandfather. After two tumultuous years of marriage, during which your mother, Naomi, was conceived, Beau died at three o'clock in the morning when his car stopped on a railroad track and was struck by an express train."

"Cosima probably murdered him," Benny said.

The colonel said, "Poor Beau's remains were in such deplorable condition and so inextricably entwined with the twisted remains of his vehicle that the coroner found it quite difficult to complete as thorough an autopsy as he preferred. Several empty beer cans and a shattered bottle of Jack Daniel's, recovered from the wreckage, along with certain tissue samples, resulted in the conclusion that he was profoundly inebriated. They decided he parked on the tracks, unaware of doing so, and took a nap from which he woke perhaps an instant before the impact killed him. This seemed an unlikely explanation, considering that Beau had abstained from alcohol his entire life."

Although Benny had thought that, in self-defense, he should have no interest in the past, this family history was intriguing.

The colonel said, "Cosima's maiden name was Clerkenwell. She is my half sister, three years older than me, and throughout my childhood, she terrified me. Although I never wished her dead, I would have smiled through her funeral."

"Amen," Benny said. He'd not had contact with his grandmother since he was nine.

"Recently," the colonel said, "it has been given to me to know the details of your childhood and adolescence."

The words *"given to me to know"* seemed an odd construction, but Benny attributed it to the fact that Clerkenwell was old enough to have come from an American culture more decorous than the pajamas-as-formal-wear culture of the moment.

"I was not surprised that, while our experiences were unique to each of us, our suffering was comparable throughout the first two decades of our lives. That is of course why it has been made clear to me that my most valuable possession must now be passed on to you. You will be receiving it by airfreight. Please be assured that this inheritance requires no legal transfer and involves absolutely no tax liability." The colonel raised his right hand, thrusting his index finger at the camera to emphasize what he said next: "*Indeed, you must keep it a secret from everyone!* Everyone except the person whose heart you trust no less than you trust your own."

Startled by the new intensity with which the colonel spoke, Benny unconsciously leaned back on his stool, away from the screen.

The old man's heretofore gentle voice abruptly roared with threat. "IF YOU CAN'T KEEP THE SECRET, THEN YOU

WILL TURN TO DUST AND BE BLOWN AWAY ON THE WIND!"

Having been captivated by the colonel's presentation and even cautiously fascinated by the prospect of an inheritance, Benny felt his spirits sag as his reputed uncle morphed into his *crazy* uncle.

"DUST ON THE WIND! DUST ON THE WIND!"

"Whoa there, Uncle Tal."

The colonel took a moment to regroup. He lowered the warning finger and cleared his throat. "I do not wish to alarm you. Forgive me if I have done so. What you are about to receive is a blessing that will transform your life. It is a wonderful thing." He smiled and nodded. "A wonderful thing. You will be receiving a call from Mayweather Universal Air Freight to arrange delivery. Eventually, you will celebrate your receipt of this great gift. Perhaps not right away. Certainly not right away. But eventually you will think of me with great fondness. In time. Given enough time." The colonel smiled and nodded. "I am already fond of you, Benjamin, even though we've never met. You have suffered as I suffered. And like me, you didn't let the pain and misery corrupt you. You have remained *nice*, just as I have remained nice. This I've been told about you by an irrefutable source. I love you for being so nice, dear nephew." He nodded and smiled and pressed a hand over his heart. Then in the kindest, nicest way, he whispered, "Now, whatever happens, no matter what—*be not afraid*. There is no reason to be afraid, though there may seem to be. There may very much seem to be. But there is not. In my experience, at least, there is not. Trust me."

The video ended. The screen went dark.

A long sigh escaped Benny Catspaw. He was not surprised to have been informed that he was about to receive a fantastic inheritance only to learn that his benefactor was three wheels short of being a fully functioning four-wheel-drive intellect. Such was life. His life anyway.

The airfreight shipment—if in fact one was impending—would no doubt prove to be a pot to piss in, broken en route, or a coupon for a free order of fries with the purchase of a Big Mac.

Well, in either case—or any other—this would be an amusing story to tell his and Jill's children and grandchildren. Benny hoped to have four children with Jill Swift, two girls and two boys, and then at least eight or ten grandchildren. Having a family, a happy family, was the most important thing of all to him, because it was something that he'd never yet experienced. Being able to support a thriving family was what drove him to work so hard.

PLUGGED AND READY

Although he had only one eye, Gordie Armstrong was a tug cart driver who had worked twenty-two years for Mayweather Universal Air Freight with not a single work-related injury or negative report on his employment record. He had sustained the loss of an eye in one of the Middle East wars that politicians were eager to fight and just as eager to lose.

In spite of being disabled, though he had been betrayed by the very leaders who sent him into battle, he never complained, and he loved his country. Being practical and economically prudent, Gordie chose not to have a decorative eye installed in the empty socket, which was permanently sewn shut. He wore an eye patch; not the usual black one, but a patch that was a miniature American flag.

Now and then, one guy or another with an unfortunate attitude would make a mean remark about the flag patch or just the flag in general, whereupon Gordie was pleased to beat the crap out of him. Tyler Looney, perhaps soon to become Tyler Pinkflower, sometimes had burgers and drinks with Gordie at his favorite bar. On two occasions Tyler had witnessed such smackdowns. He was amazed that the individual soon to be beaten always assumed the beater, having one eye, was as good as blind and a pushover even though Gordie was six feet four and as solid as an ironwood tree.

Looking up at Tyler from the seat of his electric cart, his expression as patriotic as always, Gordie said, "Yeah, it was on a wheeled pallet. I pulled it out of the way so Felix could fiberscope the beast. It's to hell and gone, bro. Hop on. I'll take you to it."

The tug cart could pull the heaviest pallet, but it also had a short cargo deck for light loads. Tyler became cargo. They whizzed away through the warehouse maze. Long ago, Gordie Armstrong's brain had reprogrammed itself to provide him with nearly as much depth perception as doctors once thought required two eyes.

In a far corner of the facility, beyond the buzz and bustle of the freight handlers, the crate in question waited. A small battery-powered drill lay on the lid.

Gordie swung off the driver's seat and stepped onto the pallet with Tyler, beside the crate. "Bro, maybe be careful with that."

"Careful? How, why?"

"There's something about it."

"What something?"

Felix Domenico had drilled a half-inch-diameter hole in the lid. Then, after inspecting the contents with the fiberscope, he'd plugged the hole with a black rubber stopper, per company protocols.

Tyler tapped a finger against the plug. "Seems like Felix must have been okay with what he saw."

Features clenched in somber expectation, his gaze traveling the length of the crate and then again, Gordie said, "Felix walks away without his drill, tosses the scope in the trash—then has a stroke or whatever. None of it's right."

Consulting the packing slip that was visible through the plastic envelope applied to the crate, Tyler said, "Going to some guy in Corona del Mar. That truck's left already. Can't deliver this today."

After a hesitation, Gordie said, "I'm not crazy, all right?"

"Maybe half. But you're not ready for an institution."

"What I'm going to tell you is just between us."

Tyler said, "Unless I can make a hit song out of it."

"This is true shit, man. Earlier, as I was towing this pallet here for Felix, suddenly I could see with both eyes."

As Gordie studied the crate, Tyler studied Gordie. "So maybe there's a televangelist in the box, come from Florida on the cheap to cure the lame and the half-blind."

"Makes more sense than anything I've come up with. When it happened, I thought, *What's this?* I don't mind saying it scared me."

"Being able to see with both eyes scared you?"

"Because I felt *known*. I mean, what was it—an offer, a bargain to be made? I get a new eye in return for what?"

Tyler had to admit the crate had made him uneasy even before Gordie shared his story. "You're saying the devil's in this box, come to California to buy souls?"

Gordie took a deep breath and exhaled between clenched teeth. "Nah, the devil's not that stupid. He'd know he's already bought most of them around here. Hell, Tyler, I just don't know what to make of it."

"Maybe you didn't see with both eyes again, only imagined you did, some kind of brain freak-out. It was only for a minute, right?"

Gordie nodded. He picked up the drill. "Whatever it was, whatever happened . . . let's move this sucker back into the dispatch sequence where it belongs. I want it out of here tomorrow."

ROMANCE

After viewing the video message from Talmadge Clerkenwell, as he considered with which of the major realty firms he would most like to be associated now that he'd departed Surfside, Benny wiped down all the kitchen counters, used a stainless-steel cleaner on the doors of the two refrigerators, and Swiffered the floor. None of this was necessary. Mrs. Shinzel, his housekeeper, came in two full days a week and was a hard worker. However, housecleaning soothed Benny. It was his meditation. He was happy when scrubbing and polishing, making his sparkling home even a little more sparkly.

He had no hobbies to take his mind off his worries and settle his nerves. His life was dedicated to work and to Jill Swift, to her dream. Currently a top agent with Belle Maison, she was determined that, by their thirties, she and Benny would form a brokerage of their own and build a platoon of agents who would storm the high-end market and dominate it for decades. "All the candy-ass firms that own the ground now will be smoking ruins when we open fire on them," she'd said recently. Jill was twenty-six and sexy and smart and stylish and loving, but sometimes Benny wondered if maybe she might be the reincarnation of General George Patton.

On this occasion, she was also stealthy. He hadn't heard her coming in the front door. She had her own key—and he had a key to her place—but she usually rang the bell as she was entering, and cried out, *"C'est moi!"* This time, she materialized in the kitchen as if she'd transported herself from elsewhere by an act of true magic.

She rounded the island as Benny was polishing the swan-neck spout at the smaller of the island's two sinks and startled him when she said, "Hey, babe." When he turned toward her, she vised his face in her hands and tongue kissed him with insistence and to a depth that was arousing but a little scary, as if she were a succubus intent on tonguing his soul out of him.

When Jill finished with his mouth, still clamping his face in her elegant but strong hands, she regarded him with such affection that his knees jellified. Her blue eyes were full of light, as if she had availed herself of a new cosmetic procedure that installed a tiny LED bulb behind each retina.

He said, "What—"

She shushed him. "Just let me look at you. I need to look at you." She seemed to stare *through* his eyes, to admire the smooth convolutions of his forebrain. She surveyed the width of his brow, dwelt for a long moment on his right ear, gazed across his brow again, and focused on his left ear. Nose, septum, lips, jaw, chin, other jaw—no element of his face was given short shrift, as if she were not his lover, but relied on a facial recognition program to identify him. A soft sigh marked the completion of her inspection, whereupon she released his face and kissed the tip of his nose and stepped back and said, "I will never forget your face. Will you forget mine?"

The most romantic response that occurred to Benny didn't sound so Cary Grant when he put it into words. "When I'm a hundred years old and riddled with dementia and don't know who I am, I will still remember you and your amazing face."

"We were great together, weren't we?" Jill said.

"We're fabulous together," he confirmed, belatedly registering her use of the past tense.

By then, she was handing him the key to his house, with which she'd let herself in. Tenderly, with a melancholy expression that made her yet more beautiful, she said, "I want you to be happy, so it's better by far you should forget me and smile than that you should remember me and be sad."

Benny vaguely recognized those words as a line from an old poem she had read to him in a tender moment. When Jill Swift was in a philosophical mood, she often relied on the artful words of poets or songwriters to convey her most profound insights into the meaning of life and the human condition.

"I don't understand," he protested.

"You light up my life," she said softly.

"And you light up mine."

"I'm totally devoted to you."

"Well then—"

"To every season there is a reason," she explained, "and a time to every purpose under heaven."

"But I love you," he said.

"Love is a many splendored thing, Benny. Love is all around us. It's everywhere we go. I will always love you. But my life and yours are paths that have taken different directions in the woods."

"Woods? What woods?"

"The woods of life, sweetheart. It tears me up, Benny. God, it really does. But the woods of life are scary, and it's easy to get lost. When one person is on a well-lit path and the other person is on a path into darkness, it makes no sense for both of them to get lost and wander in misery forever."

"Misery? Forever?"

"Take care of yourself, Benny."

"Wait. If your path is the well-lit path, then I'll take it. I'll follow you. We'll be on the same path."

The LEDs behind her retinas dimmed. "That's not an option."

He had taken a key ring from his pocket. It held two keys—one to his house, one to hers. "I don't want to give your key back. It means the world to me, having your key."

She smiled. "Then you keep it, sweetheart."

"Really? I can keep it?"

"If it means that much to you, of course. I've already had the locks changed."

He followed her out of the kitchen, along the hallway, to the front door. "I had a . . . a conversation with Handy Duroc. I left Surfside this morning. Did you know about that?"

"How could I not know, sweetie? Everybody knows. The word is out." Jill opened the door, stepped outside, and turned to him. "Don't let the bastards get you down, Benny."

"Bastards? What bastards? Who?"

"I don't know who. The usual bastards, I guess. The world's full of them these days. Take Bobby McFerrin's advice."

"Bobby who?"

She sang the title of McFerrin's number one hit. "'Don't Worry, Be Happy.'"

"You just said 'misery forever.' How can I be happy if I'm on a path of misery forever?"

"The path you're on would be misery *for me*, Benny. Maybe not for you. You'll have some kind of life, just a lesser life than the one we planned together."

"Why?"

"I really don't know why. Something you did to someone, I guess. I can't be caught in this."

"I didn't do anything to anyone. I'm not the kind who does something to anyone."

"Then maybe it was something you didn't do. Anyway, honey, there's no reason you can't have a nice little life and be happy. Most people never snatch the brass ring, yet they can be happy in their nice little lives."

"But I want a big life."

Even the pity with which she regarded him didn't make her any less beautiful in his eyes. "We all do, honey. That's why we need to be careful, very careful."

"I'm careful," he assured her.

"Evidently not careful enough. Maybe you should get a dog."

"A dog? Why a dog?"

"For companionship. People can stave off depression if they have a great dog."

"I'm not depressed, just confused."

She gave him a meaningful look. No one was better at meaningful looks than Jill. "Consider a dog, sweetie."

With that, she turned from him. Went to her gleaming, midnight-blue Mercedes in the driveway. Got behind the wheel. Drove away.

Benny stood on his doorstep, watching her go until she was out of sight. He was alone on the table, a mere dessertspoon in an incomplete and meaningless place setting.

His phone rang. Certain it must be Jill, that she realized she had made a terrible mistake, that she wanted to patch things up, he took the call. A woman from Mayweather Universal Air Freight wanted to know if someone would be at home between nine and ten o'clock the following morning to receive a delivery from Talmadge Clerkenwell of Boca Raton, Florida. "Sure," Benny said. "I've got nowhere to be."

(In spite of the cryptic and disturbing video card that Benny received from that old man in Florida, he remains able to consider the possibility that the inheritance he is about to receive will be a great good. If you're a bitter cynic or merely a sour one, you might find his hopefulness frustrating and wish to see him learn a hard, painful lesson. That is how a story can go wrong and encourage the worst of human behavior in the reader. We should hope the tale doesn't take such a turn, because Benny is one of us, after all, and wishing horrific pain on him is like wishing it on ourselves—though it's the kind of narrative drama that makes authors chortle with wicked glee.)

LISTENING TO "DON'T WORRY, BE HAPPY" IN THE WAKE OF JILL'S REJECTION, BENNY REMEMBERS HIS GRANDMOTHER

Following the murder of his father, Big Al, on a night in May, seven-year-old Benny went to live with his maternal grandmother, Cosima Springbok. His mother, Naomi, didn't need time to grieve. She had been yearning to divorce Benny's father for years but feared his violent temper. Now that Big Al had died as a consequence of a bar fight that he'd picked with the wrong man, Naomi's migraines abated. The school district where he had taught and coached football had been a snake pit of violence where students and teachers alike were often targets of the gangs that ruled the institution, and a life-insurance policy was provided as a job benefit. A double-indemnity clause increased the payout if the cause of death was either an accident or homicide. Upon receiving a tax-free five-hundred-thousand-dollar payout, Naomi quit her job at the vintage clothing store, decided she wasn't a vegetarian after all, stopped worrying that her carbon footprint might lead to the destruction of the planet, and booked a series of sea cruises to exotic ports that would keep her on the move for more than two years, until she met Mr. Right on a voyage around South America.

Enter Grandma Cosima, then forty-seven. She was about five feet eight, slim, with ink-black hair cut short and eyes as green as the plastic on certain Memorex high-density diskettes, which were still in use in those days. She always wore a full-length slinky dress or a silky Vietnamese tunic-and-pants ensemble called an *ao dai*. Cosima moved so silently and fluidly that she reminded young Benny of a cat, except on those occasions when, unaware of him, she passed through an ill-lighted room, her distorted shadow stilting along a pale wall, which suggested to him that her humanity was a disguise within which lurked a spider from another planet.

The suicide of Cosima's first husband and the death by train of her second left her financially secure, with no desire to have a man in her life. Although Benny was only seven years old when he was sent to live with her, she regarded him as a man in the making. He was unwelcome in her house, and it was her great pleasure to make him aware of that.

Benny wore black. Cosima bought his clothes, and black was the only color she provided. His pajamas were white when she purchased them, but she dyed them black. His sheets, pillowcases, and blankets were black as well, so that when he was lying abed, in the glow of the nightstand lamp, his pale hands appeared to be disembodied, as if they had been severed from the arms of another boy and placed in bed with Benny as a not-so-subtle threat.

In possession of a bachelor's degree and two master's degrees, one in psychology, Cosima was more than qualified to homeschool her grandson. Having already taught himself to read, with comprehension of text at a third-grade level, Benny didn't require that most basic instruction; he was enough of an autodidact to improve his reading skills unassisted. Therefore, on the first day of class, Cosima got straight to the subject of death. During the next nine months, using books and gruesomely explicit video documentaries, she taught him much about nature's infinite zoology of predators, with a particular emphasis on how they chased down prey, tore it apart, and often ate it alive.

Rather than instilling in the boy an abiding terror or at least a phobia regarding everything from tigers to coyotes to owls, this morbid instruction inspired in him compassion for the small, gentle creatures who were eaten and pity for the predators that nature had condemned to lives of violence by requiring them to consume a large amount of protein to survive. Tigers probably despaired at having to kill, kill, kill—but they didn't have the option to be vegans. The child's profound sympathy for prey and predator frustrated Cosima. Furthermore, he held fast to the idea that the way nature worked, as sad and scary as it was, must be the best of all ways it could work, because if there was a better way, then that would be how it would already work. This attitude not only frustrated his grandmother but also infuriated her. Although she'd bought him black sneakers, the shoes had small, white design elements that now she eradicated with a waterproof black Sharpie.

During the next nine months of homeschooling, they concentrated on geography, climatology, and planetary structure, so Benny would acquire an understanding of where, how, and precisely to what extent human and animal life could be snuffed out by hurricanes, tornadoes, tsunamis, floods, massive mud slides, blizzards, ice ages with mile-high glaciers, wildfires, earthquakes, and volcanoes. As was not unusual for a boy of his age, Benny found the spectacle of raging nature more exciting than frightening. The videos Cosima used in class during the day became Benny's preferred evening entertainment. As for the victims of these natural disasters, he figured they were in Heaven, where nature hadn't gone crazy, so they were happier than they had been down here. Around this time, his grandmother began cursing and drinking more than heretofore had been her habit.

For the next phase of the boy's education, Cosima focused most intently on biology. The number of syndromes, conditions, diseases, and injuries that could result in disability and death were quite bewildering, and the long names given to many of them were hard to pronounce and harder to remember. Although his grandmother counseled him otherwise, Benny remained certain that none of those afflictions would befall him. She could not understand his attitude, and he did not explain that, having looked into the muzzle of the gun held by Big Al's killer and survived, he felt protected and destined for a long and interesting life. Instead of inculcating in her grandson a severe case of hypochondria, she inspired in him such a sympathy for the vulnerability of humanity that he considered pursuing a career as a physician. Around this time, his grandmother began taking an occasional white pill from a pillbox and washing it down with vodka.

Intending to proceed to the subject of human cruelty and the homicidal tendency of the species, Cosima ordered documentaries on Auschwitz, Dachau, Bergen-Belsen, the Soviet gulags, the Khmer Rouge, Hitler, Stalin, Mao, and others. Before these instructive materials could arrive, Benny's mother returned from a cruise around South America, during which the captain of the ship had married her and Jubal Catspaw. The happy couple wanted to provide Naomi's nine-year-old son with a loving environment, and he was adopted by his stepfather, whereafter his last name changed from Dockenfelder to Catspaw. A new and entirely unexpected phase of his life began.

NETWORKING

Benny Catspaw knew nearly every real-estate agent in the high end of the Orange County market. He was also friendly with all of them and a true friend to several. Because he had a sterling memory and a genuine interest in people, he remembered the names of their spouses and children and pets without much effort. He recalled birthdays, not merely of those who worked at Surfside but of those at Belle Maison and the other five major firms that specialized in properties north of one million dollars. This advantage accrued to him in part because of hustle, but mostly because he found the real-estate world as scintillating as Hollywood, the agents as glamorous as movie stars, the business as his best route to success and true happiness after a tumultuous childhood and adolescence. He regularly congratulated competitors on sales that he wished he had made, and he was sincerely happy about their success because he believed that what happened for them could happen for him if he worked hard.

After Jill Swift left him with the useless key to her house, which was less painful but as emotionally distressing as a knife in the heart, after half an hour of replaying the Bobby McFerrin song didn't make him happier, and after the memories of Grandma Cosima that the song inexplicably conjured only made him nervous, he took steps to get his career back on track. Revealing his decision to leave Surfside, he texted the principals of five brokerages, all well known to him, announcing that he was open to a new professional relationship. He had an impressive two-year sales record, and they knew it, so he didn't need to make a case for himself. He restrained from texting the founders of Belle Maison because he didn't want to make Jill Swift uncomfortable by working in the same company with her.

He changed into jeans and a T-shirt and spent the afternoon vacuuming and dusting, although nothing needed to be vacuumed or dusted. He cleaned the guest bathroom though no one had yet stayed there and though Mrs. Shinzel had cleaned it the previous day. As always, housework lifted his spirits. By the time he decided to check his phone at five thirty, he expected to have three or more responses to his text messages. There were none.

This dearth of replies surprised but did not worry him. Well, in truth, it worried him a little, but it didn't unduly alarm him. The people he'd texted were all movers and shakers, at the pinnacle of the dirt business, and therefore crazy busy. Many probably didn't fully review their scores of text messages until after dinner. They had to prioritize. Everyone who made it to the top in Orange County real estate needed to be a first-rate prioritizer. Every day, they had too many property showings to squeeze into too few hours, offers to convey to sellers, counteroffers to present to buyers, escrows to monitor, home inspections to attend, hands to hold, egos to soothe, and an avalanche of paperwork cascading on them from a government bureaucracy that measured its effectiveness by the number of people it could annoy and by the degree to which it could annoy them. Benny was sure he'd have enthusiastic replies from at least two or three brokers by morning.

When he woke on Wednesday and plucked his iPhone from the nightstand, his only text message was from his dry cleaner offering a discount for three-piece suits. He'd received no emails.

(This development no doubt pleases the bitter cynics among you, but I don't like it at all. I would find it satisfying if some of those who cut Benny off were to die in a head-on collision with a gasoline tanker truck or suffer a humiliating bout of diarrhea in a public setting. However, if I did that, I would have become the kind of person I don't want to be, so we'll have to live with this sad turn of events.)

THE CRATE

After the Mayweather crew departed, Benny Catspaw was left with an immense crate in one of two empty spaces in his three-car garage. He had been expecting a package that a deliveryman could hand to him at the front door and that he would be able to carry to the kitchen island without risking a hernia.

The bill of lading identified the contents as books, offering no list of titles. Talmadge Clerkenwell had never mentioned books. He had called the bequest "a blessing" and "a wonderful thing." Benny read books and enjoyed a good novel; however, if the crate actually contained books, Clerkenwell had exaggerated the value of this gift. According to the paperwork, the old man hadn't paid for significant insurance on the shipment, suggesting the books weren't valuable, collectible editions.

The crate was well constructed, framed with solid lumber and held together with scores of screws. To take it apart or even to open the lid, he would need a power drill with a reversible motor and a countersink screwdriver bit. That would require a trip to the hardware store. When disassembled, the enormous box would still be in large pieces—too many of them to put out for the weekly trash collection; he would need to call someone and pay to have it hauled away.

Benny was beginning to feel put-upon. He didn't like feeling that way. Talmadge Clerkenwell might be eccentric, but there was no reason to suppose he didn't mean well. Benny was convinced that most people meant well, but sometimes they just didn't think hard enough about the consequences of their actions.

Furthermore, the longer he regarded the crate, the more that it disturbed him. The overhead fluorescent panels were inadequate, but the huge box seemed to *resist* illumination; it stood in shadows that appeared to be unrelated to the fall of light, as if a darkness as soft as soot seeped from the thing, gathering under and around it in a miasmic mist.

Benny was neither overly superstitious nor given to irrational fears. Even if vampires and zombies were real, life had taught him that there were worse things in the world, like husbands who beat their wives and grandmothers who hated their grandchildren and sociopaths who operated boarding schools and conducted secret medical experiments on young boys. Consequently, he told himself that the crate was a mere annoyance rather than a threat, that it contained nothing more than the gimcracks and gewgaws and fribbles that an eccentric great-uncle might feel were of enough sentimental value to dump on an unsuspecting nephew whom he had never met. He would have to buy the power drill necessary to open the damn thing and, depending on the value of the sorry contents, call Goodwill Industries or Got Junk to haul it all away. Although that task was not urgent, he decided to attend to it anyway, to take his mind off the recent hiccups in his career and love life.

Before driving to the hardware store, he went into the house to check his voice mail, email, and text messages. Nothing, nothing, and nothing.

Well, less than a day had passed since he informed the five firms of his availability. Besides, this was a Wednesday, always a busy day in the real-estate world, or at least as busy as any other; or if it wasn't as busy as any other day, it was certainly busyish. The principals of each firm would need to meet to discuss the terms and conditions under which they would bring him aboard. Because his two-year track record was excellent, they would want to craft their proposal carefully, aware that they would be in competition with other brokerages. After an initial spasm of anxiety, he now realized that the silence engendered by his text message was proof of his value in the marketplace; a less successful agent would by now have received a polite rejection or a boilerplate terms-and-conditions sheet. A day or so of silence, prior to a vigorous and satisfying response, was a sign of respect. All was for the best in this best of all possible worlds.

ON THE WAY HOME FROM THE HARDWARE STORE, BENNY RECALLS A FORMATIVE DAY IN HIS LIFE

Jubal Catspaw, who married Benny's mother, Naomi, on a cruise around South America, had inherited a fortune and dedicated himself to the enjoyment of everything money could buy. Jubal was especially enchanted by first-class travel and resided in his Beverly Hills mansion only for a week or two between what he called his "glorious expeditions." When traveling by sea, he always booked the largest suite on the ship. Flying off to Paris for a month—or to Tuscany, or to Rio—required a private jet. Training through Europe or Japan or across the United States involved a lavishly appointed private railcar with a staff of three, including a chef. Jubal adored Naomi, and Benny was happy that his mother, having endured Big Al's temper and violence and fecklessness, was highly valued and well treated.

Although Jubal adopted Benny, he was awkward with children and adamantly opposed to traveling with one. Initially, when Benny's mom and stepfather were journeying, he was left in Beverly Hills, in the care of an English butler, Rudyard Bromley, and his wife, Sally. Mrs. Bromley served as cook and the senior of three housekeepers. Benny was homeschooled by a full-time tutor named Mordred Merrick.

The mansion included a game arcade, a home theater, no cockroaches, and three acres of grounds on which a boy with a vivid imagination could have many adventures.

Although Rudyard Bromley could occasionally be found standing at a window or tending some task while quietly weeping, his pale face glistening like a ball of his wife's homemade burrata, he was a gentle presence. Mrs. Bromley was likewise kindly, although on days when she sipped too much sherry while attending to her duties, she couldn't stop singing dour Celtic songs about death and oppression, sometimes with a bitterness that scared the two housekeepers who worked under her.

The only member of the staff who seemed capable of murder was Mordred Merrick. He'd been educated at Columbia University and later denied tenure in the English department at UCLA because, according to him, he didn't hate Shakespeare enough, though he hated the bard a great deal. Mordred was a doper, though he consumed his weed in the form of brownies to avoid being outed by the distinctive scent of pot smoke. He promised to share his treats as soon as Benny was old enough for what he called "the sacred experience," which he said would be when his student turned twelve. Mordred's résumé asserted that he was a multidiscipline prodigy capable of instructing in the full spectrum of academic subjects. However, he spent much less time on mathematics than on such things as the secret history of the world (which was ruled by evil Rosicrucians), the superhero status of Fidel Castro (who hadn't died but had only taken a vacation on his home planet), and the need for children to keep meticulous notes on their parents' political beliefs and report them to the state when the revolution came. Benny found all this interesting and colorful, but not convincing. During his second month of instruction—and for the remainder of the more than two and a half years that he was homeschooled—he began to carry a sharp penknife in his pocket when in Mordred Merrick's company, just in case.

The best thing about life in that house was the music room, which contained a Steinway piano. After two years in residence, he sat down at the instrument one day, humming a pop ballad he liked, and discovered that he could play the tune note for note.

He was a piano prodigy. Once he'd heard a song through to the end, he could perform it flawlessly. Benny might have pursued this talent if Mordred Merrick had not repeatedly recounted how *his* piano teacher had molested him when he was a young boy; as a consequence, Mordred ever since had to avoid cocktail lounges and other venues offering piano music, because every time he saw someone playing, he wanted to blow that musician's brains out. Nevertheless, Benny had talent. One day that would matter.

His most formative day as the adopted son of Jubal Catspaw came on the Thursday when he turned thirteen. After a birthday party with a magician, a juggler, a guy who made origami animals out of dollar bills, a karate master who broke boards with his head and concrete blocks with his hands—but with no other children in attendance—Benny was shown a short video about Briarbush Academy. Situated in the scenic, forested mountains of Northern California, where the air was pure and nature unsullied by industry or excessive civilization, Briarbush educated only the brightest sons of the nation's richest and most forward-thinking families. The stellar faculty not only provided superior academic instruction, but also turned out young men with wilderness-survival skills and superb physical endurance and keen ambition, shaping them into the next generation of leaders.

The following day, Jubal and Naomi began a yearlong around-the-world tour that included a wealth of experiences. Their African safari would be staffed by two guides, two able marksmen to protect against predatory wildlife, six porters, a camp manager, a chef, two kitchen assistants, a classical guitarist, a flutist, and a night-soil specialist. In Egypt, they would be given VIP tours of the three most famous pyramids; the prime minister himself would serve as their docent in the tomb to Tutankhamen; they would travel by camel caravan where practical, and otherwise by armored Land Rover. Hot-air ballooning through the Alps. An expedition up the gentle slopes of Mount Fuji to the shrine at its summit. A glamorous journey by private train—locomotive and three cars—from Shimla, India, to New Delhi, to the Taj Mahal in Agra, thence through the high-country tea plantations of Darjeeling, to Calcutta, from there to Chittagong on the Bay of Bengal. And so much more.

As Jubal and Naomi jetted off to Africa, Benny was flown to Napa, California, and from there conveyed north into the wilderness aboard a Mercedes-Benz Sprinter, to the Briarbush Academy. In this primal land of vast forests and isolate lakes, daunting slopes and chasmic ravines, the nearest volcano had long been dormant even though on some nights a low grumbling issued from it, as if it were a giant who dreamed of decimating entire villages of little people. The storied academy, its majestic buildings of native stone, was modeled after England's famous boarding schools with the intention of exceeding their grandeur while conveying the impression of a last stronghold against the ignorance that engulfed the world beyond its walls. Here, 130 sons of the ruling class, between the ages of twelve and eighteen, were housed and fed and educated and morally formed for an annual fee of two hundred thousand dollars.

Benny didn't want to go to Briarbush. Nobody wanted to go to Briarbush. He didn't have a vote in the matter. And by now he was too old to find comfort in building a LEGO staircase to the moon.

On arrival, he was taken directly to the residence of the headmaster, which stood apart from the school. Dr. Lionel Baneberry-Smith was fiftysomething, tall and lean, with gray hair, yellowish eyes, thin maroon lips, and a smile as warm as a clear morning in January. Mrs. Catherine Baneberry-Smith was much younger, very pretty and pink cheeked, with foxglove-purple eyes. She served small, dry cakes that had an almond flavor, cookies that smelled like mushrooms but tasted okay, and hot tea that Benny sweetened with honey.

Although formal, the headmaster and his lovely wife were welcoming and pleasant. The only thing that troubled Benny to any extent was the collection of big, exotic insects displayed in Lucite boxes on the shelves in the drawing room, where tea was served. Mrs. Baneberry-Smith kindly explained that, in her late twenties, she had been an entomologist studying insects in Asia, until she was bitten repeatedly by a highly poisonous spider. She was hospitalized for three months, spent another three in a rehab facility, where she met her husband and, in light of the fact that her constitution would never be what it once had been, decided to leave the jungles for the settled academic life at Briarbush, where she enjoyed looking after her spouse, counseling those boys who became homesick, and teaching a class in the fifteenth-century history of Italy.

Benny had been plunged into the company of strangers and a challenging new environment. The change in his circumstances was extreme, but much in his new situation promised adventures large and small. The dramatic landscape. The presence of boys who could become his pals. The mysteries of the rambling academy, which looked as if it must have infinite attics and labyrinthine cellars and countless secret passageways. He would no longer encounter Rudyard Bromley in awkward moments when the butler proceeded with his duties while silently weeping. Mrs. Bromley's Celtic songs, sung in a venomous voice, were a thing of the past. Mordred Merrick would now have to find another boy to radicalize. All in all, Benny was enthusiastic about his new life. Then he met his roommate.

THE PLEASURE OF PHYSICAL LABOR

A career as a real-estate agent was demanding, but it didn't involve much in the way of physical labor. Physical labor could be rewarding. Benny liked physical labor, enjoyed losing himself in it. That was why he did so much housework that wasn't necessary. When he threw himself into cleaning, he proceeded feverishly, put everything he had into it. He liked to sweat as he was scrubbing, waxing, and polishing.

When he came home from the hardware store, his purchases were not limited to a power drill with a reversible motor and a variety of bits. He also brought a pair of collapsible metal sawhorses that had a vise-lock feature, a handheld circular saw, and a pry bar.

He changed into shorts and a T-shirt and protective kneepads. Without checking his text messages, email, or voice mail—to hell with them—he attacked the crate with gusto. After removing twenty screws, on his knees, he shoved the lid off the big box and let it clatter to the garage floor.

Benny gazed at a silver-gray container that was maybe brushed stainless steel. About eight feet long, three and a half feet wide. Cosseted on all sides by sandwiched slabs of dense Styrofoam. The lid wasn't ornate, but instead smooth and featureless. Nonetheless, the shape brought to mind a casket, suggesting Talmadge Clerkenwell might be even more eccentric than he had appeared in the video.

The thing was cold to the touch. When Benny slid his hand along the lid, something like static electricity raised the hairs on his arm and needled his palm. He snatched his hand back.

He removed the screws holding the planks to the crate's corner and center posts. Using a pry bar and a hammer, he disassembled the box, stacking the lumber to one side and the slabs of Styrofoam to the other side.

When exposed, the object lacked handles with which pallbearers could carry it. The lid wasn't in two sections, which would have allowed the display of only the upper half of a deceased occupant. So it wasn't a casket. With its rounded ends and curved top, it might have been the work of a pop-art sculptor, an immense hot-dog bun crafted in steel.

Benny slowly circled the container, seeking a button, a pressure latch, a slide control, any mechanism that might open it. None of those features was offered. Neither did he find a keyhole; even if one had been apparent, he possessed no key.

The line defining the lid from the body of the container was as thin as if inscribed with a pencil, perhaps generous enough to allow the insertion of a razor, but not the blade of a pry bar.

When, in frustration, he lightly rapped the hammer against the lid, the sound wasn't the hard crack of metal hitting metal, but rang through the garage like a merry carillon of silver Christmas bells, echoing wall to wall.

Benny startled backward. "Books, my ass." The eerie but not unpleasant tintinnabulation suggested that what appeared to be steel was something else—and not something he could name.

As the ringing slowly faded into the tinkling notes that might accompany a flight of fairies in a Disney movie, the head fell off the wooden handle of the ball-peen hammer.

Benny had intended to fasten the crate planks to the sawhorses and, one by one, reduce them to manageable lengths with the circular saw. Instead, he went into the house and closed the door to the garage and locked it. He was in the laundry room, holding the handle of the headless hammer. He put it on top of the clothes dryer. He looked at his hands. He flexed his fingers. They didn't fall off. He stood with his mouth open. He didn't know what to say. Anyway, there was no one here to whom to say it.

A GROWING SENSE OF DREAD

In addition to an address in Boca Raton, a phone number was included on the FedEx box that had contained Talmadge Clerkenwell's video. However, when Benny called it, a recording informed him that service had been discontinued. He tried three times, always with the same result.

The copy of the Mayweather Universal Air Freight manifest that had come with the crate cited the same phone number.

Googling Talmadge Clerkenwell was as successful as googling "Mr. Nobody N. Nobody." He was less than a ghost. He appeared never to have existed.

When Benny sat on a stool at the kitchen island and opened the video card from Clerkenwell, the screen failed to brighten. It was an automatic device with no controls. Evidently, it was programmed to erase after being played once.

Perhaps Clerkenwell's disappearing act had another explanation, but the only conclusion Benny could reach was that the colonel had taken steps to ensure that his nephew could not return the strange container or what was in it.

The old man's mellifluous voice seemed more sinister in memory than it had been when Benny first heard it: "Whatever happens, no matter what—*be not afraid.* There is no reason to be afraid, though there may seem to be. Trust me."

Benny tended to trust people until they gave him a reason not to. Sometimes he continued to trust them until they gave him two or even three reasons to distrust them. When you couldn't trust people, it wasn't easy to like them, and Benny wanted to like people. Liking people was a big part of who Benny was—and who he wanted to be.

Life had taught him that people who didn't like people were unhappy and angry. His father, his grandmother Cosima, a certain weeping butler, and various curious individuals at Briarbush Academy were unhappy and angry and, in select cases, flat-out bug-shit crazy.

Closing the dead video card and putting it aside, Benny made a conscious decision to continue trusting Clerkenwell until he had concrete evidence that his trust wasn't warranted.

His smartphone was on the island, where he'd left it earlier. He stared at the dark screen for a while. Then he picked it up and switched it on. He'd received no text or phone messages. The lone email was from Bill Palmyra at Bank of America.

Being a banker, Bill trusted no one, but he nevertheless liked people, which wasn't an easy trick. He said he could distrust people but still like them, even love some of them, because he understood the tragic nature of the human condition.

In addition to being—or having been—a real-estate agent with a full measure of hustle, Benny had bought and remodeled and flipped two houses for which Bill Palmyra provided short-term mortgage loans. The banker was old enough to be Benny's father, distrusted him as much as he distrusted anyone else, but admired his ambition, and mentored him with what seemed like genuine affection. Benny sought neglected houses in desirable middle-class neighborhoods, properties that could be improved and turned around on a tight schedule. He flipped the first in nine months, taking a profit of 16 percent, the second in six months for a 12 percent gain. He was currently in escrow on a third residence that promised to be the most lucrative flip yet.

The email from Bill was a boilerplate notice that the mortgage application had been reviewed and the loan denied. No explanation. No mentoring. It was addressed to Benjamin Eugene Catspaw and signed by E. William Palmyra, as if they never had any success together or never laughed at each other's jokes, as if this was just another pathetic scene in the dismal human tragedy.

Benny placed a call. Jennifer, Bill's secretary, to whom he'd often spoken, asked him to spell his last name. Jennifer knew how to spell it as surely as she knew how to spell her own. Benny spelled it for her anyway. She asked him to hold. He held. After a long wait, he was sent to voice mail.

SOMETHING HUNGRY

Benny was stressed. He knew that prolonged stress contributed to stomach ulcers with dangerous internal bleeding, irritable bowel syndrome, ulcerative colitis, neurodermatitis, high blood pressure, heart disease, insomnia, migraine headaches, and sexual dysfunction, all of which Grandma Cosima had explored with enthusiasm and graphic videos during the period she homeschooled him. Since adolescence, to counterbalance his ambition and hard-work ethic, Benny practiced stress-control techniques. He meditated, attended Pilates classes, took instruction in tranquility breathing, and in general strove to go with the flow, remain laid back, hold fast to a que-sera-sera attitude. Recent events were testing his resolve.

Physical activity was a reliable way to relieve stress, but he didn't want to go back in the garage and use the circular saw to cut the crate lumber into smaller pieces. Inevitably, he'd dwell on the weirdness of what had happened, with one leery eye fixed on the casket-size container, and in no time at all, a burst capillary in his stomach would start spurting enough blood to accessorize a John Wick movie.

As he was already in shorts and sneakers, he chose instead to go for a bracing one-hour walk. The October day was warm, but a gentle and refreshing onshore flow brought with it the crisp scent of the sea. The fronds of queen palms and phoenix palms swayed in the breeze, pepper trees sighed, and live oaks issued dry whispers. Red roses, white roses, lantana bright with yellow flowers, purple bougainvillea: Nature brightened the day with a full crayon box of colors. All was for the best in this best of all possible worlds, and in the interest of ameliorating his stress,

Benny said as much aloud as he walked with vigor, said it again and again. He passed a tall blonde with seriously inflated breasts and plumped lips who, withdrawing two Neiman Marcus bags from a Porsche, regarded him as if he had two heads. She said, "That must be some Jesus weed you've been smoking," a snarky comment that, these days, could have gotten her killed in a slightly less refined neighborhood. In the interest of avoiding being killed himself, he did not react to what she said, but thereafter he chanted silently.

At the end of an hour, when he returned home and let himself into the house with the intention of getting a cold bottle of water from the refrigerator, he wasn't entirely stress free, but at least the heebie-jeebies had faded, and the fine hairs on the back of his neck were lying down. Until he walked into the kitchen. He had left the place as clean as a surgery. Now it was a chaos of debris. An empty chocolate-milk carton lay on the floor, along with an empty almond-milk carton, plastic Ziploc packages that once contained slices of provolone and Havarti, a pepperoni pizza box sans pizza, an empty Ritz cracker box, as well as numerous saltines that had been trampled underfoot. The island was littered with Ritz crumbs, an overturned jar of peanut butter that had been full but was now half-empty, a jar of strawberry jam cleaned out so completely that it appeared never to have held any jam, and a drooling squeeze bottle of Hershey's chocolate syrup. The island sink contained a broken jar of jalapeños and a torn package of dry-bouillon cubes.

The front door had been locked when Benny returned. He crunched through saltines to the back door and found it locked. Unless the intruder had entered and departed through a window, he must still be here. Nobody would break into a house just to gorge himself. After satisfying his appetite, he'd probably gone in search of valuables. As Benny considered the quantity and variety of food that had been consumed, he decided there might be more than one burglar. A team. Maybe a gang of three.

He stood very still, listening. Silence.

HELP!

When Benny shifted his weight, the silence was broken by the subtle sound of saltines splintering under his sneakers.

He didn't own a gun. When he was seven, he'd seen his father shot to death. When he was thirteen, after being sent to Briarbush Academy, he'd been deeply affected by the news that Mordred Merrick, his former tutor at the Catspaw mansion in Beverly Hills, had shot nine girls between the ages of thirteen and sixteen, killing three. The attack had occurred at a boy-band concert, after Merrick posted a manifesto in which he declared *"such bubblegum music is mental colonialism via entertainment, enslaving girls and hypnotizing them into becoming lifelong consumers of the music of oppression and grooming them to be mere sex toys for pretty-boy singers who think they're cool, when they're not one-tenth as cool as intellectuals with convictions, who would be much better for those girls if given the chance."*

Instead of a gun, Benny took a small aerosol can of Sabre pepper spray from a drawer in the kitchen island. It had a twelve-foot range and was an extra-potent unit of the kind used by police, one of several provided by Robert "Fat Bob" Jericho. Keeping in mind that events of the past two days had repeatedly tested his steadfast optimism, Benny began upstairs, proceeding with caution from room to room, closet to closet, and then he searched the ground floor.

No windows had been violated. He found nothing suspicious until he came to the laundry room. On the door between the house and the garage, the oblong thumb turn of the deadbolt was vertical instead of horizontal. He'd engaged the lock when he came into the house, after taking apart the crate, but someone had somehow unlocked it. Blood glistened on the stainless-steel door handle. When he looked closer, he was somewhat—but not entirely—relieved to discover that the blood was in fact strawberry jam.

He was less afraid than offended that some slob had violated his home, gorged on his food, and left behind a mess. The situation in his kitchen was like one of those cockroach-pleasing disasters that Big Al now and then had created when he was high on a combo of pot and beer, at once famished and queasy. At least in this case, the spilled food wasn't laced with puke.

Benny turned on the garage lights and opened the door. He crossed the threshold with his index finger on the discharge button of the pepper spray. No one assaulted him. An intruder could have been hiding in the Ford Explorer or crouching on the far side of it, but Benny felt sure that he was alone.

When he walked around the front of his SUV, he discovered that the thousand-pound steel container, which could be moved only with a forklift, had vanished. In its place rested a meticulously crafted wooden box of the same size, ornately carved and decorated with colorful, exquisitely rendered illustrations. It might have been an artifact once displayed in a sideshow tent in one of the carnivals that used to travel the nation from spring through autumn, during a time before Americans had drowned in a flood of entertainment that washed into every nook and nanosecond of their lives and swept away the simpler pleasures of previous generations. Considering the enchanting quality of the art that flowed across the lid and down the sides of the container, a prosperous but eccentric individual might have commissioned this to serve as his casket. If it was in fact a sideshow attraction that had been displayed standing on end, some barker would have claimed it came from ancient Egypt or from a crypt in a lost valley shadowed by the beetling mountains of Bosnia or from a planet other than Earth, whereupon the lid would probably swing open and a genuine or faux freak would spring forth, yellow toothed and bloody eyed, to make the rubes shriek and shudder.

However. However, the mural encompassing the box was of such quality that it sanctified the object. Moment by moment, Benny found it harder to believe that this panorama was created for any purpose as base as a carnival sideshow. The artist offered numerous complex scenes in miniature, each segueing seamlessly into the next, all marvelously detailed, as if Hieronymus Bosch had collaborated with Andrew Wyeth—high fantasy rendered with meticulous attention to detail, presenting a hypnotic narrative. Street scenes melted into natural settings, bleak cities into fantastical jungles festooned with flowering vines, snowy mountain meadows into desert highways, and in all these places, men and women appeared to be in panicked flight from something. Here, three men descended the steps of the nation's capital as if pursued, their twisted shadows preceding them. And here, a desperate man swam through a river toward the safety of shore—as a dark leviathan rose under him.

Some nights, when Benny lies on the edge of sleep, an image of one thing or another comes into his mind—perhaps a lion or an old house—and as he loses consciousness, the lion bears down on him with flaming eyes or the house opens a door through which he enters, and a mere image becomes a dream full of movement and event. Exactly that now happened as he leaned closer to the painted box; suddenly, though awake, he fell away into a scene of a dimly lighted alleyway in an eerily silent city. When two men appeared, running toward him, he feared being attacked, but they seemed not to see him and passed to either side, their eyes wide with fright. Then the alley became a staircase of many flights and landings; as Benny climbed, three men and two women—each alone—descended as if Death himself pursued them with the razor-sharp arc of his scythe, and each time Benny pressed his back to the stairwell wall to avoid being knocked down. He was fully within the vivid cascading mural, a Gothic cyclorama filled with movement all around him as he pivoted into scene after scene, hurrying through a train yard full of long lines of boxcars waiting for locomotives, through a moonlit cemetery crowded with rows of gravestones and mausoleums, through a field of corn grown taller than any man. Wherever this vision took him, Benny met fear-stricken people fleeing in the opposite direction. And he sensed what he could not see—a presence of terrifying aspect and power that could, if it so wished, cause the earth to tremble with its footfalls and speak louder than the loudest thunder, moving always just out of sight among a maze of boxcars, concealed equally by the darkness and moonlight of the graveyard, screened by richly leafed and tasseled stalks of corn, but so close and coming closer, closer, until it spoke to him in a voice as cold and hard as ice calving off the face of a glacier, *"I've come for you."*

Those four words triggered a trapdoor, and Benny fell out of the vision into reality, where he discovered that his hands were pressed to the images on the casket, if it was a casket. The people and things in the miniature scenes moved under his palms and spread fingers. The voice spoke again, from within the artifact—"I've come for you"—and Benny let out a wordless cry of alarm as he shuddered backward. He expected the lid to fly open and something to arise out of the box, something that would put an end to him.

He hurried into the laundry room. He locked the door between the garage and house. He realized that he'd dropped the canister of pepper spray, but he had no intention of going back for it. He went into the dining room, grabbed a chair, brought it to the laundry room, and braced the door to the garage. He hurried to the kitchen and tramped through the debris and snatched up his phone and pressed CONTACTS and called Robert Jericho. When the detective answered, Benny said, "Help. I need help."

Fat Bob said, "Benny?"

"I got a thing here," Benny said.

"A thing?"

"A situation. A seriously crazy situation."

"What's happening?"

"I don't know. I wish I knew."

"Where are you?"

"Jill Swift dumped me yesterday, and nobody's returning my phone calls, and some mannerless intruder left a giant mess in my kitchen—"

"Mannerless intruder?"

"—and there's a casket in my garage with something in it."

"Where are you?" Fat Bob asked again.

"I'm at home. It used to be home. I don't know what it is now."

"You don't sound like yourself. You sound . . . almost angry."

"I'm not angry. I don't believe in anger. I'm nonplussed."

"I'm going to have to google that."

"I'm a little scared, too."

"You want me to come there?"

"That would be good. I mean, if it's not an inconvenience."

"I was about to go to dinner."

"I can't wait five hours."

"Is this something you should call the police?"

"Not if I want to stay out of a psych ward."

"Just remain calm. Remaining calm is who you are."

"Maybe bring a gun."

"I always bring a gun."

"Bring a really big gun."

TWO

WAITING FOR FAT BOB TO COME TO HIS AID, BENNY REMEMBERS HIS BOARDING SCHOOL ROOMMATE

On his first day at Briarbush Academy, thirteen-year-old Benny was escorted to his shared room in Felthammer House, one of the two dormitories that, with other buildings, encircled the quadrangle. The other dormitory was Kentwhistle House. In all endeavors from sports to academic achievement, the boys of Kentwhistle were the rivals of the boys of Felthammer. The master of Felthammer House, Mr. Drew Drudge, introduced Benny to his roommate, fourteen-year-old Jurgen Speer, and directed them to shake hands and recite the Briarbush anthem followed by the sacred oath of fealty to Felthammer House. Jurgen Speer knew the anthem and oath by heart, but Benny needed to read them from a card provided by Master Drudge. When this ceremony concluded, Drudge instructed the boys to tell each other about themselves, and then left them alone.

The spacious room offered an attached bathroom and two closets. There were two beds, two desks with chairs, two leather armchairs with footstools, two smaller chairs for visitors, and a four-shelf bookcase atop a small under-the-counter refrigerator.

Enthroned in his armchair, directly opposite Benny's armchair, Jurgen Speer had the air of an evil starship captain in the making, biding his time until he became old enough to command a death star and destroy entire planets. He was pale and kept his black hair slicked back with Vitalis or another styling oil. His fingernails appeared to have been filed into points until they were reminiscent of the claws of a feral cat. His ginger-brown eyes contained enough maroon pigment to be unnerving, and his stare was as discomfiting as the muzzles of two pistols.

Although Benny was pretty much the same size as his roommate and possessed of a more athletic physique, he felt swallowed up in his armchair, while Speer seemed to fill—to *dominate*—an identical piece of furniture. The floor lamp beside Benny cast a cone of hard white light on him. The reading lamp next to the other boy had been dimmed so that it bathed him in an amber glow, pooling soft shadows in his eye sockets while simultaneously conjuring an eerie glow in those maroon-brown eyes, as if a film-industry lighting specialist had spent several hours refining the scene. Both windows were covered with blinds, and darkness gathered in the corners, like congregate demons with ill intentions.

Although Master Drudge had instructed them to get acquainted, neither spoke for a few minutes. Benny's silence was a consequence of too much weird life experience, which had so precisely calibrated his weirdometer that the needle was pegged out at the EXTREMELY CREEPY end of the dial from the moment he'd shaken his roommate's hand. Jurgen Speer's cold reserve suggested he understood how to use the power of silence to make others uncomfortable and manipulate them.

When at last Speer spoke, his voice was soft and invested now with a note of friendship, yet it brought to Benny's mind the image of a serpent coiling. "There's something special about you, Ben. I see there's something special. You're so calm. Self-possessed."

"I'm just another kid," Benny said.

Speer's smile was conspiratorial, as though they shared a secret that bonded them. "You're clearheaded and centered. The masters here want us to put all childish things behind us, to be clearheaded and centered. We have classes in centeredness."

Benny shrugged.

"The funny thing," Speer said, "is that the masters are all muddleheaded. A faculty of fools and losers—and worse."

"Mrs. Baneberry-Smith seems very nice," Benny said.

"The bug lady."

"Entomologist."

"She was bitten by an exotic spider."

Benny shrugged again. "Her cookies taste good."

"The ones that smell like mushrooms or the ones that smell like onions or the ones that smell like wet dog fur?"

"Mushrooms," Benny said. "But they tasted good."

Leaning forward in his chair and out of the light, his luminous eyes going dark in their sockets, Speer said, "Never, never, never eat her cookies."

"Why not? I like cookies."

"She teaches a tenth-grade course in the fifteenth-century history of Italy."

"Yeah. She told me. So?"

"Borgias."

"What?"

"The Borgias. Catherine de' Medici. The century of poisoners. The rich, the royals, poisoning their own kind, poisoning cardinals and princesses. Everyone knows Mrs. Baneberry-Smith is *fascinated* with poisons and poisoners . . . and poisonous insects."

Benny considered the boy's implication, but not too seriously. Mrs. Baneberry-Smith was only a tiny bit as creepy as Jurgen Speer. "Do a lot of people at Briarbush die of poisoning?"

Leaning back into the lamplight, his luminous eyes souring into view once more, Speer said, "No. Murder isn't what the headmaster and his wife are about. They don't want to kill us. They want to *change* us."

"Change us how?"

"I don't know how, but I'm going to find out." He closed his eyes and punctuated his silence with a series of deep inhalations and exhalations. Then he focused on Benny again. "I believe you're sane, Ben Catspaw. I'm counting on you being sane. Are you sane?"

"Well, gee, I think so. Yeah. I'm pretty sure."

Speer tapped his chest with one finger. "I'm sane, too. There aren't many sane boys left at Briarbush. Most have been changed."

"Spooky," Benny said.

"Yes. It's way spooky. But they won't change us, Ben." He slid to the edge of his chair, palms flattened on the seat cushion, body tense, head thrust forward. "We'll look out for each other. If I see the slightest sign you're changing, I'll tell you. You do the same for me. Promise you'll do the same for me. At the slightest sign."

"I'll do the same for you," Benny promised, because at that moment Jurgen Speer was reminiscent of a tarantula preparing to jump. Tarantulas could jump five feet. Speer looked as if he might spring from chair to footstool and from there fling himself through the air onto Benny, not with any good intention. "But what . . . what would a sign look like?"

During his next silence, Speer sat with his hands curved like claws on the arms of his chair, his pointy fingernails dimpling but not quite puncturing the leather, lower lip sucked entirely into his mouth, and eyes narrowed to slits. Just as Benny was about to repeat his question, Speer said, "A sign would be like what happened to Prescott Galsbury."

"Who's Prescott Galsbury?"

"My roommate before you. He was fourteen when . . . it started."

"What happened to him?"

"It began with one of his lunula."

"What's a lunula?"

"The pale crescent at the base of a fingernail. In a week, all his lunulae turned blue. Nurse Stillhunt—she runs the infirmary—said it was an allergic reaction to the liquid soap in our dormitory bathrooms. But she's a moron and a liar and . . . something."

Benny said, "What something?"

Leaning forward again, out of the lamplight, his eyes shadowed in their sockets, Speer divided the word into two. "Some *thing*. God knows what. Galsbury's nails stopped being blue after he was caught eating ants and was put under constant watch."

"Ants? Like bugs? He was eating ants?"

"He had this jar of honey," said Speer. "He'd take it out in the meadows, where no one could see him, where there were anthills. He'd coat a soupspoon with honey and lure the ants onto it, and eat them. Spoon after spoon of ants. They're rich in formic acid. They say it was all that formic acid that turned his lunulae blue."

It was possible, of course, that Jurgen Speer was a hoaxer or even a pathological liar. However, in spite of the boy's forbidding appearance, the vulnerability that he projected seemed authentic.

The roommate's dread was real and communicable, so that Benny felt a centipedal chill crawl down his spine. "Why did he eat ants?"

"He didn't know. He was just compelled. It was something he had to do or go mad. That's what he said to me. 'If I didn't eat them when the urge came, I'd have gone crazy.'"

"Where is he now?" Benny asked.

Speer rose from his chair and went to one of the windows and stood staring at the pleated shade, as if he could see through it to the view beyond. Rather than answer the question, he said, "Prescott Galsbury thought Mrs. Baneberry-Smith was totally hot. He fantasized about humping her. You know what that means?"

A warmth came into Benny's face. "I'm thirteen. I'm not twelve anymore. But you said Galsbury was fourteen, just a boy to her."

"When the list of community service opportunities was issued, Galsbury signed up to assist Mrs. Baneberry-Smith."

"Community service opportunities?"

"Our success at Briarbush depends on the volunteer work we're dragooned into. Galsbury signed to assist in her laboratory."

"She has a laboratory?"

"Behind the headmaster's house."

"What does she do there?"

"Studies insects."

"I thought she gave that up after the spider bit her."

"She gave up jungles. Now she studies insects in the safety of a laboratory."

Benny remembered the Lucite boxes that displayed large, exotic, dead insects in the headmaster's drawing room. He was not comforted by the thought that similar specimens might be crawling around in Mrs. Baneberry-Smith's lab, even if they were properly contained.

At the window, Jurgen Speer used one finger to push aside the pleated shade just far enough that he could peer with one eye at the soccer field behind Felthammer House. Beyond the field, a primeval evergreen woodland lay in perpetual twilight even on the brightest day, a realm of Transylvanian mystery. In fact, the high grounds of the academy and the adjacent meadows were entirely surrounded by a forest so dense and deep that it seemed to grow down the steeply sloped walls of an abyss.

After a thoughtful silence, Benny said, "What does she do with insects in her laboratory?"

"No one knows," said Jurgen Speer.

"But Galsbury assisted her. What did he assist her with?"

"He wouldn't talk about it. She swore him to secrecy. He said if he kept his oath of silence, she'd eventually let him hump her."

"She's like really pretty and the headmaster's wife. Galsbury is fourteen and—what?—delusional?"

Speer moved to the other window and stared at *that* shade. "Galsbury said he needed to prove himself capable of secrecy for three months. She'd promised, 'When I trust you, I'll do you once every month thereafter, my pretty boy.'"

"'My pretty boy'?" Benny scoffed. "Who talks like that?"

"Maybe younger wives of headmasters. But Galsbury is farther from pretty than the distance between *ass* and *posterior* in the dictionary."

"So he made it up."

With one finger, Speer eased aside the shade and peered at the soccer field from another angle. "He assisted her for less than a month before his lunulae turned blue. He'd spent two hours a day in the lab for more than two months when he was caught eating ants."

Benny repeated his unanswered question. "Where is he now?"

"Supposedly, he was expelled and sent home five weeks ago."

"Supposedly?"

Speer turned from the window and crossed his arms, right hand on left shoulder, left hand on right shoulder, as if warding off an expected hard blow to the chest. "Two weeks ago, before dinner, a student named Mengistu Gidada was walking the meadow behind Mrs. Baneberry-Smith's lab, carrying a book and memorizing a poem by William Butler Yeats. He saw a face at a window, at the southwest corner of the building. It was Prescott Galsbury, who by then had supposedly been expelled. That night, Mengistu couldn't sleep. He became convinced Galsbury had been seeking help. The next morning, when he went back to the meadow, the window was boarded over *from the inside*. I'm the only one he's told because he's afraid of being sent home, where his father will demote him from first son to last son and cut off something more important than Mengistu's hair."

"You're saying Galsbury is being held prisoner?"

"Mengistu is one of the sane, and he doesn't lie."

"But come the next holiday, when Galsbury goes home, he'll tell his parents everything."

"Briarbush doesn't close for holidays. If your parents say you should go home, you go. But quite a few, like Galsbury, were sent here because they were problem kids who needed to be in residence full-time to be rehabilitated."

The word evoked a shiver from Benny. "Rehabilitated."

Speer whispered, "My word for it is *changed*."

"Were you a problem kid?"

"I didn't think so," Speer said. "But I've been here three years, and I've never been home for a holiday. Or spoken to my parents. We aren't allowed cell phones or computers with online connections."

The boy's posture—arms crossed on his chest, hands gripping his shoulders—seemed desperately defensive, as if he hugged himself because no one else ever hugged him. He was so pathetic that Benny wanted to say something to make him feel better about himself. Every reassurance that came to mind seemed stupid. Instead, he offered condolences: "I'm sorry about Galsbury. He was your friend."

In the shadows, Speer looked older than fourteen, as though each of his years at Briarbush had the abrading power of a decade. "Galsbury is nobody's friend but his own. He wasn't sent here to be changed. He was already what they want us to be. He was sent here to be *refined.* When they're done doing to him whatever they're doing, he'll return. He'll maybe become proctor of Felthammer House, in charge of enforcing the disciplinary actions Master Drudge imposes on us. Years from now, he'll maybe be valedictorian of his class. One day, governor or senator. Or the head of a hedge fund. Whatever. I'm not worried about Galsbury. I'm *scared* of him. And I'm afraid that sooner or later I'll be made into what he is."

He lowered his arms and settled again in his chair. Benny returned to his chair as well. They sat in a silence different from the one they had shared before, staring at each other until Jurgen said, "Will *you* be going home for the holidays?"

Only then did Benny realize that he didn't know if Briarbush Academy was just a boarding school to be attended during seasons of education or if it was his new home. His mother and stepfather were traveling the far corners of the world for the next year and perhaps for years thereafter. There would be no reason to go home to Beverly Hills for Thanksgiving with Rudyard and Sally Bromley, where the butler would weep for unknown reasons and his wife would sing dark Celtic ballads with bitter intensity. The only other choice was to take a holiday in Hell with Grandmother Cosima and be subjected to her efforts to depress him to the point of suicide.

Evidently, Benny's face boldly displayed his train of thought, for Jurgen didn't need to hear an answer to his question. He said, "I'm sorry, Ben. Sorry for you, but happy for me. We're both sane, and we'll keep each other sane, and while we avoid being changed, we'll have some fun."

Jurgen didn't look like a boy who knew how to have fun, but maybe he just hadn't had much opportunity to be amused.

Benny found the rheostat on the cord of the lamp beside his chair and dialed down the light until it matched the moody glow produced by his roommate's lamp.

After another silence, Jurgen said, "Can I make a suggestion?"

"Lay it on me," Benny said.

"The majority of the boys in this school are of a kind, and the others are being shaped into their kind. I'm not sure how they know we're not their kind, whether it's intuition or they smell something, but they know. We're in a hostile environment. You get me?"

"I get you."

"My advice is to develop an edgy image, as if you're mental. I've got my pointy fingernails, slicked-back hair, my silences. I often stare hard at people for five or ten minutes. Sometimes, I express admiration for Satan. Some of these guys will push you around unless they think you're unstable. In the end, they're all cowards. They'll walk wide of you if you give them any reason."

Benny's assessment of Jurgen Speer had changed dramatically in less than an hour. "In the dining hall, when meat is served, what if I hold it down with a fork and stare at it intently while I calmly stab it forty or fifty times instead of just slicing it, stab it so hard I sometimes break the plate?"

Smiling, Jurgen said, "That's a start."

MR. BEER FOR BREAKFAST

After the visions that were inspired by the carved and painted casket, waiting for Fat Bob Jericho, Benny paced his living room and front hall with a golf club in hand. Having resisted buying a gun, having dropped the little canister of pepper spray in the garage, and having felt foolish walking around with a wooden rolling pin, like an aggrieved wife waiting for her philandering husband to come home with whiskey on his breath and lipstick on his collar, he had decided that the nine iron was a better weapon than a kitchen tool that formed pie crusts. A more sophisticated version of a caveman's bludgeon, it made him feel—and no doubt look—more dangerous.

When the doorbell rang, he was so relieved that he didn't stop to consider that the visitor might be the very threat about which he had summoned Fat Bob. He disengaged the deadbolt and pulled open the door.

The young woman before him appeared to have stepped out of an ad for a Caribbean cruise. Pale-yellow sneakers with white laces. Pale-yellow jeans with an electric-blue scarf for a belt. Yellow silk blouse with white buttons. Her ponytail depended from a pink baseball cap emblazoned with one word in a dazzling shade of blue followed by an exclamation point: SMOOTH! Instead of a necklace of tiny pigs dancing across her throat, she wore a silver chain with an enameled pendant featuring the face of a golden retriever grinning and winking one eye. She was carrying a white straw purse.

"Papa Bear's," Benny said, which was the name of the restaurant where he'd met her the previous morning.

She said, "Mr. Beer for Breakfast."

Remembering her name, he said, “Harper.”

“Benjamin.”

“Most people call me Benny. What’re you doing here?”

“Bob sent me.”

“Fat Bob?”

“I refuse to call him that.”

“It’s what he wants to be called.”

“So he says. Are you going to invite me in?”

“Yeah. Sure.” He stepped back.

In the foyer, Harper indicated the nine iron Benny was holding. “What’s par for the house? Judging by the size, I’d say it’s a nine-room course.”

“I don’t have a gun.”

“It wasn’t such a bad joke that you need to shoot me for it.”

Closing the front door, he said, “Where’s Fat Bob?”

“Mr. Jericho wanted to stop for takeout, so he could eat and drive.” She walked into the living room. “Sparkly clean.”

He said, “I like clean.”

“Me too. It’s all very modern, slick.”

“I like modern things. Slick, sleek, minimalist.”

“It’s unlivable,” she declared.

“I’m sorry?”

“You don’t need to apologize. You just didn’t know any better when you bought all this.”

“I know what I like. Everyone to his own taste.”

“Do you ever sit here?” she asked.

“Why would I sit here?”

“Exactly my point. Sitting here would be about as comfortable as sitting in a dentist’s waiting room.”

"Who sits in *any* living room?" he said. "People sit in their family rooms."

"Then why have a living room?"

Benny resorted to his Realtor's chrestomathy of convincing responses, but the only thing in it was this: "Well, houses have always had living rooms."

"The view is cool," she said. "I like how you put the ocean just where you did."

He didn't know what to make of her, whether she was playing with him or maybe a little off-center. "Are you and Fat Bob . . . an item?"

"I'm twenty-one. Bob is old enough to be my father and then some."

"Not so unusual around here."

"I love Bob like you love a favorite uncle. I work with him."

"You're a private detective?"

"No. Not yet. Maybe someday, if being a waitress stops being exciting. For now, with Bob, it's a generational thing and a gender thing. He finds a young woman's perspective helpful on a lot of cases, and he's very generous."

"But you're still working as a waitress."

"Breakfast-to-lunch shift. I also have a little side business knitting custom sweaters for dogs. I like to stay busy. Can't sleep more than four hours a night. Never have, so far as I can remember. That leaves a big day to fill. What have you done to your hair?"

"Nothing."

"That's what I thought."

Following her into the dining room, Benny said, "I don't know your last name."

"Harper," she said.

"Oh. Then I don't know your first name."

"Harper."

"Harper Harper? Why would your parents do that?"

"I've never discussed it with them. Everyone makes mistakes. They're such nice people, very sweet. I never want to upset them. Your dining room is as welcoming as a morgue."

"I like minimalist."

"Do any guests come back for dinner a second time?"

"I don't have people to dinner. I take them to restaurants."

"Ah. Then maybe you should convert the dining room into a second living room."

"The kitchen is a mess," he warned her, as she pushed through the swinging door.

Saltines crackled under her shoes. She surveyed the empty milk cartons and cracker boxes, the overturned jam jars, the drooling squeeze bottle of chocolate syrup, a slice of pizza cheese-glued to a cabinet door. "If no one ever comes here for dinner, who did you have a food fight with?"

"Some intruder did this when I was out taking a walk. Raided the fridge and the cabinets, ate stuff, threw other stuff around. That's what I called Fat Bob about."

"Bob."

"Yeah. Yesterday and today, everything's gone kablooey, and I mean everything. Somehow, this has to be part of it."

"Kablooey."

"Yeah. I think whatever did this, it's in the garage now."

"'It'?"

"That's why I'm carrying the golf club. How long is Fat Bob going to take to get here?"

"Bob."

"Yeah. Whatever did this, it's probably back in its box, though I don't think it'll stay there. I braced the door with a chair, but that seems kind of lame."

Harper Harper cocked her head and regarded him with a bemused expression. "The intruder is in a box in the garage?"

"Something like a casket. It came in a crate. I opened the crate. At first the casket, if it is a casket, was this streamlined steel container, very minimalist, you wouldn't have liked it. Then it was carved and painted and . . . weird. Colonel Clerkenwell shipped it from Boca Raton. He said there was nothing to be afraid of. Maybe I'm being judgmental, but I think the colonel is a liar. Something extraordinary is going on here, maybe supernatural. That sounds crazy. But if you think I'm crazy, you're wrong."

"You're not crazy," she said.

"Thank you."

"I know crazy when I see it. You're just stressed."

"I'm very stressed. I lost my job, people don't return my phone calls anymore, and my girlfriend left me."

Putting her purse on one of the few clean counters, Harper said, "All of that's just so much blah."

"It's what?"

"Blah. Life throws a lot of blah at us, and the mistake we make is taking it seriously."

"No job, no prospects, no girlfriend. I take that seriously."

"You see? Mistake. You'll get another job, and it'll be better than the one you lost, and a new girl will come along. You know what's really stressing you?"

"You don't remember the casket thing in the garage and what might be in it?"

"Blah. Maybe nothing's in it." She spread her arms wide to indicate the condition of the kitchen. "What's really stressing you is this mess. If we clean it up together, you'll feel a lot better."

"What about Fat Bob?"

"Bob. This isn't the kind of mess Bob cleans up."

"But the mess is evidence. Isn't it evidence?"

"No," said Harper. "Where do you keep your cleaning supplies?"

He took her to the closet and opened the door.

She said, "Wow. You've got everything."

"There are so many different kinds of dirt," he said. "You need just the right product to deal with each of them."

WAITING FOR BOB

Harper was right. Benny felt better once the kitchen was clean again, but there was too much white. That was confirmed for him now. He had gone overboard on white. Maybe his obsession with white decor had offended Handy Duroc, which was why he'd been asked to leave Surfside Realty.

"That makes no sense," Harper said when he shared his white-decor theory of self-ruination.

As it was the only theory Benny had, he clung to it. "A lot of things in life don't make sense."

"That's true enough. But all this blah is related—no job, no one returning your calls, some pig of an intruder mucking up your kitchen, girlfriend gone. Did Carla Cobra have a problem with your decor?"

"Who?"

"Your girlfriend, Patty Python, did she dump you because the place looks like a hospital surgery?"

"No. She loves white decor."

"That pops your theory."

"Her name is Jill Swift."

"She sounds like a snake to me."

"Well, no, that's not fair," Benny said, following her out of the kitchen, through the dining room, into the living room, as she gave everything a sharp-eyed lookover, as if searching for a splash of color. "You don't even know Jill. She's a lovely person."

"You lose your job, she pushes you off a cliff the same day, and on your way to the rocks below, you send her a valentine?"

"You have a colorful way of talking," Benny said.

"It's part of the job."

"I've never heard another waitress talk like you."

"Private investigator. In training." As he followed her into his study, she said, "Looks like the intruder put two pale-gray throw pillows on your white sofa. We catch him, I'll kneecap the bastard."

In defense of his taste, which he was rapidly coming to find embarrassing, Benny said, "For years as a child, I lived in squalor with cockroaches. Then my grandmother dressed me all in black and made it her life's mission to depress me into suicide. Maybe white-on-white has been an unconscious effort to compensate for those oppressive experiences."

"Don't go Sigmund on me, boyfriend. Freud was a phony. The mind doesn't work that way. Most likely, you saw a magazine spread of a place done like this, and the writer raved about the cool decor, and you wanted to be cool, because you've never felt very cool, so you copied the look."

Benny was somewhat surprised and slightly chagrinned to hear himself confessing. "It was a six-page spread. High-end interior-design magazine. The Manhattan apartment of a famous playwright."

Frowning at a desk made of slabs of clear Lucite, Harper said, "I'll bet he was a pretentious mug who writes plays I'd pay big money *not* to see."

"Mug?"

"In his case a mug who commits crimes against art. The word is from a more blunt-spoken and interesting era than our prissy times."

One good thing about all this white was how good it made Harper look, dressed as colorfully as she was. Benny couldn't stop staring at her. He almost said as much, almost compared her to a parrot in a snow scene. Then he intuited that he'd be vulnerable to a critique of his ability to craft a metaphor—or was it a simile?—so instead he restricted himself to an expression of curiosity. "Your baseball cap says 'smooth.' With an exclamation point."

"That's correct."

"What's the significance?"

"I'm smooth and blue."

"Well, I guess you look very smooth, smooth in a nice way, but you aren't blue."

"I'm as blue as blue gets. You'll understand when it's time to understand, Benny."

"When will that be?"

"When it is. Now, what's the point of a glass desk with no drawers?"

"It's Lucite. The drawers are in that brushed stainless-steel unit against the wall. I just have to swivel around in the chair and scoot over there to get to whatever drawer I need."

"How charmingly inconvenient."

"The playwright's desk was made of Starphire glass, but I just couldn't afford that. His drawer unit was hidden in the floor, and it powered up into sight when he pushed a button on his chair. That was cool, but for several reasons, I couldn't make it work here."

Harper's attention shifted from the Lucite desk to Benny, and she studied his face at some length. In the traditional pattern of a conversation, it was her turn to contribute, but she didn't speak.

At first, Benny thought something was wrong with his face—like a pimple on his forehead or a booger displayed in one nostril—but then he began to suspect that, to Harper, he was as transparent as the Lucite desk, which was far more disconcerting than the thought of a prominent booger.

He said, "What?"

"You need a lot of smoothing. But though you're not fully blue, you're close."

Deciding to play her game even though he didn't know what it was, Benny said, "Well, most people are fully blue or close, so I can't take any pride in that."

"Sadly, most people are only slightly blue or not blue at all."

The doorbell rang.

"That'll be Fat Bob," he said.

"Bob," she corrected.

BEFORE THE MONSTER

In the foyer, when Benny opened the door, Robert Jericho was as reassuring a presence as always he had been. He had probably been a reassuring presence when he was in kindergarten, though most likely not as big as he was currently. Charismatic people were born with charisma; it wasn't something that could be learned or ordered from Amazon, a truth Benny had reluctantly accepted a year or so earlier.

Four inches taller than Benny and half again as wide, Bob came into the house, squinting at all the whiteness. "I always forget this is a sunglasses-required environment. How's it going, Harper?"

"I've just been holding the client's hand," she said, "until you could get here. How was dinner?"

"Terrible traffic. I didn't have time to stop. So let's have a look at the kitchen," Bob said, proceeding through the house with the majesty of an icebreaker crunching a navigable passage through the frozen Arctic Ocean. When he reached his destination, he grimaced. "White. While my pupils are shrinking to pinpoints, tell me about the mess you mentioned on the phone."

"We cleaned it up," Benny said.

"Good to know you haven't become so obsessive-compulsive that the spotless vista before me is your idea of a mess. But I'd like a description so that I might suss out a motive."

"Hunger was obviously the motive," Benny said.

So powerful was Robert Jericho's charisma that, by just raising one eyebrow, he was able to make Benny profoundly regretful that he, not being either a licensed detective or a male equivalent of Miss Jane Marple, had usurped the authority of such an experienced PI. Benny provided the needed description of the mess caused by the mannerless intruder. When he finished, Harper Harper added a few details that Benny had forgotten.

"Hunger was *part* of the motive," Bob at once deduced, "but not purely that. He left a mess in order to intimidate you, Benny, not because he wants to bully you, but because he needs your cooperation for some reason and prefers to get it through intimidation rather than persuasion. He has an anger issue. However, the object of his fury isn't you, but something larger than any one person. He has a strong personality and most likely is also physically powerful. He is impulsive, perhaps dangerously so. There was no father in the home when he was growing up. Or if there were two parents, neither of them was an adequate disciplinarian. He loves jam, but he has only contempt for saltine crackers. The jar of jalapeños, thrown into the sink and broken after he tried one, suggests not just that he dislikes hot peppers, but also that he fears them to an extent that he fears nothing else in this world. Finally, considering the volume of food consumed, it is reasonable to suspect that there are at least two of him."

At the conclusion of that analysis, Benny was further mortified that he had been so presumptuous as to offer his poorly considered psychological profile of the intruder: *Hunger was obviously the motive.*

Of course, the detective's conjectures were yet to be borne out by more than circumstantial evidence. When coming on a crime scene—or in this case the description of a crime scene that he had never observed himself—perhaps Bob was prone to pontificating as if every half-formed thought that occurred to him was an unassailable truth. Once all facts were known, maybe half or even 90 percent of his suppositions would prove to be incorrect.

Seeking some indication from Harper that Bob was fallible—a wink, a knowing smile—Benny gave her a knowing smile of his own. She appeared embarrassed for him and quickly looked away, down at the floor, shaking her head. Never had Benny seen a shaking of the head that conveyed such a richness of emotion—sadness, pity, and the keen frustration of a woman who was inclined to like him if only he could get his act together.

Just yesterday, he'd *had* his act together, had been a rising star among real-estate royalty, a respected guy whose text messages were quickly answered and phone calls returned. If only he was able to learn what he had done that had gotten him ostracized, he thought he could get his act even more together than it had been previously. No, he didn't *think* he could. He *knew* he could; he *knew* he could.

Surveying the kitchen, grimacing as if he could see the mess that had been described, Bob turned to Benny, still grimacing. "On the phone, you said there's a casket in your garage."

"A casket or something."

"You said 'casket.'"

"Yeah, okay, it's a casket or something."

"What something?"

"Well, in a casket, you tend to expect the occupant to be dead. But I don't think it's dead, whatever's in there. So maybe the box isn't, strictly speaking, a casket."

"It?"

"Whatever," Benny said. "Whatever pronoun you want to use for the occupant is okay with me. He, she, they, it."

Bob stared at him. Then he stared at Harper, who returned his stare. She didn't shake her head, and neither did Bob. They didn't need to.

Addressing Benny again, Bob said, "So how did this casket or something come to be in your garage?"

Benny recounted how Mayweather Universal Air Freight delivered a crate from Colonel Talmadge Clerkenwell in Boca Raton, Florida. How Benny had broken apart the crate. How he'd found a sleek stainless-steel container somewhat larger than the average casket. How the next time he'd seen it, the container was made of wood, elaborately ornamented with dimensional and vividly detailed scenes of terrified people in various ominous settings, people who were fleeing from some threat not depicted.

He *didn't* reveal how, when he looked closely at the amazing art, the scenes became animated, how he lost all awareness of his garage and fell away into those miniature dramas. Upon hearing such a revelation, the Bob who was a private investigator would morph into the Bob who was a concerned friend, and he would demand that Benny produce and destroy his stash of hallucinogenic drugs. Because no such cache existed, much time would be wasted when they should be focused on the *physically powerful, dangerously impulsive, unknown entity with an anger issue that was boxed in his garage!*

Bob pulled out one of the stools that was tucked under the overhang of the kitchen island. He settled on it, encompassing the seat so entirely that he appeared to have six legs, four of them polished steel. With a lack of urgency, as if they had gathered here for no purpose other than to gossip, he said, "You didn't know you had a great-uncle Talmadge?"

"No. I never heard of him. He came out of nowhere."

"Brother to your mother's mother."

"Grandma Cosima Springbok."

"Did you know your grandmother?"

"I was sent to live with her for a while."

"And she never mentioned her brother?" Harper asked, commanding a stool of her own.

"She's a narcissistic psychopath. She rarely talked about anyone but herself, never about my mother, only very little about her two husbands she killed."

"Your grandmother killed two husbands?" Bob asked.

"She wasn't convicted. She wasn't even a suspect."

Bob raised both eyebrows, an expression that was four times as charismatic and daunting as when he raised only one. "You never told me this."

Benny didn't grab a stool. He paced restlessly, hoping thereby to convey the urgency with which he felt that they should proceed. "Cosima is still alive. I don't ever want her to think I'd rat her out. I don't have any evidence. Only a few little things she said. Inferences I made. But she'd come after me anyway. She'd find me. And so I don't speak about it."

"You just spoke about it," Bob noted.

"I didn't mean to. I'm under tremendous stress."

"Your mother never mentioned Talmadge Clerkenwell?"

"No. I think she's afraid of Grandma. Sometimes I wonder if the guy who shot my father in the back had a connection with Cosima."

"You never told me your father was murdered."

Harper, hard-boiled PI in training, also had a tenderhearted feminine side. "Oh, Benny, all this is just awful. I'm so sorry."

"It's okay. He was a violent drunk. He beat my mother. He was always getting into bar fights. He would have killed someone sooner or later. It wouldn't surprise me if he already had killed someone before the back-shooter showed up while I was building a staircase to the moon with LEGOs. In fact, the back-shooter might have been another relative I didn't know about. Of the few people I knew in my family, they were all murderers or murdered."

"What about this Talmadge Clerkenwell?" Bob asked.

"On the video card, he seemed nice. A sweet old guy in a white suit. He seemed genuinely concerned about me. But you never know."

"And your mother," said Harper. "She's not a murderer."

"How do you know that?" Benny said. "You don't know that. My mother is . . . Let's not go there. The past is past. The past wasn't good to me. I don't talk about the past."

Bob said, "You've talked about it intensely for two minutes."

"Stress," Benny repeated. "I feel like I've fallen out of an airplane without a parachute. And everywhere I look below me, a fire is burning out of control."

Harper said, "You have a colorful way of talking."

Extricating himself from the stool, Bob reached under his sport coat and withdrew a pistol from a belt holster on his right hip.

"Are we going into the garage now?" Benny asked.

Robert Jericho's nature was such that even in fraught and dire circumstances, he was able to amuse himself. "Well, I might murder you here and now if I were of your lineage, but my family tends to frown on homicide, so I believe I'll go into the garage instead and have a look at the box from Boca Raton."

"What do you want me to do?" Benny asked, retrieving the golf club he had previously carried for defense. "How are we going to handle this? How can I help?"

As Harper got to her feet, Bob said, "I'll go into the garage alone while you practice your swing. If your mannerless intruder has gone, we can examine the Clerkenwell mystery casket together."

"This sucks," Harper said. "I sit through all the talk, and then I get sidelined when it comes to the action."

"This isn't a suitable situation for a trainee," Bob said. "Be patient, and I'll eventually get you into some fix where you could be killed. But I'm overly cautious when there's a chance that the proper pronoun for the perpetrator is *it* rather than *he* or *she*."

"If I owned a gun," Benny said, "I'd go with you."

"If you owned a gun," Bob replied, "I'd take it away from you."

Benny and Harper followed the detective to the laundry room, where he insisted they remain in the kitchen. They watched him as he passed through the smaller chamber. He removed the straight-backed chair with which Benny had braced the connecting door to the garage and stood listening. Then he opened the door and quickly cleared the threshold and disappeared into that realm, where Benny had earlier left the lights on. The door closed behind him.

STRESS

Here on the brink of the laundry room, the air smelled faintly of detergent and bleach and fabric softener. Warm light fell on two glossy white washers with their lids up and two glossy white dryers.

Benny said, "Fat Bob is a great guy."

"Bob," Harper said.

"Yeah. Nothing scares him."

"That's not exactly healthy," Harper said.

"What I mean is, he's courageous."

"People say he's just like his father."

"Fat Jim."

"Jim," Harper corrected.

For a few seconds, which seemed like a few minutes, neither of them said anything. No sound came from the garage.

Holding the golf club in both hands, the head of it on the floor between his feet, as if preparing to make a crucial putt, Benny said, "You don't have a gun?"

"It's hard to get a concealed-carry permit in this state unless you're a criminal, in which case you're unofficially permitted. When I get my PI license, I'll gun up."

"As a real-estate agent, I never expected to need a firearm. I guess it's the same for a waitress."

"Even waiting tables is spooky these days. Twice, people having dinner on Papa Bear's patio were robbed en masse by gunmen."

"I didn't know that."

"It's not something the restaurant advertises. There's a bigger market for food and beverages than for terror."

"Maybe we should go see what's happening," Benny suggested.

"When Bob says stay put, you stay put."

The next few seconds seemed like half an hour, and Benny broke the silence. "You called me 'boyfriend.'"

"Did I?"

"Earlier, you said, 'Don't go Sigmund on me, boyfriend.'"

"In that context, *boyfriend* is like saying *pal* or *buddy*. It doesn't mean anything."

"That's what I thought. I didn't think it meant anything. I didn't think it indicated a subconscious attraction."

"There's no subconscious attraction that I'm aware of," she assured him.

"But then you wouldn't be aware of it."

"Aware of what?"

"A subconscious attraction, because it's subconscious."

"I assume you're like this because you're so stressed."

"Exactly," Benny said.

"I sure hope you're not like this when you're not stressed."

"I'm nothing like this. You just caught me on what is one of the worst days of my life."

"One of? Well, I guess the day you saw your father shot."

"No, that doesn't even rank. How long do you think we should stay put before we have to go into the garage?"

She checked her wristwatch. "Two minutes more. Maybe three."

Wound tighter than Harper Harper's watch spring, Benny expected something horrific to burst through the door from the garage, some sight even worse than what he saw on his third night at Briarbush Academy, in Catherine Baneberry-Smith's laboratory.

(The playwright Eugene O'Neill said, "The past is the present. It's the future, too. We all try to lie out of that, but life won't let us." Benny is where he is now because of where he has been. I wish he hadn't gone to Briarbush Academy, because I find the place almost too creepy to bear. On the other hand, I like the person his experiences have shaped him into. It's good to know he wasn't torn to pieces at Briarbush, but of course he could be torn to pieces tomorrow. As could we all.)

WAITING WITH HARPER, BENNY RECALLS A MONSTROUS SIGHT FROM HIS THIRD NIGHT AT BRIARBUSH ACADEMY

Jurgen Speer's previous roommate, Prescott Galsbury—whose lunulae turned blue because he was ingesting massive amounts of formic acid by eating large quantities of ants—supposedly had been expelled from Briarbush Academy and sent home more than five weeks earlier.

In a visitor's chair in the dorm room of Jurgen Speer and Benny Catspaw, elbows on the arms of the chair and hands folded against his chest in a Yoda pose, Mengistu Gidada declared, "It is all a most egregious lie. Prescott comes from a family of such merciless overachievers that if he were to be expelled from Briarbush, his parents would not have permitted him to come home, but would either have committed him to a mental institution or dispatched him to live out his days in a monastery built by pyrolater monks."

Having learned from his roommate how to present himself with maximum drama using his adjustable reading lamp—which Jurgen called "intimidation by lighting"—Benny sat half in moody bronze light and half in penumbra, one eye full of reflection and the other hooded in shadow. "What's a pyrolater?" he asked.

"A fire worshipper," Jurgen replied from a weaving of light and shadow more artful than Benny's effort.

"There really are monasteries of pyrolater monks?"

"When it comes to human behavior," Mengistu said, "if you can imagine people doing something stupid or dangerous, then there are people somewhere who are doing it. Often highly educated people."

Jurgen said, "We call that the Gidada-Speer Law of Pointless Human Transgression."

Mengistu, a resident of Felthammer House, was almost fifteen, a year older than Jurgen Speer and two years older than Benny Catspaw, but he looked younger because he was very thin with a large head and enormous, expressive eyes—reminiscent of characters in Japanese anime or certain animated Pixar films. He was considered to be by far the smartest boy at Briarbush and was therefore envied and hated by the 95 percent of his classmates who feared he would become president of the United States before they did.

Mengistu was also, according to Jurgen Speer, one of the few sane individuals among the student body and the faculty. They met every evening during the social hours after dinner, and by this third night of Benny's incarceration, Mengistu and Jurgen were the only people he'd encountered at Briarbush on whom he would wager a dollar if the bet was on their sanity.

Better yet, both boys were nice. Although just thirteen, Benny nevertheless had come to esteem niceness as much as he did honesty and cleanliness. However, he'd begun to suspect that by holding the first two of those values, he was making a target and an outcast of himself.

Earlier, when Benny expressed that concern, Mengistu agreed. "Yes, I believe that to be true when we're speaking of the current ruling class and the institutions that prepare them to run things. During the past thirty years, they have brought the nation—and much of the world—to the brink of ruin. Rather than admit their errors, they target those who dare note their incompetence. The nicer you are when you disagree with them, the more vicious they are in their treatment of you."

"But I don't want to be mean," Benny said.

"Being mean is not the way to happiness," Mengistu said. "You must do what Jurgen and I intend to do."

"We intend," said Jurgen, "to endure until we're of age, and then bail out of the ruling class, live among people who don't want power over others, who don't think they're entitled either by birth or education to control everyone else."

"The bigger problem might seem to be surviving Briarbush without being changed," Mengistu said. "But it is not."

"The bigger problem," Jurgen concurred, "is what our families will do to us, a few years from now, when we try to bail out."

Mengistu's light, musical voice became heavy. "We want to avoid ending in a monastery built by pyrolater monks or the equivalent."

"I don't think I have to worry," Benny decided. "My family already abandoned me. My mom and Jubal, my stepfather, didn't send me here to be changed. They just wanted to get me out of the way."

Jurgen said, "How very fortunate you are if that's true."

"However," Mengistu said, "for whatever reason, you are here. Once you are here, Headmaster Baneberry-Smith, his insect-obsessed wife, and his staff of brainwashers will steep your intellect in nonsense, poach your heart in lies, Cuisinart your soul, pour you into the Briarbush mold, bake you, and send you off to university where you will be spatulated with a bitter icing of entitlement, after which you will not have any memory of the kind of person you once were and wanted to be."

"Mengistu wants to be a chef and eventually own a restaurant," Jurgen said, explaining the culinary references.

"But my parents," Mengistu said, "wish to arrange a position for me in a major media company, have me develop a suitable on-air image, and eventually move me into politics to oppress the working class if they rebel against the planned revolution from the top."

"Wow," Benny said. "That doesn't sound like any fun at all."

"No, it does not," Mengistu agreed. "It sounds like even less fun than whatever has happened to poor Prescott Galsbury in the laboratory of the headmaster's wife."

Thus the conversation returned to the ant-eating Galsbury, whom Mengistu had seen at a window of said laboratory two weeks earlier, three weeks after the boy had supposedly been expelled and sent home.

In the tradition of rebellious boys immured against their will in Gothic institutions where mysterious goings-on were going on, the three friends schemed to investigate the laboratory that very night. When the lights-out bell sounded at ten o'clock, they would all be tucked in bed, fully clothed, with the covers drawn to their chins. Felthammer House's proctor, Carter Manship, a senior and a shameless toady of the school administration, would proceed room to room with his usual fascistic enthusiasm, certifying that the occupants were abed and turning out the lights on them. The proctor himself was required to be in bed for the night by ten thirty, and he was the kind of suck-up who would rather be castrated than break a Briarbush rule. At precisely 10:45, the three conspirators would leave their rooms through windows and meet in the grove of silver firs behind Catherine Baneberry-Smith's laboratory, at the farthest end of the open meadow from the school and its dormitories.

This plan seemed too simple to succeed, but three conditions ensured its success, the first of which was the school's isolate location. Briarbush was so remote that even the most adventurous hikers never made it alive through the abysmal ravines and primeval forests to invade the—as the brochure put it—"scenic and idyllic redoubt of academic pursuits, where your loved one's mind will be enriched and his character properly formed." At the bottom of the only approach road stood a formidable gate that would withstand mortar fire, if it ever came to that, and a gatehouse at all times occupied by two heavily armed former Marine Corps snipers. Because the school buildings also featured impenetrable, cleverly concealed panic rooms, no further security was required to patrol the grounds at night. If Mengistu, Jurgen, and Benny were stealthy and quick, they were at no risk of encountering either security personnel or kidnappers.

The success of the boys' plot was further facilitated by the location of their dorm rooms, which were all on the ground floor of Felthammer House, providing them with easy egress, and also because Mengistu Gidada had a room all to himself. His parents paid a double tuition for this courtesy, ostensibly because they wanted him to be able to attend to his studies without distraction, although in fact because they feared the wrong roommate might seduce their son into a life of sexual ecstasy that denied them grandchildren. Repeatedly, his father had warned, "Sexual ecstasy before the age of twenty-one, especially with other than a female, will flood your brain with dire chemicals that, over time, will lower your IQ to that of a monkey, a very sad monkey. Sexual ecstasy must be delayed until the brain is fully formed. For one as young as you, sexual ecstasy is far more damaging than injecting heroin and eating dung, though you should never do those things, either."

Finally, the three seekers of truth were unlikely to encounter any member of the school staff or other students. Rarely did anyone venture outdoors after dark, other than into the gated quadrangle, because of the chance of being mauled and eviscerated by either a cougar or a bear. What Mengistu's father had perhaps forgotten was that, in boys of a certain age, undertaking forbidden adventures can generate brain chemicals that induce a state of ecstasy and override even the fear of being eaten alive.

And so the friends met in the grove of silver firs, which was known as the Headmaster's Hanging Ground. Rumor had it that decades earlier a headmaster, driven mad by his students, had hanged himself from a tree here. This was denied by the administration, and it was likely a baseless rumor, but because the boys wanted it to be true, it was a legend that could not be quashed. In the interest of school spirit, every institution of this kind needs to respect such lore.

Adjacent to the Headmaster's Hanging Ground stood a single-story building of considerable size, in which groundskeepers housed their machines and equipment. Because thieves and vandals were not a problem in the remoteness of Briarbush, the doors to this structure were never locked. Mengistu, Jurgen, and Benny were able to obtain two powerful Tac Lights that maintenance personnel employed when searching distant pockets of the school's vast attics for bats and for the occasional gagged-and-bound freshman or sophomore who, during hazing week (the fourth week of every month), had been secured there by upperclassmen determined to instill psychological endurance and panic control in him. They also borrowed an extendable ladder and carried it to the back of the laboratory, which stood perhaps forty yards east of the Headmaster's Hanging Ground.

This occurred under a Cheshire moon hanging over them like the bright teeth in a cocked sneer, as if the moon knew what horror waited to be revealed and believed they deserved to be terrorized for the rule-breaking hugger-muggery in which they were engaged. The air was cool and still. An eerie hush prevailed in the surrounding forest, as if the bears and mountain lions were approaching through the underbrush on tiptoe to avoid revealing themselves while the delectable prey might still be able to flee.

The two front casements of the lab featured clear glass. At one of these, Mengistu had seen a tormented Prescott Galsbury. The next day, both openings were boarded over from the inside. Throughout the rest of the building, other panes were frosted glass; they always had been. However, a large skylight on the roof, which could be seen from the third floor of Felthammer house, seemed to be clear glass. This window was the observation point into the secrets of Catherine Baneberry-Smith's laboratory that Mengistu and Jurgen and Benny—who believed themselves to be sane—were determined to reach.

The metal ladder clattered when they raised the extension, and it banged once against the rain gutter as they positioned it. The bang was louder than the clatter. The three boys froze, prepared to sprint away into the night if a voice challenged them. The lunar sneer seemed to grow sharper and more contemptuous, but Benny was pretty sure he imagined the moon's increasing derision.

Because the single-story building was wide, the pitch of the roof wasn't extreme, and the cast cobbles with which it was paved didn't splinter underfoot as slate might have done. The skylight lay on the south slope, just below the ridgeline: a double row of four panes, each two feet square, framed by what appeared to be stainless steel, separated from one another by muntins of the same metal.

The reflection of the moon sneered up at them.

As quiet as commandos scouting an enemy installation, thrilled by their bravery, so self-controlled that they didn't even whisper to one another, the boys gathered at the high window on their knees, peering into the depths of Mrs. Baneberry-Smith's laboratory. The darkness below was not absolute. Here and there, scores of tiny indicator lights on equipment of unknown function glowed red or green or amber, but these did not relieve the gloom.

Mengistu pressed the lens of his Tac Light to a pane before switching it on. This prevented glare from reflecting off the skylight glass and avoided producing so much light that a teacher who happened to look out a window of his apartment in Sikes House, the faculty residence, might suspect curfew was being broken.

Without angling the beam, Mengistu could illuminate only one small area of the lab directly below. He needed to ease along the skylight, sliding the lens across the glass, to explore the premises piecemeal, while Jurgen and Benny inched along with him, squinting into the Frankensteinian depths. In addition to arcane machinery, the room held rows of large glass boxes, like aquariums with curated environments, although they were not full of water or fish. From a height and in the inadequate light, Benny couldn't clearly see what specimens occupied these glass-enclosed worlds. He glimpsed shadowy shapes skittering and scuttling and twitching. His impression was that none of these creatures was small enough to be squashed by a stomping foot. And none was as lethargic as the toxin-crippled cockroaches his mother used to bury in a beetle cemetery in the backyard. To a one, these insects seemed highly agitated, perhaps disturbed by the sudden beam of light. Or maybe being subjected to observation and experimentation by the headmaster's wife had driven them bug-shit crazy.

Frustrated by the limitations of this method of inspection, Mengistu tilted the Tac Light and found that, at the proper angle, he was able to direct the beam farther across the room below while minimizing the glare enough that they could see through it fairly well. Which was when they discovered the human form, naked and as pale as snow, facing away from them, hanging halfway up the far wall of the lab. The individual's arms were splayed, his hands flattened against the wall above his head, legs dangling, as if he must be chained or nailed through the wrists or fixed there in some even grislier fashion, like the humongous exotic insects pinned to display board in Lucite boxes in the headmaster's drawing room.

In a voice that Benny found surprisingly steady under the circumstances, Jurgen whispered, "Is that Galsbury?"

"I do not know," Mengistu whispered. "I never saw Prescott naked."

"I never saw him naked, either," Jurgen said.

Mengistu said, "I quite assure you, I *never* want to see another human male naked, only girls."

"Only girls," Jurgen said, and Benny hastened to agree in a voice that was as cracked and shaky as he'd expected theirs to be.

"Is he dead?" Jurgen wondered.

Mengistu said, "I suspect a grave injustice has been done here, very grave indeed, even considering that the victim might be a self-adoring, preening snob like Prescott Galsbury."

Below, the self-adoring, preening snob turned his head away from the wall, swiveled it farther than any human head should be able to swivel, not a full hundred eighty degrees as might a young girl possessed by a demon and tasked with terrorizing millions of moviegoers, but plenty far enough to look over his shoulder and up at the skylight, an unearthly silver-green radiance in his eyes.

"It's Galsbury. We're totally screwed," Jurgen declared, and with one hand he clutched Benny's arm, as if he needed human contact in this inhuman moment, although he might have intuited that Benny was about to bolt to his feet, lose his balance, and tumble off the roof. With his greater strength, Jurgen anchored his roommate.

"No, no. We are not yet screwed at all," Mengistu said. "Unless, of course, the headmaster's wife discovers we have witnessed this handiwork of hers. *Then* we are screwed."

Over the tempestuous hammering of his heart, Benny barely heard himself say, "Handiwork?"

Galsbury proved not to be chained or nailed or otherwise fixed to the wall. He was hanging there by some insectile feature of his palms or with the aid of an uncanny power. His body flexed as if he had developed joints where no joints had been previously. Without arching his back, his legs still straight behind him, he snapped his feet forward, planted the soles of them on the wall, and ascended like a four-legged beetle, making his way with impressive suctorial talent.

Although Benny hadn't screamed either when he'd seen his father shot in the back or on any of the numerous occasions in his unusual childhood when a scream would have been appropriate, he wanted to scream now. Not being practiced at screaming, however, he was able to make only a wheezing noise like an asthmatic in desperate need of a medicinal inhaler.

As best he could, Mengistu used the Tac Light to track Galsbury to the top of the wall, where he moved out of sight.

"Where did he go?" Benny asked.

"Onto the other half of the sloped ceiling," Mengistu said, "beyond the ridgeline of the roof."

"What's he doing?" Benny asked.

"Coming to see us," Jurgen suggested.

"So I do believe," Mengistu concurred.

There and then, Benny decided never to ask a question to which he didn't already know the answer. "Let's get the hell out of here."

"We can't," Jurgen said, holding fast to him.

"There is much we can learn from this encounter," Mengistu said. "Much we need to know."

Prescott Galsbury—what the boy had become or maybe was still becoming—crawled partway onto the skylight and peered up at them through the double thickness of glass. Pale, hairless, moist, with gray lips and yellow teeth, he was terrifying, disgusting. Yet he remained human enough in appearance that Benny also felt pity for him. Whatever else Mrs. Baneberry-Smith might be up to in her hellish laboratory, she was the entomologist equivalent of H. G. Wells's Dr. Moreau, and the remote campus of Briarbush Academy was the equal of mad Moreau's island. Benny and his companions knelt transfixed at the skylight, stricken dumb and paralyzed by horror—until Galsbury spoke, his voice muffled by the glass but his request clear enough. "Please, please feed me," he said. "Feed me. Feed me. *Feed me!*"

All concerns about falling off the roof were in that instant forgotten. The three boys scrambled across the cast pavers as if they, too, were part insect. How they got onto the ladder and in what order they descended and with what ungodly racket Benny could not say. In what seemed like an instant, they went from roof to terra firma, the beam of Mengistu's Tac Light stabbing this way and that, here and over there, as if he expected to find that they were encircled by mortal threats.

Fright left them incapable of defense; they were jelly-spined morsels of bug food waiting to be torn apart by enormous mandibles. Nevertheless, they remained aware of the peril that they would bring upon themselves if they left evidence of their adventure, and they didn't flee pell-mell into the night. Benny had no memory of taking down the extension ladder or putting it away with the borrowed Tac Lights, but suddenly he and Jurgen and Mengistu were exiting the groundskeepers' storage building. In a frenzied stealth, they made their way back to Felthammer House, where nightmares coiled under their pillows, waiting for them to fall asleep if they could.

WHAT HAPPENED TO FAT BOB IN THE GARAGE

Standing with Harper at the brink of the laundry, Benny stared across that room at the connecting door to the garage. He was unable to banish the absurd fear that, by an amazing series of connections and transfers occurring over a decade, a further-evolved version of Prescott Galsbury now occupied the strange box in one of the empty spaces beside his Ford Explorer. That was highly unlikely because the prince of this world has so many horrors to promote that there isn't time to repeat one as specific as Galsbury, considering that repetition results in a diminishing effect.

"Well," Harper said, consulting her wristwatch.

"Yeah," Benny agreed.

"I don't like this silence."

"It's better than screaming."

"He hasn't fired any shots."

"No, he hasn't. That's good."

"Maybe good, maybe not," she said.

"You mean like someone could've taken his gun from him."

"Nobody could take a gun from Bob."

"So you mean it could be something worse happened."

"Don't say that. Why would you say that?"

"It's a legitimate concern."

"If you're going to say things like that, just shut up."

He shut up.

After a moment, she said, "We have an obligation here."

"He's a friend," Benny agreed.

Harper stepped into the laundry room and opened a cabinet and studied the contents and chose a can of spray starch.

"What're you doing?" Benny asked.

"Remember, I don't have a gun."

"You're going to starch someone?"

"If I have to. In the face. Let him inhale some Niagara Luxe."

Benny followed her into the laundry room. "I have the golf club. I'll go first."

"No you won't. I'm the PI in training. I'll go first," she said and opened the door at the far end of the room.

Benny followed her into the garage, where something was wrong with the overhead fluorescent panels. They flickered, and shadows shuddered. All was still, too still, so still that Benny knew the hush was prelude to an event or discovery that wouldn't improve the character of the day.

Harper whispered, "Bob," but Bob didn't answer and neither did anyone who might have done something terrible to Bob.

They passed the front of the Ford. Where the box ornamented with intricate scenes had once been flat on the floor, it now stood on end. Because of its shape, upright position, and ominous quality, it reminded Benny of a sarcophagus in one of those old mummy movies in which Mengistu Gidada had taken such delight. If the lid was hinged and it creaked open, however, the occupant would probably be a lot ickier and more menacing than Boris Karloff wound in tattered graveclothes, his pharaoh face as shriveled as a prune.

Spray starch at the ready, with the fully engaged intellect of a smart and highly efficient waitress determined to effect a career change into the glamorous world of private investigation, Harper went cautiously but not timidly to the big box from Boca Raton. She stood before it, marveling at the art, although she didn't touch it and thereby risk being detached from reality and plunged into the scenes depicted.

Assuring himself, not entirely with success, that he would be more effective with the nine iron as a weapon than he was with it on a golf course, Benny was standing beside Harper when she whispered, “Hey, the lid is ajar.”

Even in the inconstant light of the flickering fluorescent panel, Benny could see that indeed the lid was ajar, although not more than a quarter of an inch. The hinges were evidently concealed in the frame, and now the crack along the right side began slowly to widen.

As he backed away from the box with Harper, Benny was more sure than he’d ever been that Colonel Talmadge Clerkenwell had not sent him a sarcophagus full of books. The crack became a cleft. The cleft became a gap. The gap became a two-inch-wide fissure. Carried faster and faster by its own weight, the heavy lid swung all the way open—and there he was.

“Fat Bob,” said Benny.

“Bob,” said Harper.

The detective stood in the box, wide-eyed, mouth open as if he might be about to speak, pistol firmly gripped in his right hand and pointed between his feet. He was breathing slow and deep and steady, his big chest rising and falling.

Harper stepped forward and waved her hand back and forth in front of Bob’s eyes, but he failed to track it. “Bob? Robert? Mr. Jericho?”

Benny said, “He doesn’t see or hear us. Bob sees and hears everything. That’s who Bob is.”

“Or he sees us,” Harper said, “but he’s not able to respond.”

Benny was distressed. “This isn’t the Bob we need, the Bob we know and love. He’s like in a trance. A spell’s been cast on him.”

“Spell? You’ve got witches and wizards in the neighborhood?”

"Or like he's been bitten by some bug with paralyzing venom."

"Bug? Don't get weirder on me, Benjamin. Whatever this is, we'll snap Bob out of it."

The door between the garage and the laundry room fell shut with a solid thud.

THE MONSTER

The garage fluorescents had stopped fluttering, as if the cause of their malfunction had closed the door behind itself when it went into the laundry room.

Benny and Harper stood watching the door, not near enough to reach out and open it or to be snatched off their feet if something opened it from the other side with the desire to kill and eat them.

"Okay," she said, "for Bob, we've got to go in there and deal with this. Find the bastard who did that to him. Get it undone."

"Let's think it through," Benny suggested.

After maybe ten seconds, Harper said, "The question isn't do we go in or not. We go in. That's settled."

"Settled? Who settled it?"

"The question is whether we go in by this door or instead the front door—maybe the back door, maybe a window—and surprise him."

"Him? How do we know we're dealing with a him? How do we even know we're dealing with something human? Listen, we call nine one one and let the cops handle this."

Harper gave him the kind of look a waitress gives a customer when she suspects he's going to leave without paying the check. "And we tell them what? That a dangerous man or creature unknown is in the house, came here by airfreight, and Fat Bob has had a spell cast over him?"

"Bob," Benny corrected.

She was clearly appalled that she'd said "fat," more rattled by events than she was willing to admit.

With one finger, she tap-tap-tapped the face of her wristwatch, a gesture Benny interpreted as meaning, *Come with me now, because I'm not going to wait until you get a testosterone shot.*

He said, "Okay. All right. Let's do it."

"For Bob," she said.

"For Bob," he said.

Harper moved before Benny could. She threw open the door and cleared the threshold and swept the aerosol can of spray starch left to right, and then right to left. Brandishing the golf club, Benny followed her into the laundry room.

As Harper warily entered the kitchen, Benny felt his scalp crawling, as if it was trying to get out from under his thatch of hair. He told himself to calm down. This situation would unfold just like it did in most monster movies. The gullible audience was made to wait and wait for the first full-on appearance of the creature—teased with a distorted shadow here, a blob of discarded slime over there, a low snarl off-screen—until the big reveal, whereupon the alien or the mutant or the beast risen out of the bowels of time would be a ho-hum compilation of all the monsters perpetrated by Hollywood in the past. Having seen pale, moist, hairless Galsbury crawling the ceiling, Benny could face down anything. That is what he told himself as he followed Harper out of the laundry room, and he believed himself, was encouraged by his counsel. When the kitchen proved to be deserted, he was disappointed, just a little bit.

He admired how Harper Harper—so cute and colorfully dressed—moved lithely and stealthily, cautiously but confidently, past the refrigerator, toward the breakfast nook, where she turned left to the family room, the can of spray starch in a two-handed grip. Bob had correctly seen in her the inherent courage required of a trainee for his dangerous profession. She had moxie. She was a spunky girl. Plucky. Witty. Harper was nothing like Jill Swift, and yet so soon after she entered Benny's life, her mere presence had a healing effect; a scab had already closed the wound that Jill inflicted. The memory of Ms. Swift no longer inspired pangs of heartache, and in fact when he thought about being dumped by her, he felt strangely relieved.

A violent crashing-cracking-splintering noise came three times from somewhere in the front rooms of the house, such powerful blows that flatware rattled in the kitchen drawers.

Benny pivoted, scanning the ceiling, but nothing crawled out of the downstairs hallway or through the open door to the dining room. Nothing on the floor, either.

Energized by having something specific to chase down, Harper dashed back through the kitchen, no less lithe and stealthy than she'd been before. Passing Benny, she whispered with conviction, "Living room," and slipped away in yellow-sneaker silence, bouncing ponytail protruding through the opening in the back of her baseball cap.

The noise could have as likely originated in the study or the powder bath or the foyer as in the living room. Harper seemed to have discarded her heretofore professional conduct in favor of full-on Nancy Drew enthusiasm. If she rushed directly to the living room, the intruder could come out of the study behind her and bash her head in—or bite it off.

Less concerned for his safety than for hers, to prove that he didn't need a testosterone shot (if in fact that was what she had been thinking about him earlier), he hurried after her, along the hallway, into the foyer, and left into the living room.

The first thing he noticed was the shattered armchair. It had been crafted in Sweden of whitewashed sycamore, with a square of thin white upholstery inset in the back and another on the seat, angled to give the impression that it wasn't merely an armchair but also a means of transportation capable of conveying the occupant anywhere at rocket speed. Although it was a sturdy piece of well-made furniture weighing forty pounds or more, it had been hefted high and slammed repeatedly into the floor until it looked as though it had been left behind by a category-five tornado. Having served as the anvil on which the chair had been hammered into ruin, a couple of two-foot-square limestone tiles were chipped and badly cracked.

The second thing Benny noticed was the intruder, who had moved on from the chair to the far end of the room and stood staring at a Lucite table lamp with a white shade. If he wasn't seven feet tall, he was six feet ten. In black boots, black leggings, and a black T-shirt, he was a tower of muscle. Hands big enough to juggle bowling balls. Shaved head. Skin the color of beef bouillon. White eyebrows. When he looked toward them, his eyes were the pale blue of faded denim. His face appeared hard, forged in a furnace, as if he could break down a door with it if he preferred not to use a fist for that purpose.

Still plucky but poised to run, Harper said, "Who are you, what do you want, what did you do to the chair?"

After a brooding silence, the stranger spoke in a voice that—not because of volume but because of its quality, its character, its fundamentality—could shaketh the wilderness. "Spike," he said.

They waited for him to say more, but when the one word appeared to be all that the brute cared to share at the moment, Harper said, "Spike? What does that mean?"

The intruder repeated Harper's initial question in a perfect imitation of her voice. "'Who are you?'" Then he reverted to his true voice for his answer: "Spike."

"That's your name? Spike is your name?"

"Justice," the brute declared.

"Spike Justice?" Benny asked.

In Harper's voice again, Spike said, "'What do you want?'" In his own voice, he replied, "Justice."

As if she felt Benny might need a translation, Harper said, "His name's Spike, and he wants justice."

Benny took no comfort whatsoever from the fact that Spike had not yet attacked them and left them in the condition of the chair. His peculiar method of conversation suggested that he might be a bit slow-witted, but a lot of murderers were on the stupid side. Even if Spike wasn't a murderous psychopath, even if he was gentler than he appeared to be, that didn't mean he was just a big harmless galoot. In John Steinbeck's novel *Of Mice and Men*, Lennie has a low IQ and means no harm, but he accidentally kills a puppy, and then he offs Curley's wife a little less than accidentally. Besides, what about Bob standing spellbound in the garage?

"Broke it," said Spike.

"You broke justice?" Harper said. "You mean you broke the law?"

Resorting once more to his uncanny impression of her, he said, "'What did you do to the chair?'" That was the third question she had asked in a rush of words. "Broke it," he repeated, as himself.

To Benny, Spike didn't appear as if he was remorseful about breaking the chair. He looked as if he would break anything he wanted to break; thank you very much.

Harper seemed to think that by putting Spike on the defensive, she could get and keep the upper hand in this relationship. Benny didn't believe she was correct about that, but he didn't advise her otherwise when she took a sterner tone with the brute. "Destroying other people's property is not acceptable. What makes you think you had the right to destroy the chair?"

Spike pondered the sycamore debris from a distance and then explained, "Ugly. Uncomfortable. Ridiculous chair." Once he allowed himself the full expression of his gift for critiquing furniture, the floodgates opened, and he stopped issuing words one drop at a time. "Sit in that absurd chair too long, you'll deform your spine. It's within my authority to take such corrective action."

"What authority?" Benny asked. "I liked that chair."

Even as Benny finished speaking, Harper said, "What did you do to Bob out there in the garage?"

Spike seemed more obliged to respond to her than to Benny. "I sidelined him until I've done what needs to be done. He'll be okay."

"You can't just sideline people."

Distracted, squinting around the room as if everything he saw offended him, Spike said, "White. White, white, white," as though he might violently redecorate the house or burn it down.

"You can't just sideline people," Harper repeated.

"Yes, I can," Spike said, glowering at the Lucite lamp.

"That's an expensive lamp," Benny ventured, and Harper said, "Until you've 'done what needs to be done.' What does that mean? What are you here to do?"

"Justice. Vengeance. Cast down the wicked. Set things right."

"What things?" she asked.

"An eye for an eye," said Spike.

"Whose eye?" Benny inquired nervously.

"We'll begin tonight," Spike declared, still focused on the lamp as if it was asking for trouble. "First we'll pay a visit to Mr. Hanson Duroc."

"Handy? Handy Duroc? My old boss at Surfside?"

Spike turned his faded-blue eyes on Benny, which made Benny feel like an innocent chair about to be broken. "We'll get to the bottom of this, Benjamin."

"The bottom of what? Hey, I don't want to get to the bottom of anything. I've already hit bottom and begun to bounce back. I don't want to go to the bottom again."

"For what Mr. Hanson Duroc did to you, we'll make him sorry he was ever born."

"No, no, no. It was an at-will agreement. Each of us had the right to terminate our agreement." A minute ago, Benny wouldn't have imagined himself defending Handy Duroc. Even now he couldn't imagine himself making Handy wish he'd never been born. "That's not the kind of thing I do. What would that even entail? It would have to entail some really ugly behavior. I don't hurt people. I try to be nice. It's important to me to be nice."

To Harper, Spike said, "Does he always babble like this?"

"I don't know him that well, only since breakfast yesterday. I think he might have a tendency to babble, but he only indulges in it when he's under a lot of stress. Listen, big guy, if you're going to go off with Benny to see this Duroc or anyone else, I'm going with you. I'm not letting you out of my sight until you take the spell off Bob."

Benny regarded her with astonishment, flummoxed that she seemed to be adapting to this insane situation as though giants named Spike came into her life with regularity, talking about making people wish they'd never been born.

"I completely understand," Spike said. "You have an obligation to Mr. Jericho, just as I have an obligation to Benjamin. That is most admirable of you."

"You don't have any obligation to me," Benny protested.

"That's not for you to decide."

"Oh, really. Who *does* make the decision?"

"That's not for you to know."

"Who do you work for?"

"I'm a free agent. Right now I work for you."

"For me? Well, I'm not paying you to make people wish they were never born."

"I should have said that I'll be working on your behalf. Free of charge. I have no need of money." Squinting, with an expression of disgust, Spike surveyed the living room. Although there was no sibilant in the word, he managed to hiss it: "White, white, white."

Benny didn't get angry; he really didn't. Anger didn't solve anything. However, he wasn't an automaton; he was assailed by other emotions, plenty of other emotions like perplexity, frustration, and anxiety. At the moment he was anxious, frustrated, and perplexed all at the same time, and simultaneously entertaining so many intense emotions was exhausting. He wanted to lie down, but he needed to stay on his feet, ready to run. "What's wrong with you? Something's very wrong with you. I won't participate in murder. This is crazy. It's lunacy."

"We won't have to murder Mr. Duroc to squeeze information out of him," Spike assured Benny. "He was pressured to do what he did. The real villains are others. Properly motivated, Mr. Duroc will tell us who at least one of them was. I have helped many like you, Benjamin. I am good at this. It is my mission in life. I have no other."

"'Properly motivated'? What's that mean?"

Instead of answering the question, Spike said, "However, you must understand it's possible that, before the night is out, we'll be led to someone who will be as happy to shoot you in the head as he was to instigate the destruction of your career. Then we might have to terminate him. In such a case, that will be self-defense, not murder, but merely a justified killing."

"'Merely a justified killing,'" Benny echoed. "Well, see, it might surprise you to know I've never engaged in justified killing, and I will not be a party to it tonight or tomorrow night or ever."

Harper patted his shoulder as she might have patted the head of a basically good dog temporarily agitated by the arrival of the mail carrier. "Now, Benny, you never know what difficult choices life might present to you."

Benny gaped at her.

She patted him some more. "You're very sweet, and that's good. A girl likes sweetness in a guy. But you're quite naive, too, and that's not so good."

"Respect the little lady," Spike advised. "She's a keeper."

"You're fired," Benny said.

Spike smiled and shook his head. "You can't fire me. I don't work *for* you. I work *on your behalf.*" Sparing the Lucite lamp, the giant started across the room toward Benny, his smile seeming to be one of forbearance and genuine though tenuous affection. "Trust me, Benjamin, and I will always keep a kindliness of heart toward you even when your behavior is vexatious."

"Vexatious?"

"It means 'irritating, annoying, provocative.'"

"I know what it means," Benny said as the intruder seemed to grow in size with every step he took.

The golf club had been hanging at his side. Unaware of what he was doing, he'd raised it, though not overhead, only to chest level. As Spike loomed, Benny decided that a nine iron was insufficient to the task, that even an axe would have been insufficient to the task, and that in fact *he* was insufficient to the task.

"You won't be needing that with Mr. Hanson Duroc," Spike said.

He took the golf club from Benny, tied the steel shaft in a knot as if it were made of pretzel dough, and dropped the nine iron on the floor.

"Cool," said Harper.

Benny estimated that if he put his hands around Spike's neck, they wouldn't entirely encircle it. Not close. Instead of making an effort to confirm the truth of that observation, he hearkened back to something the giant said earlier. "'Properly motivated.' How will you properly motivate Handy Duroc to tell us who pressured him to shove me out of Surfside?"

"Intimidation will most likely work," Spike said. His breath smelled like sugary cinnamon rolls warming in an oven.

"If intimidation doesn't work?" Benny asked.

"I have other techniques."

"I want to know what they are."

Spike sighed. "Well, one of them I call 'shock and awe.'"

"I don't like the sound of that."

"I sort of do," said Harper.

"Shock and awe doesn't involve violence," Spike said.

"What's it involve?"

"Show us," Harper said. "Show us what it involves."

Benny appreciated how cute Harper was, but just then she seemed too cute, the kind of cute that slid into Holly Golightly territory and invited chaos. She had put her spray starch on the coffee table.

"Here's one thing I might do to Mr. Hanson Duroc," said Spike. "I might stand very close to him like I'm standing close to you, Benjamin. I might say something like this." His face knotted with anger and contempt. His voice grew menacing. "You tell me what you know, *Handy*, or I'll never give you a moment's peace. I'll ride your back like a demon. I'll never take my eye off you." As he finished that statement, he took his right eye in his thumb and forefinger and plucked it out of its socket. With the optic nerve, muscles, and glistening blood vessels trailing behind—an impossible two feet of them—he thrust the eyeball against Benny's right eye.

Taken quite by surprise, Benny found that he couldn't breathe even as his heart knocked as fast and loud as the hooves of a horse racing over cobblestones. For a moment he couldn't move, either, but then he stumbled backward. He encountered the sofa, and his legs buckled, and he collapsed onto a hardness of white mohair.

Bending over him, unrelenting, Spike pressed the extruded eyeball to Benny's eye again. "I can see deep in your brain, you piece of crap," Spike snarled, "and if I see you're lying, *Handy*, then you're a dead man."

Benny was saved from the embarrassment of a scream by his inability to command the function of his lungs, throat, larynx, and mouth. As Spike let go of the eye and it reeled into its socket like a tape measure slithering back into its housing, the only sound that escaped Benny was a thin *eeeeeeee* such as air makes when escaping through the pinched neck of a balloon.

Stepping back from the sofa, smiling, Spike said, "So what do you think?"

Harper stood nodding like a bobblehead doll, ponytail waving behind, but then she found her voice. "Shock and awe. You didn't oversell it. That was definitely shock and awe."

"Thank you," the giant said. "It's not my best stuff, but you can see how it would be effective."

Benny struggled up from the sofa, swaying. He expressed his confusion and concern. Their puzzled looks brought him to the realization that the sounds he was making weren't words.

As if psychic, Harper spoke for him. "Hey, big guy, you scared the bejesus out of me."

To Benny, that did not appear to be true. She had not collapsed onto the sofa and hadn't made the air-escaping-the-pinched-neck-of-a-balloon sound. She looked as though she had every bit as much bejesus as she'd had before the eyeball trick.

She continued, "What are you, Spike? What the hell are you?"

"Craggle," he said.

"Spell that." He spelled it, and she said, "Spike Craggle."

He corrected her. "Spike the craggle. It's not a last name. It's like saying, Benjamin the human." Focusing on Benny, he produced a terrifying smile. "I am your craggle, your bodyguard, lifeguard, paladin, defender. Many of your friends will be fair-weather friends, Benjamin, but I will be there in bad weather, in worse weather, in any weather."

(This book was originally titled *Spike the Craggle*. No one in the marketing department was enthusiastic about that. I am pleased to be able to say that Spike made no attempt to intimidate me into calling it *Spike the Craggle* anyway. He's not that kind of entity.)

So then . . .

ON THE ROAD

So then they were aboard the Explorer. They had been standing in Benny's white-on-white living room, and he had blinked, and in the fraction of a second that his eyelids were closed, the three of them had been transferred into his SUV. They were cruising down the hill from Cameo Highlands to Pacific Coast Highway, Spike driving, Benny riding shotgun, the sky ablaze with stars, the moon full, the coastline bejeweled with lights.

From the back seat, Harper said, "The fun keeps on coming."

Once he was free from Briarbush Academy and disentangled from everyone who remained in his dysfunctional family, a new spiritual buoyance had swelled in Benny. Since then, he'd thought of himself as a fun guy, not a raucous party guy swilling champagne and shaking his booty on a dance floor, but a guy with a keen sense of humor and a positive attitude and a heck of a lot of interesting life stories to tell. He knew what fun was, and he was always up for fun, but—with all due respect to Harper—this wasn't it.

"How'd you do that?" Benny asked.

Spike turned his head to look at him, both eyes inserted where they should be. "Do what?"

"We were there. Now we're here."

"Just a time thing."

"What time thing?"

"Sort of an origami time-fold trick."

"Clear as mud."

"That's all I can say. It's a craggle secret."

The giant hulked so large that it didn't seem possible he could fit in the driver's seat, but there he was, hunched over the wheel so that the top of his shaved head wouldn't be pressed against the roof. Although he hadn't hitched himself into his safety harness, the Explorer wasn't warning him, either with a strident tone or a flashing instrument-panel symbol, that he was breaking the law; it didn't dare.

Harper said, "Okay, so what's a craggle?"

"Me," said Spike.

"Could you be more specific?"

"That's about as specific as it gets, little lady."

"Are you from another planet?" Harper asked.

Spike laughed and laughed as he pulled to a stop at Pacific Coast Highway and waited for the traffic light to change. He had a husky, whiskey-soaked kind of laugh that Benny would have found contagious under other circumstances. Then he said, "Why would you think I'm an alien?"

"Oh, I don't know," Harper said, "maybe the eye thing and the time-fold trick."

"Just standard craggle tactics."

"Where do craggles come from?" Benny asked, feeling as if he were trapped in a collaboration between J.K. Rowling and Monty Python.

"Where does anything come from?" Spike said, obviously taking pleasure in being obscure. "It's all a mystery, isn't it? Mysteries within mysteries."

Harper said, "How many craggles are there?"

"At all times, there are as many craggles as the world needs. Actually, quite a few at the moment. The world is currently in a most sorry condition. So many urgent missions to be undertaken."

The light turned green, and Spike swung right onto the coast highway, and Benny said, "Missions? What missions?"

"There are ever fewer nice people," the giant said. "Millions are falling into one mass-formation psychosis or another. The world desperately needs nice, sane people. When a nice person is too nice for his own good, like you—"

"I'm nice, but I'm not all *that* nice," Benny protested, as if he'd just been called a Goody Two-Shoes.

"—and when that super nice person, humble and naive, is shat on by one of the many psychodoodles out there—"

"I haven't been shat on."

"—has been shat on in an attempt to destroy him or her, but thinks it's all a big misunderstanding, then a craggle is assigned to the case so that the very nice person will have support and won't sink into despair and become one of them."

"Psychodoodles?" Benny said.

"We take our work seriously," Spike said, "but we don't take ourselves seriously."

Glancing at the computer screen, Benny realized the navigation system was engaged without the audio assist. The selected address was the home of Handy Duroc. They were really going to subject Handy to shock and awe.

"I don't feel right about this," Benny said.

"Of course you don't, being the way you are."

"It isn't my niceness making me doubt."

"Of course it is."

"It's what Handy will do after we leave. Why won't he call the cops on me?"

"He won't remember we were ever there. He won't remember us or what information we wrung out of him."

"You have the power to make people forget encounters with you?"

Spike shrugged. "Why wouldn't I?"

After a silence, Harper said, "This is all so great, so cool, so life changing. I don't want to forget you."

"You might not," Spike said. "You could be a special case. We'll know as the night unfolds."

"What special case?" she asked.

"For me to know and you to find out."

For someone who apparently spent significant amounts of time in a box, and in spite of being crammed into a seat that was about as accommodating to him as a child's high chair to a full-grown bear, Spike was a superb driver. Evening traffic on Pacific Coast Highway was heavy, complicated by the fact that maybe 15 percent of the motorists were undocumented aliens with forged driver's licenses and no firm understanding of the motor-vehicle laws of California, while another 15 percent were well-documented drunks and drug addicts who either had contempt for the motor-vehicle laws of California or thought they were on a yellow-brick road in Oz. Spike wove from lane to lane, always finding an opening in the flow when he needed one, progressing swiftly and smoothly, never delayed at an intersection by a red traffic light, while all around them grid-sapping four-thousand-pound Teslas and lighter-weight gas hogs moved through the night like weary red corpuscles shuddering through arteries clogged with cholesterol.

Benny said, "Why don't you just origami time-fold us to Handy's place?"

"I like to drive. It relaxes me. I used that other trick just to slide past all the jabbering and get us on the road."

"Jabbering?"

"You and the little lady are such question monkeys, we might never have gotten out of the house. It saves time to do the Q and A on the road. No offense intended."

From the backseat shadows, Harper said, "None taken, big guy."

"When this is all done, this mission of yours," Benny said, "will I forget you and all that's happened?"

"No, no, of course not. Your enemies will forget how they've been handled. And any bystanders who witness them being handled will forget. Only they, not you, will be mystified by how you routinely defeat their nefarious schemes."

"I'm no damn bystander," Harper asserted quietly but firmly.

"Indeed, you are not," Spike agreed, "and nobody with a brain would ever mistake you for one. You are something unique, Harper Harper. Together, in the perilous hours ahead, we'll discover what you are. And I, for one, believe that discovery will delight the three of us."

"'Nefarious schemes,'" Benny said.

"'*Nefarious,*'" the giant said, "has been rendered a trite word by its overuse in the bombastic movies of our time. Nevertheless, I like it, and it's more expressive of your enemies' plans than are the words *criminal* and *unlawful*. Perhaps the word *abominable* might be appropriate as well, except that it brings to mind such silliness as the abominable snowman and Bigfoot."

"'Silliness'?" Benny said.

The glance with which Spike favored him virtually dripped with incredulity. "Benjamin, surely you don't believe in such nonsense. Reassure me that you don't."

"Not wholeheartedly, no. I'm somewhat skeptical. It's just that, all my life, things that seemed to be impossible have proved to be possible."

"The abominable snowman and Bigfoot are modern myths," Spike said emphatically. "They do not exist. They are pure silliness. Case closed."

Harper was concerned about another word Spike had used. "Uh, 'perilous.' In what way are the hours ahead perilous?"

The giant was as adroit at modifying his statements as he was at maneuvering the Explorer through the blacktop jungle. Glancing at her in the rearview mirror, he said, "My error. I should have said *precarious*, which isn't an acceptable synonym for *dangerous* or *perilous*, but only means *uncertain*. The events that may befall us in the dark hours ahead are uncertain, but not necessarily full of peril."

"Ah," said Harper.

"Unless a bogadril shows up, which is most unlikely."

"'Bogadril'?" Benny asked.

"Here we are," said Spike.

"What's a bogadril?" Harper asked.

The giant pointed through the windshield. "Mr. Hanson Duroc's house is ahead on the left."

The giant parked in the driveway. "You'll both come along. We're destiny buddies now. But once we're inside, leave the torture to me."

Benny flinched, blenched, and shrank a little in his seat. "Torture?"

"Psychological torture. Intimidation. Just the usual craggle techniques," the giant assured them. He got out of the Explorer with a sound like a tight cork being extracted from a bottle.

DUROC REDUX

Handy Duroc, former lifeguard and currently a dirt salesman extraordinaire, lived in a house on Newport Harbor with its own dock and a boat slip that accommodated a fifty-foot coastal cruiser. The property was worth many millions. Many. Year by year, as long as government programs promising equity and social justice did what they were actually designed to do, which was transfer wealth from the poor and the middle class to those at the top of the economic ladder, this residence would be worth ever more fantastical sums, until it had greater value than any city with a population of one hundred thousand in the nation's heartland—or until the US dollar collapsed and you could then purchase the place with a year's supply of canned food and whiskey.

Uncharacteristically, Benny was feeling a little cynical as he approached the house on foot with Harper and their destiny buddy, Spike the craggle. He also felt unsteady, shaken by a sense of unreality, as perhaps were those who operated under the influence of crack cocaine or crystal meth, though he had achieved this quasi-delirium without using illegal drugs.

In the weak onshore breeze, the queen palms and phoenix palms produced a soft sound, as if shushing the hoi polloi of a clamorous world and warning them not to disturb the serenity of this favored neighborhood. The night smelled of salt air and roses and steaks grilling on a barbecue.

Fronting the shrubbery to the right of the main entrance, a small sign advised that the property was protected by a security company providing an armed response; an image of a snarling dog implied that each agent would arrive with a firearm in one holster and a Doberman in the other. To the left, a sign virtue signaled the homeowner's commitment to an environment free of carbon dioxide, though presumably he did not mean *so* free of it that all plant life would perish and therefore production of oxygen would cease.

The first entrance was not into the house itself. An ornate oiled-bronze gate provided access to a courtyard. The gate was locked. A backlit button glowed on a call box.

"Handy won't want to see me," Benny said.

Spike said, "We're not asking."

The electronic lock could be disengaged by entering the correct code on a keypad or released from inside the residence in response to a call-box request. Spike placed one immense hand on the armature containing the electromagnetic assembly and regarded it with quiet consideration, in a pose reminiscent of a faith healer with his hand on the head of a seated paraplegic who hoped to walk again.

Benny didn't yet know what to make of this craggle business. He might never know what to make of it, but certain expectations flowed from what he had seen of Spike thus far. He imagined that the giant, whether a supernatural or science-fictional entity, possessed the psychic ability to interrupt the current and thus demagnetize—and thereby disable—the lock.

Instead, the giant violently twisted the assembly once, broke the several welds that fixed it to the gate, and threw it away into the yard.

"Wow," said Harper.

Benny said, "I thought you were going to disrupt the current and demagnetize the lock."

"My fundamental nature," Spike said, "is to be direct, blunt, and physical."

"Evidently so. Won't that have set off an alarm?"

"The gate isn't alarmed. The doors and windows of the house itself will be. But with so many lights on, it's likely that Mr. Duroc hasn't yet set the alarm for the night." He pushed open the gate and smiled at Harper and said, "You first, little lady."

Benny followed Harper into the courtyard, where more palm trees were up lit. Three life-size dolphins, carved out of white marble, spouted water from their blowholes into a surrounding fountain.

She said, "You know who Spike reminds me of?"

"I've no idea. Samson? Hercules?"

"John Wayne."

"He doesn't look anything like John Wayne."

"No, but he's got that John Wayne smile, that courtliness, that sort of sideways walk, and how he says 'little lady.'"

"I've seen maybe three John Wayne movies," Benny said. "The comparison wouldn't have occurred to me."

"You've gotta see more. Like a year ago, most girls my age, we were swept up in this intense John Wayne craze, binged on dozens of his movies. There aren't a lot of guys like him these days. If there were, you'd see a heck of a lot more babies, babies everywhere you looked." As Spike closed the damaged gate and joined them, Harper said to him, "You remind me of John Wayne."

"That is a high compliment, ma'am."

"Do you date?" she asked.

"Indeed. I date back eighteen hundred and fifty years."

Harper frowned. "What's that mean?"

"It means I'm eighteen hundred and fifty years old."

"Huh. You sure don't look it."

"A craggle is what he always was. We always are how we came into the world. The year I came into the world was a bad year for nice people. They needed us."

"Okay, but by 'date,'" she said, "I meant like with girls."

Spike smiled—Benny had to agree—like John Wayne. He patted Harper on the head and said, "That's not the craggle way, Miss Harper. Like others of my species, I've no interest in reproducing."

"Maybe you haven't met the right girl," she said, as if the previous two millennia were known to have been lousy for romance.

"It's simpler than that. A craggle has no reproductive organs. That kind of thing would distract us from our vital mission, which is championing those people who are so nice that by their niceness they can make this a better world—if they can stay alive."

Benny felt an unworthy but not at all mean satisfaction when he saw the look of disappointment that overcame Harper.

"Now," said Spike, "let's go terrify Mr. Duroc."

"But not torture," Benny said.

"Not physically," Spike concurred.

"Intimidation," Benny said.

"Big time," Spike said, and he grinned more like Jack Nicholson in *The Shining* than like John Wayne in anything.

INTIMIDATION

Benny heard music throbbing inside the house. Muffled by the limestone-clad walls and the multilayered bullet-resistant glass installed to foil burglars, the melody remained unidentifiable, while the bass beat thumped out a carnal rhythm.

The front door was a slab of teak set in a carved-limestone surround. Mounted above it, a security camera fixed the destiny buddies with an incriminating stare.

"Security video is often stored for thirty days," Harper said.

"For our visit," said Spike, "I'm emitting an electromagnetic signal that disables all security cameras."

"Yeah? How do you do that?" Harper asked.

"Think of it as a long, uninterrupted, odorless fart composed not of gas but of microwaves that issue from my ears."

"What if he has a gun?" Benny asked.

"All the more fun."

"Well, the thing is, Harper and I aren't bulletproof."

"I am aware of that sad fact about human anatomical design. I will do my best to prevent you from being bullet riddled, stabbed, bludgeoned, strangled, set on fire, or crushed by large falling objects."

Benny wasn't sure whether Spike was joshing or mocking him. He decided it must be the former. Therefore he didn't resort to mockery of his own by saying, *Yeah, but* we've *got reproductive organs.*

The brushed stainless-steel hardware on the door featured a lever-action handle. The lock was engaged.

"Maybe we could just ring the bell," Benny said.

Pointing to the camera, Harper said, "When Handy sees who it is, he's not likely to open the door."

Spike applied himself. Teak cracked as if it were balsa wood. Spanner screws stripped their threads and sprang from their holes and pinged across the courtyard paving. The latch assembly and the escutcheon—with cylinder, plug, and keyway—tore out of the door. Examining the ruined hardware, Spike said, "Mr. Duroc will have no memory of us after I'm done with him. Little things like this will mystify him and make him nervous for years to come." He dropped the mortise lock on the stoop.

The door swung inward of its own weight, and Spike led them into a foyer that, like every room on the main level, was floored with polished cream-colored marble.

The music flooding the rooms through the all-house sound system was loud, but it wasn't the volume that inspired Spike to grimace and snarl with contempt, "Electronic dance crap."

Benny had been here twice for Surfside corporate parties. On both occasions, the place made him nervous. The interior designer believed in color and lots of it. Copper-leafed and silver-leafed and faux-malachite ceilings. Chandeliers like cascades of tentacular sea creatures. Glistening lacquered walls in apricot and peach and raspberry. Oversize plush furniture. Heavily veined quartzite end tables. The enormous abstract expressionist paintings—spatters, streaks, whirls, and blocks of color thrown and squirted and spatulated onto the canvases—might have been produced by psychotic monkeys with access to a wide spectrum of acrylics, but in fact were the work of an acclaimed Los Angeles artist.

They stepped out of the foyer into a hallway that led left and right. Directly ahead, a wall of glass in the spacious living room provided a view of Handy's coastal cruiser in its slip and the dark harbor ringed by twinkling shore lights.

The compressed, repetitive melody and pounding rhythm masked any sounds that might lead them toward human activity. Benny half expected a dance line of time travelers from the late disco period to come strutting their stuff along the hallway, the guys in black ankle boots and white suits, their shirts open to mid chest, the girls in spike heels and slit skirts and silk blouses with deep necklines and rhinestone-encrusted chokers.

Then the music stopped. The sudden cessation of ear-splitting sound triggered in Benny a reaction similar to the manner in which he would have responded to silence abruptly shattered by a shrieking security-system alarm. He startled, pivoted this way and that, as if he had been caught in the act of theft. He considered—though only briefly—bolting from the house. When he realized Harper was looking at him as if making an assessment, he straightened his back, squared his shoulders, and strove for a steely-eyed Clint Eastwood look.

The silence lasted maybe six seconds. Then male laughter issued from somewhere to their right, and a different kind of dance music—piano and strings and a swooning saxophone, with a less insistent beat—filled the house, but at a more reasonable volume.

"Now it's the last dance at the senior prom," muttered Spike, evidently having become something of a music snob over eighteen hundred years.

"If I remember the layout," Benny said, "that laugh came from the kitchen."

"Lead the way," Spike said.

Harper surprised Benny by taking his hand. He didn't think she was scared and needed reassurance, not after she had reacted to the craggle's eyeball trick as she might have to a magician conjuring a dove out of a pocket handkerchief. For maybe two seconds, he thought his Eastwood squint had impressed her with his potential manliness, but of course not. As they approached the entrance to the kitchen, she solved the mystery by whispering, "If Handy assaults you on sight, just know I took a course in how to treat gunshot and edge-weapon wounds. I can probably keep you alive until EMTs get here."

"Good to know," he said.

The immense kitchen had everything a high-end kitchen ought to have, then had it all again: four Sub-Zero refrigerator-freezers, two microwaves, four regular ovens, two islands with a vegetable sink in each, two larger sinks elsewhere, two griddles, two grills, two woks, two icemakers, two trash compactors. This was what a sales brochure might call a "kitchen equipped for major social events." So if you had a thousand close friends in for a sit-down dinner on the patio, you didn't have to work yourself to exhaustion, but could rely on a caterer and have a lovely evening for a mere quarter of a million dollars, including a fancy dessert about twice the size of a thimble as well as good but not exceptional wines.

On this occasion, a bottle of fine champagne was nestled in an ice bucket on the smaller island. Two Lalique flutes stood beside it, tiny bubbles rising through the golden liquid. Handy Duroc had only one guest. He was slow dancing with her through the generous workspace surrounding the islands.

More accurately, they weren't dancing so much as they were rubbing their bodies against each other as they moved through that culinary wonderland. Benny was impressed with Handy's ability to lead his partner faultlessly in a figure eight around and between the islands, considering that both of them had their eyes closed and were making the kind of lower-body contact that tended to cloud the mind with desire or, again more accurately, lust.

In any other circumstances, their performance would have been amusing, even laughable, like two cold-blooded assassins earnestly trying to delude themselves and each other into believing that they were embarked on a romantic evening and that both of them had their virginity to lose. None of this was funny, however, because the one who wasn't Handy Duroc was Jill Swift. The same Jill Swift who, just one day earlier, had been Benny's future bride, who was a top agent not at Surfside but at Belle Maison, who apparently regarded her former fiancé's misfortune as a career opportunity.

Handy must have sensed something amiss. He turned off the power to his rotating pelvis and opened his eyes and looked at Benny with far less delight than he displayed when admiring the half-life-size model of a McLaren Speedtail in his office. "What the," he said, and then again, "What the," unable to decide which third word would properly complete the question.

Jill wasn't able to shut off her pelvis and breast works until Handy's second "what the," and when she opened her eyes, she had to turn her head to see Benny. During their courtship, Benny had never seen her lovely face contorted all at once by surprise and anger and vicious intent, as it was now.

Before his ex could think of a line from Taylor Swift or Lady Gaga, Benny reached farther back in pop-music history and recited a line from Dion's "Runaround Sue."

The dancers were so stupefied by this interruption that they decoupled in slow motion from each other's arms and hips, like a space shuttle disengaging from the airlock of the International Space Station in a zero-gravity environment.

The aplomb, graciousness, and professional congeniality of a highly successful real-estate agent deserted Jill. Taking a step toward them, she became a venomous, sneering harridan out of a bad soap opera. "Puppy dog Benny shifts into stalker mode. Watch your manners, puppy. Don't pee in the house. And who is this perky little refugee from a Disney after-school special?"

Before Benny could respond, his companion astonished him by saying, in an entirely perky way, "Remember those times he was making love to you and he called you Harper? That's me."

"Ah," said Jill, "little Miss Funny Hat has a sharp tongue."

"Don't be bitter," Harper implored tenderly. "You've lost the only man who ever satisfied you, but you'll find someone else."

Harper had knowingly pressed a psychological button that Benny hadn't realized existed. For reasons that he could not understand, Jill the Beautiful abruptly uglified herself and became Wicked Jill, who would have elicited a scream from him if he had encountered her in a dark alley. Her exquisitely contoured body twisted subtly yet profoundly into the spiky anatomy of Cruella de Vil. Her face hardened, and every feature grew sharp, and the blood drained out of her as if she had just provided a banquet to Dracula. She'd been so triggered that she said something quite other than what she meant to say. "For your information, Braindead Barbie, I've satisfied a lot of men, *a lot*." Handy appeared surprised, although not in the way a person looks when given a nice gift, and Jill appeared as mortified as she was angry. She hastily revised her statement, though it still failed to convey the information she wished to impart: "I mean a lot of men *have satisfied me*."

Benny felt such sympathy for Jill that he wanted to give her a hug and tell her everything would be okay. Because he intuited that she might bite off his fingers, however, he resisted the impulse.

Rather than correct herself a second time and plummet deeper into misstatement, she said, "Handy, dammit, do something. This is *your* house. What're they doing here?"

On the nearest cooktop, a skillet rested on a cold burner, as if later in the evening Handy intended to sauté something or flambé black cherries for a jubilee. He grabbed this unconventional weapon of home defense and brandished it and said, "Benny, I don't want to hurt you. We've always had such a cordial relationship."

"Until yesterday," Benny said.

"You were like a son to me, almost like a son, like I'd want a son to be if I'd ever fathered one."

"You don't want to be my father," Benny said. "It's a dangerous gig. My father was shot in the back, and my stepfather was stabbed in the back."

"Don't go dark on me, Benny. We parted amicably. Let's put on our big-boy pants and admit what happened was beyond our control. We have so many good memories to cherish. Let's not sully them."

Following a growl of exasperation, Jill Swift said, "Good God, give me the skillet," her clear intent being other than sautéing or flambéing.

With an incomparable sense of timing and a flare for making memorable entrances, Spike the craggle stepped through the archway and into the kitchen.

This apparition inspired a long moment of thoughtful silence before Handy Duroc responded as he might have when he'd been a young surfer and lifeguard. He smiled warmly at the giant and gave him the two-finger peace sign. "Dude. Wha'sup?"

Benny said, "This is our friend, Mr. Spike," because maybe the word *craggle* was proprietary information. "He's not an attorney or anything like that. You don't have to worry this is about anyone suing anyone. We just need to come to a better understanding about why my career was destroyed."

Returning the skillet to the cooktop, Handy said, "Cool. Be a better world if we all tried to understand one another."

"Where do you go these days," Jill asked bitterly, "when you need a man for the job?" She picked up the skillet.

Spike wagged an enormous finger at her. "That will be of no avail to you, Ms. Swift," he rumbled.

"You're a big sonofabitch," she said, "but you don't scare me. Now get out of here, all of you."

One arm extended to full length, palm toward Jill in a talk-to-the-hand gesture, Spike spoke in what might have been Latin or an even more ancient language. To Benny, in his agitated and stressed condition, the tumble of words sounded something like, "Wop bop a loo bop a lop bom bom," but he wouldn't swear to that if the evening ended in a police interrogation.

Pulses of amber light issued from Spike's open palm, washed onto Jill Swift's face, formed two whirlpools, and drained into her eyes.

Face contorted in anger, mouth hanging open as if a series of additional obscenities were on the way from her brain to her vocal cords, Jill was cast into stasis. She stood there as motionless as the Statue of Liberty, though with a skillet raised instead of the torch of freedom. She was in the same condition as Bob Jericho, who still posed with his pistol in the garage of the house in Corona del Mar. When she was released from this spell, she wouldn't remember anything of what had happened, including how she'd been mortified, which was the only thing that gave Benny hope for the future of humankind.

Taking a step back from the giant and a step sideways from Jill, Handy said, "I am seriously psyched out."

"She's just in stasis," Benny said. "He sidelined her. She's breathing. She'll be fine when Spike releases her."

"She'll still be a conniving bitch," Harper said, "but she won't have been harmed. You can trust Spike. I do, and I'm a good judge of character."

Fear wound the Realtor's psyche backward thirty-five years, to when he'd been an adolescent grommet, a young surfer who didn't yet have the hair to ride the biggest waves. "Please don't Popsicle me, dude."

Spike went to the sidelined woman, took the skillet out of her hand, and said to Handy, "Name an animal."

"What?"

"Name an animal, any animal. An animal you like."

Handy looked as if he had been asked to specify what body part he could do without. "Don't hurt me."

"Relax, bro. Just name an animal."

"Squirrel," Handy said. "I like squirrels."

The craggle's big hands were amazingly dexterous, moving too fast for Benny to follow all the intricacies of his art. He pinched and pleated and folded the skillet for perhaps a minute, producing a torrent of tormented sounds, and when he finished, the fry pan was reshaped into a work of metal origami. "Squirrel," he said, and it was indeed a charming cast-iron rodent, although its tail wasn't convincingly bushy. "A goodwill gift from me to you, Mr. Duroc." He set his creation on the island beside the silver ice bucket in which the champagne chilled.

Handy stared at it, speechless and trembling.

"All we need is a few minutes of your precious time," Spike rumbled. "A few answers. Give us a little cooperation, make nice, and we will leave you to dance the night away."

SPIKE'S FOLDING OF THE SKILLET REMINDS BENNY OF MENGISTU GIDADA

Nineteen hours after venturing onto the roof of Mrs. Baneberry-Smith's laboratory, the boys convened in Jurgen and Benny's dorm room, in the subdued lamplight they preferred. They were drinking Coca-Cola spiked with aspirin, even though they didn't fully credit the rumor—which the other boys of Briarbush considered dogma beyond questioning—that this combination produced an alcoholic beverage.

Ostensibly, they gathered during this social period, prior to lights-out, to play a version of partnerless pinochle, though no one brought forth the necessary cards. For almost an hour, they slumped in their armchairs, discussing subjects of little interest compared to the issue that was foremost in their minds and that they were loath to confront. Proposed: that the school nutritionist, at the direction of Headmaster Lionel Baneberry-Smith, daily laced the food served to students with saltpeter or another substance to suppress their libidos. Although this belief was widely held among students, the consequence of certain eventful dreams seemed to disprove it, as did the popularity of the soft-core girly magazines that one of the landscape crew, Vigor Maitre, purchased during his expeditions to civilization and resold to students at six times the cover price. On the other hand, considering the proven duplicity of the academy's administration, neither Jurgen nor Mengistu nor Benny could dismiss the possibility that the cumulative effect of eating Briarbush food during adolescence would be permanent impotence by graduation day. The best they could do to cope with this fear was open another Coke, drop another aspirin, and hope for inebriation. Proposed: that the headmaster and the masters of Felthammer House and Kentwhistle House were secret (a) satanists, (b) extraterrestrials, (c) descendants of Hitler, (d) intelligent fungi. Unanimous conclusion: Without a doubt, they were intelligent fungi satanists who venerated Hitler, but they weren't intelligent enough to be extraterrestrials capable of inventing faster-than-light space travel.

Throughout these discussions, Mengistu busied himself with one-dollar bills that he folded into miniature wonders of origami. He'd been taught this art by his father, Solomon, who now supplied him with three hundred crisp bills every month. Solomon required his son to create these works and present them to fellow students, teachers, and academy staff as expressions of gratitude or friendship. Solomon said that such thoughtfulness would ingratiate Mengistu with members of the faculty who could eventually assist in getting him into one of the most prestigious universities, and would help him make friends with other boys who would eventually be the honored elites who ran the world. Although Mengistu intended somehow to avoid university and become a chef, although he thought the other boys here—with the exception of Jurgen Speer and now Benny—were self-important dolts who would bring civilization crashing down around them, he did what his father directed because he was a dutiful son. He crafted origami even though he suspected that another reason Solomon required this was to fill some of the spare time during which Mengistu otherwise might be seduced into a life of sexual ecstasy of a kind that would deny his parents grandchildren. So Mengistu created dollar-bill birds, bunnies, butterflies, boats, crickets, chickens, elephants, monkeys, roses, stars, and an origami depiction of a popular Russian hors d'oeuvre called *zakuska*. Briarbush Academy would have been the repository of the world's largest origami collection if the students had not conspired to unfold Mengistu's creations and use the heavily creased bills to purchase smutty magazines from Vigor Maitre.

During all this discussion of saltpeter and intelligent fungi, accompanied by the swilling of spiked Coca-Cola, Jurgen from time to time rose from his chair to go to a window and ease aside the shade. He studied the soccer field and the forest beyond as light drained down the western sky, but Benny and Mengistu knew that Jurgen was on the lookout for the very thing none of them could bring himself to talk about.

At last, Mengistu threw aside an unfinished wild boar and said, "Prescott Galsbury. The hideous creature that he has become. What must we do about Galsbury?"

"It's a predicament," Jurgen said, turning from the window.

"It is worse than a predicament," Mengistu declared. "It is a dilemma offering only unfavorable choices for us."

Straightening up in his armchair, Benny said, "It's a dilemma wrapped in a quandary."

"Even that," said Mengistu, "is an inadequate description of what we face. But it is good to have friends smart enough to be capable of making such distinctions."

They smiled at one another, three geeks who had lucked into a meaningful friendship, but their smiles faded.

"Galsbury is a menace," Mengistu said, "but also a suffering victim. There is a moral issue before us."

Pacing, Jurgen said, "He begged us to feed him. But how the hell can we do that?"

Mengistu's large eyes became larger. "We will make no attempt to feed him, Jurgen. It is not our job to operate a soup kitchen for monsters."

"What I think," Benny said, "is I think what he wanted to eat was us."

"I believe so as well," Mengistu said. "Immediately Galsbury said it, he licked his lips with that disgusting tongue."

Jurgen returned to his chair and sat on the edge of it. "It's okay to have sympathy for the poor sonofabitch, but we need to remember Galsbury was a creep even when he was more human. He might be a deadly threat now. The adults will have to handle this."

"What adults?" Benny asked.

That thorny question resulted in an uncomfortable silence as the friends contemplated an answer that wouldn't at once strike them as ridiculous.

Finally, Jurgen said, "I guess we've known for some time that no adult at Briarbush can be trusted."

Benny sighed. "Our parents have consigned us to an asylum, not an academy."

"A den of iniquity," Jurgen said, "but not any kind of iniquity that might have a fun side. What if we call the county sheriff?"

Mengistu shook his head. "Not an option. Yes, we are three boys who, through hard experience, have gained a clear-eyed understanding of the troubling nature of humanity and the broken condition of the world. However—"

Benny interrupted. "I never thought of putting it that way. It's true, and it's not a bad thing to be wiser than our years, but it's a little sad."

"It's very sad," Jurgen said.

"Cease and desist right now. We will not engage in a pity party," Mengistu said, and he continued on his previous track. "*However*, for all our experience, we are nonetheless boys, kids.

When kids claim they have seen a pale, hairless man-bug with gray lips and yellow teeth, there is no chance whatsoever that the nine-one-one dispatcher will send out a SWAT team."

The expression of this truth resulted in another silence that was broken only when Benny said, "We need a photograph of Galsbury. If we can get a camera, we go on the roof of the lab again and lure Galsbury to the skylight."

Jurgen sank back in his chair. "They'll think the image is Photoshopped."

The silences were growing more frequent and longer.

Jurgen got three more Cokes from the refrigerator.

"No more aspirin," Mengistu said. "My blood will be so thin, I'll die of a paper cut."

A possibility had occurred to Benny some time earlier, but he hadn't immediately wanted to dwell on it. Undesired images crowded into his mind nonetheless, so he said, "Do you think Galsbury might have eaten Mrs. Baneberry-Smith?"

Jurgen clamped his hands over his ears as if to block out the grisly suggestion retroactively. "He took the job in the lab to have a chance to hump her, not devour her."

"His needs might've changed with his physiology."

"Well, she probably would taste a lot better than her cookies."

"Her cookies were okay," Benny said, "even if they smelled like mushrooms."

As usual, Mengistu brought logic to the discussion. "If the headmaster's wife was eaten by a monster of her creation, that would have resulted in considerable commotion even at Briarbush Academy. There has been no commotion. There has not been so much as a faculty meeting to discuss who will teach Mrs. Baneberry-Smith's course in the history of fifteenth-century Italy.

Faculty meetings always get ferociously noisy. We would have heard the uproar."

Jurgen sank even deeper in his chair. "Here's another thing that'll make you soil your shorts if you think about it too much. In books and movies, when there's a laboratory full of monsters or a hotel full of murderous ghosts or whatever, it always ends in fire. It has to end in fire, everything and everybody burned up, so the threat is eliminated."

"Sometimes the place is nuked," Benny said.

"I'd rather be nuked, vaporized in an instant," Jurgen said, "than slowly burn to death."

"We are not going to be either nuked or burned," Mengistu said, as if he could fold fate to his liking as easily as dollar bills. "At least not within the next day or two. Or even three. Meanwhile, the moral issue of Galsbury's suffering remains before us. We must continue to think about that overnight and arrive at a course of action by tomorrow."

Although wise beyond his years, Mengistu Gidada could not see the future. The violent resolution of the Prescott Galsbury problem occurred later that very night, after lights-out.

(I must tell you Spike notes that the final lines of this chapter are an example of a plot device called "foreshadowing," which is useful for setting the mood and creating an atmosphere of uneasy expectation. Spike suggests that if you are in a readers' group, you might want to make this a point of discussion and compare these lines to the dialogue of the three witches in the first act of *Macbeth*.)

ON THE ROAD AGAIN

After Handy Duroc had spilled his guts, figuratively speaking, he was left in the kitchen in a bespelled state, in the arms of Jill Swift—and she in his embrace—in a classic dance position. The only details incongruous with the romantic tableau were the expressions fixed on their faces. His was a mask of terror, hers a torment of rage.

Spike considered the duo and then adjusted Duroc's right hand, moving it from the small of Jill's back to her butt, where it had been when they were swanning around the kitchen earlier. "The instant they become motile, their expressions will change. His terror will be forgotten, as will her rage, and they will flow right in step with this excruciating music, engaged in their grotesque vertical seduction as if we had never interrupted them." He shuddered. "It's in moments like this, in observance of specimens like these, that I am deeply grateful that craggles have no organs of reproduction."

Only minutes earlier, Benny could not have conceived that a time would come when Jill would not seem like a perfect package of total wonderfulness, to be longed for even after she'd rejected him so decisively. Now the sight of her made him shudder, made him want to laugh and, oddly enough, weep a little for her, all at the same time.

Benny and Harper followed Spike through the house and out by way of the broken front door. By the time they were crossing the courtyard, under the bright and glowering moon, Handy and Jill had returned to the dance.

Having come from Boca Raton, Florida, in a crate, Spike took an almost childlike delight in driving the Explorer. "There's nothing quite so invigorating, so *freeing*, as piloting a gasoline-powered vehicle along an open road. Years from now, when all the vehicles are electric, when tens of millions of acres of Earth's surface have been destroyed by open-pit mining for the enormous quantities of lithium and cobalt and nickel and copper required for EVs, when thousands of new landfills have been crammed full of batteries that can't be recycled and are leaking horrifying toxins into the water table, when thousands of square miles of windmills have made extinct hundreds of species of birds with disastrous environmental effects, I will still—always, always—remember this special and exhilarating night, chauffeuring you two hither and yon in the dogged pursuit of justice, my destiny buddies."

From the back seat, Harper said, "I am strangely moved—and I do mean *strangely*."

By the time the destiny buddies were heading south and inland, out of the ocean-side city of Newport Beach proper and toward the annexed community of Newport Coast, Jill and Handy had perhaps paused in the rubbing of their bodies together long enough to drink champagne, whereupon they would surely have noticed the mystifying origami squirrel that had once been a cast-iron skillet.

How curious it was, Benny decided, that from one day to the next, Jill Swift could fade from being the sunshine of his life to an increasingly dim figure no brighter than a low-wattage bulb in a bathroom night-light made of pressure-molded plastic in the shape of, say, a miniature antique lantern or an outhouse with a crescent moon cutout in its door. No less curious was that Harper Harper, in that same span of time, had evolved from a cute and perky waitress into an intriguing woman, still cute and perky, but also possessed of a sharp wit, good judgment, the courage of a first-rate private investigator in the making, with mysterious depths, who was terrific fun to talk to and look at. Benny didn't know if the rapid rise of Harper in his affections meant that, at the age of twenty-three, he was developing a more accurate and mature appreciation of character, personality, and beauty—or whether he was so shallow that he could discard one love for another as easily as throwing away a Kleenex and plucking a new one from a box. He wanted to think that, in the ongoing crisis, he was being shaped into a better man by the stress of events, but he knew that the human heart was deceitful above all things, a truism he'd first read on a slip of paper from a fortune cookie, at the age of twelve, and had at once known was the essence of wisdom. Well, if he was to have a future with Harper Harper, only time would tell, and more than anything else, it would depend on whether, at the end of this night, he was dead.

While Harper was prominent on the stage of Benny's mind, other important issues jostled with her for his attention, including the phrase "destiny buddies," which had troubled him since Spike first spoke it. Now, as they made their way to the home of the attorney whose name they had gotten from Handy Duroc, he said, "So, Spike, what happens if I get my career back?"

"Not if. Never if," the giant admonished. "*When* you get it back. Cragglethink allows no possibility of failure."

"Not even if a bogadril shows up?"

"In that event, things can get messy. Terribly, terribly messy. But you will nevertheless get your career back or something better."

"What is a bogadril?" Harper asked from the back seat, as she had asked earlier, on the way to Handy Duroc's house.

"To discuss those creatures at length is to draw one of them to us. We do not want to draw one of them to us. End of discussion."

"Okay," Benny said, "but what happens when I get my career back or something better?"

"Don't think you'll be happy ever after, everything wine and roses for the rest of your life."

"I was disabused of that fantasy a long time ago."

"You'll be happy for a while, very happy, and then you'll be assaulted by nefarious forces."

"Them again."

"What's new is this—these people aligned against you aren't ordinary nefarious forces. They're organized. They remain anonymous and yet produce a newsletter that can be read by only those with an implanted identity chip, have an awards banquet, and meet biannually in person under the most stringent secrecy. Antwerp in the spring, Aspen in the autumn. They have many targets, not just you. They possess the resources to torment thousands like you. From time to time, we'll have to take countermeasures and set your life aright once more."

Benny neither doubted Spike nor was disheartened to learn that the misfortunes besetting him all his life were no longer the acts of merely random dark forces, but were engineered and executed by a conspiracy of powerful individuals. Although he was very much an optimist, he had expected something like this sooner or later.

"So then, when this is done," he said, "you're not going away."

"I would never leave you," the giant said. "Don't worry about that, my friend. Cragglethink places great value on duty."

"How long were you with my great-uncle, Talmadge Clerkenwell?"

"Seventy years, from his nineteenth birthday."

"But you left him."

"His time had come to move on from this world. I could do no more for him." A single tear slid out of the craggle's right eye, down his cheek, to the corner of his mouth. He licked it away and smacked his lips a few times and said, "Your uncle was a lovely person. So nice. Like you, niceness was his curse. He became a special target. They wanted to grind him down, ruin him, leave him so depressed that he would kill himself. But Talmadge had me, as you . . . as you, another special target, now have me on your side." His voice grew huskier and caught on a snag of emotion, and then he said, "Destiny buddies. You cannot survive without me, but you don't have to try. You no longer have to walk alone through the darkness and storms of this world. I will never let you down."

"That's sweet," Benny said.

"When you get to know me," said Spike, "you'll find that I *am* sweet. Oh, sure, I'm big and kind of scary looking, and when I need to, I can intimidate the shit out of anyone, but the real me, in my heart, I'm a muffin."

Behind them, Harper said, "I'm an emotional wreck back here."

Benny was determined not to get sentimental until he understood what being destiny buddies entailed. "So what arrangements will I need to make? I mean, you know, as regards the box you came in and everything."

"Well, I could stay in my time-out tube—"

"Your what?"

"Time-out tube. My box. I could stay there, in a corner of the garage, no trouble at all, and come out whenever things go to hell in your life and you need me. That would be fine. I have no problem with that." He hesitated as he braked to a stop at a traffic light, at the corner of Pacific Coast Highway and Newport Coast Drive. "But if it wouldn't be too much trouble, there is something I would like better, a different arrangement from the box."

"Tell me."

"I don't mean to be pushy. Tell me if I'm being pushy."

"I will. I'll tell you."

"Well, it would be nice to have my own room in your house. It doesn't have to be a big room. A modest space. Just a bed to lie on. A chair to sit in. A footstool would be appreciated. I'd like to have a shower. I find showers relaxing. But I don't need a toilet."

"Excuse me?"

"Don't fret," Spike said and patted him on the shoulder. "If you made an indelicate noise, I didn't hear it."

"I mean—why no toilet?"

"The internal plumbing of a craggle is different from yours. I never evacuate from bowels or bladder. I don't have either."

"But you eat like a horse."

"And I metabolize a hundred percent of every molecule with no waste products. Neither do I sweat or produce mucous or belch or shed skin cells into the environment. I do not mean to be bragging, but I'm a neat individual."

"May I say?" Harper asked.

As the light changed to green, Spike wheeled the Explorer onto Newport Coast Drive. "Of course, little lady. What is it you want to say?"

"I helped Benny clean up the kitchen. It's unkind of me to put it this way, but do you always eat like a pig?"

Accelerating up a long hill, Spike sounded mortified by the memory of the mess he had left. "I'm ashamed. Genuinely, truly humiliated. I assure you, it will never happen again."

"Why did it happen the first time?" Benny wondered.

"Well, see, I was crated and in transit for five days. I was hungry, famished. And when I'm cooped up like that, with no chance to stretch my legs and feel the sun on my face, I go a little nuts."

"Who wouldn't?" Harper said.

"Thank you for understanding. And it was all much worse because Talmadge sent me off knowing he would die within days. I wanted to be there with him when he passed, but he insisted I be shipped off to you while he was still well enough to make the arrangements. And then, while I had every confidence that I would like you, Benny, one never knows. Over the centuries, I have provided my services to some I did not like all that much. They were nice. Some of them were even nicer than you. But they were not wise. Nice and wise are different things. It is frustrating to serve someone who is nice but a fool, who wouldn't recognize a nefarious person if said nefarious person was robbing an old lady at gunpoint on the steps of a church. None of this excuses my going a little nuts and leaving that mess, but perhaps you will consider that there were mitigating circumstances."

As Spike turned left onto Pelican Hill Drive North, Benny said, "After all that you've done for me—or are trying to do—I'd be an ingrate if I kept you in a box in the garage. My house has four bedrooms, each with a bath. One of them can be yours."

"Thank you, thank you, thank you, Benny. I will never forget this. Craggles are incapable of forgetting anything, but even if I weren't a craggle, I'd never forget your kindness in this matter. We can remove the toilet from my bath."

"Why would we do that?"

Spike appeared puzzled. "You did understand what I said about never needing to potty?"

"Yes, I did. Nevertheless, we'll keep the toilet for when I sell the place someday."

Pounding the steering wheel enthusiastically with one huge hand, Spike said, "Keep it for resale! That is wise! So wise!"

"I'm going to have to start taking notes," Harper said. "I'm not a craggle, and I don't want to forget any of this."

"When we're finished with this evil attorney," Spike said, "maybe we can discuss a couple other issues."

"What issues?" Benny asked.

"Like maybe having a regularly scheduled boys' night out."

"Actually, I saw that coming."

"A movie now and then. Bowling. Or an afternoon of golf."

"Only if it's a fair competition. I never want to think you're letting me win. If I lose every time, that's all right, as long as I know that if and when I do win, it's all my doing."

"It's a deal, my main man. Just so now and then we do something fun together. But listen, don't worry that I'm going to be hanging around all the time, dominating your social calendar. This is your life, and I'm just like an old friend you went to college with or to war with, or maybe we both loved the same girl, she dumped both of us, and we bonded. Does something like that work for you?"

"Yes."

Spike swung the Explorer onto a long two-lane palm-lined driveway leading to a gated guardhouse, beyond which lay a private community of expensive estates.

"We have a problem," Benny said. "The only way anyone gets in there is if their names have been left with the gatehouse."

Spike pulled an Incredible Hulk face, except not green. "Some guard tries to stop me, I'll tear his head off and shove it up his ass."

"Uh," Benny said.

Slapping his companion's knee, Spike said, "Loosen up, buddy. It's a joke. Thrown out of college, survived a war, dumped by the love of our life—we need to keep our sense of humor."

PARTY TIME

The guarded and gated community was called Pelican Crest. Benny thought a guardhouse must be a serious problem when you were engaged in sneaky business. Spike regarded it as a chance for a bit of fun.

He powered down the window and smiled at the young man standing in the open door of the building, one of two personnel currently on duty. "How are you this evening, Ehud?" he asked, reading the name tag on the guard's jacket.

"I'm well, sir. What can I do for you?"

"Ehud isn't a name I hear often anymore."

"If ever," Ehud agreed.

"Do you carry a double-sided dagger?"

"No need. King Eglon has been dead for many centuries."

"Marvelous! You know the derivation. Could it have been an ancestor of yours, a long-ago Ehud, who freed the children of Israel from the horrid king of Moab?"

"I doubt it, sir. It's always been the women in my family who take on the tough jobs."

"That's usually the case, but seldom recognized."

Charmed by this banter, Ehud stepped out of the guardhouse doorway for a closer look at Spike. "Who're you calling on this evening, sir?"

"The self-important and thoroughly corrupt attorney, Oliver Lambert, is having a party," Spike said, having learned of the celebration from Handy Duroc. "I'm his brother, Fielding, and I have with me two companions who will be vastly more interesting than the pompous snobs Oliver calls his friends."

Ehud strove to maintain a sober expression, but he couldn't repress a smile.

According to Handy, Oliver Lambert was an unlikable man who traveled in the company of other unlikable people, all of whom pretended to love one another until such a time as they could stab one another in the back. The young security guard's reaction seemed to confirm that assessment.

"One moment, sir," Ehud said. "I'll check the guest list for the event." He returned to the guardhouse.

Benny said, "The party started more than an hour ago. What if Fielding already passed through and was checked off the list?"

"You heard what Mr. Duroc said. Oliver is desperate for his brother's approval, and his brother takes pleasure in withholding it. Best guess—Fielding was invited and will enjoy not showing up."

"But what if?"

"You've seen cragglethink in action with Ehud, but sometimes we need a little craggleluck."

"Actually," Harper said, "that business with Ehud is kind of like something Bob would do."

"Are you referring to Mr. Fat Robert Jericho?" Spike asked.

"Robert Jericho, Bob, yes."

"I believe I would enjoy getting to know him if one day there's a justifiable reason to make him a destiny buddy and reveal to him the existence of my kind."

Ehud returned to the Explorer with a pass to be displayed prominently on the dashboard. "Have fun at the party, Mr. Lambert."

"Well," said Spike, "I suppose it might be the occasion when Satan shows up to collect the soul my brother sold, but that'll probably be a night when I have the bad luck not to be present for all the fun."

The ornate gate rolled open. Spike powered up his window and drove through, and colonnades of palm trees flanked them again.

Benny knew the neighborhood well. He'd sold a twelve-million-dollar house here. One of the lesser residences. The architecture of these homes was often unfortunate, but the views of the Pacific and of the light show that was Orange County came at a cost.

They cruised higher into the community, and soon the streets were lined with the luxury vehicles of partygoers. A platoon of young valet-parking attendants in white shirts and black slacks waited in front of the Lambert residence in expectation of generous tips and the fun of driving glittering sedans and sports cars that cost far more than an average house anywhere in the Midwest. They didn't look crestfallen at the sight of the Ford Explorer, merely stunned that anyone in such a plebian conveyance would have been invited to an affair where the other guests were grandees or at least social-climbing swells with only a few rungs of the ladder remaining above them.

Stacked on an acre with a hundred-eighty-degree view, the house was grand in scale and vulgar in execution. As required by design guidelines of the community, it was Mediterranean—or was said to be, which apparently was good enough. In fact, it more resembled a residence in a cartoon Candyland where marshmallow qualified as an approved building material and where the definition of "accurate detail" had been decided by an architect who was literally a silly goose. Long ago, on the innocent side of puberty, Benny had realized that wealth and good taste were not necessarily linked.

Under the pitying gazes of the valets, he and Harper stepped out of the SUV and joined Spike, where he accepted a car check from an attendant. Gone were the craggle's black boots, black leggings, and black T-shirt. He wore black patent-leather shoes, a tuxedo, a ruffled shirt with French cuffs, a black tie, and a cummerbund.

"Will you look at that," said Harper, and Benny said, "A cute trick, but not as impressive as the business with the eyeball."

Wide-eyed at the sight of the tip he'd just been given, the valet said, "Uh, sir, you accidentally gave me a C-note."

Pulling a thick wad of hundreds from a pants pocket, Spike said, "Sorry about that." He peeled off a second hundred and passed it over, but then changed his mind and put the entire bankroll—maybe two thousand dollars or more—in the young man's hand. "Spread it around among your fellow car jockeys. Just don't dent a fender. The Ford belongs to my destiny buddy. He's such a perfectionist, if the paint is scratched, he'll piss a brick."

Pretending to be struggling against a fierce wind in this calm night, a pair of mimes—a man and a woman—met them at the entrance to the walkway and led them to the front door, apparently with the intention of assuring them that entertainment of a tedious nature would be provided without surcease during the event.

When Benny and Spike followed Harper into the spacious foyer, leaving the miserable mimes to perish in a tornado, a dozen long-legged showgirls in skimpy costumes featuring enormous pink feathers were posed on the curve of the grand staircase. Timing their movements more or less to the music of a band playing elsewhere in the house, the beauties descended as in a Busby Berkeley number from a 1930s movie, circled the three newcomers, smiling and blowing kisses, and paraded up the stairs from which they'd come, molting only slightly in the process.

The ten-piece band performed on a stage skirted with black velvet, in a courtyard decorated with maybe two thousand black and white balloons, doors open on all sides to flood the house with their music. The chatter of tuxedoed men and glamorously gowned women swelled louder than the band. The abundance of cavernous cleavage was a stirring testimony to the skill of Newport Beach's legions of cosmetic surgeons. Liveried waiters glided among the bejeweled and Botoxed celebrants, effortlessly carrying trays laden with fine wines and hors d'oeuvres. Guests were drinking champagne or chardonnay or cabernet, while others were eating skewered shrimp or lamb lollipops or chunks of ahi in wasabi sauce. Young sylphs in black body shirts and leggings circulated with supernatural grace, relieving guests of empty wineglasses, skewers, and soiled napkins. At various nooks in the mansion, women costumed as Romani read palms, dealt tarot cards, and perhaps cast curses on the enemies of the party guests for a price. The immense swimming pool must have been drained and then filled with saltwater, or otherwise the two dolphins frolicking in it would have been dead. A mustachioed and goateed man with fake horns spirit-gummed to his forehead and a red rubber tail protruding from the back of his pants, making balloon animals, might have seemed out of place if he hadn't been using bottled oxygen to inflate a variety of condoms with which to create his menagerie, but everywhere he went, gales of laughter greeted his act. Three or four times, Benny heard someone say the whole shebang was right out of *The Great Gatsby*, which meant they had never read Fitzgerald's novel.

Holding hands again, mainly to avoid being separated and lost forever in this sea of hilarity, Benny and Harper followed Spike as, from his higher vantage point, he searched for Oliver Lambert, whose photo Handy Duroc had earlier pulled from the internet. The attorney was eventually found in the kitchen—one rather like that in Duroc's house, but larger—where a busy cadre of cooks labored to ensure the guests had a selection of delectables with which to accompany excess alcohol consumption throughout the evening. So many delicious smells laced the air, Benny wouldn't have been surprised if he gained a pound just by breathing. Lambert was at one of the islands, sampling a fresh-from-the-oven savory, in the company of the caterer, Chaz Champlain, for whom Benny once listed and sold a house.

Spike approached the attorney and put a hand on his shoulder. Lambert looked up, chewing something, and Spike bent down to whisper in his ear. The lawyer swallowed, and a glazed look came over his face. With Spike's arm around his shoulders in a brotherly fashion, Lambert exited the kitchen by the back stairs.

Benny smiled at Champlain and said, "Great job."

He and Harper followed the craggle and his distinguished captive to the second floor, along a hallway, to a spare bedroom. Harper closed the door behind them as Spike encouraged Lambert to sit on the edge of the bed.

At fifty, the attorney had a coiffed mane of dark-brown hair as it might have been when he was twenty, the still-smooth yet seasoned face of a thirtysomething barrister, the poisonous methyl-green eyes of a centenarian who had spent a hundred years looking upon wicked work committed by himself and others, the patrician nose of a Boston Brahmin, the ripe mouth of a born libertine, and the prominent jaw of a proud longshoreman. He appeared to have been stitched together in an experiment, handsomer than the creature Victor Frankenstein summoned to life, but a man who was designed to be all things to all people—and nothing reliable.

When Lambert sat on the bed, he looked around the room, clearly puzzled about how and why he happened to be there. Then he focused on Harper, liked what he saw, seemed to reach the bizarre conclusion that he had been invited to a ménage à quatre, winked at her, and patted the mattress beside him.

"Oh, yuch," she said. "Spike, shake and bake this toad, and let's get out of here. I don't want to breathe the same air he's breathing any longer than I have to."

If Lambert had still been somewhat in the mists of a craggle spell, Harper's insult woke him fully to the reality of the moment. He began to get up from the bed, but he sat down again when Spike put one massive hand on his chest and politely positioned him.

Suddenly alert to the possibility that even an individual of his social position and power might be in danger in his home, he fumbled in a pocket of his tuxedo trousers and then in the other pocket. He still didn't seem to be alarmed, only irritated.

With a magician's flare, Spike produced an object about the size of a tube of lipstick. He thumbed open the flip-top of the object to reveal a button. "When I press this, how many bodyguards does it summon?"

"How did you get that?" Lambert demanded. "You have no right to that. Who are you? Who do you think you are?"

"I'd say at least eight security agents during an event of this size. Two of them should always have been within sight of you. But you felt so safe in this crowd of your own kind that you assigned all eight to the perimeter."

"You won't escape this house. You won't get away. You're finished."

Spike's voice got more craggily. "Don't be tedious. I have no patience for tedious people. I like to have fun. You are not being fun." To Harper and Benny, he said, "Am I missing something? Is he being fun, and I just don't get it?"

"He's no fun whatsoever," Harper said.

"You're no fun at all," Benny told the attorney. "You ruined my life. I never did anything to you, and you waltzed in and ruined my life."

Lambert raised his chin and looked offended that the life of anyone as inconsequential as Benny should be of interest to him. "Ruined your life? Why would I ruin your life? I've never met you. I don't even know who you are."

The attorney sounded as though he was genuinely baffled, but Benny wasn't as easy to deceive as he'd once been. When your mother turned out not to be the person you thought she was, when she would have called animal control and consigned you to the dog pound if only you'd been canine rather than human, when she cut you loose at thirteen, what naivete still pooled in your heart was flushed away as abruptly as the contents of a space-shuttle vacuum toilet.

"Oh, you know who I am," he told Oliver Lambert. "You put the screws to Handy Duroc and others to turn me into a nonperson. I'm Benjamin Catspaw."

Lambert's bafflement swelled into astonishment. "*You?* Why would they go to the trouble of erasing you? You're an obvious nonentity."

"I'm an entity, all right," Benny objected. "I'm very much an entity."

"You're a mediocrity," Lambert said, his expression of disgust precisely what it would have been if he spooned a dead mouse out of his bouillabaisse. "Look at you. Those clothes. Your posture. That *hair*. You're a nobody."

"He's cute," Harper said.

"Thank you," Benny said.

"Had I seen a photograph of you, even just a blurry photo," Lambert said, "I would have suggested to them that it was a mistake to waste time and effort on an insignificancy like you."

"You never even saw a photo of me?"

"Your values and principles might be those we must oppress if we are to have a better world, but you're a lightweight jackstraw incapable of serving as an example to others, incapable of spreading your dangerous ideology."

"Ideology? What ideology? I don't have an ideology."

His nostrils flaring as though he could smell the moldering truth of his unwanted visitor, the attorney said, "You're a *walking-talking* ideology, but you're no danger to the new world being shaped because you have no charisma. You are no great matter, a *peu de chose*. The most ineffectual kind of nullity. *Look at you.*"

Benny never got angry. Life was too short for anger, and rage accomplished nothing worthwhile. However, he felt a need to defend himself, especially after Harper said he was cute. "I've had two years of excellent sales. I was rising fast in the dirt business before . . . before this."

"I have antique automobiles worth more than any house you ever sold," Lambert said. "I have a Jackson Pollock painting worth more than *all* the houses you've sold put together. You are an obscurity, a trifler, a piddler, and I am profoundly put out that I wasted an entire day directing your erasure."

"You know, everything isn't about you," Benny admonished. "*This* isn't about you."

"Don't be stupid. It is *only* about me," Lambert said. "You came to me. I didn't come to you. Everybody comes to me. Your father was a dipsomaniac, and your mother was a *souillon*, a wanton trull, and you are nothing but the consequence of their mutual inebriation."

Oliver Lambert possessed inexhaustible energy for argument and vituperation, not to mention a colorful vocabulary. The lawyer would continue to defame, revile, and slander long after Benny retreated in exhaustion from the conversation. And so Benny said only, "You are not a nice man," and was done with it.

Lambert swelled with pride at that accusation. "I'd rather be dead than nice. Niceness is the refuge of fools. Humility is for losers. This is a hard world that can be run effectively only by hard people. Whatever you came here to extort from me, you'll fail to achieve, a piddler like you. Now *get out*."

Almost inconceivably, Oliver Lambert had become so enthusiastic about disparaging Benny that he seemed almost to have forgotten the seven-foot tower of tuxedoed muscle who had whispered him away from the kitchen and placed him on the bed.

Said tower now asked, "Them?"

Lambert shifted his attention from Benny to Spike. "What?"

"You said that if you'd even just seen a photo of my friend here, you would have 'suggested to them that it was a mistake to waste time and effort' on him. Them who?"

Benny's retreat to the simple accusation that Oliver Lambert wasn't nice seemed to convince the attorney that he should also stand up to Spike. He rose from the bed. "You have no idea with whom you're dealing. If you don't want to be arrested, jailed, and held without bail, charged as a national security threat, then get the hell out of my house."

This was a mistake.

With his left hand, Spike seized Lambert by the throat and lifted him off the floor as though he weighed five or ten pounds. Then, as only a craggle could do, he grew his arm—along with shirt and coat sleeves—to a length of perhaps six feet as he hoisted the attorney to the ceiling, lightly bumping the man's head against the plaster.

As terror and astonishment contested for control of his facial features, Lambert clawed at his assailant's wrist with both hands, but to no avail. He looked down from on high at Harper and didn't wink, at Benny and didn't sneer, at Spike and said, "Gah."

"You're just a glorified messenger boy," the giant said. "Tell me who decided to erase Benny's career and happiness. Tell me how they were able to coerce people like Handy Duroc to screw him over. Be quick and succinct, or I'll squeeze until blood squirts out your eyes, brains drool out your ears, and your head pops off."

Benny was pretty sure the threat wasn't sincere, that it was only intended to intimidate Lambert. Nevertheless, he said, "Uh, Spike?" The giant gave him a look of mild vexation, and Benny said, "Well, I had to ask."

Dangling at the end of the elongated arm, Oliver Lambert was forced to divulge the required information through clenched teeth, because the primary force of Spike's grip was upward, under the attorney's chin, rather than around his throat. Although Lambert sounded somewhat like Donald Duck, the tenor of his voice conveyed fright rather than the exasperation that frequently sent the fabled duck over the edge.

When Spike's questions had been answered, he said, "Ollie, old boy, being a forgiving soul, I'm inclined to let you live, even to limit your pain to humiliation. Take off your clothes." When the suspended man expressed dismay and reluctance, the hand that held him grew larger; thick fingers spread up his face, like the petals of a blooming flower. No words were necessary to convey the message that sealing his mouth and nose shut would be neither difficult nor an act that would cause his executioner to lie awake at night in the grip of regret.

His legs dangling like those of a boy hanging from a tree limb, Lambert struggled out of his tuxedo coat. It fluttered to the floor. He freed himself from his cummerbund, untied his tie, tore open his ruffled shirt, fumbled with his cuff links, and those items fell away from him. His trousers slid down surprisingly thin and bowed legs, but they hung up on his shoes.

When Spike abruptly released him, Lambert fell to the floor with a sound like—but with less grace than—a sack of potatoes.

As his swollen hand and elongated arm shrank to their previous size, the giant said, "Little lady, you might want to avert your eyes."

Harper's smile suggested she foresaw much that might amuse her and nothing likely to offend her.

Benny knew it was unworthy of him to take pleasure in watching the vain and arrogant Lambert humiliated. Although he was nice, even if some thought he was too nice, he never claimed to be saintly. He didn't look away.

After Lambert slipped out of his shoes and threw aside the tangled pants and stripped out of his undershirt, he stood in his red-and-black harlequin-patterned briefs, trembling and bewildered. His cultivated suntan now overlaid a ghastly complexion, rendering him a dull grayish bronze. "No more," he said, faking defiance.

Looming over Lambert, Spike pulled the here's-looking-at-you-kid trick, this time with both eyes.

Letting out a thin shriek, as if he had shed forty-five of his fifty years and changed genders in an instant, the attorney stumbled backward two steps and came up against a wall.

With his eyes glaring on the ends of fibrous stalks and swaying like cobras an inch from Lambert's face, Spike said, "If I have to take those fancy underpants from you, I'm sure to grab more than the fabric, and I'll tear off whatever I close my hand around. Presto, esquire becomes eunuch."

On second thought, their host shucked out of his shorts.

The eyes reeled back into their sockets. Heavy lids closed halfway over them. Spike lowered his face to Lambert's.

Breath wheezed in and out of the attorney in ragged gasps as his tormentor grabbed his head in both hands and turned it sideways and murmured something other than endearments in his ear. When the naked man stopped shaking and began to breathe normally, Spike released him and stepped away.

"Benjamin, he will remember that you and Harper were here, but he will recall nothing of me. He will not understand how you could have bespelled him into doing what he's about to do, but he will now forever live in fear of you."

A bead of sweat depending from his nose, his face glistening like a glazed doughnut but not as appealing, Lambert looked around as if not sure where he was. After a moment, in a voice eerily normal, he said, "Well, I better get back to the party."

Wearing nothing but black socks, like a performer in a sleazy 1950s stag film time-warped into a new century, he crossed the room and opened the door and stepped into the upstairs hallway.

Spike, Harper, and Benny followed Lambert down the back stairs to the kitchen.

The attorney paused at one of the islands, where a chef was hovering over a silver tray, arranging sticks of zucchini that had been breaded in sweet-potato starch and Parmesan before being deep-fried. He picked up one, bit off a piece, chewed, swallowed, and said, "Superb." He headed toward the nearer of two swinging doors, the one that would take him not into the butler's pantry and then the dining room, but into a hallway that served the several chambers where his guests partied.

Lambert hadn't yet finished chewing the zucchini before Chaz Champlain and his staff had fallen silent and still, like mannequins in a diorama. All eyes followed the attorney as he sauntered out of the kitchen, and no one seemed to notice Benny and his companions when they passed through the other swinging door.

In the dining room, on the right, a wide archway led to the hall. They proceeded instead to the far end of the room, to a door that opened to the immense foyer where the showgirls waited on the staircase. Benny was aware of the roar of conversation diminishing in stages as elsewhere the bare-assed barrister made his way among the celebrants with zucchini stick in hand.

When Benny followed Spike and Harper Harper out of the house, the Rolls-Royce that had occupied the place of honor in the street had been replaced by his Ford Explorer. A valet, serving as spotter, called out to his fellows. A squad of attendants sprang into action, opening the doors and starting the engine. If they had possessed whisk brooms, they might have hurriedly swept the path.

As before, the two energetic mimes flanked the destiny buddies. The silent pair no longer struggled against a nonexistent wind, but instead moved sideways, polishing nonexistent walls of glass that supposedly enclosed the walkway.

Nearing the Ford, as the ten-piece band faltered to a sudden unmelodic conclusion, Benny glanced back and saw a colorful flock of women in glamorous dresses and stilt heels wobbling out of the house in great haste, clinging to tuxedoed men for support.

Harper scrambled into the back seat, and Benny climbed into the shotgun position, and Spike the craggle crammed himself behind the steering wheel, and the grateful valets slammed the doors one-two-three, and somewhere Oliver Lambert was coming to the realization that he was naked except for black socks, with no memory of taking off his clothes and no slightest idea why he'd done so.

LEAVING THE PARTY OF THE CENTURY, BENNY REMEMBERS THE HORROR IN THE HEADMASTER'S HANGING GROUND

So after an intense evening of Coca-Colas with aspirin and the crafting of dollar bills into origami animals, having arrived at an understanding that they had a moral obligation to put an end to the suffering of Prescott Galsbury, now also known as "Bugboy," Benny and Jurgen—and Mengistu Gidada in his private room—were awakened the following night by excited but distant voices and two muffled sounds that might have been shotgun blasts. After hardly more than an hour of sleep, they erupted from their beds and flew to their windows, from which they glimpsed several flashlight beams sweeping the night in the vicinity of Catherine Baneberry-Smith's laboratory.

With uncanny synchronization, they threw on dark clothes and unlatched their windows and arrived simultaneously at the massive, spreading pine that stood fifty yards from Felthammer House. The sky was ornamented with a crescent moon, as on the previous night, but this time it seemed, to Benny, less like the sneer of the Cheshire cat and more like a harvesting blade. The four or five searchers had receded beyond the laboratory and now their lights carved the darkness across the last of the meadow, moving toward the grove of silver firs known as the Headmaster's Hanging Ground.

Mengistu said, "I do not delude myself that we are in no real danger. We are in mortal danger. One of us might die this night."

"One or all," said Jurgen Speer.

"Or none," Benny said. "We might all live long and prosper."

"I believe that to be highly unlikely," said Mengistu. "I am not a fatalist, Benjamin, merely a realist. Which is why I brought with me this pressurized can of Spectracide insect killer that I liberated earlier today from the janitorial-supply closet in our dormitory. The nozzle is set on STREAM rather than on SPRAY and promises a range of twelve to fifteen feet. I do not expect that it will kill a human-insect hybrid of Galsbury's size. However, if the unfortunate creature should attack with the intention of devouring us, I have some confidence this will repel it and allow us time to flee with our limbs and virtue intact."

"Ten months ago," said Jurgen, "I managed to steal this chef's knife from the kitchen and conceal it under a loose floorboard in my closet. I didn't know what the hell I'd need it for, but I knew sooner or later my survival would depend on having it. I just didn't figure it would be anything as weird as Bugboy."

"Should the Spectracide fail to deter the creature," Mengistu said, "it will fall to you, Jurgen, to use your cutlery to slash at whatever seems the most vulnerable part of the hybrid's anatomy. You have an opportunity to be most heroic, but I do not envy you enough to trade my insecticide for your knife."

Their faces mostly shadowed in the dim moonlight that found them through gaps in the pine limbs, Jurgen and Mengistu regarded Benny expectantly.

"Today," Benny said, patting his jacket pockets, "I bought four candy bars in the school commissary. A Clark Bar, an Almond Joy, a Hershey's bar, and a Reese's cup. See, after a lot of thought, I decided that when Galsbury said, 'Feed me,' he didn't necessarily mean with our own flesh and blood. I'm hopeful he's still human enough to have a sweet tooth. If we can befriend the guy, you know, maybe persuade him to join forces with us, then we have a chance of somehow getting him in front of the media to expose the crimes—the evil—of the headmaster, his wife, and Briarbush Academy itself."

His friends stared at him in silence for a longish moment, and then Jurgen said, "Man, you sure do march to the beat of a different drum."

"I like to be positive, give everyone the benefit of the doubt no matter who or what they are."

Mengistu said, "I find it most impressive that you have made it to your thirteenth birthday."

"If we're all alive tomorrow," Jurgen said, "I'd like to hear more about how you've gotten this far, Benny."

"Meanwhile," Mengistu said, "if Bugboy should perhaps take us by surprise and if you are his first target, I would suggest that the chances of your candy plan succeeding will depend entirely on offering him the Reese's cup first."

"Definitely the Reese's cup first," Jurgen agreed.

"Under no circumstances," Mengistu warned, "should you start with a Clark Bar."

"Under no circumstances," Jurgen emphasized.

Thus armed and with basic strategy in place, they raced off into the meadow, approaching the laboratory on an arc trajectory, the better to avoid any searcher who might be posted in the dark between Felthammer House and Mrs. Baneberry-Smith's little shop of nightmares.

Although no more than a can of insecticide, a kitchen knife, and four candy bars stood between Benny and a potentially horrific death, he ran through the night in a state of euphoric exaltation. Indeed, he didn't understand the reason for his exhilaration when the prospect of a gruesome death was very real. Eventually he would come to realize that he was inebriated not as a delayed effect of aspirin dissolved in Coca-Cola, but because he had drunk the rarest of all wines, the wine of true friendship, which until now he had never known.

By the time the boys arrived at the laboratory, the searchers had followed their probing lights into the grove of silver firs.

The front door had been torn off three of its four hinges and hung askew. Something had broken out of the building, and the odds were against the escapee having been something like an exotic spider the size of a tarantula or an Amazon rainforest butterfly.

"Bugboy broke out," Jurgen said, and no one disagreed.

It might have been commonsensical to creep into the nearby groundskeepers' building to borrow Tac Lights of their own, as they'd done the previous night when they had laddered themselves onto the roof of Catherine Baneberry-Smith's wicked domain. However, in spite of their high intelligence and keen recognition of peril, common sense wasn't central—or even peripheral—to this outing. They were in a swoon of adventure and derring-do and camaraderie. Although Mengistu had declared that one of them might die this night, none of them believed the worst could happen. Besides, if they employed Tac Lights, the search team would see them, and that might be worse for them than encountering the thing that had been Prescott Galsbury.

Their eyes had dark-adapted to a night with a lean moon, for there were stars aplenty. If they ventured into the silver firs and stayed close to the posse in pursuit of Bugboy—although not close enough to be detected—the lights of those searchers would provide an adequate view of what events might unfold.

In part, they had rushed into the night because they recognized a moral obligation to end or ameliorate Galsbury's suffering. That motive, if not forgotten, had become an appendix to the larger issue of curiosity, a virtue that had allowed humanity to rise from caves to the surface of the moon, while also resulting in deaths beyond counting. Then there was the attraction—the thrill—of all things mysterious, dark, hidden, and occult. Especially for young people trapped and being propagandized in the stupefying depths of modern education, the unknown and the unknowable offered the possibility of discovering the meaning of life that they had thus far been told did not exist.

Across the mowed yard, through the tall grass, they fled the humdrum. They crept into the forest, through an undergrowth of snowy woodrush and ribbon grass and bead fern, cautiously drawing closer to the search party, which by now they were able to count. There were four men and Mrs. Baneberry-Smith.

The headmaster's wife wasn't dressed as demurely as she did at school functions, nor was she in laboratory whites. She wore black boots, black jeans that looked as if they had been sprayed on, and a black T-shirt with a V-neck suggesting breasts that would qualify her for a ten-page spread in one of the smutty magazines that Vigor Maitre peddled to students at an unconscionable markup from the cover price. Although she was engaged in abominable and insane experiments, though she had transformed Prescott Galsbury into Bugboy, though she made cookies of questionable ingredients and gifted them to students with perhaps wicked intent, she was at the moment more alluring than Benny had ever imagined she could be, her golden hair streaming like an oriflamme that would hypnotize men to go to war for her. She stirred in Benny an unworthy desire.

However, one thing about the woman was so scary that it ensured Benny wouldn't have unchaste dreams of her. In addition to the Tac Light in her left hand, Mrs. Baneberry-Smith carried a bullwhip in her right and seemed impatient to use it on someone, anyone. As she moved, she now and then lashed out. The end of the whip flared in the backwash of light, suggesting it was tipped with steel, and fir-tree needles erupted off a shaken branch or the bark of a trunk was scored or fern fronds were severed. This seemed to be an odd weapon, unsuitable for a monster hunt—unless she had no fear of Bugboy and had good reason to believe that, with the whip, she would be able to subdue the beast and force it into captivity. She certainly looked fearless as she strode with great authority through the undergrowth like the Roman goddess of the moon and the hunt, Diana, abroad without her wolf pack.

The four other members of the posse were armed more appropriately, two with shotguns and two with what might have been AR-15s. They were big guys with hard faces. Benny had never seen any of them at Briarbush. They wore body armor, and they didn't seem to be as fearless as Mrs. Baneberry-Smith. They advanced more cautiously than she did, so that she repeatedly had to stop and wait for them, impatiently cracking her whip. With the Tac Lights that were fixed to their weapons, the gunmen warily probed the tree limbs overhead and the wild shrubs that grew tall where the conifers relented. When the firs gave way to other evergreens, and the search party was drawn deeper into the woods, the men appeared to grow more nervous at every swale in the ground and every cresting hillock and every rock formation behind which something might be lying in wait, their anxiety revealed by the way the Tac beams jittered or swooped abruptly toward some imagined movement or sound.

The gunmen's anxiety inspired them to sweep the night behind them with their lights almost as often as they reconnoitered the way ahead. That prudence complicated the pursuit Benny and his friends had undertaken, requiring the boys to shrink back farther than they would have liked. They hurried in a crouch from one point of cover to another, sometimes crawled, sometimes dared to dash openly and upright, grateful for the fog that began to gather in the vales between the series of ever-rising slopes.

Eventually, Benny was amazed at how far they traveled before it occurred to him that the great danger wasn't Bugboy. They were less likely to be gutted by a Lovecraftian horror than to be mistaken for Prescott Galsbury and shot by the posse. So intoxicating was this adventure—*the chase, the unknown, the danger, the courage required of them!*—even the realization that he could be gunned down at any moment didn't diminish his enthusiasm for their mission. He had read in a magazine that the human brain didn't finish developing until the age of twenty or thereabouts, and he had taken offense at that claim. Now he knew it was true. The reckless abandon with which he continued to throw himself into the pursuit, his determination not to appear cowardly to his friends—it was totally nuts. He was deranged. They were *all* deranged, their brains not yet equipped with adequate risk governors, reason overwhelmed by hormones, swept away by the fantasy of a heroic quest, and *it was soooo great.*

Crouched between Benny and Jurgen in a vale where fog pooled, with the four gunmen and Baneberry-Smith maybe twenty yards upslope in clear sight, Mengistu indicated a mass of dense shrubbery about ten yards ahead. "Mountain pieris," he whispered, evidently having identified the plant when the Tac Light beams had played over it. Mengistu taught himself all manner of things that he wasn't required to learn, that no one else had an interest in learning. As one, they rose out of the fog and broke for the next point of cover.

The boys were halfway to the mountain pieris when something came down out of a tree behind the gunmen, apparently making not a sound to alert them. Silhouetted against the light of the Tac beams, the pale creature was veiled in shadow. It seemed to be similar to what the boys had seen in the laboratory the previous night, though changed in ways Benny couldn't fully perceive. For sure, the thing was bigger, almost twice the size of Prescott Galsbury, and it had more limbs or appendages or whatever. At the sight of it, the boys halted halfway to the pieris, and Benny meant to shout a warning, but the new-and-improved Bugboy was lightning quick. It seized one of the gunmen, who screamed in terror and agony, unable to fire a shot before he was hauled off his feet. The beast had not entirely descended from the tree canopy, but seemed to depend from it by one or more limbs. It reeled itself up and out of sight, with the gunman in its fierce grip.

As the bloodcurdling scream cut off with a fatal abruptness, four flashlight beams played through the dense canopy of tree limbs, seeming to track a target as the three remaining shooters opened fire with two rifles and one shotgun. With a fervor equal to any that a *male* mad scientist could have exhibited, Mrs. Baneberry-Smith shouted, "Stop! Stop, damn you, you'll kill it, you fools!" But the gunmen failed to obey her, having determined that their survival required them to make the thing very dead indeed. Thunderous gunfire echoed through the forest, and evergreen debris showered down, and Crazy Catherine cracked her whip in a high dudgeon, and the three boys stood shocked and for the moment paralyzed. The snatched gunman reappeared, falling out of the trees in three installments—first the body, and then an arm, and finally the head. The bullet-riddled former resident of Felthammer House followed its prey, slamming hard to the earth, on its chitinous back, its four legs and two armlike limbs twitching. The pale and horrid creature seemed to be trying to right itself and commit further mayhem. However, the two riflemen possessed extra magazines, and the guy with the shotgun had a supply of spare rounds. Gross bug bits and thick gouts of slime spattered across the forest floor in such abundance there could be no doubt the threat had been eliminated.

Before the headmaster's wife or one of the remaining gunmen might look up from the drooling carcass of the monster and discover they had witnesses, the three boys dropped flat and squirmed forward and burrowed into the lush foliage of the mountain pieris. Huddled in that leafy sanctuary, they strove to stop shaking, fearing that their tremors might raise enough noise from the shrubbery to draw unwanted attention. Mengistu dared to murmur, "We're not out of the woods yet." The irony of that cliché caused Benny to titter, and Jurgen clamped a hand over his mouth.

GASSED UP

Leaving the estate of Oliver Lambert, having squeezed from the attorney the identity of his superior in the let's-destroy-Benny conspiracy—F. Upton Theron—the destiny buddies were unable to predict how many sinister individuals in addition to Theron they might have to visit before Benny's life was put back on track. Therefore, Spike determined that they needed to fill the vehicle's fuel tank. Benny gave him directions to a service station, and Harper suggested another route.

Attired once more in his less formal garments, Spike preferred to follow the advice of the navigation system. "She sounds like a nice lady. I don't want her to feel like we don't value her input."

Although he hesitated, Benny then said, "You do know that's just a kind of recording, not a live person making recommendations and talking you real time through the route."

"Who doesn't know that? Nevertheless, whoever gave the system her voice was a real person. We should honor her contribution."

"You think so, huh? Really? Okay then."

Frowning, Spike said, "Harper?"

"Right here."

"Don't you think she sounds like a nice lady?"

"She sounds very nice. I don't know what Benny's problem is."

"What is your problem?" Spike asked Benny.

"I don't have a problem. Not with a recording, anyway."

Harper said, "Maybe something about her voice reminds him of Jill Swift."

"She doesn't sound anything like Jill," Benny objected.

Harper said, "He came back a little too hard on that, don't you think? Like it touched a nerve."

"It didn't touch a nerve," Benny said.

"Even if she reminds you of your faithless fiancée," Spike said, "that's no reason to take it out on our guide lady."

"Okay, yes, you're absolutely right," Benny said. He leaned toward the dashboard computer. "I'm sorry. I'm grateful for your contribution."

Spike was pleased. "See? That wasn't so hard."

"Not hard at all," Benny agreed.

Harper said, "I like a man who can admit his mistakes and rectify them."

Holding the steering wheel with his left hand, Spike nudged Benny with his right elbow and winked theatrically, as if to say, *She likes you.*

"'Admit mistakes and rectify them,'" Benny said. "I am reminded of my chair."

"Chair? What chair?" Spike asked.

"The sleek, Swedish, bleached-sycamore chair that used to be in my living room."

"Ah, yes. That ugly, uncomfortable chair was another mistake."

"From my point of view, the mistake was destroying another person's furniture."

"If you sat too long in that chair, it would deform your spine. Why would I encourage you to deform your spine?"

"You're going to be with me the rest of my life, right? That is the deal as I understand it."

"Yes. To put your life back on the tracks when other people, wicked people, derail you."

"I'm grateful."

"You're welcome."

Benny said, "We can be friends and go bowling, play golf now and then—"

Spike said, "Maybe get a cat."

"We'll discuss pets later. The thing is—this won't work if you're going to nanny me."

"I never would."

"Well, that's exactly what you did with the chair."

"Is not."

"Is too. If I want to deform my spine by sitting in a cool chair, I will."

"That is not a wise choice."

"If I want to set my hair on fire, I will."

"That is even less wise."

"Besides," Harper said, "your hair isn't *that* bad."

"Your job," Benny said to Spike, "is to protect me from other people, not from myself."

"Oh, my main man, it's not a job," Spike said. "It's a calling and an honor."

"No nanny."

Spike sighed extravagantly. "Benjamin, you're just like your great-uncle Talmadge, bless his soul. He insisted on the same condition."

"Then we understand each other?"

"I can't say I fully understand a man who would set his own hair on fire, but I agree to your condition."

As the combination service station and convenience store appeared in the next block, Benny said, "One more thing."

"Is it the cat?"

"No. I'm wondering where all the money came from that you gave to the parking valets."

"It came from my pocket."

Harper said, "I can vouch for that. I saw him take it out of his pocket."

"I mean," said Benny, "how did all that money get in your pocket?"

Pulling off the street, coasting toward the island of gasoline pumps, Spike said, "There's always money in my pocket, whatever amount I need, whenever I need it. That's just part of being a craggle. No toilet, plenty of money."

"It's good being a craggle," Harper said.

"It's very good," Spike agreed, "except when you have to lie too long in the time-out tube and you can't turn your mind off, and you start mulling over all the I-sure-wish-I'd-done-that-differently moments from eighteen centuries."

Fishing a credit card out of his wallet, Benny said, "I'll get this. I need some fresh air. I need a lot of fresh air."

After a day in which he'd felt for the most part powerless, a mere pawn on the chessboard of life, Benny took real pleasure in the task of efficiently fueling the Explorer. It wasn't pleasure equal to an orgasm or eating filet mignon, but it was real. He slid his credit card in the scanner slot and took the pump-hose nozzle out of the nozzle boot and flipped open the little door on the Explorer's fuel-tank access and took off the cap. He inserted the spout of the automatic nozzle in the tank-filler neck and squeezed the trigger and breathed deeply of the gasoline fumes and took pride in his competence. Admittedly, the task was small and millions of people accomplished it every day, but the successful completion of this mundane chore had the surprising effect of lifting his spirits and increasing his confidence. Despite how he had been brought down by recent events, he didn't have to be forever a pawn on the chessboard of life. He could be a bishop or a knight, certainly not a queen or a castle, but maybe eventually even a king if only he stayed smart and made the right moves.

As he capped the fuel tank and shut the little access door and returned to the pump and seated the nozzle in the nozzle boot and got his receipt, his mood continued to improve, his self-assurance to swell. Then he dropped his credit card. As he stooped to retrieve it and stood and put it in his wallet, a car came off the street too fast and braked with a shriek of tires. Three thugs erupted from the no-doubt-stolen sedan, all in their late teens or early twenties, admirably diverse as to race but not as to gender and probably not as to religion, none of them presenting the appearance of a person who went to a church or synagogue or mosque. One was armed with a pistol, another held a machete, and the third gripped a tire iron.

In the harsh light that flooded down on the pump island, the guy with the gun was as pale as a corpse and gray around the eyes, but he compensated for this colorless condition with green lipstick and bright-orange hair waxed into a fright wig that made Benny's thatch look like the five-hundred-dollar coiffure of a *GQ* model.

"I want your car, asshole."

Although Benny's high spirits were plummeting, he was still buoyant enough to think it would be amusing if he replied, *My car doesn't have an asshole*, but fortunately he said, "Okay, sure, I understand, no sweat."

The driver's door opened. Like a Norse god being born out of rock, Spike emerged from the Explorer.

Harper opened the back door, and Spike told Benny to get in with her, and the guy with the gun said to Benny, "Hey, hey, hey, give me the key."

"He doesn't have the key," Spike said. "I've got the key. If you want this vehicle, you have to ask me nice for it."

"I'll stand with you," Benny assured Spike.

"Please don't," the giant said. "Get in with Harper. This won't take long."

"You some mush-brain dimwit?" the guy with the machete asked Spike.

"Why?" Spike asked. "Are you starting a club?"

Benny decided to get in the back seat with Harper.

AS BENNY GETS IN THE BACK SEAT WITH HARPER, HE REMEMBERS HIDING IN THE MOUNTAIN PIERIS

Two of the three surviving men loaded the pieces of their slaughtered compatriot into a body bag that they had brought for the purpose of transporting the corpse of Bugboy. As that grim task was undertaken, Mrs. Baneberry-Smith and a man whom she called Kimball, seeking privacy for a conversation, had come downhill from the gore-splashed area where the confrontation recently occurred. They stood beside the mounded mass of mountain pieris in which Benny, Jurgen, and Mengistu had taken refuge.

Their Tac Lights revealed their approximate location, but the density of foliage prevented Benny from seeing anything of them.

Kimball said, "After we haul Hawthorne's body out of here, we'll come back at first light to collect what's left of the freak."

"Leave it," said the headmaster's wife. Her voice was not soft, as previously it had been, but possessed the lacerating effect of her whip. "And don't call it a freak. It was a masterwork of cross-species engineering, one of the many wonders of Regulus technology."

"But if anyone finds that thing—"

"No one will. Carrion eaters will be at it, and what they don't consume will rot away quickly. I don't want anyone seeing ISA agents on or near the campus in daylight."

"No one will know we're ISA. We'll dress as hikers, hunters, whatever."

"If you cock-ups dressed as fairy princesses, everyone would still know exactly what you are. Having you here at night is risky enough. If you hadn't screwed up and lost control of my beautiful *olla podrida*, you would have him in your truck now, alive, and be halfway to Area Fifty-One. This shit, your stupidity and ineptitude, has set my work back six months or even longer."

This black-clad whip-carrying obscenity-spouting woman was dramatically different from—and much more exciting than—the Catherine Baneberry-Smith who, in a flower-print dress, had served cookies and tea in her drawing room. She almost seemed to be a different person, perhaps a wicked twin.

Benny understood now why Galsbury wanted to work in her lab. She was hot in one sense and cool in another. However, it was important to remember that something happened to Galsbury in her company that drove him to eat ants until his lunulae turned blue—which was the least of it.

Agent Kimball endured her tongue-lashing, perhaps because she was hot and he was one of those men for whom being whipped was a source of pleasure. Or maybe because she was so important to the dark operations of the Internal Security Agency that he dared not anger her.

After she finished excoriating him, they stood in silence for half a minute or so. Then Kimball repressed whatever anger he might have felt and spoke to her in a voice suggesting concern or even compassion. "In that jungle, twelve years ago, it wasn't just some spider that bit you. What was the thing really like and how were you . . . attacked? What did you endure that day, Cathy?"

Following a hesitation, during which it seemed Mrs. Baneberry-Smith might regret the sharpness of the rebuke she had directed at Kimball, she proved instead to have no remorse. "What happened to me would have left an absurd specimen like you squirming on the ground, shitting your pants and vomiting up your entrails. None of you ISA types has the intellectual capacity to endure what I endured. The physical pain you might have survived, but the mental torment and emotional anguish would have destroyed you."

Deep in the mountain pieris, Benny had more sympathy for Mrs. Baneberry-Smith than he might have expected. There were her faults and her insane experiments that had to be considered, but she also made tasty cookies, even if they smelled strange, and she served good tea with honey to sweeten it, and she welcomed him to Briarbush with what seemed to be genuine warmth. He assured himself that her lovely foxglove-purple eyes and the way she perfectly filled out her skintight black clothes had nothing to do with the tenderness that her words evoked in him. She had not always been a foulmouthed mad scientist. Once she'd been an innocent girl and then an adventurous young entomologist, and it was for *that* Catherine, the Cathy before the mysterious event in an Asian jungle, that Benny felt compassion, even pity.

"Imagine, if you can," Mrs. Baneberry-Smith continued, "what it would be like to be bitten and injected not with mere venom—if only it had been venom—but with a fluid that's a data-storage medium so vastly superior to silicon-based memory that a few milliliters can contain the entire history and all the knowledge of an alien race whose civilization is thousands of years more advanced than ours. Stretch your pathetic little mind to consider being plunged into a sea of bizarre revelations, strange science, freaking weird alien perspectives and customs, so that you think you're going mad, your entire concept of reality turned inside out and upside down. You feel as though your true self is being subsumed into some hideous hive mind, as if you're drowning not physically but intellectually."

By this point, Jurgen Speer had clutched Benny's right arm to express fear and amazement at the woman's revelations, and Mengistu Gidada had clutched Benny's face with the same intention before finding his companion's left arm and seizing that. They trembled with dread that wasn't entirely unappealing and inhaled wonder with every breath. They virtually crackled with a kind of excitement that adults had long forgotten if they had ever felt it.

Mrs. Baneberry-Smith snapped her whip, snapped it again, as if trying to make the terrible memories relent, but she could not lash them away. "During those three months in hospital and three more in rehab, none of the shit-for-brains doctors were sure what they were treating me for or how to treat it. As I gradually repaired myself, I came to understand that I'd been attacked by a being that was the only survivor of a crashed vessel, and it too had then died. Along with all the knowledge its species had acquired, I'd been injected with an imperative to use their science to populate Earth with their kind, and with the precise location where I could find a secreted capsule containing their DNA. Well, to hell with that. My willpower is greater than the imperative they implanted in me. This is my world now, and I'll do with it what I want."

When the headmaster's wife snapped her whip twice again, Benny realized that she wasn't trying to lash away terrible memories, but was declaring her mastery over all things and her intention to rule with merciless fervor. The sympathy he felt for her began to ebb.

"It's what all of us want," Kimball said. "The way you want to shape the world is the way the ISA and people like me intend it to be shaped. It's the way the parents of the boys we've brought to you want it shaped. They want it so intensely that they'll sacrifice the free will of their sons to see your vision fulfilled."

Jurgen's and Mengistu's hands tightened almost painfully on Benny's arms.

"With all due respect, Cathy," Kimball continued, "we only wish you could master this alien science somewhat faster."

"Damn you, don't pressure me, Kimball. I won't tolerate it. I'll deal ruthlessly with insubordination. I possess the knowledge, but it's complex beyond your feeble ability to comprehend. I've got to be careful in the application of it. I've given you a few things of great value in the area of weaponry. I've altered hundreds of young men from elite families, hollowed them out, so they can be elevated rapidly into the social order and used by us as if they were sock puppets. But I'll move at a pace that I—and only I—determine to be prudent."

"You halted the aging process in yourself eight years ago, when you were just thirty-two. Look at you—timeless. Yet you won't share with us how that can be done, how we can live three or four hundred years. Your refusal has caused anger in the ranks. We need to feel we're in this together."

"Feel what you feel. It doesn't matter to me. I'll share that miracle when I'm confident my position is unassailable. Perhaps within a year."

Kimball said, "If we brought in other scientists—"

"No."

"—and you shared a fraction of your knowledge from the Regulus civilization—"

"No."

"—and assigned them projects, we could advance our cause so much faster."

"Knowledge is power, Kimball, especially knowledge as absolute as this. I'm as averse to sharing power as you'd be in my position. I'll give you miracles from time to time, miracles of my choosing, only when I wish to grant them."

"But—"

"Enough. Don't hector me. I'm the only doorway through which you can receive any of the knowledge you covet. I can shut you out. And never forget—I can kill you and everyone who knows about me, kill all of you faster than you can say *Please let us live*."

After a silence, as if wounded, Kimball said, "Cathy, all that we once were to each other . . . doesn't that matter to you?"

Her voice sounded so cold that Benny imagined snow crystallizing from the breath she expelled with her words. "What we were isn't what we are now. What I will become is nothing you can ever be. Know your place, presume nothing, and never dare touch me."

A new voice said, "We bagged Hawthorne. Pretty sure we didn't miss any pieces."

The three agents and Mrs. Catherine Baneberry-Smith departed, their lights dwindling into the darkness quicker than the sounds of their passage faded into the silence of the post-midnight forest.

Jurgen and Mengistu let go of Benny's arms. They didn't speak, as if they weren't convinced they had escaped discovery, as though Mrs. Baneberry-Smith would at any moment whisper their names and part the foliage and lash out at them with arms that had become whips.

For fifteen minutes or longer, they sat wrapped in the foliage of the mountain pieris, each lost in his thoughts.

Benny ruminated about all the people he'd expected to kill him but who had not done so. His father. Grandma Cosima, who no doubt murdered two husbands. His tutor, Mordred Merrick. Bugboy. A person couldn't expect to glide through life, good luck always breaking his way, the worst kind of bad luck befalling only other people. Sooner or later, you had to take it in the shorts, as they say, bite the bullet or maybe even bite the dust. A moment of grave misfortune must be near at hand.

(Additional note to readers' groups: The line immediately above is another, subtler form of foreshadowing, like the lines previously drawn to your attention by Spike. Just sayin'.)

"I believe," Mengistu said at last, "that it is now safe to come out of hiding. Even with their grisly burden, they have surely progressed far enough that we will not be heard or seen making our way back to Felthammer House."

"Let's wait a little longer," Jurgen said.

"I quite agree," Mengistu said.

Perhaps five minutes passed before Benny said, "What if it's not as dead as they thought?"

Jurgen said, "They must've pumped like a hundred rounds into the damn thing, blew it to bits, all that slime, it just can't be anything *but* dead."

"Yeah, but you know how it is in the movies," Benny said. "Just when they think the monster is dead, the thing comes at them one more time."

"This isn't the movies," Jurgen said. "The monsters in movies aren't really monsters. They're just CGI crap. In real life, real monsters can be killed and stay dead."

"That's just a theory," Benny objected.

Mengistu disagreed. "I fear that Jurgen's statement is not even a hypothesis, let alone a theory. A hypothesis is a statement of what is deemed to be *possibly* true, but it cannot be taken for the truth until all related facts and further evidence are brought into comparison. As we have no facts, no knowledge, of how or whether the life force in Bugboy can be extinguished, I am confident when I say that Jurgen's statement is mere speculation."

A ululant shriek quivered through the forest.

As one, the boys exploded out of the shrubbery and sprinted maybe twenty yards downhill before they recognized the howl of a coyote or perhaps a wolf. That realization brought them to a halt. When they looked back the way they'd come, even the meager moonlight confirmed that Mrs. Baneberry-Smith's masterwork of cross-species engineering had not risen again. Relief had the same effect on each of them, and they stepped to three different trees to unzip their pants and empty their bladders.

HOODLUMS

Being in the back seat with Benny, one of his hands in both of hers, was sweet. It felt right.

Harper Harper had been getting smoother and bluer year by year until she was now fully smooth but not quite yet fully blue, which is why her baseball cap was emblazoned with just the word SMOOTH! Very few people knew what smooth and blue meant, although individuals who were on the smooth-and-blue path recognized others progressing along it as well, whether or not they announced it with words on articles of their clothing. It wasn't a cult; they never attended meetings or produced manifestos or intended to drink poisoned Kool-Aid together. Quite the opposite. Smooth and blue described a condition of the mind and the heart that all but ensured a more stable and happier life than most people experienced.

The funny thing about Benny—one of the funny things—was that he was on the smooth-and-blue path, but he recognized neither that she was nor that he was himself. He seemed ignorant of the entire concept. Harper's assumption had been that he was by nature smooth and blue but failed to recognize the need to perform maintenance on those qualities, allowing a little rust to form and some of the color to fade. He was a true lamb of a person, but perhaps he had not been able to cultivate those qualities because his life had been so full of extraordinary turmoil.

She decided that she'd be the one to make him aware of his innate smoothness and blueness, and bring him along the path toward the fullness of both. As confirmed by the rollicking events of this evening, that task was likely to be arduous, even dangerous, but her determination wasn't pure magnanimity. She had a selfish reason to help him be his best and happiest self because, to her surprise, she had in mere hours begun to fall in love with him.

As for the three hoodlums attempting to jack the Explorer, they were as far from smooth and blue as anyone could get. She pitied them, but she was not prepared to tolerate their kind. If Spike hadn't come into Benny's life, and if she and Benny had nevertheless ended up together this evening, and if they had encountered these thugs, she would have had to take them down. Even considering her extensive martial arts training and quick mind, she would likely have sustained one or even two serious injuries, not least of all because of the machete. A firearm required that it be aimed with a precision that many shooters lacked, and the awkward shape and heft of a bludgeon like the tire iron conferred on he who wielded it the disadvantages of bad aerodynamics and negative gravitational effects inherent in its design. Large-edge weapons with expertly forged and tempered blades, however, were easily manipulated by piteously stupid people, and they made it difficult for even a master of tae kwon do to get in close and personal enough to damage the assailant.

As Harper and Benny observed the action framed by the driver-side windows of the Explorer, the first attacker to be disarmed was the one with the pistol. For a person of his formidable dimensions, Spike the craggle proved surprisingly quick. Before a shot could be fired, he seized the gunman's hand and squeezed so hard that Harper thought she could hear fingers breaking like breadsticks. The thug cried out and let go of the gun, the barrel of which appeared to be bent when their destiny buddy tossed it aside. He picked up the would-be carjacker by the throat and crotch and threw him at the snarling fool with the tire iron, and both hoodlums tumbled backward, through the gap between two gasoline pumps.

"It's a shame he doesn't have reproductive organs," Harper said. "He would be perfect for Chrissy Wenwald."

"Who is Chrissy Wenwald?" Benny asked.

"She's the breakfast and lunch hostess at Papa Bear's. The tall blonde with the nose job that came out just right, so that you don't look up her nostrils all the time like with so many nose jobs. She's really sweet and pretty, but she's so darn unlucky at love it's heartbreaking."

"Of course, I've seen her," Benny said. "She seems nice."

"She *is* nice. But most men these days are a mess. The sexual revolution relieved them of the burden of responsibility, not to mention chivalry."

The third attacker, a grinning and oily individual with the black and rotting teeth of a methamphetamine addict, took advantage of the distraction provided by Spike's need to hurl the gunman at the basher with the tire iron. Long-legged and long-armed and as lean as an arachnid, the crook spidered forward, intent on cleaving his adversary's skull. Exhibiting the nimbleness with which he had changed from casual wear into a tuxedo, Spike shifted out of the path of the blade without seeming to move—was just here and then there—startling his assailant. This clever evasive tactic resulted in a demonstration of the primary problem with an otherwise effective edge weapon. With all the force the thug could muster, he brought the blade down on the roof of the Explorer, against which it rang like an iron bell. The compressed vibrations traveled through the blade, through the haft, into the would-be killer's hand, causing instant if temporary numbness and weakness extending past his wrist. His fingers spasmed, and he lost his grip, and the machete bounced off the vehicle. Spike snatched it out of the air, by the haft, and slung it away into the night.

"When you asked Spike if he dated," Benny said, "I thought you were, you know, interested in him for yourself."

Amused, Harper said, "Really? Oh, he's wonderful, very John Wayne and all that, but he's not my type."

"Why not?"

"For one thing, he's a bit too unpredictable. Chrissy Wenwald is up for unpredictability more than I am."

Tire-iron guy had disentangled himself from the gunless gunman with the broken fingers. Having failed to process recent events to an extent that would have led to an understanding that the towering target of the carjacking was not a common variety victim, the thug still had confidence in the efficacy of his weapon, which indicated low intelligence and a high degree of stubbornness. Holding the L-shaped tool by the short end with the lug wrench, he could choose to use it as a club or, because it ended as a bladed pry bar, drive it forward with the full force of his body and skewer his enemy. Clutching the makeshift spear with both hands, he chose the second tactic. He was understandably surprised when Spike's right arm abruptly elongated, hand raised in the gesture that is universally recognized as a command to halt. When the blade pierced the open palm, Spike smiled, and his hand closed bloodlessly around the bar, halting the attacker and instantly converting his forward momentum into leveraging energy. Because the attacker held fiercely to the weapon, he went vertical, arcing over Spike's head, flipped loose of the tire iron, and crashed onto the roof of the Explorer with a sound that suggested he would welcome the swift arrival of an ambulance.

As the chastened thug rolled across the roof and fell past the starboard windows to the ground, Benny said, "'For one thing.'"

Harper said, "For one thing—what?"

"You said that, for one thing, Spike was too unpredictable. Was there another reason, before you knew he lacks reproductive organs, why he wasn't your type?"

"Well, you know the answer to that, silly."

"If I know it, I don't know that I know it."

"He isn't my type, Benjamin, because you are."

His expression was priceless. He really was a lamb.

"Of course," she said, "my type, assuming that certain small alterations can be made." She leaned sideways and kissed his cheek.

The gunman with the spiky orange hair and green lipstick and damaged hand had gotten to his feet and was staggering around in a widening gyre, frantically searching the pavement for something.

Meanwhile, the spidery dude, whose machete had been slung away into the night, had evidently not seen the tire iron pierce Spike's hand without drawing blood or inspiring a cry of pain. He was sure to regret his inattention, because he had the temerity to extract a knife from a belt sheath and shout, "Gonna gut you like a pig," a threat he followed with a vicious obscenity that accused Spike of having copulated with his nearest relative, an insult the giant was not likely to take lightly even though he had no relatives.

As Harper watched the lopsided but entertaining battle unfold further, she wondered why the giant hadn't just bespelled these men, sidelined them as he had Bob Jericho and others, leaving them to emerge from the bewitchment five minutes later and puzzle over the sudden inexplicable disappearance of the Explorer and everyone in it. He had claimed craggles didn't kill people; to be fair, none of the would-be carjackers appeared to have suffered mortal injuries. Nevertheless, the current melee seemed to exceed even the most liberal definition of *intimidation*, which he had implied—or even claimed—was his sole technique.

Distracted by the consideration of that issue, Harper hadn't registered the maneuvers by which Spike relieved the meth freak of his knife and brought him to a collision with the driver's side of the SUV. She startled when the drug-wasted collection of bony limbs slammed against the back door, his face pressing to the window hard enough to distort his features, gazing in at them as if he were an ugly and exotic fish peering out of an aquarium. He opened his mouth to allow half a dozen black, rotten teeth to dribble across his lips, and then he slid out of sight.

Benny said, "'There is no reason to be afraid, though there may seem to be. There may very much seem to be. But there is not.'"

Harper squeezed his hand. "You okay, sweetie?"

"That was something my great-uncle Talmadge said on the video card, when he informed me that he was sending my inheritance by airfreight. Uncle Talmadge claimed I could trust him. I believe I can. I think I can. I sure hope so."

The gunman who had come on as if he were a droog out of *A Clockwork Orange* now hobbled around in widening circles like a broken windup doll, searching the pavement. Spike called to him, "Hey, my friend. Is this what you're looking for?" In his right hand, he held up the key to the hoodlums' junky old car, stolen wheels that could be abandoned when they jacked something better. With his left hand, Spike made a come-to-me gesture. "You give me a hug, and I'll give you the key. We can meet here every year on the anniversary of our evening together and reminisce."

No longer a confident droog in pursuit of ultraviolence, the gunman didn't run away into the night, but instead fled toward the convenience store associated with the service station. On another occasion, he might have been inclined to point a pistol at the head of the cashier and demand the contents of the cash register, but now he evidently perceived value in citizens standing strong together in a shared spirit of community.

Machete man, perhaps spitting out more teeth, appeared on his hands and knees, crawling after the gunman.

Harper supposed Tire-iron guy was lying by the starboard side of the Explorer, waiting to regain consciousness or playing dead.

Spike got behind the wheel and pulled the driver's door shut and said, "You okay?"

"I'm okay," Benny said.

"We're great," Harper amended. "Fabulous."

"I'm hungry," Spike said and started the engine.

DINNER

Crossing the parking lot from the Explorer to the restaurant, and again when they entered the restaurant, Benny felt his heart quicken in expectation of he knew not what. Life now seemed to consist of an endless series of unexpected dramas accelerating toward a hard wall of fate.

Those who dine out in Southern California tend to eat early, and restaurant traffic diminishes significantly after eight or nine o'clock. Even as little as half a decade ago, this dining habit was a consequence of the fact that Golden State culture was so rich with options that most people chose to get on with their favorite forms of fun rather than linger over dinner. In recent years, however, safe streets had become but a bittersweet memory, and those with a true sense of the tenor of the times preferred to get home early and lock the doors.

In the establishment to which the destiny buddies took their appetites, three-quarters of the tables were untenanted, but a noisy crowd still populated the adjacent bar. The role of excess alcohol in personal ruination, destruction of families, deadly arguments, and traffic deaths had long been understood. Less attention was given to the fact that, in depressing and perilous times, legions relied on communal consumption of alcohol to provide a sense of well-being and confidence in the future that, false as it was, made them easier targets when they ventured homeward through a world in which the predators were either sober or, worse, wired on drugs that made them hyperalert to which were the most vulnerable animals in the herd.

"I'd like some wine," Benny said after the hostess led them to a booth, where he'd settled beside Harper and across from Spike.

"I haven't felt so wound up since the night the ISA agents killed Bugboy. But under the circumstances I want to have a clear head."

"Bugboy," Harper said. "Sounds like a memory worth sharing."

"It's not suitable dinner conversation," Benny assured her.

Their waiter, Shane, was a handsome twentysomething guy with well-manicured beard stubble that, although currently fashionable, reminded Benny of the throngs of homeless men who pitched tents in parks or sprawled insensate in bedrolls on sidewalks littered with empty ampules of drugs. He didn't understand many fashion trends, like eyebrow rings and shoes without socks and suits with shorts instead of pants, unless the point was to say *Look at me*, which in Benny's opinion was always a mistake. When you called attention to yourself, there were bad people who would decide to do things to you that you didn't want to be done. Anyhow, Shane proved as efficient as he was stubbly, took their orders, and then delivered exactly the food they wanted instead of his interpretation of their desires.

Harper received the Cobb salad, and Benny had a double-patty cheeseburger with bacon and extra-crispy French fries. Spike tucked into two orders of filet mignon accompanied by Broccolini and baby carrots, with two sides of fried mozzarella, followed by sautéed salmon with basmati rice and brussels sprouts, followed by two pepperoni pizzas with extra cheese. And one entire meatloaf.

Of a generation that considered it a virtue not only to ignore but even to applaud the excesses of others (which was also Benny's generation, although he didn't feel a part of it), Shane made no comment about the volume of comestibles arriving in waves on Spike's side of the table. Fat-shaming still existed in some unenlightened corners of society, but muscle-shaming had never been engaged in by a significant number of people, especially not when the potential target of such comments was as dangerous looking as Spike.

"Back there at the service station," Harper said, "I was rather surprised by the violence of your reaction to those carjackers."

"I didn't kill anyone," Spike replied gruffly.

"But you sure broke some bones."

As though to mollify her with a change of tone and the addition of an honorific, Spike smiled and nodded and looked penitent and said, "Yeah, but I didn't kill anyone, little lady."

"A lot of bones," she said.

"Bones are bones. They break. Doctors set them. Life goes on."

"I was also a little surprised," Benny chimed in. "I was under the impression that you used only intimidation. Maybe you didn't say as much. I can't recall. But you seemed to imply it."

"Most of the time," the giant said, "intimidation is enough. But those bad boys didn't intend just to take the Explorer. They meant to kill you and me, then kidnap and gang-rape Harper."

Benny put his burger down, not sure that his appetite would be sustained.

Pausing with a fork of Cobb salad halfway to her mouth, Harper said, "Murder and rape? How can you know what they would've done?"

Spike answered her with one raised white eyebrow.

"Oh," she said, "because you're a craggle."

When Harper was able to continue eating without further pause, Benny picked up his burger. After two bites and some consideration, he said, "Why couldn't you just have sidelined them, put them under a spell until we could get away?"

"And when they reanimated," Spike said, "they would still be wired and crazy and eager for action. They would have found someone else to murder, someone else to rape. We wouldn't want that on our conscience, would we? Now they're out of commission for a week or two. And because I allowed them to remember me and all my little craggle tricks, they have a newfound sense of the deep strangeness of the world, perhaps an appreciation for the truth that life has meaning. Given time, sure, they'll slide back into depravity. But before then, one might die of an overdose, and one might be killed when he picks a fight with another of their kind. Or maybe they'll cross our path again and give me the chance to blow their minds, scare all the courage out of them, destroy their self-confidence so the only crimes they'll dare commit will be speeding in school zones and running red lights. I can't do more. My mission is to protect you, Benjamin, not to save the world. None of us can save the world. The world has to save itself. It knows the way."

Knife in one hand and fork in the other, Spike turned to what remained for his attention, the meatloaf, and began to demolish it.

Benny went to the men's room, and Harper went to the women's, and Spike remained at the table, efficiently metabolizing every molecule he consumed.

When Benny and Harper returned, the dirty dishes had been taken away. Nine of the ten desserts offered by the menu were plated on the table, all at the moment untouched.

Spike felt it necessary to explain why he hadn't ordered ten. "White chocolate sucks. It isn't really chocolate. White chocolate is a fraud."

Benny sampled the pear tart, and Harper sampled the mandarin-orange cheesecake, and they drank coffee while they watched Spike prove that craggles had no fear of diabetes.

"This F. Upton Theron guy," Harper said, "is supposedly worth billions and billions. According to Oliver Lambert, he's a weird old dude, pretty much a recluse. His house is a fortress. Big-time security, way more than Lambert. We aren't going to be able to walk in on him like we did Handy Duroc, and he won't be throwing a party we can invite ourselves to. Are you sure we can get at the creep?"

"Piece of cake," Spike confidently declared as he ate a piece of cake. After he consumed the last morsel, he wiped his mouth with a napkin and leaned back in the booth and sighed. "That was much better than the meal I had at your house, Benjamin. I believe I will leave a four hundred percent tip."

"Shane can buy a new car," Benny said.

"Will my extravagance embarrass you?"

"I'm beyond embarrassment."

"You are a humble man," Spike said.

"I'm an *exhausted* man. I need to conserve my energy for more important things than embarrassment. Like terror."

Shane brought the bill, and Spike said he'd pay cash. As the big guy peeled hundred-dollar bills off a fat bankroll and as the gratuity kept growing, the waiter's studied cool was tested. In the best tradition of the Unimpressible Generation, Shane maintained the deadpan expression of one who had seen everything there was to see a long time ago and who soldiered on, world weary and indifferent to material pleasures. When he picked up the pile of cash, he said only, "Decent of you, sir," as if he had morphed into a British butler with the mastery of understatement required of that position.

When Benny stepped out of the restaurant, anxiety rising, he surveyed the night for the equivalent of the three carjackers who had targeted them at the service station.

Seeing his companion's uneasiness, Spike said, "Please relax, my friend. Over these many centuries, I've served as the protector of twenty-nine others like yourself, men and women who were too nice for their time and culture. Twenty-seven lived long lives full of accomplishment and prosperity."

Harper said, "What about the other two?"

"They were murdered horrifically," Spike said.

Although they were perhaps forty feet from the Explorer, with the potential battleground of a parking lot all around them, Benny halted.

Massaging the back of Benny's neck with one hand, Harper said, "Jeez, Spike, that's a ten percent failure rate."

Clearly hurt by her observation, the craggle said, "That's kind of harsh, don't you think? I haven't lost ten percent of the people assigned to me. It's more like seven percent. Besides, it wasn't anything I did that got them murdered horrifically. Gee whiz, guys. I'm dismayed you'd think it was anything I did."

"What . . . what was it then?" Benny asked.

"They wouldn't listen to me."

"Who wouldn't?"

"The seven percent. They had free will, you know. I wasn't the boss of them. There were things I told them to do, but they wouldn't do them, and they were murdered horrifically."

"Stop saying they were murdered horrifically."

"Well, they were. Don't ask me how. I'd be obliged to tell you. If you knew how, you might never sleep well again."

"Even that's too much information," Benny said. "Why did you have to tell me two died? Why didn't you keep that to yourself?"

"I have to be honest with you, honest at all times. That's an important craggle protocol."

"Some craggle protocols," Harper said, "are maybe a lot like white chocolate." She stopped massaging the back of Benny's neck and patted his shoulder as though to reassure him that he wouldn't die horrifically—or as though she was expressing a sad little bye-bye.

"Honesty is always the best policy," Spike insisted. "You know that's true." He placed both hands over his heart, as if to suggest he was wounded. "Cut me some slack here. Anyhow, it's a long time since I lost the second one."

"How long?"

"Nine hundred years. And the first one was nine hundred years before that, when I was a newbie."

"So," said Benny, after a brief pause for calculation, "one might conclude that you lose someone every nine hundred years. And now it's time again."

"Not at all, Benjamin. It's not a *pattern*."

"It kind of looks like a pattern," Harper said.

"Well, it isn't. Some nice people can be wonderfully nice but not wise. And I can't make them wise. That's all. It's very sad. But that's the way it is. Niceness plus free will minus wisdom equals sudden and horrific death. But that won't happen to you, Benjamin, because you're wise. If I tell you there's something you must do to save your life, I'm sure you'll do it. You know, this relationship isn't all about me. It's a partnership. We're in this together. We share responsibility. You and me against the forces of evil."

To Benny, Harper said, "Now that he's walked us through it, I have to agree with him. You need to trust Spike. He'll do right by you."

"Thank you, Miss Harper."

"You're welcome. Benny, a guardian angel can protect you from all kinds of trouble, but not from yourself."

Although Benny knew she was right, he remained spooked by the revelation of a 7 percent failure rate. "Okay, but what kind of guardian angel beats the shit out of bad guys?"

"I'm not a guardian angel," Spike said. "I never claimed to be a guardian angel."

"He never claimed to be an angel," Harper agreed.

"I'm a craggle."

"He's a craggle, Benny."

"I *know* he's a craggle. I don't know what craggles are, where they come from, what their backstory is, but I know he's a craggle." An involuntary sigh escaped him. "All right, we're in this together. I didn't mean to be a jerk. I'm grateful to be given a ninety-three percent chance of getting my life back on track, and I'll do my part. I'll be as wise as I know how to be."

"We'll play golf sometimes, right?" Spike asked. "Go out to a movie now and then, right? Like we agreed?"

"Yeah, absolutely. Take a walk on the beach. Go bowling. After we get through this crisis."

Spike opened his arms wide. "Give us a hug."

"Ah, man. I'm not really a hugger."

"You're totally a hugger," Harper said. "A hugger is exactly who you are, sweet thing."

After surveying the parking lot and determining that neither thugs nor potential victims like himself were currently going to and fro, Benny said, "So, Spike, if I don't give you a hug, if I'm just not in a hugging mood at the moment, I'll still have a ninety-three percent chance of surviving, right?"

"A hundred percent," Spike assured him. "But I'll be sad." His smile faltered. "Very sad."

Harper stepped forward and hugged Spike. "I don't want you to be sad. Benny, there's no reason for any of us to be sad. This has been a great evening, and it's only going to get better."

After they completed a group hug and stepped apart, Spike said, "I'm so invigorated. Let's go put Mr. F. Upton Theron through the wringer and see what we can squeeze out of him."

ON THE WAY TO SEE F. UPTON THERON, BENNY REMEMBERS A BRIARBUSH MOMENT

As the boys hiked back to Felthammer House through the high forest, clouds crept out of the northwest, robbing the sky of stars and stealing the light of the moon.

Because Mengistu Gidada didn't want to be alone in his room during the rest of that night, he followed Jurgen and Benny through the window by which they had departed hours earlier. Jurgen locked the pane and drew down the shade. Benny turned the lamplight low. According to the bedside clocks, it was 2:05 a.m. Having raced into the night in a spirit of high adventure, they now collapsed into their chairs in a spiritless concession to the truth of their dire circumstances.

Prescott Galsbury was stone-cold dead. The surviving ISA agents had departed the school grounds with the decapitated corpse of their comrade. Mrs. Baneberry-Smith had taken sanctuary in her laboratory or in the headmaster's house, an insane entomologist stuffed full of dark knowledge from the far end of the galaxy, determined to reshape civilization and install herself as the ultimate power in the nation, perhaps in all the world, while at the same time indulging in pointless cruelties like cross-species engineering just because she could.

"Briarbush might have been only a casually evil boarding school at one time," Mengistu said. "However, it is now also an institution of unprecedented horror and a fascist project to transform the sons of prominent families into . . . into . . ."

When Mengistu seemed unable to speak the unspeakable, Jurgen said, "Sock puppets. I've known this place changes boys in some way. When they come here, most are conceited, but some are meek, in both cases because of how their parents screwed them up. The conceited become more certain of their superiority but also less obnoxious in the way they express their pride, more politic. The meek become very sure of themselves. Those who were colorful become less colorful. Those who were colorless become just a little colorful. The loud speak more softly. The soft-spoken speak with more force. Week by week, with the exception of Mengistu and me, every boy here becomes more like every other boy at Briarbush. Sometimes I get the feeling none of them have souls anymore. And now we know they've been robbed of their free will. A human hive."

"Jurgen and I do not wish to be changed. We certainly do not want to be made into sock puppets."

"When we're with the other guys," Jurgen said, "we try to act like them, so they won't suspect we're different."

Mengistu raised a fist above his head, a gesture of resistance. "If Jurgen or I should see the other changing for real, we will make a break for it. We have a plan."

"What plan?" Benny asked.

"Details of the plan will be revealed on a need-to-know basis. At this time, you have no need to know, Benjamin. But if Jurgen and I see you changing, we will break out and take you with us."

Benny said, "Whatever's being done to the others—why isn't it working on you guys?"

Jurgen shrugged. "We don't have a clue."

"We live each day," Mengistu said, "fearing that a change will start in us simultaneously and, being in the same condition, neither of us will notice the change in the other. Life at Briarbush Academy is not conducive to sound sleep, good digestion, or the avoidance of frequent constipation."

"My father," Jurgen said, "being who he is, could press the attorney general to investigate Briarbush on any number of grounds. But if I raised the subject, I'd only be announcing to the staff here that whatever's changing the others isn't changing me."

Benny assumed his stepfather was the villain in this matter. Although his mother had never been all that mothering, he refused to believe that she would have knowingly sent him away to have his soul removed. "Why would our parents want this to be done to us?"

In the dialed-down light of his reading lamp, Jurgen's pale face seemed to pale further. "When Mengistu and I figured that out, we made a pact never to talk about it again."

"Speaking of it," Mengistu said, "only causes pain, and pain leads to sadness, and sadness leads to depression, until depression cannot be sustained, whereupon it becomes anger, whereafter anger escalates into rage, and one begins to consider murdering one's parents, which is neither moral nor rational, or for that matter easily accomplished without serious risk of incarceration. In time, you will no doubt arrive at the same answer that we did, Benjamin, and it will soon enough become a scar on your heart."

A bleak and somber silence settled on the room. If they had been weary enough to fall asleep in their chairs, the silence would have been brief and tolerable. After the shocking events of the night, however, sleep might elude them all the way till dawn. For something to do that might result in a resumption of conversation and an end to the silence, Benny searched his jacket pockets and retrieved the four candy bars he'd purchased to ensure his survival in a confrontation with Bugboy. He offered the candy to his friends. Mengistu took the Almond Joy, and Jurgen took the Reese's cup.

Peeling open the Hershey's bar, Benny said, "There's still the Clark Bar."

"Yes," said Jurgen.

"Inevitably," said Mengistu.

With the subject of treacherous parents now behind them for the time being, they fell into conversation again until, at some point between three o'clock and three thirty, they did indeed fall asleep in their chairs.

In the morning, at breakfast, a rumor circulated among the students in the dining rooms of both dormitories that later was confirmed by a formal announcement. During the night, Dr. Lionel Baneberry-Smith, the headmaster, had apparently gone sleepwalking and had fallen down the stairs, breaking his neck. The school flag was lowered to half-mast, and classes were canceled for the day.

THREE

F. UPTON THERON

Word had come to F. Upton Theron that something curious might have happened at the home of Handy Duroc. And of course he had heard about Oliver Lambert capering in the nude with a stick of fried zucchini in front of two hundred guests, a performance the attorney could not explain even to his own satisfaction, but which seemed to have nothing to do with either inebriation or sudden dementia. Upton and thousands of others who shared his beliefs were waging a secret war against those retrograde individuals who were—or were likely to become—a serious negative influence on society. In all modesty, Upton and crusaders like him called themselves "the Better Kind." From time to time, developments suggested some reactionary organization unknown to the Better Kind was resisting their efforts. If an outfit was operating on behalf of Benjamin Catspaw, an especially sinister and dangerous young man, they seemed to be working up the chain of command, in which case their next stop would be Upton's doorstep.

It was in his interest to learn all that he could about the clandestine defenders who sometimes schemed with success to undo the damage done to men and women like Catspaw. In previous situations, even highly professional security forces had failed to insulate the Better Kind against these mysterious agents; neither had schemes to find and slaughter said agents been successful; incredibly, they were able to purge their images from security-camera video. Some of the Better Kind had been exposed to outrageous ridicule akin to what Oliver Lambert suffered. However, none had been physically harmed, a fact that gave Upton the courage to prepare this drawing room for an eventual visit from these enigmatic enemies.

For thirty years, since he turned sixty, Upton had kept two full-time physicians on payroll, not only to provide immediate emergency care if needed, but also to ensure that he was able to obtain a prescription for any medication he wanted, for whatever purpose he might wish to use it. One of the current pair of doctors, Alistair Pinch, who received more than one million dollars a year, visited Upton half an hour earlier to install a catheter in a vein in the crook of his left arm, without presuming to inquire why. Dr. Pinch also refrained from asking about Arabella, who often sprawled in Upton's lap during long evenings of mutual affection. She was currently safe in the primary bedroom, where she would remain until this nasty business was done. Following the physician's departure, Upton fully loaded a pair of hypodermic syringes, the contents of which he could inject into the catheter in less than a minute.

He was ready for a confrontation.

He sat in a Biedermeier armchair in the sixty-by-forty-foot drawing room that offered a stunning view of the Pacific during the day. Currently, ten Tiffany lamps provided a magical ambiance that encouraged in him a nostalgic mood. He found himself thinking back over a life well lived.

When F. Upton Theron was just in his twenties, yammering fools in the media would already on occasion say that he had more money than God. Whenever this came to his attention, he held Arabella in his lap and said, "My darling girl, I have no knowledge of the Lord, but considering that He never steps forward to refute the claim that my fortune is much greater than His, I must assume that He is indeed poorer than I. And because money is power, who then is the greater power, my sweet?" Arabella always declared that her dear Uppie was the greater power; she never called him Upton. He would then say, "Let God keep to Heaven, and I will see that Earth is run as it ought to be." He never failed to be amused by this little dialogue. Because Arabella enjoyed it quite as much as Uppie did, they always followed this with a marvelous cuddle. During this wanton snuggling, he often buried his face in her belly and stroked her ears, and no matter how long their mutual adoration lasted, Arabella never once vacated her bowels in his lap.

When truly loved and adequately schooled, a sixteen-pound white rabbit, of the breed called "Flemish giant," could be potty trained. The great house, in which Upton was born, had been renovated after he inherited it when he was twenty-seven, so that a room on each of the three levels served as a toilet for Arabella. The doors were always left open, and the floors paved in sealed limestone with a central drain. A trusted member of the fourteen-person household staff checked each *toilette de la lapin* eight times a day to collect the pellets and wash the urine into the drain.

Even with loving care, a Flemish giant lived only a few years. Upton contracted with a breeder to produce an uninterrupted series of white Flemish giants and hold them off the market. A new Arabella must always be on the brink of adulthood and fully toilet trained, to be placed in Upton's arms the very day that the current Arabella passed away. Rabbits could be stoic in decline. Often Upton didn't know he'd lost a beloved Arabella until, at the end of a frantic search, he found the cooling body. Such shocking discoveries were distressing. When he knew his sweet Arabella was ill, after the veterinarian confirmed that nothing more could be done to extend her life, Upton spared her from dying alone, euthanizing her as tenderly as he knew how. He and he alone dug her grave and placed her body in it. Every Arabella was buried in the same corner of the estate, near the first Arabella Rabbit. The first Arabella had come to him with the silly name Powderpuff, and he'd changed it.

When Upton's father built the estate, he had called it Casa Something Something, a romantic and foolish name for such a grand house. Upton resorted to the Italian language when he renamed it Palazzo del Coniglio, Palace of the Rabbit. Over the decades he lived in happiness with many Arabellas. A stone wall encompassed five acres with a spectacular view of the San Clemente coastline.

The vaguely Tuscan house provided over sixty thousand square feet of living space, a space that was more than comfortable for a confirmed bachelor like Upton, even though he seldom left the property. Those people he wished to see were invited to Palazzo del Coniglio or induced to come there by application of the carrot-and-stick tactic, or reduced to swift obedience by a credible threat to destroy everything they held dear. Upton had no interest in travel for business or pleasure; rather than see the world, he wanted to own a large portion of it.

His father, H. Ellsworth Theron, had left him a considerable fortune, and he had industriously multiplied it year after year. In pursuit of his goals, Upton was ruthless, deceitful, utterly without conscience. He experienced no doubt or regret, no shame, because he knew his ultimate intention was noble—to amass enough power and influence to reset the world from what it was to what it ought to be, and make people do what was best for them, whether they wanted to do it or not. Some people called him evil, but their judgment meant nothing to Upton because he had healthy self-esteem, and he was smarter than they were, therefore better able to see the truth of things. His goodness was uncontestable, as proved by the time, money, and unconditional love that he devoted to bunnies.

Upton was self-aware enough to understand that he was in part motivated to be a good man because his father was such a bad one. Ellsworth built Casa Blah Blah largely to placate his wife, Upton's mother, Pelagia. She could reign as a doyenne of high society, her grand estate a draw for celebrities and artists and politicians who came for long weekends of partying with like-minded people who shared the most enlightened views. In return, she never complained that Ellsworth spent much of his time away from home with one or another of his mistresses.

Although he had hardly known his father, Upton knew his mother too well and despised her more than he did Ellsworth. Because Upton strongly resembled his father, Pelagia could not bring herself to grant him even a fraction of the affection that she lavished on his younger sister, who didn't resemble Ellsworth but looked remarkably like a movie star who visited Casa Silly Name often for a week at a time. Sister got everything she wanted, and Upton got what Mother decided he deserved.

Sister was seven when she received the rabbit she desired and named it Powderpuff, while her ten-year-old brother continued to be denied the dog for which he had been pleading for years. One night while everyone slept, Sister ventured from her room and evidently fell, hitting her head on the pool coping and plunging unconscious into the water, where she was found drowned in the morning. Grieving for his sibling, Upton honored her memory by assuming responsibility for Powderpuff. He renamed the white rabbit Arabella, after the lost girl.

When Upton was fifteen and had just received his third rabbit, Ellsworth divorced Pelagia, keeping both Casa Doobee Doobee

Doo and custody of their son, while settling on her thirty million dollars per the terms of a prenuptial agreement. Thereafter, Upton never saw his mother again, though every year on his birthday, until she died, she sent him a different photograph of his sister.

Although Upton occasionally saw his father after the divorce, he was raised by Mr. and Mrs. Gumfrey, who served in loco parentis. Norbert Gumfrey was the estate manager slash butler, and Zenobia Gumfrey was the cook. They were not by nature kindly people, but they knew a good thing when they fell into it. They made sure that young Upton had everything he wanted, which was more than he needed, and he in turn never reported what he knew about the many games they played with the expenses of the estate and the sums they embezzled.

Twelve years after the divorce, Ellsworth died, and Upton came into his inheritance. The Gumfreys, with the survival instincts of two rabbits in a world of wolves, suspected they might be fired and replaced with honest employees. Zenobia issued a warning cloaked as an innocuous comment: "Ah, dear boy, look at you now, the handsome master of Palazzo del Coniglio. How fast time passes. It doesn't seem possible your parents entrusted you to Norbert and me twelve years ago or that it's been seventeen years since your beloved sister was drowned." Even if the left corner of Zenobia's mouth hadn't curved into the vaguest suggestion of a sneer, Upton would have understood the threat inherent in the locution "was drowned" when a mere "drowned" would have been the correct way to express an accidental death.

He responded to that subtle extortion by giving the Gumfreys an immediate 20 percent raise and generously expanding their paid-vacation benefit from two weeks to four. Later that year, while they were on holiday in Las Vegas, staying in a presidential suite with a twelve-foot-square spa, they died in a freakish electrocution when the pump motor malfunctioned and a failure of the spa insulation allowed electric current to be introduced into the water.

Through an intermediary, photographs of the deceased were quietly provided by the hotel engineer, Ivan Krucknick, who was responsible for keeping the extensive mechanical systems functioning without surcease. The pictures were satisfying because the Gumfreys had paid a proper price for treachery, for not being the better kind of people, chiseling such minor sums in an inelegant ill-conceived fashion, revealing themselves to be little more than grubby street criminals in livery.

Because Upton had been interviewing new couples who could serve as estate manager and cook, he was able to replace the Gumfreys the day after the timely incident in Vegas. Management of the eighteen-member staff, including those in the house and the groundskeepers, proceeded without a hitch.

Thereafter, for the next sixty-three years, F. Upton Theron's life had gone smoothly, a busy and fulfilling affair defined by the unconditional love of large white rabbits, the accumulation of ever greater wealth, and the vigorous cancellation of the careers of the retrograde individuals who possessed the qualities and potential to rise into positions from which they could challenge, in one way or another, the steady progress toward utopia that was being crafted by their betters. At ninety, he felt fortunate to have led a life of purpose and meaning.

The hypodermic syringes lay on the table beside his armchair, under the colorful canopy of a Tiffany lamp. His shirtsleeve was rolled up to expose the catheter that Dr. Pinch had installed in his left arm.

Also on the table was a small remote-control device rather like a garage-door opener. It offered two buttons, one red and one green.

Upton owned numerous companies, including the relatively small Ob & Ob—short for Obstruct and Obliterate—that installed security systems with defensive *and* offensive capabilities, as well as panic rooms that could survive even a tactical nuke if one detonated no closer than sixty-four yards. They worked mostly on properties owned by members of the Better Kind, though there were some vicious dictators whom it made sense to oblige. Ob & Ob had done great work on this drawing room.

To their consternation, the regular security guards had been sent home with the assurance that Upton would be safe this one night without them, though he gave no explanation. He believed they were genuinely concerned for him because they knew he was a great man.

As he waited for a showdown, he held a bottle of root beer, sipping the treat through a straw. He enjoyed root beer floats with French vanilla ice cream more than the unenhanced beverage; however, on this occasion, the larger glass and the long spoon required by a float would be more difficult to set aside than a simple bottle. He needed to remain quick and dexterous to meet a sudden threat. All these years later, he remembered how much Sister enjoyed root beer floats, but of course she couldn't have them anymore. He intended to prepare a float later, when his visitors, whoever they might prove to be, were all reliably dead.

A tone sounded throughout the house, revealing that a vehicle had turned off the street and entered the driveway.

He must assume that those who evidently represented Benjamin Catspaw and who earlier humiliated Oliver Lambert, Esquire, had dared to venture into his web.

After taking one more deep draw of the soda, he set the bottle aside and picked up one of the hypodermic syringes. He pressed the plunger just enough to squirt a brief stream of the contents out of the cannula, ensuring that he would not inject an embolism into his bloodstream. He married the needle to the catheter and administered the full dose. He repeated this procedure with the second syringe, providing himself with a total of sixty cubic centimeters of antitoxin. He put the empty syringes under his chair, rolled down his sleeve, and placed the special remote control on the seat of his chair, against his thigh, where it was unlikely to be noticed.

DO NO HARM

So after they enjoyed a group hug outside of the Newport Beach restaurant, they got in the Explorer. Spike drove out of the parking lot and turned left, and they were instantly twentysome miles south of Newport, exiting Interstate 5 at San Clemente.

The origami time-fold trick was no less startling than it had been before. Benny found himself gripping the edges of his car seat as if the fundamental structure of the universe was unstable, as if the vehicle might spontaneously disassemble and gravity might fail, whereupon he in his seat might soar out of Earth's atmosphere. A good dinner and a hug hadn't to any extent relieved his stress.

A two-lane cobblestone driveway served the walled estate of F. Upton Theron. A guardhouse stood to the left. The massive ornamented gate was meant to leave lesser mortals abashed at the splendor of the wealth it represented. An entire clan of bronze workers must have been contused, sprained, abraded, and badly herniated during its construction. At the moment, the halves of this barrier stood open.

In the lane farther from the guardhouse, someone had left a black Mercedes sedan. The engine was running, and the parking lights glowed, but no one occupied the outbound car. The vanity license plate declared PINCHME.

As they approached, a man in his forties stepped out of the guardhouse. In a superbly tailored dark suit and white shirt and necktie, with his short hair styled without ostentation, beardless, with no visible tattoos or face jewelry, shoulders back, posture perfect, he might have been Benny's older brother from another mother or a time traveler just arrived from the 1950s. He blocked the inbound lane and waved them to a stop.

"His suit," Spike said, "is cut to conceal a pistol carried in a shoulder holster, yet he clearly isn't a guard. This should not be a conversation conducted through an open window."

"Is this a bogadril moment?" Benny asked.

"Pray it's not," Spike said and disembarked from the Explorer.

Instead of doing the rational thing and skedaddling, Benny and Harper exited the vehicle as well, because that's the kind of night it was.

The idling Mercedes was an EV, exceedingly quiet as long as its toxic and unstable batteries failed to burst into flame. The night was also hushed, the faintest of breezes whispering through the cascading fronds of the phoenix palms, as if carrying secrets from one tree to another.

No less self-possessed than Clark Kent, Superman's alter ego, the stranger exhibited neither surprise nor concern about Spike's size. "May I ask who you're here to see?"

"Mr. Theron is expecting us," Spike said.

"He invited us," Harper said.

With astonishment, not being practiced in deceit, Benny heard himself reaching deep into his storied past to craft a lie. "Upton generously funded the vital research of my mother, Dr. Catherine Baneberry-Smith, the Nobel laureate. You undoubtedly know of her, might even have seen her on one of her many PBS appearances. We've come here tonight to share with Upton the exciting news that Mother has made a breakthrough of historic nature."

By the time Benny finished, Spike and Harper were staring at him as if he had rattled all that off in flawless Chinese.

The stranger appeared to receive this preposterous announcement without suspicion. "I'm Dr. Alistair Pinch, Mr. Theron's personal physician. Indeed, he's my only patient. I'm a bit concerned about his behavior this evening. I came here to . . . to attend to a request of his. Mr. Theron often has unusual requests, but there's never any negative repercussions. In spite of his age, he is sharp minded and determined to live at least to a hundred. The thing is, the usual guards were on duty when I arrived, but they were going home at Mr. Theron's direction by the time I was leaving. He further instructed them not to close the gate, though he is always security conscious. I've been here for twenty minutes, trying to decide whether I should return to the house and check on him. But he resents being what he calls 'mothered,' and he can be . . . caustic."

Enchanted by his newfound ability to lie convincingly, Benny said, "I can put your mind at rest, Dr. Pinch. Upton is aware that we are bringing him news of such importance that it will change the world, bring an end to disease, and lead humanity to lasting peace and plenty. The guards know us from past visits, know my mother from her amusing appearances on *Saturday Night Live* and her TV commercial for milk. They are aware that Upton is her greatest supporter. So he was concerned that they might infer from our late-evening visit that Mother has either wrought another scientific miracle that will earn her a second Nobel Prize or has, at the very least, been signed to her own reality TV program. The guards here are good people, very loyal employees. But as you can well imagine, there is serious money to be made by tipping off various media to major developments in the lives of people who are as famous as Mother and as wealthy as Upton. Given the momentous nature of what we have come here to tell

Upton, I shouldn't have revealed even what little I have to you. We are relying on your discretion."

"Yes, all right," Pinch said, "but there's also the issue of Arabella, which I find troubling."

For whatever reason, the physician addressed that statement to Harper, as if she impressed him as being the one most likely to have an understanding of the singular importance of Arabella.

Harper smiled and nodded. "Yes. Arabella."

"Although she has an independent spirit and business of her own to attend to now and then," Dr. Pinch said, "Arabella is always with Upton in the evening. They are inseparable. She's either in his lap while he strokes her while she quivers all over, or she's draped around his neck like a contortionist, seemingly boneless, or on the floor in front of his chair as he wiggles his bare toes all over her. But not tonight."

Still nodding but now frowning with concern, Harper said, "Really? Not tonight?"

"I asked him where she was," the physician continued, "and he said she was safely in the bedroom, watching TV, and changed the subject. 'Safely.' I wondered about that word. He always wants her with him. Do you think the word *'safely'* could be a euphemism?"

Harper said, "You know, I'm largely uneducated." She pointed to Benny. "My brother, Elmer, he'd know about euphemisms."

Before Benny could launch again, Pinch said, "The thing is, he's given his heart to so many Arabellas over the decades, death after death after death, all buried on the estate as a constant reminder of loss. Maybe there comes one loss too many, and he decides he can endure no more. Could the word *'safely'* imply that Arabella is dead, safe from pain and suffering, and he's placed her in his bedroom, where he intends to lie down beside her, inject himself through the catheter in his left arm—some drug he got that I never would have prescribed—and just fade away?"

"That doesn't sound like the Upton I know," Benny said. "The Upton I know is—"

The doctor tramped on whatever fabulousness Benny might have conjured. "I must say, when I first became his physician, I didn't find rabbits particularly appealing. But those Flemish giants are quite endearing and very beautiful."

"Ah, *rabbits!*" said Harper, Benny, and Spike in sudden mutual understanding.

"Gradually," Pinch continued, "I came to see why Upton would prefer them to dogs or cats. When the first Arabella under my watch died, I'm not embarrassed to say I was more moved than I expected to be."

"Dr. Pinch," Spike said, taking control of the situation as was his nature and his mission, "I spoke to Upton not ten minutes ago, to advise him we were soon to arrive, and he said that Arabella will be there. He knows how much my sister, Elvira"—here he indicated Harper—"adores that rabbit."

"Arabella," said Harper, "couldn't be more magical if she had been pulled from a top hat."

The physician looked from Harper to Spike to Benny. "You're all the children of Dr. Bradbury-Smith?"

"Baneberry," Benny corrected. "She's our mother, but we're all adopted. Mother suffered a terrible laboratory accident back in the day, when she was earning her master's degree, and she's unable to have children of her own. If you'd ever met her, you'd know how sad that is, because she loves children even more than doing science and winning Nobels. Children are immediately charmed when they meet her, as though she's Mary Poppins."

"She sings as well as Julie Andrews did in the movie," said Harper, apparently taking advantage of the opportunity to hone the skills of deceit that she would require to be an effective private investigator. "She could have had a career in music, but with the world-class scientific research and raising us as a single mom and writing her series of children's books, wherever would she have found the time? God, I love her so much."

Alistair Pinch was beginning to look bewildered, though not suspicious. "The thing is, I take the Hippocratic oath seriously, not in a dogmatic sense, but pretty darn seriously. 'First do no harm.' Being Upton's personal physician, on call at all times, can be challenging, considering the things he wants, but I'm grateful for the opportunity. 'First do no harm.' I want to be sure that I never do him any harm."

As he had done in the kitchen at Handy Duroc's house when he'd sidelined Jill Swift, Spike thrust one arm toward the doctor in a talk-to-the-hand gesture and spoke words in some ancient language. Pulses of amber light issued from his palm, washed over Pinch's face, and whirlpooled into his eyes.

"Was that necessary?" Harper wondered. "I think he was about to drive off and leave us to it."

Spike raised one eyebrow in an expression that was by now as familiar as its message was unmistakable. "The two of you made our fictional mother so interesting that Dr. Pinch would have googled her at his first opportunity and discovered she didn't exist. Police would have been swarming through this place in minutes."

Keenly annoyed by her failure, Harper drove her right fist into the open palm of her left hand. "Yes, you're right. Bob always says the best lie is a simple one. I just got carried away listening to Benny, his power of invention."

"Bob would be Fat Bob Jericho?" Spike asked as he opened the back door of Alistair Pinch's Mercedes.

"Robert Jericho, yes. Bob. Bob Jericho."

Even in these circumstances, Benny could not help but notice that Harper managed to look deeply chagrinned without appearing any less cute than before. Already, hardly more than thirty-six hours since Jill Swift had dumped him, Benny could not get a clear picture of his former fiancée in his mind's eye, or understand what about her had enchanted him. He wondered what his fascination with Jill said about his character, if it said anything other than that he had been gullible and had taken far too long to add the words *and wise* to the word *nice* in his résumé.

Spike returned to the sidelined—and stiff—physician, picked him up as if he were a papier-mâché figure, carried him to the Mercedes, and slid him onto the back seat. Closing the door, he said, "I'll wake him when we leave."

When they were all in the Explorer once more, Harper said, "'Baneberry-Smith.' How did you come up with such a name?"

Benny could have said: *I needed a name that sounded kind of like a scientist. Mrs. Baneberry-Smith was a real person, the only scientist I've ever known, mad or otherwise. She's been dead for some years, accidently blew herself up along with several boarding-school boys, which probably saved the world from being enslaved by the weird science of an evil extraterrestrial race.* However, if he had said as much, they would have demanded an explanation that would have kept him talking until dawn. Because they needed to get to F. Upton Theron in a timely manner, Benny said only, "There was this girl I knew once, when I was thirteen."

"So you had a thing for her?"

"No, I didn't have a thing for her."

Perhaps practicing her interrogation skills, Harper said, "You had a thing for her, all right, if after all this time her name popped into your mind just like that."

Benny said, "*She* was the one who had a thing, not a thing for me, just a thing. You wouldn't have wanted to see it." He decided to shut up.

As they cruised toward the immense house, Spike said, "Although he didn't realize it, Dr. Pinch told us everything we need to know to avoid Theron's trap and keep you two alive."

Puzzled, Benny said, "What trap?"

Leaning forward in the back seat, Harper said, "The catheter-in-the-left-arm-Arabella-safe-in-the-master-bedroom trap."

"Oh, that trap," Benny said knowingly, because he didn't want Harper to think he had one oar too few to row his boat and could only go endlessly in a circle.

Glancing at the rearview mirror, Spike said, "You know what you need to do?"

Harper said, "You two find Theron. I find the bunny rabbit as quick as I can and bring it to you."

"You've got what it takes, little lady."

"Right back at you," she said.

An unworthy ember of jealousy abruptly glowed bright in Benny. He almost said, *Yeah, he has what it takes except for genitals,* but he didn't say it because that would have been unkind and crude.

Spike parked in front of the mansion. They got out of the Ford and gathered at the foot of the limestone steps that led to a broad receiving terrace.

The many windows of the great house featured panes with beveled edges and in some cases exquisite, leaded designs that glowed along every polished facet like assemblages of jewels. Every room sent a warm resplendence into the night, which should have been a charming, inviting spectacle, but was not. In this age when powerful forces were determined to destroy the energy industry and impoverish their enemies, consolidating economic and political power in an oligarchy, this extravagance of light was the equivalent of presenting a stiff middle finger to the masses.

The front door stood open wide, but the effect of this gesture seemed more like a threat than a welcome. Inset above the entrance, a limestone panel artfully bore a carved image of a rabbit, and even this playful detail loomed ominous.

Spike said, “Remember what I told you, Benny.”

“What did you tell me?”

Harper said, “About why ten percent of the people assigned to him have been murdered horrifically.”

“Seven percent,” Spike corrected. “And do you remember why, Benjamin?”

“Because they wouldn’t listen to you.”

“Niceness plus free will minus what equals what?”

“Minus wisdom equals death.”

“Equals horrific death. Okay then, let’s pay a visit to F. Upton Theron.”

AS HE ENTERS PALAZZO DEL CONIGLIO, BENNY REMEMBERS THE BRIARBUSH REGIME CHANGE

Years before he had fallen down the stairs and broken his neck, Headmaster Lionel Baneberry-Smith had overseen the conversion of the school chapel into a theater in which movies were shown on weekends. Therefore, his memorial service was conducted in the gymnasium. His casket rested on trestles and straddled the division line between Felthammer Court and Kentwhistle Court. Students were required to attend, but because the headmaster had been a rather remote figure, those who planned the affair saw no need to place boxes of Kleenex at strategic points in the bleachers.

The service began with a recording of John Lennon singing his touching anthem “Imagine.” This was followed by a stirring tribute to the deceased from the chief groundskeeper, Finn Finbar, who too insistently claimed that the departed was one of the greatest men of his generation and who expressed his undying gratitude that the late headmaster had drastically reduced the number of times per year that seasonal flowers were changed out, thus lifting a serious burden from the landscape crew. At this point, the sound system delivered Elton John singing “Don't Let the Sun Go Down on Me,” which led to an appearance by the widow, Catherine Baneberry-Smith. She walked to the casket, a dramatic figure in a floor-length long-sleeved white dress. She took the microphone from its stand, as if she might sing, but she did not sing. She said that she wore white as a statement of defiance in the face of death, that it was her belief that science would one day defeat death, and that it was Lionel's rotten luck to fall down the stairs and break his neck before an immortality serum could be developed. She completed her remarks by informing students and faculty that the board of Briarbush Academy had appointed her to her late husband's position, as the first head*mistress* in the long history of the institution. As she returned the mic to its stand and walked off the court, the house lights dimmed. Darkness gathered in the gymnasium, and a spotlight focused on the casket. Mourners were asked to rise and stand throughout the playing of a third song, "Don't Come Around Here No More" by Tom Petty and the Heartbreakers.

In the morning, Lionel Baneberry-Smith would be trucked away to a town in Kansas, there to be buried near Lester and Bertha Smith, who were said to be his parents, though for some reason they lacked the first half of his surname.

Meanwhile, subsequent to the service, dinner in the dining hall featured five courses and seven dishes that were Lionel Baneberry-Smith's most favorites, which he would never be able to enjoy again. Faculty, although not students, were served a series of fine wines that, in their grief, they imbibed to excess.

Later, Mengistu Gidada joined Jurgen and Benny in their dorm room to discuss the events of the evening. They had eaten little in the dining hall, because the ceremonies left them with the fear that life at Briarbush was about to become even stranger than it had been heretofore and with the suspicion that the memorial dinner, more than any other, was likely to be heavily spiked with saltpeter or something worse. They feasted on what they had purchased in the commissary: potato chips, corn chips, Ritz cracker sandwiches with peanut butter, Planters peanuts, and Cheese Doodles.

They also did a bad thing.

Recent events suggested they were living in their own personal End Times, that Mrs. Baneberry-Smith would resort to her trove of unearthly knowledge to create horror after horror. They were not permitted to have phones, and even if they possessed phones, their parents were unlikely to accept their calls. Even if their parents might take their calls, none of the truths they had to tell about Briarbush or its headmistress would be believed. They had been sent here by parents who thought of their offspring not as sons but as raw material to be forged into useful tools in the great game of wealth and power. Such people, craving power more than all else, believed only what they wanted to believe, and truth didn't matter to them. They would never be a light in any darkness.

That was the realization Mengistu and Jurgen had come to some time ago, which they had not wanted to talk about on the night that Bugboy was killed, the realization they had told Benny would be a scar on his heart when he arrived at it on his own.

So they had done a bad thing, which they had never done before and would not do again. After the memorial service, they purchased a pint of vodka from Vigor Maitre, the landscaper who dealt in smutty magazines. Now, intending to drown their fear and find their way to greater hope, they washed down all the junk food with spiked Coca-Cola.

They didn't get profoundly drunk, only tipsy, and they didn't puke, but they also didn't drown their fear. That night and in the days ahead, their fear was always simmering and sometimes boiling. Neither did the vodka lift them to a higher rung of hope. However, they remained as hopeful as ever because any boy who is bonded in the best way with at least one other boy has an ally against the world.

(Spike wishes it to be known that, had he been present, this behavior wouldn't have been tolerated. Even the horrors conjured by Mrs. Baneberry-Smith do not justify the reckless consumption of intoxicants by young men whose brains, not yet fully developed, could be forever stunted by inebriation. To dissuade the boys, he would have opened his abdomen, extracted his stomach—an organ with its own teeth—and set it loose to chase them around the room until they collapsed, exhausted by terror.)

As the weeks passed and mountain summer drew toward an end, Dr. Catherine Baneberry-Smith was out and about more than she had been as the headmaster's wife. She purged from her wardrobe the white she'd worn at the memorial service, dressing in black at all times. These weren't the garments of a widow respecting her lost spouse, but the decidedly erotic costumes of the kind she wore on the night of the bug hunt—snug jeans, tight sweaters with V-necks. Firm breasts without need of support provided deep cleavage and lessons in fluid dynamics that, in a boy's boarding school, should have been inappropriate in the extreme, that should have been the number one topic among the horny inmates, and yet neither the faculty nor the students dared to comment on the headmistress's unorthodox attire, as if they sensed that doing so would bring upon them the wrath of gods unnamed and unknowable.

It was Mengistu who perhaps put his finger on it when he said, "It is not gods they fear, but the woman herself. On a deep level, they all know that something about her is profoundly wrong, in some way not fully human. Intuition tells them she is a mortal danger to us all. Her provocative dress does not excite them because, in spite of all her physical attributes, she seems somehow not to be one of our species. They are cowed by her because every one of them is here alone, with no true friend in this place, with no bonds like those we have forged among us. That capacity has been somehow educated or brainwashed out of them, and each alone dares not speak about what others are not speaking, for fear of condemnation or something unknown but worse than condemnation."

Soon the headmistress strode the campus in black leather boots that came almost to her knees. More and more often, she sheathed herself in leather pants as tightly fitted as anything a flamenco dancer might wear, a black silk blouse with the top two or three buttons undone, and a leather jacket with lines of silvery studs decorating the collar and lapels. She painted her fingernails black and began to wear black lipstick. If it seemed she was *soliciting* criticism or censure in order to establish herself as yet another victim of discrimination based on gender or sexual identity and thus have grounds to sue for compensation, the three friends agreed that was not the case. Something less tedious and far stranger than profit seeking compelled her on this course.

That speculation was confirmed when the first of the zombies appeared around her. They weren't the flesh-eating kind of zombies, not the rotting and unclean walking dead. They were four seniors from Kentwhistle House, well scrubbed and properly dressed in their gray slacks and blue blazers and white shirts, but not in class where they ought to be. MacAskill, Ferragamo, Ellison, Calacalis. They didn't shamble, but matched Catherine Baneberry-Smith's brisk pace, shoulders back and apparently committed to a serious, urgent mission. They murmured to one another and to their headmistress, but as far as could be seen, she never spoke to them, as if she might be able to direct them to her purpose without the need to speak.

On the ninth of September, standing at a second-floor window of the school library, the three friends watched as a squad of zombies accompanied the striding headmistress from the faculty residence to her laboratory. These four were from Felthammer House. Ramirez, Blankenship, Cho, Heggenhougen.

"Not zombies," Mengistu whispered. "They serve her somehow, not in any way that Vigor Maitre might find exciting, but as if they are programmed, following some genetic imperative, without either fear or sexual attraction, as if she is the queen of the hive and they are sexless worker bees."

On the evening of that day, Mengistu and Jurgen and Benny made a shocking and dismaying discovery during dinner in the dining hall. Santiago Ramirez and Andrew Heggenhougen were among the five other boys assigned to their table every night. Santiago's eyes had always been a warm brown. Now they were lead gray. Previously as blue as Nordic skies, Andrew's eyes were the soft gray of tarnished silver. Otherwise, these worker bees seemed unchanged, their personalities intact, Santiago boisterous to an annoying extent, Andrew quick with a sarcastic and cutting quip, Santiago eager to talk about soccer as well as the legs and butts and breasts of women in the entertainment world, Andrew more inclined to talk about politics and himself, both of them insufferable.

The other three boys at the table—Knacker, Hisscus, and Nork—appeared oblivious of the ocular transformations that Santiago and Andrew had undergone. Jurgen fished for a reaction by complaining that his eyes were itching because of autumn pollens and asking if anyone else was having the same problem. Benny repeatedly inserted comments about the beautiful eyes of the entertainers whose legs, butts, and breasts so obsessed Ramirez, until Nork asked him if he intended to become an ophthalmologist.

Although Mengistu was the most verbally gifted of the friends, he seemed to realize that subtlety—even blunt statements—wouldn't evoke thoughtful consideration and intelligent responses from the other five dinner companions. Leaning over the table, head craned forward, with the intent expression of a cop interrogating a murder suspect, he chose silence as he repeatedly engaged the gray-eyed duo in staring matches that they broke off after five or ten seconds. Benny never saw them regard Mengistu with the contempt of the half-alien children in that old movie *The Village of the Damned*; rather, they appeared puzzled by his behavior and seemed to chalk it up to an increase in his geekiness. This convinced Benny that even with the evidence that mirrors provided, *they didn't recognize what had happened to their own eyes*. They didn't know that they were being transformed into . . . Into what?

When the dinner hour ended with a dismissal tone broadcast over the sound system, Jurgen wove quickly through the crowd to look at Felix Blankenship, one of the other worker bees who had scurried around with the headmistress earlier in the day. The boy's once blue eyes were now the gray of mouse fur.

Benny managed to check out the fourth, Marshall Cho, whose ink-black eyes had faded to ash gray.

Minutes later, in Mengistu's dorm room, the three were slumped in armchairs, each boy half in soft lamplight and half in shadow, precisely as in Jurgen and Benny's room, an ambiance that appealed to an adolescent sense that the world was a twilit realm drifting one day toward pale hope but the very next day toward darkness and annihilation. Benny had no candy, either for comfort or to use as a weapon; neither did Jurgen have close at hand his stolen steak knife nor Mengistu his can of powerful insecticide. They had arrived at the disturbing conclusion that any weapons available to them were inadequate to the threat.

"Whatever's happening," Jurgen said, "whatever she's scheming toward, it's all accelerating."

"Indeed," said Mengistu.

Benny said, "Everyone at Briarbush, the faculty and staff and students, everyone but us, seems to be under a spell, hypnotized to accept whatever she does, whatever happens, as just a new normal, nothing to be concerned about, nothing to see here."

"Manifestly," said Mengistu.

"I can only assume," said Jurgen, "that if she knows with total confidence that she holds them in some kind of spell of ignorance and illusion, with whatever alien technology, then she also knows the three of us are not as blinded as the others."

"Indubitably," said Mengistu.

Benny said, "At some point, when she feels the time is right, she'll come for us, and we'll either become like the rest of them, or we'll wind up like her husband, not necessarily buried next to Lester and Bertha Smith out there in Kansas, but buried somewhere."

"Unquestionably," said Mengistu.

"Are we screwed?" Jurgen asked.

"We're screwed," Benny confirmed.

Mengistu said, "We have one potential weapon—knowledge."

"What knowledge?" Jurgen and Benny asked simultaneously.

Mengistu said, "We must seek clues as to how she exercises the power she possesses and how she might be foiled. We must search for that knowledge, and expeditiously. I do not believe it would be wise to seek understanding in her laboratory, where we might encounter another Bugboy or his ilk. But when she is working in the lab, we might find it fruitful to break into her house and search the shit out of it."

PALAZZO DEL CONIGLIO

When he stepped through the open door and into Palazzo del Coniglio, Benny felt as if he not only shrank physically but also diminished in value as a human being. The architecture and interior design seemed to be calculated to render him submissive. He wasn't humbled by a sense of majesty and wonder and mystery as he would have been in any great cathedral, where humility tended to expand the spirit. Although the scale of the house was grand, Benny felt burdened by the mass of it, even vaguely claustrophobic, and wanted to be gone from there.

The foyer measured maybe forty feet in diameter. The gold-leafed domed ceiling arced more than thirty feet above the floor. Polished mahogany walls. Limestone floor with a checkered border of malachite and black granite. In the center stood a six-foot-diameter walnut table, French, perhaps two hundred years old and inlaid with ivory and mother-of-pearl and silver wire.

"The architect and interior designer were geniuses," Spike declared. "They spent spectacular sums to create an impression of grandeur, while employing countless cunning techniques to mock H. Ellsworth Theron by overdoing everything to the point that sublime proportions and details were exaggerated precisely enough to become tawdry. They imbued the faux grandeur with an oppressive quality equal to anything the most ominous Gothic building could impose. They must have despised Ellsworth Theron a great deal."

"So white, white, white has some appeal after all," Benny said.

"None whatsoever. It's just a different kind of awfulness from this."

At the far end of the foyer, two curved staircases with several tons of gilded bronze railings offered different routes to the same second-floor gallery. Harper dashed past Benny, hurrying upstairs to find the bedroom where the umpteenth Arabella was confined for her safety.

To the right of the foyer, doors stood open to a vast library with a mezzanine, Persian carpets in jewel tones, and several pairs of massive French armchairs upholstered in fabric with such patterns as fleur-de-lis. Although it was as old as the rest of the house, the room appeared to be recently assembled and as yet unused.

To the left of the foyer, beyond another pair of open doors, lay what might have been a gentlemen's lounge with a massive black granite fireplace. Ruby-red leather sofas and matching armchairs. A billiards table. A bar with eight stools. Behind the bar, a colorful mural depicted uniformed men on horseback charging valiantly across a landscape littered with dead soldiers and ribboned with cannon smoke, perhaps inspired by Alfred Lord Tennyson's "The Charge of the Light Brigade." Men might gather in this chamber, without their ladies, for after-dinner brandy, cigars, and conversation so stuffy as to put them at risk of suffocation if a window wasn't open.

Benny and Spike crossed the foyer to another pair of doors, beyond which lay a drawing room larger than a professional tennis court, with several seating areas. Illumination descended from two immense crystal chandeliers and radiated from a bedazzlement of gorgeous Tiffany lamps. As planned, Benny paused in the doorway while Spike proceeded across the threshold.

Even from his perspective, he could see the man sitting off to the right in an armchair beside an occasional table. At ninety, F. Upton Theron didn't look his age. He looked much older. Perhaps his head wasn't a large potato that had shriveled until its moisture content was immeasurably small; however, the swags of puckered and brittle skin festooning his face required closer inspection before the potato hypothesis could be disproved. Whatever color his hair had once been, it most likely had turned white for a time before it had finally acquired the unhealthy yellow tint of the stringy silk from a diseased corn plant. Because Benny wanted to be generous, he assumed that Theron's nose had once been as straight and sculpted as that of anyone who had been born from the headwaters of New England society and that its current appalling condition was either evidence of a degenerative rhinological malady or the consequence of decades of extreme alcohol abuse. Swollen, shapeless, strangely folded at the tip, darker than the pale face that surrounded it, webbed with prominent red capillaries, it could have been no more disconcerting if it had been a nose that was bitten off by an iguana, swallowed, retrieved from the reptile's stomach, and sewn back on by a surgeon who never completed medical school. Theron's unfortunate appearance opened a tap of compassion in Benny. Dripping with sympathy for one of the people who intended to ruin his life, he felt stupid, but the sympathy dripped anyway, like a leaky faucet.

"Gentlemen, I've been sitting here enjoying a root beer and anticipating your arrival with pleasure." Theron's robust voice was as appealing as his face was off-putting. "Please sit with me, and let's resolve this misunderstanding. Come in, Mr. Catspaw, come in. Perhaps you gentlemen would like a root beer."

Benny remained in the doorway, looking around the drawing room, pretending to be awed by the splendor of the place. "What a room. What a house. What a night to remember." If he entered the chamber before Harper arrived with the giant white rabbit, he would probably be dead sooner than later; dying would be unfair to his personal craggle, whose failure rate would then be closer to 10 percent than to 7.

Spike stood to one side of Theron's chair, staring down at him as though at an abomination that crawled out of a sewer grating.

Peering up at the giant, Theron produced a smile like a slit in a deflating beach ball. "And what is your name, sir?"

"Spike."

"Mr. Spike, may I ask what your position is in relation to Mr. Catspaw?"

"No."

"He's my interior designer," Benny said. "I have an inability to coordinate colors, so everything in my place pretty much ends up white, white, white. Except for whatever wine and food stains resist removal. I finally have to admit I have no talent for decor. I've made mistakes with women, too. In our relationship, Jill was a steak knife and I was a dessertspoon, just like Fat Bob said. Bob. Just like Bob said."

Where is Harper Harper?

THE HOUR OF THE RABBIT

The second floor of Palazzo del Coniglio offered a bewildering number of rooms in three wings. Elegantly furnished guest rooms, each with its own bath. A model-train layout with what seemed like a mile of track winding through miniature villages, mountains, and valleys, through tunnels, across bridges. An arcade with twenty pinball machines.

She yanked open a door to a bed-sitting room, where a game show was underway on a TV. A fiftyish woman in a bathrobe and slippers startled up from her chair, ice rattling in a glass of whiskey that she held in her right hand. Judging by the fact this lodging was smaller and less well appointed than others, Harper deduced she was in the servants' wing.

"Who're you?" the woman asked.

"Your worst nightmare," Harper said, and knew even as she said it that she sounded ridiculous.

"Honey, my worst nightmare isn't dressed all in yellow with a pink baseball cap and a ponytail."

"Don't screw with me. Don't you dare screw with me. I'm looking for Arabella. I'm taking her."

"A kidnapper? Oh, this is sweet. This is delicious. He'll pay a million. He'll pay ten!"

"I'm not asking for ransom advice." Harper decided to go total hard-boiled. "If you don't want your throat cut, *tell me where I can find Arabella!*"

"Honey, you do know—Arabella is a rabbit."

"Yes, I am aware. Large, white, furry, likes carrots."

"She won't be here with any of us in the servants' wing."

"Ah, hah! Servants' wing," Harper said, pleased that her powers of deduction were better than her ability to talk tough.

"Arabella will be with the beast," the woman said.

"Beast? What beast?"

"Theron."

"You call your boss a beast?"

"He's a turd. We all think so."

"Then why work for him?"

The woman winked. "Benefits."

"Stealing him blind, huh?"

"Doing our best. My name's Tanya."

Harper gave her two thumbs up. "Listen, Tanya, the rabbit isn't with him. She's in his bedroom. Can you show me where his bedroom is? I didn't mean that about cutting your throat. I wouldn't cut anyone's throat. I wouldn't even know how. I'd make a mess of it."

Tanya put down her glass of whiskey. "We've been told to stay in our rooms tonight. To hell with that. Come on, sister."

The primary bedroom was slightly smaller than a six-car garage but not as plain. In addition to the usual furnishings, there were maybe a hundred plush-toy rabbits of various sizes, in a rainbow of colors.

When Tanya called, "Bella," a large white rabbit with enormous ears hopped—*thump, thump, thump*—out of what might have been a bath or a walk-in closet, crossing the bedroom with exuberance. The woman scooped Arabella off the floor. "Can't hate her just because that turd loves her. She's a bundle of joy." She started to pass the rabbit to Harper, but hesitated. "Hold her for ransom, but don't hurt a hair on this hare."

"I won't. I never would. She's so cute."

"If you hurt her, I'll find you. I'll cut *your* throat. And believe me, *I* know how."

The rabbit twitched its nose and allowed Harper to cradle it like a baby, gazing up at her with soulful brown eyes. The long ears were soft pink on the inside, flexing left and right as if they were radar dishes seeking a signal. "She's a giant furry marshmallow."

"She's strong. She can kick, but she won't. She likes you."

As Tanya returned to her room, Harper hurried down to the main floor, Arabella in her arms.

Benny stood on the threshold of the drawing room. He turned his head as she approached. The rabbit elicited from him a sweet smile, or maybe it was the sight of the rabbit and Harper in concert that together pleased him, even now when they were about to put their lives at risk. She liked to think it was the latter, that she, as well as a fluffy white rabbit, could brighten his spirits even with the prospect of death looming for all of them. This was an almost mawkish middle-school desire, the kind of yearning she thought she'd put behind her when she was thirteen. She had never liked bad boys; nevertheless, she was surprised to discover niceness, to the degree Benny embodied it, should have such appeal. In one evening, her heart seemed to have overruled her brain and had assigned her goal of becoming a private investigator to second place on her list of ambitions while inserting romance at the top.

Benny stepped into the room, and Harper followed close behind him. She saw Spike standing about six feet from an armchair, looking down at an entity so wattled and warted and wrinkled that it might have been a fungus of some kind, except that it was dressed in what appeared to be a Prada shirt, Giorgio Armani pants, and tasseled loafers by Salvatore Ferragamo. This was one of those individuals whose ears grew larger or became misshapen with age, so that now they hung on the head like masses of indigestible gristle that had been coughed up by a meat-eating predator. As the ears colossalized with time, the lips seemed to have shriveled and lost much of their elasticity, so that the mouth was more like a hole, reminiscent of the end of a vacuum-cleaner hose. Under it spilled chins resembling a small stack of pancakes, each offset from the one before it. With F. Upton's countless facial creases, his morning shave must be more difficult than grooming a Shar-Pei.

Harper remembered something her parents told her: How you live your life will earn the face you have in years to come; if you think you're superior to others, if you can't live and let live, if your arrogance inspires perpetual anger and resentment because others do not agree with you, then you'll age into a face that reveals the corruption of your soul. To have earned the face he now had, Upton Theron must have been infuriated since infancy.

TO LIVE FOREVER

Although irritated by the impudence of Catspaw and his hulking friend, who appeared to be a professional wrestler from some down-market cable channel, F. Upton Theron was in a fine and fearless mood. For one thing, he controlled the situation. Having injected himself with the antitoxin, he was impervious to the nerve gas with which he would execute these foolish men after obtaining from them what information he required.

For another thing, his conviction that he would never die gave him unshakable confidence regardless of the circumstances in which he found himself. Scientific breakthroughs were occurring so often and technology was advancing so rapidly that long before he'd lived a century, he would have immortality options. A Methuselah enzyme or elixir would be discovered; the effects of aging would be reversed; life eternal would be his. Between now and then, there might be a period when he needed to be sustained by the transplantation of a pig heart and other porcine organs; the sows providing the organs had been genetically engineered to have enough human DNA so tissue rejection was not a concern and the risk of smelling like ham had been eliminated. He and others of the Better Kind had ensured that enormous government sums had been devoted to such a project. Being augmented with pig parts as needed could buy time until his brain could be transplanted into a robot body. Not enthusiastic about being a cyborg, more machine than human, some of the Better Kind wanted to explore the possibility of having their brains put into pigs, as a temporary measure to sustain them if their bodies began to fail. The size and shape of a pig skull and differences between porcine and human nervous systems presented insurmountable problems.

Personally, Upton would be okay with having his brain stuffed into a healthy pig, strictly as an interim home, until human cloning was perfected, whereupon the brain of the clone could be removed and Upton's brain installed; physically he would then be twenty with many years of good health during which to wait for the Methuselah elixir to be invented. There might be psychological problems related to having been a pig, even one that had lived in a mansion and been well cared for by servants, but if that were the case, drugs would be invented to erase those memories.

Catspaw, that insufferable nonentity with strange hair, finally stepped off the threshold and entered the drawing room.

Unable to repress a smile of triumph, Upton snatched the remote control off the seat of his armchair. He pressed the green button. Installed by Ob & Ob, two pneumatic steel panels whisked out of the doorjambs and engaged each other. Similar barriers dropped out of window headers and locked into sills.

The drawing room was now hermetically sealed. After extracting from his visitors the answers he required, when Upton pushed the red button, nerve gas would flood this space but not leak into the rest of the house. The lethal toxin had such a dramatic and prolonged effect that the demise of the intruders would be entertaining. These enemies of the Better Kind were about to discover their truths would not save them. In the world as it had become and was becoming, what were virtues had been transformed into vices, vices into virtues, and resistance to this progress was futile.

Then the woman appeared from behind the loathsome Catspaw, and for a moment Upton was frozen by enchantment, focused on her lovely face. Through the completion of his eighth decade, although not as often during the past ten years, he had enjoyed having a woman. His occasional and always short-lived relationships were never about companionship; he had his rabbits for that. The sex was satisfying; however, he was primarily excited by waging a subtle but intense psychological war against each lover, instilling in her doubt about her worth, leading her to wonder if the best things about her were instead the worst, humiliating her while making her think she was the only agent of her humiliation. Upton taught her the new virtue of absolute tolerance. When in a few months she believed in nothing and disapproved of nothing and found purpose in nothing, when he had pulled her up by the roots from her past, he cast her out into a world unlike the one she'd been a part of before coming under his thrall, without the hope that might have made it possible for her to regain the world she'd lost. Not surprisingly, to one degree or another, these women resembled either his mother, Pelagia, or his sister, Arabella. This perky, ponytailed woman with Benjamin Catspaw looked less like Sister than others had, but she was particularly exciting because she possessed those qualities that most enfevered Upton Theron's lust for destruction—beauty, winsomeness, grace, and innocence.

Enchantment gripped him so firmly he didn't at once realize what she was carrying. When he saw Arabella captive in this bitch's arms, the strobing lights of an ocular migraine squirmed through his field of vision. A high-pitched tinnitus shrilled like cicadas deep in his ears. His mouth went dry. His heart raced. His stomach turned over as if it were some sleeping animal adjusting its position, his kidneys swelled with an excess of processed root beer, and his testicles nearly retracted into his body. He was stricken by the irrational but powerful fear that eighty years of achievement had been undone, that before him stood his sister as an adult, not with her lungs filled with the water in which he drowned her when he was ten, but his sister—the first Arabella—breathing air and holding Powderpuff, returned now that Upton was old and vulnerable. She had returned to thwart his plan to sustain his life with appropriate pig parts and robot bodies and a clone whose brain had been scooped out to make room for his own. Upton was displeased, then irritated, then angry, then enraged, then infuriated, and then filled with a godlike wrath so mighty that he wanted to rain fire and brimstone on them, shatter their bones as those inhabitants of Sodom and Gomorrah were said to have been shattered. However, F. Upton Theron was not a god. There was no such thing as a god in his belief system. He was only the next best thing to a god, and all he could do to these intruders who would, if they could, deny him eternal life was to push the red button and deliver unto them an agonizing death by nerve gas.

A SUDDEN DEATH THAT UPENDS ALL EXPECTATIONS

As ancient as F. Upton Theron had looked, fury aged him even further. He appeared not merely like a wattled, warted, wrinkled fungoid variant of humanity, but like a fungoid variant of humanity who had also died, been preserved with the same techniques applied to the cadavers of Egyptian pharaohs, awakened after three thousand years, and stripped off his windings. He would henceforth need to wear a face mask if he wanted to get a table in a good restaurant.

When Theron saw Harper holding the rabbit, his mouth fell open in a silent howl of protest and rage. Then a geyser of obscenities erupted from him. It was such a brazen, vulgar, obscene spew that Benny felt as though he ought to bathe in a tub full of sanitizing gel as soon as possible. The old man sprang to his feet, not in an athletic fashion, but with a flapping of arms and repeated thrusting of his head that bestowed on him the grotesque aspect of a startled chicken.

On his feet, squawking curses, Theron thrust out his right arm, in which he held the remote control that had sealed off the doors and windows. If his intention might have once been to lure them into Palazzo del Coniglio and extort from them an explanation of how they had identified him as one of Benny's organized enemies, that purpose was abandoned in his fury. He meant to press a second button on the remote and evidently either render them unconscious or dead with an infusion of a gas into the drawing room.

Spike didn't take a threatening step toward Theron, but his arm stretched out as if he were Rubberman, the long-forgotten comic-book superhero whose limited powers were too silly to immortalize in movies. He broke the old man's thumb and plucked the remote control from his hand. The giant's arm shrank to its previous proportions. When he pressed the green button, the pneumatic barriers retracted into the window headers and doorjambs.

Between cries of pain, Theron expressed outrage that anything so horrendous as what had happened to him could have been allowed to transpire. "You broke my thumb! My thumb! You broke it!"

"You are correct," Spike said.

"What were you thinking?"

"That your thumb needed to be broken."

"You can't do that."

"Evidence suggests you're incorrect."

"Who the hell are you?"

"Mr. Catspaw's interior designer."

Belatedly, Theron realized his assailant was standing at too great a distance to have broken his thumb. The assault had occurred when the old man had been vomiting forth a stream of obscenities and blasphemies, so transported by fury at the sight of Harper with the rabbit that he had insufficient peripheral awareness to notice that something of an unnatural nature had occurred. Cradling his injured right hand in his left, his shriveled face difficult to read but his voice rich with perplexity, he said, "Hey. What the? How did you?" At last, the fear he should have felt at first sight of Spike came upon him, but he was too proud to back down. "Get out of my house, get out, get out now, you piece of shit."

"Uh-oh," said Harper.

"Please do not call me names," Spike said.

"Freak," said Theron. "Piece of shit. *Peasant.*"

"I must insist that you apologize."

Theron glared at Harper and then returned his attention to Spike. "Tell the slut to put down my Arabella."

After a moment of silence, Spike said, "To whom do you refer?"

Unable to let go of his anger long enough to assess the truth of his position—or perhaps, in spite of his broken thumb, unable to imagine a grandee like himself in peril—Theron said, "There's only one stinking slut in the room holding a rabbit. The slutty slut in the pink hat. Tell the bitch in the pink hat to put down my rabbit, and all of you syphilitic freaks *get out of my house.*"

"Uh-oh," Benny said.

"She's a lady," Spike informed Theron. "Do not speak such filth to a lady."

Ninety years of ever-increasing self-esteem had resulted in the extinction of any self-awareness Theron might once have possessed. The maniacal purity of his arrogance was a wonder to behold. "Lady? *Lady?* When my people get done with you, *you'll* be a lady."

To Benny, Harper said, "Good grief, he's no better at tough talk than I am."

Spike tossed the remote control to Benny, who gasped at the thought of what might happen if he dropped it. He caught it.

Without taking a step, the big guy reached out about ten feet with his right arm and seized the master of Palazzo del Coniglio by the throat, reached an equal distance with his left arm and gripped him by the crotch. Lifted him off his feet. Lifted him high. Turned him upside down. Joggled Theron as though to shake some sense into him. Turned him right side up. Dropped him into the armchair.

This time, the old man could not help but see the arms elongate and then return to their proper proportions. From him issued feeble and pitiable sounds of a small animal in grave distress, but those whimperings could not mask the drizzling noise that accompanied his decision to empty his bladder without bathroom or bedpan.

When he spoke, he couldn't command his language to be coherent. "Don't me touch. Back stay! What, what you? How you what?"

Spike towered over him, careful to remain beyond the stain that spread slowly through the antique Persian carpet. "I don't want to hear your political opinions, your theories of social organization, your definitions of progress, your absurd vision of utopia, your justifications for destroying people and tearing down civilization to rebuild a better one. I don't *need* to hear them. For more than eighteen hundred years, I've listened to the same stupid, heartless words from others of your ilk. I want to know just a few things, a very few. First, Mr. Theron, what do you connivers call yourselves? You have some name for your crusade. Your type always does. A name that makes you feel enlightened, superior, above the common herd. What do you call yourselves?"

Incredibly, when Upton Theron achieved coherency, he still stubbornly resisted. Sounding shaky but nonetheless haughty, he invited Spike to consume a dinner of excrement.

Ignoring that offensive invitation, voice calm but no less ominous than before, Spike said, "I also want to know how many delusional narcissists are in your organization and what resources you have available to spend."

Upton then suggested Spike stick his head up a feature of his anatomy that no one would find pleasant to inspect in such an intimate fashion.

Although Spike was an extraordinary contortionist who might have accomplished that incredible feat, he had no need to potty and therefore lacked the feature that Theron so rudely named.

The prospect of being murdered with a poisonous gas had passed, yet Benny grew more tense with each exchange between the craggle and the crackpot.

He glanced at Harper. She smiled. So did the rabbit.

To Theron, Spike said, "Finally, I want to know the name and whereabouts of the person at the top of your gaggle of imbeciles. Who decided that Benjamin's career and life must be destroyed? Who gave the go-ahead? I want to settle this tonight."

Remarkably defiant in his urine-soaked pants, Theron advised Spike to copulate with himself, give birth, and send the baby to a zoo where it would belong.

Benny didn't fully grasp the logic of that insult, but there was a lot about Upton Theron and his kind that eluded understanding.

Thus far, Spike had shown more forbearance than Benny expected, but the giant had reached the end of his patience. He glowered down at the old man as though he might tie him in a Gordian knot and then sever it with a sword.

Clearly frightened but drawing some courage from the power of his contempt, Theron glared up at Spike from the sodden and reeking armchair of mortification.

"Perhaps," said Spike, "you fail to understand my commitment to Benjamin, how very much he matters to me. Maybe it would help you to understand if I showed you what's in my heart."

With the style of legerdemain particular to cragglekind, Spike thrust a hand through his black T-shirt, into his chest, and tore out his heart. He held it toward Theron, a pound or two of blood-dripping muscle that continued to beat slowly, steadily. The rip in his shirt revealed a hideous cavity.

Every weary swag of flesh in Theron's face was enlivened by terror, his eyes as wide as the lidless eyes of a fish, his mouth agape and trembling.

"If you won't tell me what I want to know," said Spike, "I will feel the need to extract *your* heart and study it to understand what secrets it contains."

So it was that even a man as armored in arrogance, insulated from reason, and divorced from reality as F. Upton Theron could be brought to an understanding that he wouldn't live forever and might not live another minute.

First haltingly and then with increasing haste, Theron divulged the information that Spike demanded, his stare fixed unwaveringly on the beating heart. They called themselves "the Better Kind." There were fifty-two of them, led by a woman named Llewellyn Urnfield. Their combined assets totaled two-thirds of a trillion dollars. Handy Duroc and Jill Swift and others like them were riffraff, trash, *ignobile vulgus*, not in the exclusive club of the Better Kind. They were merely tools, strivers who could be intimidated or bribed or otherwise manipulated into assisting the Better Kind in the destruction of anyone deemed to be a threat to the New Truth, the New Way, the New World, the glorious and inevitable New Future. Potential enemies of the New Future, such as the monster Benny Catspaw, were defined by criteria established by the Better Kind, and then identified by an algorithm applied to all social media, government records, and corporate data troves.

"Monster?" Benny said. His feelings shouldn't have been hurt when his accuser was a lunatic like Upton Theron; nonetheless, they were a little bruised. "I'm not a monster. I'm just a guy trying to have a life."

"A good guy," Harper added.

"Not a perfect guy," Benny said. "Nobody is. But I like to think I'm on the good end of the spectrum."

"He's way out there on the good end," Harper insisted.

"Not way out there, but sort of comfortably in the middle of the good end of the spectrum," Benny said, embarrassed that he felt the need to insist on his virtue and the limits of it.

Even though terror still gripped Theron, he remained capable of rage. He was so angered by the assertion that Benny wasn't a threat to the happiness and welfare of all humanity, he thrust up from his antique urine sponge and jabbed an accusing finger at the man he'd labeled a monster, excoriating him in a loud voice dripping with hatred and bitterness. "You stand there with your boyish face, your innocent little-girl eyes, your silly mop of hair, pretending to be as harmless as a bunny rabbit, but in your h-h-heart, you know what you really are, what a revolutionary, what a threat to the hope and progress of humankind. You are *nice!*" He hissed the word *"nice"* as though he considered niceness to be the worst of all depravities. "You are foolishly, absurdly, dangerously *nice*. You are also wise, you smug little shit, wiser than you know. And it's the wrong kind of wisdom, based on truth that isn't the New Truth. When you realize how wise you are, you'll be wise and *nice*, you preening little pile of angel puke. When you're wise and *nice*, you'll have charisma. When you have charisma, you despicable Goody Two-Shoes, you might inspire *niceness* in others, open their h-h-hearts to a way forward that IS NOT OUR WAY! Despicable scum like you will bring us an Armageddon of *Niceness* based on stupid wisdom of the dumbest kind. You'll muck up everything. I find you repugnant. You nauseate me. I detest you, despise you, loathe you, abhor you, hate you, hate you, hate you. You're an abomination, and I want you to die hard, your brain to explode, your h-h-heart to to to—"

Having been terrified by the heart still dripping in Spike the craggle's hand, and then having further excited himself by flying into a rage and indulging in hatred all while nonetheless terrified, Upton Theron proved that, as a man of ninety, he didn't have the oomph to encompass so much emotion in one snarling fit of outrage and carry it off to satisfaction. The hand with the accusing finger swept away from Benny and clamped on Theron's chest. His mass of wrinkles scrunched into an expression that said *Uh-oh.* His mean eyes rolled back in his head, as though to examine his conscience before it was too late. It was too late. He fell facedown, which would be a blessing to whoever found him.

"Neat," said Harper.

"Overdue," Spike said as he tucked the bloody heart back into his chest. The wound closed. He smoothed his T-shirt, and the tear disappeared.

Benny said, "There was a time when I'd have thought, because I came here and confronted him, I was somewhat responsible for this, and I would have felt bad."

"Now?" Spike asked.

"I feel somewhat responsible, but I don't feel bad. I'm sort of surprised I don't feel bad."

"You have arrived at cragglethink," Spike said with approval.

The rabbit was so comfortable in Harper's arms that it snored softly.

She said, "I better talk to the housekeeper who helped me find Arabella. The staff needs to know about the poison gas or whatever it is, so they don't accidentally trigger it. Plus they don't have much time left to compensate themselves for having to work for that creep." She started to turn away and then said, "Oh, and I'm keeping this sweet bunny," before hurrying from the room.

"I believe," said Spike, "we will bring an end to this current war on you, Benjamin, by paying a visit to Llewellyn Urnfield. If you're ready to chance it."

"Chance what?"

"What every human being chances every morning that he or she wakes up—death."

"Well, at least I guess my odds are good. With you on my side, a ninety percent chance of surviving."

"Ninety-three," Spike corrected.

"Just one thing."

"Which is?"

"If I have to die, I'd like it to be quick and clean, not prolonged and horrific."

"We can hope," Spike said as they crossed the drawing room toward the foyer.

"Something you said makes me a little nervous."

"What was it? How can I put your mind at ease?"

"You said we'll 'bring an end to this current war' on me. The word *'current'* seems to imply there might be other wars like this in the future."

"Maybe I didn't imply it. Perhaps you only inferred it."

As they stepped into the foyer and stood waiting for Harper, Benny said, "It sounded to me like you bluntly implied it."

"Well, I was trying to set your mind at ease, my friend, but I guess you won't let me do that. Once we can break these Better Kind fanatics or badly disrupt them, we can put your life back together. But they can always regroup. Even if their project implodes, there are always others like them, some wealthy, others who aren't wealthy but have political power and can use the resources of the government to harass you and others like you."

"Tormenting nice people who just want to get along—they get off on that?"

"Yes. But they're also afraid of people like you. Theron had it somewhat right. When kindness and decency—also known as *niceness*—are coupled with wisdom, you have charisma of a good kind. When charismatic people also have plenty of courage, they can inspire others and, with them, do great good things. That scares the hell out of Theron and his pals, who claim to be doing good even when they're doing great evil."

"So it's all about money and power to them?"

"Not entirely. Some know they're doing evil, but some don't. In each case, they're all the same—impatient, shortsighted, reckless fixers. Seeing themselves as fixers gives their lives meaning."

"Fixers?"

"They're people who can't let anything be as it is. No matter how good the thing is, it's never good enough for them. Everything they look upon seems either not quite right or wrong, and they're convinced they know how to fix it. Most of the time, they utterly destroy it before rebuilding something less good from the rubble."

"What sense does that make? If my car has a broken windshield wiper, I don't blow up the car before starting repairs. And for sure I don't want my life blown up and fixed. Even with you on my side, what kind of life will it be, always a target?"

Spike pinched Benny's cheek affectionately. "It'll be *life*, my main man. Who in this life isn't a target one way or another? You'll do fine, Benjamin. We've got this. Say 'We've got this.' I want to hear you say 'We've got this,' and really mean it."

"I don't feel like we've got this."

"Sure we do. Say 'We've got this.'"

"I don't want to say it. Saying it will jinx us."

Spike gripped Benny's lips with one thumb and two fingers and gently massaged them as if shaping the words he wanted. "Say it for Uncle Spike. Say 'We've got this.'"

Benny endured the mouth massage until it stopped. Instead of saying what was requested of him, he said, "'Plenty of courage.' According to you, the formula for success is niceness, wisdom, and plenty of courage. But I don't have gallons of courage. I have like maybe one cup of courage, maybe not even a full cup."

"You'll have oceans of courage when you need it," Spike assured him. "When anyone has something more to lose than just his life, the fear of losing that bigger thing gives him great courage."

"Bigger than my life? What more could I lose than my life?"

Spike looked to the spectacular staircase and smiled, and Benny turned to see what the smile was about, and Harper was descending with the rabbit in her arms. He was rocked. He was hammered. For a moment he could not breathe. He had been aware that this woman was growing on him, not like a fungus or anything gross, but growing on him in a good way, the best way, growing *closer* in mind and heart, growing more precious and with surprising speed, considering under what circumstances their courtship had been conducted. Could one date be called a courtship? One date chaperoned by a craggle? It wasn't even a date by the standard definition. Yes, they'd eaten dinner together, while Spike had eaten ten dinners, but they hadn't gone to a movie or dancing. They had invaded Handy Duroc's house, and they had stripped Oliver Lambert naked and sent him off to shake a deep-fried zucchini stick at his party guests, and together they escaped being fatally gassed by an evil old man who was now lying dead in urine-soaked pants, but a quick review of the evening's activities failed to reveal anything that could credibly be called *romance*. Benny had been aware that something was evolving between him and Harper Harper, a sweet mutual attraction, even something that might be described as a *relationship*. However, as he watched her gracefully descending the stairs with a large white rabbit, he was rocked so profoundly by emotion that the thought of losing her was intolerable. His passion had nothing to do with the rabbit; it was all about Harper. He would do anything to protect her, anything, including sacrificing himself to save her life, which he would most likely never be called upon to do—he sure hoped not—but he would take the bullet for her if it came to that.

When Harper descended the final step and set foot in the foyer, breath came to Benny, and he said, "We've got this. I've got this."

"You make me proud," said Spike.

LEAVING PALAZZO DEL CONIGLIO IN HIGH EMOTION, BENNY REMEMBERS AN EMOTIONAL TIME AT BRIARBUSH

Every week, another few boys joined the growing hive of worker bees, their eyes transformed to one shade of gray or another. Of the teachers, staff, and students, only Benny and Jurgen and Mengistu seemed to be aware of this transformation. And only they thought it was peculiar that these gray-eyed minions attended to mysterious tasks at the direction of the headmistress rather than pursuing their studies or horsing around as boys their age were wont to do.

Autumn always came early and passed quickly in those mountains. That year when Benny was thirteen, most species of birds migrated south in the same two-day period, perhaps because instinct warned that winter could arrive abruptly and with brutal force. The sudden departure of 90 percent of the birds effected a change of no big material impact. However, the silencing of their songs and flight calls, their erasure from the sky, where the sight of them on the wing could lift your spirit, was one of many reasons that the mood at Briarbush Academy became darker by the day. The food in the dining hall, previously the best thing about the school, gradually grew less flavorful, as if the chef and everyone on his staff had lost their culinary mastery and motivation. At times, Benny and Jurgen and Mengistu heard an ominous bass throbbing that rose from the earth and persisted for an hour or longer, as though an immense machine had been constructed in a previously unknown cavern beneath Briarbush and was now laboring at a sinister task. Eerie electronic sounds riddled the night, originating somewhere beyond Felthammer House, but they never lasted long enough to be tracked to their source. No one but Benny and Jurgen and Mengistu heard either the throbbing or the electronic keening. Or if others heard it, they were programmed not to react or remember; increasingly, the three boys suspected that, except for themselves, everyone at Briarbush was being programmed; by what method, with what intention, and for what purpose they could not say.

Though all but three minds were clouded to the truth of weird goings-on, the incident of the bears was perhaps too dramatic to be deleted from the memory of those who witnessed it. For days it remained a topic of conversation among everyone at the school. The black bears that roamed these mountain forests and high meadows weighed about three hundred pounds, and they could be dangerous if they were angered or felt threatened. They had long shied away from Briarbush Academy, which Jurgen said must be because their instinct told them most of the boys under formation there were too tasteless to be worth eating. Until the last Monday of that September, nobody had ever seen more than a single bear at a time wandering along the meadow near the forest. On the afternoon of the visitation, seven black bears appeared in the tall grass, lined up like the statues on Easter Island, standing erect, swaying slightly, facing the school with their heads raised as if heeding a sound only they could hear or drawn by a scent only they could detect. Students and staff gathered at windows and on balconies and even in the open yard to observe the phenomenon. As though under an enchantment, the bears held their position for almost an hour before they dropped to all fours and lumbered away into the woods.

That was not the end of it.

A few days later, at half past the witching hour, Benny's nightmare broke apart as if it were a jigsaw puzzle, bright pieces spinning down into a black void. He woke with a start, threw aside the covers, erupted from bed, and stood trembling in the dark dormitory room. All that he remembered of the dream was a dry and susurrant voice speaking in a language he didn't know. Awake, he still heard it, not as loud as when he'd been lost in sleep, but insistent and strange.

"What is that?" Jurgen asked, and Benny realized his friend was standing on the far side of the room, presenting the shadowy shape of a boy in the dim glow that issued from the digital bedside clocks. "It's the same creepy voice as in the dream."

"Mine too. What was your dream?"

"I don't remember."

"Me neither."

"If a snake could talk, it would have a voice like that," Jurgen said.

Benny said, "Or an iguana."

"Some kind of reptile."

"Not a friendly reptile," Benny said.

The character of the voice wasn't the worst of it. Benny failed to sift meaning from the whisperer's language—nor perhaps could any linguist on Earth—but its constructions and edgy rhythms raised his hackles, inspired in him a conviction that this language had been created by a cruel and evil race. And yet . . . in spite of the fear gripping him, the flow of words was compelling. Not charming. Not pleasant. But agreeable. It was as though in the human brain nestled a small and heretofore undiscovered gland or some simple fornix with a secret function to which the whisperer spoke with the confidence that it could influence the listener even as it terrified him.

"Refuse to listen!" Jurgen said, as if his thought was on a parallel track to Benny's.

A soft knock came at the door, which had no lock, and Mengistu rushed in without waiting for an invitation. "You hear it? Refuse to listen. Refuse, refuse."

"It's for sure not French or German," Jurgen said.

Benny said, "Doesn't sound Spanish or Chinese or anything."

Making his way to a window, Mengistu said, "Did you see? No? Then look, look. You have to see this."

Beyond the mowed yard and the cobblestone driveway, in the tall grass of the meadow, the bears stood in line as they had done on their previous appearance, but nearer the school this time. Because they were black and the pale moon hung like an incomplete ballroom globe, Benny might not have recognized that they were bears if this had been their first visit. Even known for what they were, the seven remained nonetheless mysterious—tall forms of inscrutable intent, darker than the night, each with two dots of animal eyeshine.

"If we're hearing what the bears are hearing," Jurgen said, "how long until we're the way they are?"

"Unlike bears," said Mengistu, "we possess the mental capacity to resist being hypnotized or whatever has been done to them. In fact, intuition tells me that, when we hear this whispering, it is important for us to get together as quickly as possible. We may be vulnerable individually, but together we have the power to resist."

At the window, Mengistu stood in the center of the trio, one arm around Benny's shoulders and one arm around Jurgen's, each of his friends with an arm around Mengistu's shoulders, watching the bears in the meadow. The moon beamed down, and the stars ranked outward through the Milky Way, across uncountable galaxies beyond, to the edge of the universe. The whispering faded away. The boys waited, inviolate, and soon the bears dropped from their sentinel stance and departed on all fours.

Through the increasingly bizarre days and nights at Briarbush, the friends maintained their determination to invade the house of the headmistress. They meant to search for knowledge that might lead to her destruction or provide them with protection and a chance to flee when everyone else at the school had been bewitched. For when Mrs. Baneberry-Smith would turn her full attention to the only three in the hive whose eyes were not yet gray.

Day after day, no opportunity to search her residence presented itself—until the second week of October. Rumor spread that Mrs. Baneberry-Smith would be meeting with the academy's most generous benefactors, leaving Tuesday and returning Thursday. Indeed, at two o'clock Tuesday afternoon, a rhythmic clatter carved away the quiet of the mountains when a large corporate helicopter settled on the driveway in front of the school. Twin engines. High-set main and tail rotors. Advanced glass cockpit. The craft appeared to have the capacity to carry eight or ten passengers. Only the headmistress boarded it.

Benny, Jurgen, and Mengistu watched from a second-floor window of the library as a gray-eyed worker bee carried a suitcase to the aircraft and the copilot loaded the bag. For this expedition, the headmistress dressed more demurely than had recently been her habit, although she was still attired in black clothes that did little to conceal her enticing form.

As the chopper rose off the driveway, Jurgen said, "There's no company or agency name on it. No registration number on the engine cowling, the fuselage, or the tail boom. They're above the law."

Referring to what they had learned when they had been hiding in the mountain pieris, the night that Bugboy was killed, Benny said, "She's not going off to meet the school's most generous benefactors. She's scheming with the Internal Security Agency."

"Manifestly," said Mengistu.

Jurgen declared, "We're running out of time to make a break for freedom."

"Indubitably," Mengistu agreed.

"We might never have another chance to search her house," Benny said. "We've got to do it before she returns."

"Unquestionably," Mengistu confirmed.

The worker bee who carried the headmistress's luggage stood on the driveway after the helicopter cruised out of sight, staring at the sky into which the craft had disappeared, his face a mask of yearning. After two or three minutes, he raised his arms and grasped at the air with his hands, as if by some magic he could draw her back to him. Suddenly he issued a wretched pule like the whine and whimper of a dumb animal in severe pain. The sound was louder than one that a wounded dog would make, and whereas a dog's complaint would inspire pity, this cry, for the half minute that it lasted, induced a chill in the three friends at the library window.

They needed a couple of hours to prepare for the justified crime of breaking and entering. Autumn nightfall came early. They worried that the use of flashlights in the Baneberry-Smith residence might draw unwanted attention. None of them needed to give voice to the truth that undertaking a search of her house in the dark was just too damn scary. They would wait until early light.

If they claimed to be ill, they would have to report to the nurse in the school infirmary. Instead, they made use of one of the five personal-study days available to every student, exempting them from attending classes on Wednesday.

Sleep didn't come easily that night. They weren't disturbed by sourceless whispering in an unknown language or by bears that might intend to occupy the boys' beds in a reverse Goldilocks scenario. No human-insect hybrid tapped on their windows, asking to be fed. From time to time, however, one voice or another in Felthammer House let out a miserable cry like that of the worker bee who had mourned the departure of Mrs. Baneberry-Smith, and always an answering cry came from elsewhere in the building. Neither the master of Felthammer, Drew Drudge, nor anyone else ventured forth to investigate those expressions of despair, as if everyone knew the reason for them and grieved no less than those who voiced their pain, even if most chose to suffer in silence. The same was surely happening in Kentwhistle House, in the faculty apartments, and in staff residences. A hive without its queen was a failed construct without any purpose, its inhabitants left to dwell on the meaninglessness of their existence, to die from anguish and disorder if she did not return.

Eventually, a slow-rising tide of dirty light along the eastern horizon revealed that storm clouds had gathered during the night, trailing gray beards of mist, for the moment withholding their rain.

Exiting dorm rooms by the windows, the three friends met again under the giant spreading pine, fifty yards from Felthammer

House. During the weeks they had planned for this moment, they'd stolen a roll of painters' tape and a claw hammer and a screwdriver from the maintenance crew's supplies. Jurgen also had the chef's knife with which he'd armed himself for a previous adventure, and Mengistu carried the aerosol can of insecticide that might deter a large bug or a human assailant. Benny had refrained from purchasing a fresh supply of candy bars. Thus prepared, they set out through the fast-waning night for the house of the headmistress.

They approached the rear of the residence and crouched behind shrubbery to reconnoiter the backyard. Under the sooty sky, with no sun to stretch or shrink shadows, the black of night melted into a dreary grayness, as if an acceleration of time had eliminated the morning and afternoon, marrying dawn to dusk. Although Benny had once thought this place appeared stately, it now loomed like the desolate, oppressive House of Usher imagined by Edgar Allan Poe.

"There is enough natural light to allow us to navigate the rooms," Mengistu said, "and with the storm impending, we cannot expect brighter conditions. Why are we delaying?"

"We know why we're delaying," Jurgen said.

"We know," Benny agreed.

"Of course we do," Mengistu said. "My question was rhetorical, intended to shame us into exhibiting greater courage. If we do not exhibit greater courage and get on with this before the headmistress returns, sooner than later we will fall under her spell as others have done. We will be alike to the millions who, in this culture, have trammeled themselves with infinite absurd bureaucracies, regulations, and rules to give their existence meaning after their ancestors declared no need for meaning two and a half centuries earlier. Shall we become termites in a colony, living for no purpose but to devour what little remains of our once glorious civilization, or shall we grow into men of responsibility?"

"Why don't you go first?" Jurgen suggested.

Pressing two fingers to his forehead, Mengistu said, "I am more of an inspirational philosopher than a man of action, a truth that I am humbled to discover just now."

Benny rose from behind the sheltering shrubbery and sprinted across the yard to the back porch. He made that charge not in the spirit of the Marines who raised the flag on Iwo Jima, but because he was overwhelmed by a sudden fear that seven bears, whispering in an alien language, would loom behind them, fall upon them, and tear them limb from limb, a fate that seemed more terrible than any that might await them in the house.

The back door was locked, but it featured four panes in the top half. Benny began tearing strips from the roll of painters' tape and applying them to the square of glass nearest the lock.

When Benny's friends joined him, Jurgen said, "We were kind of locked back there. You unlocked us."

"Not me," Benny said. "Bears."

"What bears? There aren't any bears."

"The possibility of bears," Benny explained.

"There is at all times a possibility of bears," said Mengistu. "We act, or we are acted upon."

"Exactly," said Benny.

When the glass was covered with blue tape, Benny used a single strip to form a hinge linking the pane to the wood frame.

Benny stepped aside, and Jurgen swung the hammer. The pane shattered with a quiet crackling sound. The glass adhered to the tape. When Jurgen pressed on the pane, it drooped inward, well secured by the hinge, and did not fall noisily to the floor.

Mengistu said, "Allow me to rehabilitate my damaged reputation by being the first to risk death inside these walls."

Benny and Jurgen were all right with that.

Mengistu reached through the empty pane, felt for the thumb turn, and disengaged the deadbolt. The door announced the violation with an extended creaking as it swung open. They would have been amazed if it had been silent.

They began in the basement with some reluctance. In stories of this kind, bad things happened to people in basements. If a basement harbored a secret, it was a secret best left undiscovered, and if you uncovered it anyway, it would tear your face off or do something worse to you. Because there were no windows in that subterranean space, they could turn on the lights, the better to see one another being eviscerated. The steps led into a room with a gas furnace and water heater, and although there was no statue of Satan or bloodstained altar, there were three closed doors. Three doors for three nosy boys. Benny could not shrug off the feeling that the house had been built not for any headmaster, but for him and his companions, with the foreknowledge that they would one day open these doors and get what was coming to them. With a spirit of shared risk, each chose a door, a fate. In stories of this kind, one intruder always dies, and two escape to encounter death elsewhere. This was not a story, however, but real life, so there was no reason that mortal threats might not lurk in each room, with three lives taken in the next minute. Three doors were opened, three light switches flipped, and no one died. Such an anticlimax was a great relief and, in the strangest way, slightly disappointing.

On the main floor once more, they began in the kitchen, where neither of the refrigerators contained a collection of eyeballs floating in mason jars full of embalming fluid. They did not find either a collection of poisons in the pantry or cookbooks with recipes for cannibals. Go figure.

Room by room, closet by closet, cabinet by cabinet, drawer by drawer, carefully examining every object to be sure it was only what it appeared to be, the friends conducted an exhaustive search for evidence that might convict Mrs. Baneberry-Smith. For a document or device that would explain the powers she gained by exploiting the knowledge from another world that was injected into her during that long-ago jungle expedition. For some clue as to how to defeat her.

After spending two hours on the main floor without arriving at even the smallest revelation, they began to lose confidence that the house contained what they hoped to find. If they found nothing on the second floor, they would have no option remaining but to search the laboratory. They *knew*, as surely as anyone can know anything, that if they went into the lab, they would either be carried out dead or come out transformed and no longer themselves, whether Mrs. Baneberry-Smith was on campus or not.

Before proceeding upstairs, they used the half bath to "pee" (Benny) and "take a leak" (Jurgen) and "relieve the pressure of a distended bladder" (Mengistu). They took cans of Pepsi from a fridge and stood at the kitchen island to drink. They considered eating a store-bought cake that was still in its original container, but after a lengthy debate, they agreed the headmistress might have opened it, contaminated it, and wrapped it up again. After twenty minutes spent in this fashion, they acknowledged that they were avoiding the second floor not because they feared finding nothing, but because they feared finding something.

An hour later, they found the locked room at the back of the house. Jurgen used the hammer and screwdriver to assault the lock assembly. The chamber contained a shiny black column about two feet square and five feet high. No immediate threat appeared, though the boys were profoundly unnerved by the severed head.

Any severed head would have curdled their blood, but this one was especially disturbing for three reasons, of which only two were at once apparent. First, this was the head of Dr. Lionel Baneberry-Smith, who had supposedly broken his neck when he'd fallen down the stairs while sleepwalking. Second, the head terminated in a two-inch wide metal collar and floated in a glass sphere that itself floated a few inches above the column with no visible support. As unsettling as a floating, bodiless head might be, it was also the kind of thing that most boys of a certain age would find irresistible, and the young men of Felthammer House were no exception.

"She sends the body off to Kansas," Jurgen said, "but she keeps the head. Why does she keep the head?"

"I do not believe she has kept it for sentimental reasons," Mengistu said. "A photograph would require less maintenance and be more poignant than this."

"Why is the head locked into that collar?" Benny wondered. "How is it preserved? How can the sphere just float there like that?"

"If she can't turn us into gray-eyed worker bees," Jurgen said, "maybe we'll end up like this."

The third—and not immediately apparent—reason the head was so disturbing became evident. The eyes opened and moved left to right as if scanning the boys. From the mouth issued the voice they heard on the night of the bears——a sinister, whispery chanting of words no human being had ever spoken, somehow conjuring in the mind images of reptiles.

In their haste to exit the room, the three friends nearly wedged together in the doorway before bursting into the upstairs hall. They thundered down the stairs, raced along the ground-floor hallway, crossed the kitchen, and fled the house.

By the time they sprinted halfway to the school, they realized that being seen in full, frantic flight would raise suspicion and invite inquiries that, in their current condition, they wouldn't be able to answer with convincing equanimity. They slowed to a walk, almost to a saunter.

Clouds piled up, dark gray with coaly veins, seeming as solid as charred timbers and soot-blackened masonry, as though this world existed under the ruins of another. The thunderheads were for the moment mute, the lightning sheathed, the wind pent up in preparation for a long and violent exhalation.

"We're in very deep shit," Jurgen said. "Even deeper than we realized. I mean, I knew we were in shit up to our hips, but in fact we're in it up to our necks."

Less interested in the depth of the shit than the purpose and meaning of the horror before them, Benny said, "What the hell did she do to his head? Why does he talk in that weird voice? Yeah, yeah, I know it's not the headmaster talking, but . . . but . . . *what did she do to his head?*"

"I believe," Mengistu offered, "that his head—to be precise, his brain—has been adapted to function as a receiver of messages transmitted far faster than light from a world elsewhere in the Milky Way, or perhaps from another galaxy altogether and through a wormhole. I would venture to say that the transmissions are neither something as innocent as the audio of an alien game show nor a warm greeting from one intelligent species to another."

That made sense to Benny. If his father hadn't been Big Al and his mother hadn't been Naomi, if he had not been for nine months in the care of his bitter death-obsessed grandmother Cosima, if Mordred Merrick hadn't been his tutor during the Beverly Hills years or Mr. Rudyard Bromley his weeping butler, he might have found Mengistu's speculation unconvincing. However, the people and events of his life had shaped him into a boy who was immediately receptive to the idea of a severed-head intergalactic radio receiver.

As they drew near the school, they became aware of a stretch limousine, a black Cadillac, parked in front of Felthammer House. None of them had seen such a vehicle on the grounds before. Given the dire situation in which they found themselves, they were quick to assume that the limo conveyed to Briarbush Academy yet another threat.

"What if it's her?" Jurgen said. "Maybe she knows what we've done. Maybe she knew the moment we broke the pane in the kitchen door, and now she's back."

Benny shook his head. "She's not supposed to return until tomorrow. And she's more likely to come back in the helicopter."

"I fully concur," said Mengistu. "Let us not be distracted by an ominous-looking car. Time is running out. It is imperative that we put our plan in motion and escape from Briarbush today."

"The plan," Benny said. "Your plan. I guess the time has come that I have a need to know about it."

"Jurgen has a special uncle."

"Special how?"

"He's nice," said Jurgen. "He's nothing like the rest of the family. He's nice, and he's sane, and none of the rest of them will have anything to do with him. They hate him. He'll take us in and never tell them."

"The school won't release you to him."

"Of course not," Jurgen said. "We'll need to escape here and get to him. He lives in Arizona, far from the rest of the family."

"We intend," said Mengistu, "to fade into the forest and hike south approximately seventeen miles to the small town of Smuckville, where we will find the means to make a phone call to Jurgen's uncle, who will then come to transport us to Arizona."

"There's a town named Smuckville?"

"You would not think so, but there is."

"Seventeen miles in these forests might as well be a thousand," Benny said.

"We have a compass and a trail map," Mengistu said. "At this time of year, snakes will not be a problem. We are aware that we must remain on the lookout for bears and cougars. We do not dismiss the possibility we might encounter a depraved and heavily bearded individual who resides in a ramshackle cabin, who lives off the land, and whose unnatural lust compels him to kidnap young girls and boys to be sex slaves until such time as he murders and eats them. However, we are not stupid, and we are determined. We will have our wits and the hope of Arizona. We remain convinced that we will get to Smuckville and ultimately to Arizona unless we both suffer broken legs in a fall or drown in a flash flood or encounter an entire cult of depraved individuals of such number that we are overwhelmed."

Jurgen said, "So are you with us?"

"Absolutely."

They had come to the limousine, which looked long enough to accommodate eight passengers. The engine was idling. The tinted windows were so dark that nothing could be seen of the occupants.

A back door opened, startling the boys, and a woman in a chic black-and-white coat with a fur collar stepped out of the vehicle.

Benny said, "Mother?" She was supposed to be on a one-year around-the-world adventure with Jubal.

"Your stepfather is dead," she announced. "My inheritance is less than I expected. We are no longer able to afford Briarbush. I have disenrolled you from the school, and we must leave now."

Although Benny had become accustomed to a life path marked by sudden switchbacks and hairpin turns, he wasn't ready for this. "But I can't," he objected. "Things are happening here. Important things. I have friends here."

Naomi smiled at Jurgen and Mengistu, but it was such a cold and brittle smile that Benny would have been horrified but not surprised if her lips had cracked apart like fractured ice and fallen off her face. Her coat wasn't tailored from the skins of a hundred and one Dalmatian puppies, but she had a new villainous quality that was darker than the indifference with which she had often treated him. For the first time, his mother reminded him of Grandmother Cosima.

"I've already packed everything in your room, Benny. Omar has put your bags in the trunk. I have an appointment this evening in San Francisco. We must leave at once. Be a good boy and get in the car."

"I have friends here," Benny said plaintively. He'd never had friends before. He'd never really understood what true friends were like until he met Jurgen and Mengistu. Now, after less than three months, he was being taken away from them. He needed to cast his lot with them, risk being eaten by bears, cougars, and heavily bearded degenerates in order to earn a new home in Arizona.

Omar, the black-suited chauffeur, had gotten out from behind the wheel and had come around the limousine as if willing to handle Benny like baggage. A squat, muscular specimen with a beetling brow, he looked as if he ought to have tusks.

Unmoved by her son's plea, Naomi tapped one foot impatiently on the cobblestones. "Say goodbye to your friends and get in the car."

How terrible it was to be young and dependent. How hopeless it seemed when those who had custody of you knew little about you and didn't care to learn more.

Benny couldn't bring himself to say goodbye. He saw unshed tears in Jurgen's and Mengistu's eyes, and his vision blurred, a monumentally embarrassing development. Boys of their age must never admit to the capacity for tears let alone shed them. They stared at one another, struck speechless by the suddenness, the awfulness, the injustice of this development. Benny was seized by the irrational fear that, if he said goodbye, he would never see them again, that the word would be a curse and they would die in the forest. So then if he didn't say goodbye, if they didn't exchange any words, not one, and didn't hug one another and didn't shake hands, maybe they would all survive; perhaps years from now, in some far place, when they least expected it, they would find one another and revive their friendship.

Benny climbed into the limo and slid across the seat, and Naomi got in and sat beside him. Omar closed the door and went around the car and settled behind the wheel.

They drove away.

Benny did not look back.

As the driveway descended from the high meadow into the forest and the gatehouse appeared below, lightning flashed-flashed-flashed so bright that it might have been the announcement of an impending judgment of all things. The crack of thunder was immediate, as if Earth's core were rended pole to pole. In the dazzling storm flares, the trees cast off layer after layer of shadows that seemed to be blown away by a sudden and ferocious gale. Mere wind-driven raindrops rattled against the limousine roof and windows as if they were hard bullets of hail.

This wasn't a day when two boys should engage in a seventeen-mile battle against Nature and all her armory. Nor was it a day when they dared to delay. Benny yearned to be with them.

ONE LAST STOP ON THE JOURNEY TO JUSTICE

As Spike drove away from Palazzo del Coniglio, where F. Upton Theron sprawled dead of a heart attack in the drawing room, Benny Catspaw was amazed that the memory of a lengthy Briarbush incident could pass through his mind in great detail during the two or three minutes he and his companions took to return to the Ford Explorer and cruise off the property. If he'd decided to write a book about the adventures of his youth, typing just the account of his last day as a student at Briarbush would have required a week.

Because he had visited the school five years after the rainy morning when his mother had taken him away, he knew that Jurgen and Mengistu hadn't shown up for dinner that day. When Marshall Cho, one of Mrs. Baneberry-Smith's worker bees, reported seeing them hiking into the woods, they were declared missing. In spite of the valiant efforts of sixty-two trained search-and-rescue specialists, no trace of the boys was found. The wilderness they faded into covered more than twenty-two hundred square miles in which a handful of small towns lay at great distances from one another. Most of the terrain was forbidding. Much of that vastness was so remote, the searchers could have labored half a year, seven days a week, and not visited all the places where the bones of two boys might be moldering. Such endeavors were expensive and couldn't go on forever. The search was called off after ten days.

Benny preferred to believe that his friends had survived and been taken to Arizona by the nice uncle, who somehow acquired for them new identities. He liked to believe they were happy in their new lives. There were more than a few things Benny liked to believe that weren't likely to be true, but he believed them anyway.

Curiously, as they drove out of San Clemente toward the Pacific Coast Highway, one thing Benny had recently begun to hope might be true now became manifestly true, yet initially he found it harder to believe than that Jurgen and Mengistu miraculously survived. The believe-it-or-not moment began with the need to rename the rabbit.

From the back seat, where she sat with the Flemish giant in her lap, Harper said, "I'm not going to keep calling her Arabella. It's a stupid name for a rabbit as cute as she is."

"Call her Snowball," Benny suggested.

"She's not cold. She's snuggly warm."

"Is she sweet?"

"She's very sweet."

"Then call her Sugar."

"Not quite."

"Sugarpie."

"No."

"Sugarplum."

"Hardly."

"Sugarfoot."

"Enough with sugar."

"Creampuff."

"You're terrible at this."

"Fluffy, Floppy, Fuzzy, Frappé, Cottonball—"

"You won't be naming our children."

"—Cottontail, Honeybunny, Blanch. Wait. What did you say?"

"You know what I said."

Spike chimed in. "You know what she said."

Disconcerted, Benny said, "Well, gee, I mean, we sort of met cute, like in the movies, and I like you, and I sort of thought you liked me, but it's not as though we grew up together or like we've been dating for years and years. I haven't, you know, proposed. And yet you're planning a family?"

"Don't be old-fashioned," Harper said. "You don't need to propose. I just did."

"Is that what that was—a proposal?"

"Well?" she said.

"Well what?"

"I won't ask again," she said.

Spike said, "Don't be a dumb Benny."

"What's that mean?" Benny asked.

"You know what it means."

Benny said, "How can we talk about this when I might be dead before the night is out?"

"Hey, hey, hey," Spike protested. "Twice in eighteen hundred years is not a pattern. We already settled that."

Harper sighed. "I'd rather you were my dead fiancé and not just my dead friend. My almost husband. That would give me something to hold fast to in my grief. But you're going to live because I won't have it any other way."

Although a warm, fuzzy feeling came over Benny, he said, "For God's sake, we only met earlier today. How can we know we're right for each other when we haven't known each other an entire day?"

"We met yesterday in Papa Bear's when I served you breakfast."

"Oh, that's right. We've known each other a whole day and a half. Why aren't we already on our honeymoon?"

"It's marriage first with me, mister. You know, I would never have imagined that I'd propose to a man who ordered beer with his breakfast. However, now that we've been hanging out a little and I see how crazy your life is, I understand why you have a problem with stress now and then."

"Benjamin," Spike said, "you should know by now that I'm all about making your life as happy as it can be. That's my mission. My reason to exist. So hear me now when I tell you, Harper and you were made for each other. I knew it from the moment I first saw the two of you, when you came into your living room after I'd just smashed that hideous Swedish chair."

"I'll count to three," Harper said.

Benny said, "This is a huge decision, the biggest decision of our lives."

"One."

Spike let go of the steering wheel with one hand and pinched Benny's cheek. Hard. "Just because Jill Swift dumped you and made a fool of you and wounded your heart doesn't mean that'll happen with Harper. Harper isn't anything like Jill. Anyway, if you discover maybe you're not compatible, you can call off the wedding."

"Like hell," Harper said. "Two."

"My head is spinning," Benny said.

Taking the steering wheel in both hands, Spike said, "Now that you mention your head, that's another thing. With hair like yours, you're not going to receive a lot of proposals from girls as great as Harper."

"Three," she said, and Benny said, "All right!"

"All right what?"

"All right. Am I nuts? I'm not nuts. Of course I'll marry you. I want to marry you. I like you. I've always liked you. I think

I might love you. I'm pretty sure I do. I mean, why wouldn't I? You're great. I'm not sure why a girl as great as you wants to marry me."

"You're fun."

"I'm fun? That's it? Fun is my entire portfolio?"

"Being fun is a big deal, Sugarpie. You're also nice and kind and getting wisdom, and you're just sexy enough."

"Just enough?"

"Too much is always a problem. You're just right."

Spike hooted with delight. "This is so great. You came into the living room and saw the smashed Swedish chair, and I was thinking about destroying that hideous Lucite lamp with the white shade. I saw you two and knew right then you'd be together forever." He took a deep breath and sighed. "Now, about the rabbit."

Harper said, "What about her?"

"Well, she's white as a calla lily. Maybe call her Lily."

"Lily. I like that. Lily. That's pretty. Thank you, Spike."

"*De nada.* When it's time to name the kids, you think I could maybe have a little input? I won't be hurt if you say no."

"Sure. Why not?" Benny said. "Decorate the nursery, too. After all, you're going to be doing a lot of babysitting."

"I'm a very good babysitter. I've been babysitting for many centuries. My previous destiny buddies always found my babysitting skills to be a most useful service in addition to my preventing bad people from destroying them."

"Just don't ever," Benny said, "think that babysitting kids is the same as sidelining them like you did with Fat Bob."

"Bob," said Harper.

The suggestion seemed to offend Spike. "I would never sideline children. That would be a violation of cragglethink."

Harper said, "Your eye trick, pulling your heart out of your chest, that kind of stuff—it might negatively impact psychological development."

"Little kids, sure," Spike agreed. "But most of them, when they get to be nine or ten, they just love that stuff."

"We'll discuss it when the time comes," Benny said. "Now, why are we driving to San Diego instead of time-folding there?"

Spike was chagrinned. "I got so caught up in naming the bunny, and then how the discussion segued into romance, I forgot Llewellyn Urnfield. I'm a sucker for romance. That was a beautiful moment. I'll never forget being part of that beautiful moment, not even a thousand years from now when you're both . . . you know . . . gone."

"I am very touched," Benny said.

So then the coastal highway folded away, and a suburb of San Diego folded into view around them. They coasted to a stop at the address that F. Upton Theron provided.

"This can't be right," Harper said.

They were on a street lined with California live oaks, in a pleasant middle-class neighborhood, in front of a house that could have been a cottage transported out of a Thomas Kinkade painting. The humble but exquisitely quaint structure featured a slate roof, stone walls, sculpted dormers, and French windows of beveled-glass panes that sparkled with amber light. Nestled in a meticulously attended garden of flowers and flowering shrubs, with a lawn that seemed to have been trimmed to perfection using hand shears, the house was magically, subtly illuminated, as was every corner of the landscape. In contrast to the homes around it, the place seemed to have been transported out of a land of elves and hobbits.

"She's a billionaire," Benny said. "So where's the guarded gate, the palatial digs, the ocean view?"

"Maybe there's a sixty-thousand-square-foot basement," Harper said.

(Spike wishes it known he wasn't surprised by Ms. Urnfield's effort to conceal the truth of her enormous wealth behind humble architecture. Over the centuries, he has met many people who are so certain of their righteousness and their entitlement to power that they do not know the truth of themselves. They become convinced of their humility, although they possess none, and of their wisdom, though they have none. They believe passionately in their goodness, though they are evil; they believe they are motivated by a noble desire to make the world a better place, when in fact they merely insist on shaping it to suit their preferences, and to hell with everyone else. According to our resident craggle, they seriously scare him. If you're in a reading group, consider a discussion of the issue.)

As Spike, Harper, and Benny got out of the Explorer, the front door of the cottage opened, but Llewellyn Urnfield didn't appear—unless she was a gray-brindle whippet. The dog padded to the end of the lamplit flagstone entrance walk, stood looking up at them for a moment, then turned back toward the house. When they didn't at once follow, the whippet halted and looked over its shoulder as if to say, *What do you want, a written invitation?*

As they followed the dog toward the open front door, Benny said, "I have a bad feeling about this."

Harper tousled his already disarranged hair. "You have a bad feeling about everything, sweetie."

"Not about you. Not yet. I don't think I ever will. I hope."

"My Romeo."

APPROACHING THE HOME OF LLEWELLYN URNFIELD, BENNY REMEMBERS LEAVING BRIARBUSH WITH HIS MOTHER

Omar hulked in the driver's seat of the superstretch limousine, perhaps regrowing the pointed tusks that had been surgically removed from his face. Benny and his mother sat side by side in a passenger compartment large enough to accommodate them plus everyone in their family who had been murdered over the years. The tinted windows that were almost opaque from outside were clear enough from the inside. The world beyond the car appeared to be coming apart as trees thrashed, debris flew, rain shattered through the day in blinding sheets, and the black underbellies of the clouds were ripped by stilettos of lightning.

"Jubal died in Cairo. Jubal, your stepfather," Naomi clarified, as if Benny was known to suffer from short-term memory loss.

"What happened?" Benny asked.

"He was stabbed to death in an alley in a disreputable part of the city."

"Who stabbed him?"

"We will never know. It is a country that offers no justice to foreigners, and often not to its own people."

"What was he doing in a disreputable part of the city?"

"I am sorry to tell you that your stepfather was not the man I thought. Behind my back, he indulged in perverse practices."

"What practices?"

"Every perverse practice you can imagine. I won't corrupt your young mind by describing or even naming them. When he was brutally murdered, he was on his way to an assignition."

"Ass ignition?"

"It means 'a secret rendezvous for an erotic purpose.'"

"I think it means what some kids do when they gather in a dark dorm room to light their farts."

Putting one hand to her breast as if to calm her shocked heart, Naomi said, "Whatever kind of sick school did Jubal send you to? Do they groom boys at Briarbush to be as perverse as he was?"

"Not really," Benny said. "I never saw a fart-lighting party, but I heard about them. At Briarbush, they're up to weirder stuff than that. Anyway, I think the right word is 'assig*nation*.'"

Naomi's expression soured further. "Just three months in that hoity-toity boarding school, and you think you know more than your mother. I won't tolerate being condescended to by my own child."

"I'm sorry. I just thought—"

"It's best that you don't think. Thinking too much can get a boy in a lot of trouble."

After a mutual silence, Benny said, "When is the funeral?"

"There was no funeral. Who organizes a funeral for a stinking pig? He was cremated in Cairo. I was so disgusted, so repulsed, by what I learned about his sick desires, on which he spent *fortunes*, that I emptied his ashes into a sewer drain and donated the empty memorial urn to a beggar boy for whatever use he might make of it to improve his life."

"And now we're broke?"

"It isn't good." From her Gucci purse, Naomi retrieved a small, round, ceramic pillbox and a tiny silver spoon. She unscrewed the lid of the box, spooned a white powder from the container, inhaled it through her left nostril, and repeated the process with her right nostril. "A prescription for my irregular heartbeat. I've been so stressed you can't imagine." She returned the paraphernalia to her purse. "The creep spent so lavishly on his lifestyle, as if there was no end to the money, and he spent even more lavishly to fulfill his hideous, demented, unspeakable desires. In the end, he pissed away a four-hundred-million-dollar inheritance. By the time the house in Beverly Hills is sold, as well as the residences in Rio and on the Côte d'Azur, when the estate is settled, I will be left with only sixty or seventy million."

Benny did a little math. "Briarbush costs two hundred thousand a year."

"Plus your allowance, your uniforms, books. It's exorbitant. Outrageous. I've made other arrangements for sixty thousand a year through your eighteenth birthday."

Alarmed, Benny said, "Not Grandma Cosima."

"No, no, no. That old bitch would want twice as much. Anyway, I have cut her off entirely. I no longer talk to my mother and intend never to see her again. She'd pry and pry and pry until eventually she'd figure it out, and then there would be no satisfying her, the greedy old witch."

"Figure what out?"

"Never mind. You wouldn't understand, Benny. You're too young to understand. Anyway, there's nothing to figure out."

Mile by mile, the storm intensified until it seemed as if it were not a meteorological event, not mere weather, but a planetary catastrophe: as though the trees were thrashed not by wind, but by the ground beneath them quaking violently; the rain not rain at all, but the oceans cast from their depths and thrown upon the land by a wobble and abrupt change in the rotation of the Earth. It was not a time to be alone—or with a mother who made you feel alone.

"I had friends," Benny said.

"What do you mean?"

"Two friends at Briarbush. I never had friends before."

"Of course you had friends before."

"No. Not ever before."

"Well, if you've had no friends, it's because you've always been standoffish."

He disagreed. "It's because I never had a chance before."

He was aware of her staring at him with analytic severity, but he focused his attention on the clenched fists in his lap. He was perhaps beginning to figure it out, the business in Cairo, and he didn't want to see anything in her eyes that would confirm what he was thinking.

She said, "Sometimes you're such a strange boy, Benny. I don't always understand you, but I try. Do you realize how much I try to understand you?"

He dared not answer that question. He said, "Where are you taking me?"

"From San Francisco, you will fly south to Los Angeles. You're going to live with a woman of great learning, Fernsehen Liebhaber, who will homeschool you."

"What kind of name is that?"

"You can call her Dr. Liebhaber or Mrs. Liebhaber. Don't call her Fern unless she invites you to."

"Where are you going? Where will you be living?"

"I have had a hard life, honey. Under the thumb of Cosima until I met and married Big Al. You remember your father, Big Al?"

"It's only been six years since I saw him shot in the back."

"Six years," she mused. "It seems like a lifetime ago until you put a date to it. Anyway, Big Al was a domineering brute. Cosima and Big Al and then Jubal, the pervert. I've had a hard life."

Benny still stared at his hands. He hadn't consciously opened his fists, but they were open. They were on his thighs, palms up. Something about his hands was sad. They looked like hands that had forgotten how to grasp and hold, like hands that had given up trying to do anything.

"I've had a hard life," Naomi repeated. "But I've found a place that makes me happy. Happy at last. I've bought a house on Lake Como in Italy. The rooms are full of light, and the view is lovely. The food, Benny! Such wonderful restaurants within a short walk, one for every day of the week, and wines the equal of the food."

"When will I see you?"

"Oh, often, often. Whenever I'm in the States, we'll have fun together. We'll do exciting things."

Benny didn't want to go to Italy. He no longer wanted to be with his mother as he'd once so very much wanted to be with her. Nevertheless, he had to ask, "Why can't I go to the house on Lake Como?"

"Oh, honey, it's very different in Italy. You don't speak the language. The customs. The way people are. You'd be lost. You would never make friends there. You need to finish homeschooling here in America—and *then* the world is your oyster."

"I guess that makes sense," he lied.

"It makes perfect sense. You'll love Dr. Liebhaber, and you'll be a cultivated young man when she's done with you. So . . . it's at least four more hours to San Francisco, even as fast as Omar drives. Tell me about Briarbush, I want to hear all about it."

"You wouldn't believe me if I told you," Benny said.

"Of course I would. Why wouldn't I believe you? You've always been a truthful boy."

"Well," he said, "in some Asian jungle, Mrs. Baneberry-Smith was bitten by a dying extraterrestrial that injected her with all the knowledge of its race. So then, back at Briarbush, she starts doing transspecies experiments, and Prescott Galsbury—"

"Wait, wait. Who is Mrs. Baneberry-Smith?"

"She *was* the wife of Lionel Baneberry-Smith but—"

"And who is this Lionel?"

"The headmaster. But he supposedly fell down—"

"Headmaster? What's a headmaster?"

After a hesitation, Benny said, "That's what they call the person who runs a school like Briarbush."

"Why wouldn't they call him the principal?"

"I thought you would have met him."

"Jubal made all the arrangements. I wouldn't have known about boarding schools, how to find the right one, how to handle that. Now what about Mrs. Baneberry-Smith's experiments?"

Benny's hands rested on his thighs, palms up, fingers curled like the legs of some pale, dead insect. "See, that was just a movie I saw. I was gonna try to make it sound like something that really happened at Briarbush."

"Why would you do that?"

"Well, I guess to entertain you. Briarbush was a boring place. I just wanted to make it entertaining for you."

After a silence, Naomi said, "The limo has a fabulous audio system, and it's got Sirius radio. Why don't we listen to music?"

"That sounds nice."

"What kind of music do you like?"

"Whatever you like."

"I'll pick something fun."

"Okay."

"In the ice there, we've got bottles of water and coconut water and unsweetened ice tea. Get whatever you'd like."

"I will."

"We've also got snacks. Healthy chips, some French crackers, sunflower seeds, meatless jerky made out of something or other."

"Sounds good," he said.

San Francisco seemed as far away as Cairo.

Because of its warm color, the lamplit flagstone path reminded Benny of the Yellow Brick Road in the movie, but he didn't feel like dancing along it. He followed Harper, Spike, and the whippet, which glided on its long legs, head high, tail wagless. The dog led them into a residence with numerous bookshelves crammed full of volumes.

Otherwise, the inside of the house had nothing in common with the exterior. There were tens of millions of dollars' worth of scary-as-hell expressionist and abstract expressionist art on the walls. As they passed canvases, Spike said, "Francis Bacon. Never learned to draw. Used smudges, whorls, jagged slashes, and disturbing shapes to alarm the viewer. Edvard Munch. Lived most of his life on the edge of insanity, spent time in an asylum, serious alcoholic. Ah, Jackson Pollack. Had very little instruction in art. Threw the paint at the canvas, dripped it, applied it with sticks and even turkey basters. Serious alcoholic. Died in a car accident. All three adored for the incoherence represented in their work, and highly collectible."

The dog led them into a kitchen as stark as Benny's, although it was black and white, rather than all white. On the far side of a central island, a woman was standing between two commodious swivel stools with backs and arms.

A book lay open in front of one of the stools. Beside it were a glass of red wine, a fork, a napkin, and a white dish that contained what appeared to be steak tartare garnished with capers and chopped onions.

The woman picked up the whippet and placed it on one of the stools. The dog delicately licked her hand before it curled up as though to sleep.

"Llewellyn Urnfield," said Spike.

"Who else?" she asked. "I am who I am." She sat on the second stool with the imperious expression of a judge, and they stood on the other side of the island, facing her, as if they were attorneys summoned to the bench to be reprimanded for courtroom antics.

She was fiftysomething, almost as thin as an issue of *Vogue*, her shoulder-length blond hair styled without bangs and as straight as if she slept hanging by it from a ceiling fixture. In her youth, she must have been an austere beauty with a mystical quality. Now, with her flawless skin and chiseled features, she was still lovely, though severe.

"Upton informed me about what happened to Oliver Lambert at his most recent ill-conceived celebration of excess. Upton expected you, Mr. Catspaw, to visit him in the company of this colorful little jejunity. I have not heard from him since then, but evidently you have visited him and somehow obtained my name from him."

"He's dead," Spike said.

"I have not addressed you," Urnfield said. "You will have the courtesy to wait until I do."

Benny said, "We didn't kill Mr. Theron. Not technically. He died of a heart attack. We adopted his rabbit. She's in the car."

"Please attend me carefully, Mr. Catspaw. If Upton is indeed deceased, that is an inconvenience to our movement. However, I am not to any degree emotionally affected by the death of a ninety-year-old man who, while sharing my views on the reorganization of society, was otherwise repellent both in appearance and personal habits. Nor do I care how he died, whether of a heart attack or a hatchet to the head. As for his rabbit, its future care, and its current whereabouts—in my experience, your talent for tiresome conversation is second to none. If you insist on injecting endless details of no significance that extend this meeting beyond reason, then I shall be most displeased. Do you understand me?"

"Yes, ma'am."

"You will excuse me, Mr. Catspaw, if I have little confidence in your ability to understand anything. What is it you think that you understand about what I have just told you?"

"You're in charge of this meeting—this confrontation, powwow, whatever it is—and we're not to speak until spoken to."

"And?"

"And. Uh." She looked nothing like Grandma Cosima, but Benny wouldn't have been surprised to learn they had been conjoined at birth and shortly after had been surgically separated. "Well, I guess, we're supposed to keep our responses on point and succinct."

Her raised eyebrows conveyed the same emphasis as would have two exclamation points on a written reply. "Whatever lies between your ears is gaseous, but at least it provides minimal function."

Harper said, "I know what 'jejunity' means. It's the noun form of the word *jejune*. You've just called me juvenile, immature, and insipid."

Llewellyn Urnfield produced a smile sharp enough to sever a carotid artery. "I am aware that little learning occurs when you attend a government institution, especially when your school day is interrupted by cheerleader practice and daydreaming about copulation with the football team. Therefore, I can only admire that you have taken a course to improve your vocabulary in the wake of your sad miseducation. However, I encourage you to consider that I have had the benefit of the finest finishing school followed by degrees taken at two superb universities, and that my family has possessed great wealth for generations, ensuring both that I could devastate you in a battle of wits or have you killed without consequences. You would be well advised to heed my advice to Mr. Catspaw."

Benny half expected Harper to fling herself across the kitchen island and take Llewellyn Urnfield out of her barstool. Of course she did no such thing, and even with his gaseous brain, he could deduce why Harper restrained herself. Urnfield had such confidence in her authority over other people that anyone might infer it must be based on more than the mere assumption of superiority, that the woman possessed a lethal power enabling her to turn an attacker to ashes in an instant. Besides, at least in the short term, Urnfield's vitriol was strangely entertaining.

"Mr. Catspaw," she said, "those of us who have taken it upon ourselves to develop algorithms that identify dangerous individuals such as you—we aren't stupid. Indeed, we're the best and brightest. Yet we are often surprised by how ineffective you people are when we destroy your careers, how little most of you are able to grasp that a powerful organization has devised your destruction. Perhaps this is because we choose our targets early in their lives, before they have acquired much wisdom, when they regard everyone with good will and don't yet understand that some of us do not regard them in the same let-live spirit. Indeed, we work tirelessly to identify them ever earlier in their lives, so that we can eliminate the threat they pose to a perfect society before they even begin to know what they believe, before they develop the ability to influence others, when they're still naive fools as pathetic as you."

"Gee," Benny said, "that's a little harsh, don't you think?"

"I *do* think, Mr. Catspaw, and quite deeply about many things that you have never thought about in your life. In time, we hope to identify our targets when they are in elementary school and disable them psychologically at such an early age they will achieve nothing of which they were once capable. We have been aware for some time that there must be a mysterious organization assisting some of our targets, undoing our fine work, promoting creatures like you into successful lives on the very path that we find unacceptable. Never, however, has one of them identified us so quickly, and none has dared to come after us and confront us as you have this night."

"I'm proud of being uniquely dedicated to my destiny buddies," Spike said.

"Shut up," said Llewellyn Urnfield. "Mr. Catspaw, you will tell me how you have accomplished this, and you will withhold nothing if you value the life of this perky piece of fluff in her pink cap."

Benny said, "Hey, you can't—"

"I haven't given you permission to speak, Mr. Catspaw." She looked at Spike as he opened his mouth. "Nor have I yet asked to hear a word from *you.* If you think I'm intimidated because you look like Bigfoot after a full-body shave, you don't understand who I am and what terrible power I possess. This ponytailed popsy is a dead girl standing if that's what you want. Now, we will pause in our discussion."

She picked up the fork, ate some of the steak tartare, ate some more, put down the fork, sipped the wine, and then savored another sip.

The whippet had fallen asleep, as if so accustomed to her mistress's rants that they no longer entertained her. She was snoring.

After patting her lips with the napkin, Urnfield said, "Very well, Mr. Catspaw, now you will tell me how you made your way from Handy Duroc, that hopeless striver, to Upton and hence to me."

Recalling his uncle Talmadge Clerkenwell's admonition never to reveal the truth of Spike to anyone, Benny said, "I can't say. I'm under an enjoinment in the matter."

"'Enjoinment,'" said Harper, "meaning he's under an injunction not to speak about this."

"A sacred injunction," Benny said.

"'Sacred'? Are you out of your mind, using such an excuse with me of all people?"

Spike said, "Before our friend, the perky piece of fluff, is instantly incinerated, allow me to explain who I am, what I am, and how we came to be here. Unlike Benjamin, I am not enjoined from doing so."

WAITING WHILE MS. URNFIELD EATS MORE STEAK TARTARE, BENNY REMEMBERS DR. FERNSEHEN LIEBHABER

For five years, until he turned eighteen, Benny lived in a suburb of Los Angeles with Dr. Fernsehen Liebhaber, while his mother found her bliss on the fabled shores of Lake Como, in Italy. Naomi never returned to the United States during those five years, but she sent Benny a check for five hundred dollars on every birthday and one thousand at Christmas, always with a different postcard of some picturesque spot in that far corner of the world. On each postcard she wrote a few endearing words. Toward the end of her second year abroad, she wrote, *Vittorio is everything Big Al and Jubal were not. I am the luckiest woman alive! Merry Christmas and Happy New Year to you and to the good doctor.* Naomi did not explain who Vittorio was, but by then Benny was fifteen and could figure it out.

Fernsehen Liebhaber was a retired child psychologist, not a medical doctor, but she was good. Good enough. She didn't torture Benny either physically or mentally. She was pleasant but not companionable. On Benny's first day in her house, she said, "Child, I have nothing against you. But I don't want to spend more than fifteen minutes of the day talking to you. I will provide you with excellent meals, but we won't take them together. Please understand that I spent thirty-five grueling years counseling the children at the finest, most expensive private school in Los Angeles County, listening to their whiny complaints, quieting the many fears their parents actively instilled in them and the fears their parents unintentionally saddled them with, treating their neuroses, walking on eggshells around those among them who had developed into full-blown psychopaths. While I do wish you and all young people the best of everything, I am exhausted, burnt-out. While I believe you are different and unspoiled, I am nonetheless sick to death of children. Read the schoolwork I give you, complete assignments diligently, stay out of trouble and out of my hair, and we'll be happy together, or as happy as anyone can be in this mad world populated by legions who have lost all understanding of why they're here, where they're going, or what it all means. Do we have an understanding?"

"Yes."

"This house," she continued, "contains a few thousand books. They are mostly novels. I grew so disillusioned with psychology and all the social sciences that I trashed every book of that kind. At one time, I enjoyed reading history, but most of what is published these days is so unhistorical that one of my primary arteries, less elastic year by year, will pop if I read more of that. I engaged a document-disposal company to come by with a truck-size shredder and watched while they turned all those volumes into confetti. I came to the conclusion that truth could be found only in good fiction, and for years I took enormous pleasure in reading well-written novels. But a moment came when I'd had more than enough of the truths those works conveyed, and since then I have read nothing other than books of jokes intended to be left by the toilet for those occasions when one's system is not functioning optimally. I've kept all the novels for sentimental reasons. You may read any you wish, but you must never attempt to have a conversation with me about them. Is that clear?"

"Yes."

"I have now said more to you than I am likely to say in the next two weeks. If there is anything you need or desire that is not an urgent matter, write your request rather than come to me with it, and fix it to the door of the fridge with the magnet that looks like a waif out of a Dickens novel. Are you all right with the terms as I have outlined them?"

"Yes."

"Do you have any questions?"

"No."

"I like you already, child. Now go be happy like me."

Dr. Fernsehen Liebhaber had two interests that, fully indulged, made her so happy that sometimes she broke into song, upbeat tunes like "What a Wonderful World" and "Somewhere Over the Rainbow" and "Crocodile Rock." The first of her passions was food. In her youth and even to the end of her career, she'd been tall and thin, a bit long in the face and lanky, but attractive. Now she was as round faced and rosy cheeked and ample as Mrs. Santa Claus, matronly and fun to look at because she was pleased with her life. She was so light on her feet that she seemed always to be dancing. Her second enthusiasm was television. Every room of her house featured a set with a screen as large as could be accommodated. She spent her days watching game shows, old film comedies, hit TV comedy series from decades ago, and talent competitions. She said that by filling her brain with works of merriment and frolic, she might be able to empty it of everything she wished she had never put in it.

During that half decade, Benny read all the many novels that Dr. Liebhaber had collected. He learned more about her from the books she liked than from the interaction he had with her. More self-schooled than homeschooled, he lived in her residence as if they were two hermits in a hermitage. He gained no friends during those five years except for the acquaintances he made in the pages of his favorite stories. Considering the nature of his former life under the roofs of Big Al and Cosima Springbok and Jubal Catspaw (where he was tutored by Mordred Merrick), this period provided him with a peace he'd never known before, an absence of sociopaths and the dark dramas they so effectively authored. In the strangest way, the loneliness was medicinal; those years were a time of healing.

Of course it came to an abrupt end.

When Dr. Liebhaber's five-year contract with Naomi expired, the good doctor said, "You must be out of my house by noon Friday, your eighteenth birthday. You have been an exemplary tenant, clean and quiet, in no way any bother. I wish you well, but I'll be relieved to be rid of you. For five years, there has been something about you that troubled me. During the second year of your time here, I put my finger on it. Niceness. Unrelieved niceness. You're too nice to be real. For two years, I couldn't be rid of a certain tension arising from the conviction that such niceness must be a pretense, a ruse, a cloak under which hid someone more complex and problematic. I have lived all my life among dissemblers, pretenders, impostors, and deceivers. I know what to expect of their kind. Incredibly, halfway through your fourth year, I realized your niceness was genuine. To no degree whatsoever a pretense. This unsettled me more than the possibility that you might be a monster masquerading as an angel. I have seen what life does to those who are sort of nice but much less nice than you are. They suffer. I don't wish to suffer. With concern that your niceness might exert a damaging influence on me—that it might, so to speak, rub off on me a little—I began making a greater effort to avoid you, and in my private moments, I have practiced mean thoughts about you and the world in general."

Bewildered, Benny said, "But you *are* nice. You've always been very nice."

Dr. Liebhaber's expression of abhorrence would have been more appropriate if Benny had flung a handful of feces at her. "Do not put that burden on me, young man. I am a selfish old bitch, and I love who I am. Don't you go trying to change me. Between now and noon Friday, we will see no more of each other and exchange not another word."

And so it was.

On Thursday morning, an attorney named Emmet Spoils rang the doorbell. Thin and hairless, he looked like a gecko in a suit. He was accompanied by a slinky notary public named Imogene Mott. Benny welcomed them into the parlor. Mr. Spoils represented Naomi Catspaw. He had brought a cashier's check for $206,455. This sum would be settled on Benny as a gift to get him started in his adult life.

"To receive it," Spoils said, "you must sign a nondisclosure agreement, a release, and other documents required by your mother."

"Okay," Benny said.

"You must read them first, in front of me and Miss Mott, who will witness your signature. You will be acknowledging that this is an act of pure generosity, that you have no rightful claim to your mother's estate either when she is living or after she is dead."

"Sure," Benny said.

With the stern expression of a Scandinavian adolescent activist predicting planetary destruction on TV, Spoils said, "You must agree never to speak negatively about your mother in public and never to write negatively about her for publication."

"Why would I?" Benny asked.

The attorney's face pleated in an expression of manifold suspicions. "You will also be agreeing never to seek her out or to make any attempt to contact her. Should you do so, you will then be required to return this gift in full, with interest at whatever rate has prevailed in the time you have had its use."

"All right."

After a silence, Spoils said, "Mr. Catspaw, it is important that I can swear under oath, if it comes to such an occasion, that you signed these documents with full awareness that your mother's fortune is now worth in excess of ninety-five million dollars."

"Oh, good," Benny said. "She's made some great investments with the seventy million from Jubal's estate. I've always known she was smarter than people gave her credit for."

Spoils and Mott exchanged a puzzled look, and then the lawyer said, "And you understand that everything you will ever realize from that estate is two hundred and six thousand four hundred and fifty-five dollars. Does that seem adequate to you?"

"Wow, yeah. It's a lot more than I expected. I didn't expect anything. One thing worries me."

"Ah," said Spoils, as Mott said, "Here we go."

"Is Mother's health all right? Is she well?" Benny asked.

"Well? Yes. She's perfectly well." The attorney's eyes narrowed as though Benny had begun to emit a dangerously bright light. "Why would you ask? What do you mean to imply?"

"It's just, you said I have no claim while she's living or after she's dead. I thought maybe she's ill."

"No, no. That was just a statement of terms. She is not ill. She's in excellent health."

Benny sighed with relief. "That's great. You had me worried there, the way you phrased it."

After making coffee for Spoils and Mott, serving it with a plate of St. Michel French butter cookies with sea salt, Benny read the documents while his guests sipped and nibbled.

He signed the various papers. He inked his thumbprint in Imogene Mott's record book. He accepted the cashier's check.

Subsequent to the attorney and the notary's departure, Benny spent an hour writing a thank-you-and-goodbye note to Dr. Liebhaber. He placed it on the kitchen table with five hundred dollars of his unspent birthday and Christmas money, so she could buy something special that she enjoyed eating.

One day ahead of schedule, he left Dr. Liebhaber's house with his luggage. He found a motel and rented a room for one week. He selected a bank and opened an account with the cashier's check.

After five years of hermitry, he found the world to be much bigger than he remembered, with unlimited possibilities. Of the numberless things he could have done, he chose first to return to Briarbush Academy.

URNFIELD UNCHAINED

When Llewellyn Urnfield finished most of the steak tartare with all of the chopped onions and capers, she saved a portion of the meat for the whippet, whose name turned out to be Virginia Woolf. Benny thought Sylvia Plath would have been just as literary a name and less precious, but because it wasn't his whippet, he kept his opinion to himself. Virginia Woolf finessed the meat from Urnfield's fingers with admirable delicacy. The dog accepted the second morsel, licked her lips discreetly, put her head down on her paws, and went to sleep again.

After patting her mouth with a napkin and taking another sip of red wine, Urnfield surveyed her three visitors, where they stood on the far side of the kitchen island. Her disdain was of such pungency that Benny's nostrils twitched.

"Mr. Catspaw," she said, "you have no idea how much I detest you and your kind."

Benny said, "I have a pretty good idea."

"You do *not* have an idea. You only think you have an idea. You're incapable of conceiving of the weight and complexity of my contempt for you. Do you know what the difference is between you and me, Mr. Catspaw?"

"I'll probably be wrong about that, too, but I'll give it a try. People keep telling me I'm nice."

"That's better, but it does not define the fullness of our difference. And what has being nice ever gotten you?"

"I don't know. Not much, I guess."

"Then why do you continue on that unfortunate path?"

Benny shrugged. "I can't seem to help it."

"How wretched your life must be. Another and more important difference between us is that you work for your money, and my money works for me."

"You inherited billions."

"Wealth is genetic, Mr. Catspaw. If it hadn't passed to me from my parents' estate, I would have earned it quickly in some high-tech endeavor. Having inherited it has allowed me to devote myself to the betterment of the world. With no need to labor to meet my quotidian needs, I spend my time thinking about issues that have perplexed humanity for centuries—and finding solutions. My IQ is a hundred eighty. I won't embarrass you by asking what yours might be."

"Thank you."

"'Quotidian' in that context," Harper said, "means *everyday*. That's all it means. Your everyday needs."

Urnfield said, "You are a tedious person. If you wish to live long enough to give birth to the next generation of space fillers, do not interrupt me again. Now, Mr. Catspaw, indulge my curiosity by answering one more question as best you can. I am a billionaire many times over, and yet I live in a middle-class neighborhood. I have no live-in help, only a day staff. To all appearances, I do not employ any extraordinary security. Why do you suppose I choose to live in such humble circumstances?"

After considering a Francis Bacon painting above a counter, between two Sub-Zero refrigerators, a composition so unnerving that it would give nightmares to an axe murderer who'd always enjoyed sweet dreams prior to seeing it, Benny said, "It's humble except for a couple hundred million worth of paintings by deranged alcoholics."

Urnfield's sigh conveyed contempt no less effectively than her words. "Please refrain from pretending that you know anything about art, Mr. Catspaw. Pollock, Munch, and the others whose work hangs here were alcoholics, but Mr. Bacon was not. Are you unable to answer my question?"

"I guess you live here because you want to appear humble."

"You have just said something of such profound ignorance that your ability to dress and feed yourself is called into question. Allow me to enlighten you. I do not care whether I am thought humble or brilliant or elegant. Other people's opinions of me matter not at all, because if I did care about that, I would be just like them. I occupy this residence because I have no interest in status symbols and lavish expressions of wealth. I see enormous wealth as having one and only one useful purpose—power. Every civilization currently in existence has been misbuilt and grossly mismanaged. I mean to use my power—and encourage others like me to use their wealth—to set the world right, reset it, remake it so that what we create can never be unmade or in any way altered."

"That's a big job," Benny said.

"Yes, I am aware. However, I'm not afraid of how much work lies ahead. We have numerous programs, not just the one by which you were targeted. But we will persevere. We will not let the little people defeat us."

"You shouldn't worry about the little people," Benny advised. "There aren't that many of them, and their life expectancy is often not good. Besides, they never have a lot of money unless they play elves and hobbits in hit movies."

Llewellyn Urnfield stared at him, slammed by a rare moment of befuddlement. "I can make no sense of what you said, Mr.

Catspaw. Are you *trying* to be stupid, or is it simply that you can't help it? Never mind. That was a rhetorical question."

To Benny, Harper said, "She really thinks she's untouchable, invulnerable."

Either Urnfield didn't hear that statement or was incapable of hearing it. She turned her attention to Spike. "You. What did you say your name was?"

"Spike."

"You said you could explain yourself, who you are, how you came to be here. I am now prepared to listen, though I advise you to be succinct, as I am a busy woman."

Spike obliged. "I am a craggle."

"You appear not at all craggy. You have polish, and you look like a big lump of muscle."

"Craggle. Not craggy. As best it can be explained to one of your species," Spike elucidated, "a craggle is for the most part a benign supernatural creature whose mission is to help nice people lead safe and meaningful lives when they find themselves thwarted and abused by such as yourself—nice people who could contribute to the world in ways that improve it and lift the spirits of others, do good where you would do evil."

Having sampled her wine during that speech, Llewellyn Urnfield put her glass down. "Good and evil are relative concepts, therefore meaningless. To hurry your recitation along, I should tell you that I am quite impervious to insults."

"As I observed earlier. In short, I'm Benjamin's bodyguard, friend, and destiny buddy. I am about to show you abilities that will convince you that you're overmatched and should back off, quit tormenting your moral betters, and retreat to whatever snake hole you came from. If you don't die of a heart attack or go mad from what you are about to see, then you won't remember what I've told and shown you. However, the terror will remain with you, festering into such a host of phobias that you're no longer competent enough to carry on with your schemes to remake the world as you wish."

Again, Urnfield produced a smile as sharp as a razor and as curved as a chef's mezzaluna. "I forget nothing. I remember every resentment I've harbored since the cradle."

"Then your heart must be very black," Spike said. "Mine is not. Here, I'll show you."

As with F. Upton Theron, he tore his beating heart from his chest and held it out to her, blood dripping on the island.

Urnfield twitched but didn't flinch, eased back an inch in her seat but didn't recoil. "What trick is this?"

"Trick?" said Spike. "No, I think it's very real, but I'll take a closer look."

His eyes reeled out of his sockets on tethers of muscle and blood vessels and optic nerves, hovering around the throbbing heart, peering at it from this angle and that.

Evidently, Llewellyn Urnfield was far more detached from sanity than she had seemed heretofore. She regarded this display as though it was of interest but not as shocking and horrific as things she witnessed every day. Like maybe a long flow of snakes slithering out of a water faucet. Or her daytime employees butchering live babies to eat for lunch. Or floors and walls swarming with huge cockroaches that had human heads. The kind of things chronic alcoholics saw when they suffered delirium tremens.

She said, "You'll draw a crowd when you go to Comic-Con, but the reaction will be much greater if you take the time to design a better costume than the clothes you're wearing now."

Then she proved to have a vicious surprise of her own. On her side of the island, from a shelf concealed under the countertop, she withdrew a pistol that had a round already chambered, and she shot Harper Harper.

WHEN HARPER IS SHOT, BENNY IS TOO SHOCKED TO DWELL ON MEMORIES OF HIS RETURN TO BRIARBUSH, BUT HERE IS PART OF WHAT HAPPENED BACK THEN

During the fourth of his five peaceful years with the good Dr. Fernsehen Liebhaber, Benny had emerged from hermitry long enough to take driving lessons and get a license to operate a motor vehicle.

Now, on Saturday, after two days on his own, one day after his eighteenth birthday, he purchased a used Honda and started the long drive north to Briarbush Academy. He didn't entirely understand why he felt compelled to return to the campus. He didn't yet know that Mengistu and Jurgen had vanished into the forest on the day Naomi had come in the limousine to take him away, and he did not know that a team of sixty-two search-and-rescue specialists had been unable to find the slightest trace of them.

(It is vital to keep in mind that the disheartening information about Mengistu's and Jurgen's fate was previously imparted during a sequence set in the present day, long after Benny made the journey that is about to be recounted here. In that scene, he was recalling the one now unspooling. This is sometimes how stories must unfold, and there's nothing to be done about it but to issue a clarification and friendly reminder as provided here.)

Even if the boys hadn't died in an attempted escape, they would no longer be at Briarbush, for Jurgen would be nineteen and Mengistu would be twenty. No student remained at the academy past the age of eighteen. In part, Benny made the journey in the hope that he could persuade the alumni affairs office to provide him with the current addresses for the only two friends he'd ever made.

He was also curious, of course, as to whether Mrs. Baneberry-Smith was still the headmistress and whether she had turned the entire student body into gray-eyed worker bees, as well as to what extent and purpose she had been able to apply the extraterrestrial science that had been injected into her with a vicious bite.

(It is no less vital to keep in mind that in the present-day chapter titled "Do No Harm," it was revealed that the headmistress blew herself up along with several Briarbush students, a tragedy for the boys who were killed but perhaps a happy development for a world spared from the evils of alien technology. This current chapter is set earlier in Benny's life than "Do No Harm," when he hadn't yet learned about the explosion.)

Considering the horrors Benny witnessed during his short time as a student at the remote boarding school, one would be excused for finding it curious that he would return there knowing that he might be risking his freedom and even his life. However, friends are what make life worth living; when a person has had only two friends—and then for less than three months—the desire to reconnect with them after half a decade can be irresistible regardless of the danger.

Furthermore, he felt drawn by something he could not name. The figure of the astonishingly well-proportioned headmistress, clad all in black and carrying a whip, loomed vividly in his mind's eye. He didn't want to believe that he was in the grip of a debased erotic compulsion, but he knew himself well enough to know that he didn't fully know himself. At times during the long drive, he could hear the voice that had spoken to him and his friends in the language of another world and had issued from the head of Lionel Baneberry-Smith as it floated inside the levitating glass sphere; most likely, what he heard now was a memory of that voice, though he could not rule out the possibility that it was more sinister than a mere memory.

For whatever reason in addition to those, he drove north from the suburban sprawl around Los Angeles, stayed overnight in Santa Rosa, north of San Francisco, and continued early the next morning toward the unknown.

Sunday afternoon, Nature acknowledged Benny's brave but perhaps foolish return to Briarbush by creating an atmosphere identical to that on the day when his mother had whisked him away in a limousine. The overcast was the disturbing gray of morbid tissue and riven by black lesions. A funereal pre-storm calm lay over all, and the dark evergreens were like gigantic monastic mourners whose robes hung motionless in the still air.

At the bottom of the approach road to the school, the windows of the guardhouse were boarded over, and the security gate stood open, seeming to indicate that nothing was as it had once been at Briarbush. On the high plateau, the extensive lawns had not been mown in a long time, the grass having grown as tall everywhere as always it had been in the wilder meadow. The school, dormitories, and other buildings forming the quadrangle were as impressive as ever, monuments to the mastery of the masons who constructed them and to the institution's storied past. However, though not fallen into ruins, the structures were without signs of life and appeared to have been abandoned.

Benny parked his Honda on the driveway, where weeds bristled between the cobblestones, and went first to the main entrance of Felthammer House. The great wooden door proved to be locked and in need of maintenance; the carved image of a knight astride a horse was weather damaged, in need of fresh coats of stain and sealant. The windows revealed no lights inside, no sign of occupants. He would have liked to visit the room he had shared with Jurgen five years earlier. But perhaps it was just as well he didn't take this sentimental journey only to discover, as he surely would, that it led to melancholy rather than a warm nostalgic wistfulness.

He waded through the tall grass to the nearest quadrangle gate and opened it and stepped into that vast limestone-paved courtyard. The center fountain stood waterless. The eight marble statues of famous philosophers, once placed at intervals, no longer stood on their plinths. Surely they had been sold to an art dealer. But Benny smiled as he thought the eight might have come to life and, keenly aware that they didn't belong in this place of little learning and much indoctrination, had hiked away to another institution where they were appreciated.

Although Benny was sure now that his visit here would not gain him any knowledge regarding the whereabouts of Jurgen and Mengistu, that he would have to seek a lead on them elsewhere, he nevertheless crossed the quadrangle to Seidlitz Hall, which had housed classrooms and administration offices. If the academy's files hadn't been destroyed but instead packed up in hope that the school might one day reopen, maybe they were still here, where he could access them.

As he was trying the locked door, a voice behind him said, "May I help you, young fella?"

Startled, Benny turned and saw a man wearing a long-sleeved ankle-length white tunic belted with a cincture and over that a full-length white cope fastened across the upper chest by a clasp. The cope featured a hood that was at the moment not raised.

White socks and sneakers completed the outfit. He carried a wooden staff as might have a shepherd on a Greek isle in the distant past.

"My name is Knute Pebbity, but I prefer to be called Brother Sunshine since I ordained myself in the church."

"What church is that?" Benny asked.

"The Church of Earth."

Brother Sunshine's hair and beard were white, his face tanned and weathered. His left eye was blue, and the right was green, and they were open very wide. He might have been fiftysomething.

"I'm Benny. I used to go to school here. For a short while."

"I myself never attended Briarbush. I'm a former Army Ranger and currently an employee of the Internal Security Agency, which some people refer to as the American gestapo, though I don't see myself as a fascist, especially not since I ordained myself. I've been assigned to live here, stand watch, monitor developments, and report weekly to my superiors regarding unusual occurrences, if any—of which there are plenty. I don't believe you're unusual enough to report, but we'll see."

Benny didn't want to be judgmental, though he could not help but be wary of Brother Sunshine. "I'm surprised that the Internal Security Agency hires clergymen as agents."

"Oh, I wasn't self-ordained when I started here. That happened after a few months because of what I saw. Washington assigned me to Briarbush not because they needed a clergyman in the position but because I was functionally insane."

"Ah. What does that mean—'functionally insane'?"

For whatever reason, Brother Sunshine looked at the storm sky, raised his staff, shook it, and shouted, *"Fulgur Prohibeo!"* Then he turned his attention to Benny. "I'm insane but capable of doing my job. Thus functional. I'm not one of your *dangerous* madmen types."

"That's good to know."

"I was driven insane by the war."

"What war was that?"

"The secret war I'm not allowed to talk about. They sent me here to Briarbush after the explosion because if I ever write a book about the creepy things I've seen here or talk to the media about it, no one will believe me, considering that I'm certifiably insane. Which is ironic, because I never lie."

Benny's life had so well prepared him to talk with a functional madman that he felt he was in the lap of destiny. "I've never heard of the Church of Earth."

"I formed it," said Brother Sunshine. "I am the pope, the only clergyman, and at the moment the sole adherent of the faith. But if the ETs from the planet circling Regulus ever break through to us, my church will swell in numbers and be the spiritual army that saves Earth from domination."

"That's a big responsibility."

Brother Sunshine shrugged. "Someone has to do it."

The night Bugboy had been killed, when Benny and his friends had been hiding in the mountain pieris, Mrs. Baneberry-Smith had referred to Regulus technology when talking to Agent Kimball.

"Brother, you said that you were sent here to stand watch 'after the explosion.' What explosion?"

"The headmistress was conducting an experiment, and something went wrong. She blew up herself and seven students. The ISA, which secretly owned Briarbush Academy, sent the remaining students home—those who had not been blown to bits—and fired the staff and closed the school forever. I don't know what they did with the bits. I guess they scooped up the bits and sent those home, too."

"When was that?"

"Four years ago next Tuesday."

A chill climbed Benny's spine. "The boys who were killed. Do you know their names?"

"I knew them once, but now I'm not so sure. I'd have to go through the files in the administration vault."

"Do the names Mengistu Gidada and Jurgen Speer ring a bell?"

Brother Sunshine's solemn expression cracked into a smile. "I know those names! I read about them when I was researching the school's recent history. They didn't die in the explosion."

Relief flooded through Benny.

"They must have been very stupid boys. Those two numbskulls ran away into the forest," Brother Sunshine continued. "During a storm. I can't imagine what they were thinking. That's a true wilderness. Sixty-two search-and-rescue specialists set out to bring them back, but no one ever found hide nor hair of those boys. Not a tooth or a fingernail. Neither a decaying nose nor a finger bone. Those two are deader than dead. Probably cougars tore them asunder and ate them and then shit them out a year before the explosion."

THE FATEFUL BULLET

More than fifty years of a charmed existence had not inspired gratitude in Ms. Llewellyn Urnfield. Instead, she felt entitled to fifty more. She'd always gotten everything she wanted. The easy fulfillment of her every desire left her drifting somewhat due south of sanity, afloat on delusions of invulnerability and immortality. With maniacal confidence, she drew a pistol from under the counter, took it in a two-handed grip, and fired point-blank at Harper, no doubt intending to shoot Benny a second later and the google-eyed craggle with his heart in his hand two seconds after that.

Because Urnfield believed in nothing but herself and her power, she had no capacity to accept the existence of a supernatural being even when he performed miraculous feats for her. She dismissed him as nothing more than a close-up magician and card mechanic executing the equivalent of tricks with a stacked deck. Benny could have told her that a person, any person, is never at greater risk than when he or she believes in nothing other than himself or herself. Of course, if he'd tried to convince her of that hard truth, she would have shot him before he managed to say more than *a person is*.

When the pistol appeared, Benny thought the crack of the shot was also the sound of his last chance at happiness crashing to ruin. In the same instant, however, pulses of amber light radiated out of Spike's dripping heart and whirled into Urnfield's eyes. Not only did the crazed woman lock in position, a vicious sneer of contempt frozen on her face, but the bullet also was sidelined. It hung in midair, halfway between the muzzle and Harper's face, its kinetic energy for the moment only potential energy, a pale plume of vapor continuing to mark the progress it had made from the gun.

As Spike retracted his eyes into their sockets and returned his heart to his chest, Benny let out a few syllables of sound alike to the whimpering of a dreaming dog having a nightmare. Then he found words. "Oh God, that was close, too close, the crazy damn witch!"

"It's not done," Spike said solemnly, almost in a whisper.

"What? What're you talking about? You stopped it. You can do anything."

"Look at Harper," Spike said.

Benny turned his head to stare at her as she stood at his side. Like Llewellyn Urnfield, Harper was sidelined. Blue eyes gone wide at the sight of the pistol. Mouth open in a cry of alarm that she hadn't been able to let out. One hand half raised to ward off the shot before it was fired.

On the second barstool, Virginia Woolf, the whippet, was as bespelled as her mistress.

The digital clocks on the ovens no longer counted off minutes. Benny looked at his watch and saw the second hand no longer swept from check to check. When Bob Jericho had been sidelined, when Handy Duroc and Jill Swift were bespelled, time continued its inexorable progress. Now time had stopped for everyone but him and Spike.

"What the hell is this?" Benny asked, the anguish in his voice suggesting that, subconsciously, he knew the answer to his question.

"This is a time-out, Benjamin, a chance to step out of who you have been and into who you can become. A time when even the nicest of nice men must do a hard thing that his heart doesn't want to do but that his mind knows is the *right* thing. As your paladin, I have the power to exempt only you from this spell, not Harper. If you try to move her, you will find you can't alter her position by even as much as a thousandth of an inch. She stands there now, embodying all the weight of the life she has lived and all the weight of the life she might still be able to live if this terrible situation can be well resolved. I can't wind time backward, Benjamin. How I wish I could. But that's beyond my power. Neither can I kill a human being, not even a cold-blooded murderer like Urnfield. That violates sacred craggle protocols. It is forbidden. I can intimidate and terrify and mortify and break a few bones, even have fun doing it, but never kill. I can only sideline the principals in this awful drama, the shooter and the shot, and in fact the entire world, because every human fate impacts every other, so you are all principals in every such drama. Now there's no potential hero here but you."

Although Benny was cold to the bone, sweat beaded on his brow. His hands were clammy. His mind raced; it seemed to be hurtling toward a cliff, an abyss of despair.

He leaned against the kitchen island and reached out with his right hand, as if to block the bullet.

"Think, Benjamin. If the round smashes through your hand, it might be deflected enough to miss Harper—or not. Given the fierce velocity of a bullet leaving the barrel, you are likely to lose your hand. At the very least, you'll never again have full use of it."

"I can live with that if she's spared."

"But she might not be spared. The bullet could pass through your hand and still kill Harper. And whether she is spared or not, you'll never play the piano again. When you were twelve, you found that you were a piano prodigy. That's not a gift to throw away."

"I haven't played a piano in eleven years. I've never had one since Jubal's music room. No time for that with houses to sell."

"Look. Think about this." Spike reached across the island and picked up the book that Urnfield had been reading. He put it down in a different place.

Benny stared at the book.

"You can't move people like dolls, like *things*," Spike said. "People have physical weight but also moral weight. But inanimate objects are of a different order."

Benny turned his attention to the bullet suspended in midair. Hesitantly, he reached for it.

"Think," Spike warned. "Angle it toward the ceiling, and when the instant time-out ends, Urnfield squeezes off another shot, another, another, before even I can reach her and seize the gun."

Benny looked at Llewellyn Urnfield.

"The pistol is fixed in her hand. When she's in a time-out, you can't take it from her any more than you can lift her and move her. This is not a mere sidelining."

The book. The empty dish. The fork. The wineglass. None of them offered Benny an advantage that he could see.

He felt as if he were in a vise invisible, the steel jaws being cranked tighter, tighter. Pressure stressing his skull, compacting his chest. Pain around the heart. Lungs compressed, every inhalation harder to draw than the one before it.

He looked from the wineglass to Spike. "Please."

"This is your turning point, Benjamin. It's not mine. This is the moment where your wisdom matures to equal the other best quality you possess—or doesn't."

"The laws of physics," Benny protested feebly.

"The velocity is in the bullet. So it will remain, even if to a degree diminished."

Reaching uncertainly toward the projectile, Benny said, "This is as much magic as science."

"Hasn't your life shown you that's the truth of the world? The known and forever unknowable are entwined. Quantum mystery lies at the base of all things. Scientists tell us that, down in the quantum level, there is no such thing as matter. It all appears to be as ephemeral as thought waves. This is your moment."

His hand trembled. The adjustment had to be precise. He looked at Harper. So vulnerable. Like everyone. He stilled his hand.

The 9 mm round should have been blistering hot when he pinched it between thumb and forefinger, but it was so cold that he feared it would freeze to his skin when he tried to let go of it. With exquisite care, he turned the slug so that the nose was directed toward Urnfield. He adjusted it ever so slightly, trying to set it on a trajectory above the muzzle of the pistol.

When fate perhaps had been foiled, if ever it could be, Benny looked at Llewellyn Urnfield, horrified by what was about to happen, unsettled by the satisfaction of impending retribution that freed him from the feeling of being crushed in a vise. Retribution was not the same as revenge. It was impersonal and righteous. He understood the difference. And yet . . . Looking at her, though he knew her to be evil, he also knew that she wasn't a monster from another world. She was human, as human as he was, although certainly not humane. "Wait, wait," he said, lest Spike might revoke the spell. Benny tried to imagine what he'd feel and do if Urnfield's face hadn't been contorted in a sneer of hatred and contempt. What if she had looked distraught, anguished about what she was doing? And what if Harper hadn't been precious to Benny? What if Harper had been a stranger or even someone he disliked? But Harper was an innocent, and Urnfield was not. Benny could find no refuge in what-if, no reason to back off from the responsibility that he had shouldered. In the end, the choice to murder an innocent was an inhuman act, and the murderer of an innocent forfeited her or his human rights. How many others had Urnfield murdered either herself or by proxy? There was no virtue in granting mercy to such murderers, and nothing *nice* about anyone who failed to protect the innocent. He put his hands on Harper's shoulders and said to Spike, "Okay, all right, do it."

The instant the spell was broken, as echoes of the gunshot rattled the kitchen, Benny thrust Harper aside, not because he feared the first bullet, but in expectation that another would be fired as the first left the muzzle. Too close to seem other than simultaneous, glass panes shattered in a cabinet door behind him, a consequence of the second shot, even as he saw Llewellyn Urnfield's face implode as she pitched backward with the barstool and fell out of sight.

Harper staggered, kept her balance, and said, "What the *hell*?"

The last green number in the oven-clock readout changed. Time goes on.

Still aboard its barstool, the shivering whippet made a thin sound of distress. *Life* goes on.

Spike's expression conveyed a knowing compassion that combined the tenderness of pity with the dignity of sympathy and the active quality of mercy. He gave Benny one thumb up.

Although Benny's stomach fluttered and his heart knocked hard and his vision blurred, he gave Spike two thumbs.

Adjusting her pink cap, Harper said, "Hey, clue me in. How come not me, but her? What happened to her?"

Having plucked the frightened whippet from its stool, holding it in one arm and against his chest to comfort it, Spike said, "She shot herself. Llewellyn Urnfield has been shooting herself all her life."

BENNY'S RETURN TO BRIARBUSH, PART TWO

When it came to things biblical, Benny didn't know whether he took Revelation seriously or not, but he knew the book claimed that, in the End of Days, the devil would come *down* unto the earth with great wrath, rather than up unto it. Now, over Briarbush, the heavens swelled ever darker and more malignant, as though the depths of Hell had been raised overhead and, when the storm broke, blood would fall instead of rain, or a plague of scorpions.

In the quadrangle, seeming to glow in his white vestments even as the day darkled, Brother Sunshine raised his staff and shook it at the sky, and again he cried, *"Fulgur Prohibeo!"*

"What is that about?" Benny asked.

"I am forbidding lightning to strike us," said the pope of the Church of Earth.

"Oh. Good. Thank you."

Brother Sunshine swept his staff in an arc as he said, "Here they appear from time to time. Not in their full reality, but mere projections."

"Who does?"

"Those who haunt Briarbush but are not ghosts."

"What are they if not ghosts?"

"I believe the headmistress almost opened a way for them to come from their world, not by journeying hundreds or even thousands of years in their ships, but by a more expedient form of transport. You may call it a gate, though it is not a gate, and I wouldn't call it a gate if I were you, because educated people might laugh at you, and being laughed at is a painful experience, as I'm sure you know too well. It's more like a wormhole than a gate. Not a wormhole built by worms, you understand. That is even more ridiculous than calling it a gate. In this context, a wormhole is a hypothetical structure in space-time that connects two points that are separated by an enormous distance in space and time. You may think of it as a tunnel through space-time, although it is not anything as simple as a tunnel. I wouldn't call it that aloud, if I were you, and make a fool of yourself all over again. I believe the wormhole had to be opened from this end, between Earth and some foul planet revolving around Regulus, but Mrs. Baneberry-Smith blew herself up before she quite achieved that breakthrough. I have seen them! From time to time, they manifest like spirits at a séance, shadowy horrors, as though peering into one corner of Briarbush Academy or another from the far side of a looking glass, yearning to be here but unable to pass through the incomplete portal, one final membrane defeating them. That membrane, that lens, is clouded. The Regulons can't be seen in the fullness of their monstrousness. Thank God for that! What can be seen of them would drive me mad if I weren't already functionally insane. I have often seen them! Even seen through a glass darkly, they are hideous beyond imagining."

Benny said, "That's disturbing."

"'Disturbing'?" Brother Sunshine said. "'*Disturbing*? Is that what you said? Did I hear you right? '*Disturbing*?"

Benny's life had been an eighteen-year-long dark carnival aswirl with eccentrics, cranks, freaks, sociopaths, and maniacs—among them Big Al, Grandma Cosima, Mordred Merrick, Bugboy, and Catherine Baneberry-Smith. None had been safely light-years away, held off by an impenetrable membrane. All had been up close and personal. He had survived them. He'd thus far also survived his mother, who perhaps had stabbed his stepfather in an alleyway in

Cairo, Egypt, or hired someone like Omar the chauffeur to stab him. After all that, Benny just couldn't get too worked up about evil extraterrestrials who were grinding their mandibles and stamping their eight clawed feet in frustration because they weren't able to open a gate that was not a gate, travel along a tunnel that was not a tunnel, and conquer Earth.

Nevertheless, he made a concession to placate Brother Sunshine. "Worrisome," he said. "It's very worrisome."

"*'Worrisome*?" The clergyman looked aghast. "'Very *worrisome*'? *It's fucking terrifying!* Do you think my hair was white when I came to Briarbush? It was not! I was functionally insane, but my hair was chestnut brown and beautiful. *What's wrong with you?* You are not a serious person. Get out of here with your 'disturbing.'" In less than a Christian spirit, Brother Sunshine shook his staff at Benny. "Get out of here with your 'very worrisome,' you callow young fool. *Get out!* Go sell whatever it is that stupid, unskilled people sell to make a living. Go sell used cars or gym memberships, while the Earth is ever on the brink of alien Armageddon. Go sell shoes, sell your soul, sell guns to babies, sell real estate that monsters from another planet can build their hives on. *Get out, get out, get out!*"

And so Benny got out of there.

The darkest vein in the sky ruptured, and fierce light burst from it—again, again, again. With those sudden flares came sudden shadows, and the one shaped like Benny repeatedly tried to leap away from him, as though he had embarrassed it. He ran to his Honda as thunder crashed onto the mountain with such power that the fibers of his bones reverberated with it.

As Benny got behind the wheel and started the engine, rain fell in torrents. He switched on the wipers and the headlights, put the car in gear, and drove away from Briarbush, never to return.

On the way south to his motel room in a suburb of Los Angeles, with long hours of driving ahead of him, he didn't want to dwell on memories of Jurgen Speer and Mengistu Gidada and thereby mourn them; he preferred to pretend they were alive somewhere. Instead, he pored through many other moments of his strange and storied life until, south of San Francisco, he began to think about the future. Because he had a bankroll, he didn't need to sell his soul, a transaction to which he was opposed on principle. Even if babies had money and a desire to purchase guns, he would not have sold firearms to infants. Nor was he of a mind to traffic with hive-building monsters if they should ever open a gate-tunnel thing between planets. However, there was something appealing about selling homes to nice people, places where they could raise families, be safe, and be happy in a world where safety and happiness were in short supply.

Seven months later, he had moved to an apartment in Costa Mesa, obtained a license to sell dirt, landed a sweet position at Surfside Realty, under the mentorship of Handy Duroc, and was mere weeks away from meeting Jill Swift. He had turned a page, opened a door to a new life, found a path to prosperity. All was for the best in this best of all possible worlds.

THE GARAGE

So with Harper Harper contentedly ensconced in the back seat in the company of Lily Lapin and Virginia Woolf, they cruised away from the charming cottage that was a shrine to soul-shriveling art in a suburb of San Diego.

Spike said, "With Urnfield dead, Theron likewise, and Oliver Lambert humiliated as well as discredited, the other conspirators who call themselves the Better Kind will scuttle for cover and lie low for a while, waiting to see if the rest of them will be taken down. Like all bullies, they're cowards. Eventually, they'll crawl out of their holes and get on with the destruction they enjoy. They might let you alone, Benjamin. In fact, I think they will. And they better. But there are others like them. Many others. You are and always will be an irresistible target. So we will be vigilant as we get on with your life. Yours and Harper's. It won't be all going to movies and bowling and playing with the cat, if in fact we all agree on adding a cat to the menagerie. There will be crises and dangers, stress and sadness. But because you now possess a wise variety of niceness and will listen to my advice in moments of peril, your risk of being murdered horrifically is much lower than it was."

The origami time-fold trick pleated them from the San Diego area to Corona del Mar, and as they pulled into the driveway of Benny's house, he said, "I like selling homes to people, but maybe I've done enough of that. I mean, I got into it because the pope of the Church of Earth suggested it, and I didn't want to sell guns to babies—or my soul, for that matter—or shoes, or gym memberships. I'm only twenty-three. I'm sure there's something I can do that will be even more satisfying than what I've been doing."

While Spike just stared at Benny, Harper said, "Why would you even consider selling guns to babies?"

"I didn't consider it. I never would. Not even to elementary school kids, let alone to babies. I'm just saying it was suggested by the pope, Brother Sunshine. He was functionally insane, able to do his job, you know, but the second part of 'functionally insane' is 'insane,' which I always kept in mind."

As Spike used the remote to put up the garage door, Harper said, "I can see I've got a lot of catching up to do, learning all about your past."

Fat Bob—also known as Bob, officially Robert Jericho—stood in the colorful, illustrated casket, glazed eyes open wide, taking slow and deep and steady breaths. To anyone awakened to the truth of craggledom, Bob might have been mistaken for a craggle in training.

Benny, Harper, and Spike gathered in front of the detective, who had been sidelined about seven hours.

Spike said, "What is this man to you, Benjamin?"

"He's my friend. My only remaining friend—before tonight."

"And to you?" Spike asked Harper.

"My friend and mentor. He's nice but not too nice. He's almost smooth and halfway to blue."

Benny said, "He's wise, wiser than I am or ever will be, but he's never arrogant like those Better Kind people."

"Can he keep a secret?" Spike asked.

"He makes a living uncovering secrets *and* keeping them," said Harper.

"Does he have any serious faults of which you're aware?"

Benny nodded. "He makes fun of my hair."

Spike said, "Perhaps making fun of it is his way of advising you to do something about it, in which case that isn't a character flaw but a virtue."

"Huh."

"Did he assist you in choosing the decor of your house?"

"No."

"Did he approve of that terrible chair?"

"No. It was a lovely chair, but he mocked it."

"Did he approve of the Lucite lamp with the white shade?"

"He mocked that, too."

"I like this man," Spike said.

"You've never met him."

"Harper can introduce me to him."

"*I* could introduce you."

"No offense, Benjamin, but he doesn't know the new you yet. He knows the Benny who was in thrall to Jill Swift, wanted to be Handy Duroc, and had not yet given his heart to a rabbit and a whippet. He will take what Harper says more seriously than anything you say."

"I can't argue with that," Benny said.

"Of course you can't. So I have decided to bring him into our little family, explain cragglekind to him, and dispel any disbelief he might have by giving him a demonstration of my unique physical abilities."

"He'll enjoy that," Harper said. "But he didn't have a chance to grab dinner on his way here last evening. When you've done your shtick and stuffed your heart back in your chest, he'll be hungry."

Spike patted his stomach. "I myself am already hungry. It's been a busy few hours."

"Well, then before we wake Bob, we better order in an early breakfast and have it all ready."

Benny plucked his wallet from a hip pocket. "I can put it on my credit card. But the delivery guy usually likes the tip in cash."

"Bob's generous," Harper said. "He tips forty percent."

"Then I'll tip forty," Benny said. "But I only have three hundred in my wallet. I'll need maybe five hundred more."

"Easy peasy," Spike said, counting hundreds off his eternally fat bankroll.

ENGAGEMENT PARTY

As a detective who had investigated scores of women over the years and had conducted scores of investigations on their behalf, Bob understood that gender better than Benny did, and he had a good sense of Harper Harper's taste, so he accompanied his friend to the jeweler's to choose an engagement ring.

The ring delighted Harper. She said yes. To Benny. On that happy occasion, Bob felt the need to advise the future groom not just to hand the ring to Harper but instead to put it on her finger, and Benny was able to execute this maneuver without injury to either himself or his fiancée, or to any bystanders.

Spike planned and paid for the engagement party, for which he booked a table that turned out to be at a restaurant in Scottsdale, Arizona. This was not inconvenient. A friend of Harper's was willing to babysit Lily Lapin and Virginia Woolf. Benny, Harper, Spike, and Bob time-folded to Scottsdale in the Explorer.

Although Harper Harper wasn't a giggler by nature, she giggled a few times during the two-minute trip, while she and her fiancé snuggled in the back seat. As it turned out, her amusement wasn't because Benny proved to be an awkward snuggler, for he was certainly adequate, but because she knew a secret that he did not.

The reservation Spike had made was actually for a private room at the restaurant, where the table was set not for four, but for eight. Although ten years had passed, Mengistu Gidada and Jurgen Speer were instantly recognizable.

Fantasy stories of recent vintage featured fearsome dragons and blood-soaked swordsmen with enormous dirty beards; there was usually a magical object that, if one possessed it, granted dominion over the kingdom or even the entire world, although it often looked like a badly designed Christmas ornament crafted in a Chinese sweatshop. Benny's adventure involved none of those things. In nearly every such story these days, which extended to as many volumes as the author could write in a lifetime, an enormous cast of characters produced protagonist after protagonist, each of whom was, in his or her turn, vigorously beaten to death or hacked to death or burned to death or stoned to death or tortured to death, or a combination of the above. In Benny's story, the people who were nice and sane had managed to survive unscathed at least until this emotional moment in a restaurant in Scottsdale, Arizona.

Although Jurgen and Mengistu were only twenty-four and twenty-five, they owned the restaurant. It was an enormous success. Jurgen managed the operation, and Mengistu served as the highly creative chef. On escaping Briarbush, they had been taken in by Jurgen's nice uncle in Arizona, the one despised by everyone else in the family, who knew how to obtain new identities for them and who raised them as his own, eventually financing their enterprise. They would soon open a second restaurant.

Bob Jericho's skill as a detective and Spike's special powers, when combined, resulted in their spending more time at long, lavish lunches than they had needed to find Benny's former schoolmates.

The evening was rich with emotion, about which no one felt the least awkward. There was much laughter, as rarely occurs in those stories involving blood-soaked swordsmen with enormous dirty beards, because Benny and his friends weren't contesting with one another to rule a kingdom or be the first to rape and subjugate a princess, and none had recently—or ever—had a limb amputated by a dungeon master and cauterized by fire.

Mengistu's guest at dinner was named Stone, and Jurgen's guest was named Mace. To the best of Benny's recollection, this was the first time he had been in a room where approximately 38 percent of those present were seven feet tall. Neither Stone nor Mace looked anything like Spike; however, when the evening came to an end and the restaurant staff were gone, when the group of friends had the premises to themselves, it was no surprise that the three tallest of those assembled knew all the words to the Craggle Anthem. They sang it with such feeling that there was not a dry eye in the house, though all eyes remained in their sockets.

WEDDING DAY

In spite of the eventful nature of Benny and Harper's brief courtship, there isn't much story value in the wedding. Weddings are all alike, except for those where gunfire breaks out or the groom's first wife from whom he was never divorced shows up uninvited with their seven children. This ceremony wasn't one of those exceptions. Here's the church; here's the steeple; open the door, and see the people. The ring bearer was a whippet. Spike served as best man. Harper's dad gave her away, and her mother was the maid of honor. Robert "Fat Bob" Jericho fulfilled the role of bearer of the witness rabbit. Though the minister wasn't as colorful as Brother Sunshine, he was sane and threatened no one with a shepherd's staff.

Vows were taken. Bride and groom were pronounced husband and wife. Happy tears were shed. Organ music accompanied the couple as they walked the long aisle through the nave, basking in the smiles of their friends. They were almost to the narthex when a bogadril manifested from the Dark Dimension, a creature so hideous that mere words could not describe it adequately. Even if a description could be cobbled together that did justice to the monster, the image thus conjured in the mind would result in a significant percentage of readers suffering nervous breakdowns or spiraling irretrievable into a depth of madness usually endured only by characters in the fiction of H. P. Lovecraft.

Many might have perished and the church might have been damaged beyond repair if there hadn't been *three* craggles in attendance. The minister, organist, Harper's parents, and the guests standing in the rows between pews were at once sidelined. The presence of a single craggle would have resulted in a fierce and extended battle that would have been thrilling to a ten-year-old but tedious to almost everyone else. The bogadril was surprised to find a trio of craggles where it expected one. Instead of a glorious battle, imagine this: three big men chasing a scurrying cockroach, trying to stamp on it before it could find a crack in which to hide. The bogadril wasn't anything like a cockroach, and it was gigantically bigger than any beetle, but the action was pretty much as herewith suggested. No one attending the wedding was injured. None would have a memory of the incident. The invader was dispatched in less than three minutes, but those who had been sidelined needed to remain in that condition for almost an hour while Spike, Stone, and Mace swept up the bogadril debris and hosed the slime out of the church.

The wedding reception proved to be everything that a wedding reception ought to be. The celebration unfolded in a ballroom in a five-star hotel, with an open bar and food that even Mengistu Gidada found impressive. The bride was beautiful, and everyone complimented Benny on his new haircut even when they weren't sure about it. So many gorgeous flowers had been incorporated in the event decor that those guests with serious allergies needed to resort to double doses of their medication. The place settings at the tables did not, not, not include little cups of those almonds in hard-candy shells that are usually provided at wedding receptions, the absence of which contributed to everyone's good mood. There was much laughter and reminiscing, toasts raised and drank, plus dancing to the music of Tyler Pinkflower and the Cooltones, an LA group that Spike had known about and booked.

The music was so exceptional in fact that Benny felt compelled to take a turn at the piano, freeing Tyler Pinkflower—the pianist and lead vocalist—to concentrate on his singing for three numbers. This was the first time Benny had sat at the keyboard since he had lived in the shadow of Mordred Merrick. Something magical happened, as you knew it would. Benny, now too old to be a child prodigy, was a more gifted pianist than Tyler Pinkflower. He inspired the other four musicians to play at a level they had never quite achieved before, and Tyler brought greater power and deeper emotion to his singing. As was always the case in such moments, the wedding guests at first mockingly applauded the groom as he sat at the piano, for they assumed he'd drunk too much and would make a fool of himself, but then they quickly realized he was a terrific pianist, and soon everyone was on the dance floor, totally rocking out.

We have all been conditioned to expect dramatic developments like that to unfold in a certain way, and those expectations were fulfilled when Tyler and Benny and the boys launched into the next number, a profoundly stirring piece like something the Righteous Brothers might have recorded. The jubilant dancers quieted and stood very still, gazing at the band, in a condition of wonder, gripped by a suspicion that they were present at a moment of pop-music history. And of course they were. The third number was so fabulous that it made the first two sound like elevator music, and those assembled stood in awe, almost bovine in their fixation: Really, it was like when scores of cows in a field face the same direction, their heads raised, having ceased chewing their cuds, hypnotized by whatever it is that entices cows into a mass trance. If it had been a scene in a movie, the camera would have moved in for a close-up of the bride, whose eyes would be shining with tears of joy, her face a portrait of love and pride for her special husband. When the third number ended, you'd expect the crowd to soar out of the trance and erupt into wild applause, which they did. What else would you expect them to do—torch the place, murder one another in a mad ecstasy? Benny and Harper's story was not that kind of story, which is something you can get anywhere these days but you can't get here. You would expect Tyler Pinkflower and Benny to hug, which they did, each aware that he had found a spiritual brother and that something big was going to happen for them.

After that, the fabulous wedding reception became even more fabulous, because there were still no almonds in hard-candy shells being forced on attendees *and* they knew that Benny, Tyler, and the Cooltones would come up with a new name and soon be the biggest stars on the music scene. These were not stupid people that Harper and Benny invited—mostly Harper, as she had far more friends than Benny did. The people in that crowd were smart and tuned into the culture, and they knew where a meeting of talents like this would inevitably lead. They knew that, by Monday, Benny would realize he could write great pop music. They knew that, by Wednesday, the band would listen to him play his first two compositions, and they would just about go nuts. If you'd been there, you would have known it, too. By Friday, Benny would realize he could sing as well as he could play and would do backup vocals for Tyler. Robert "Big Bob" Jericho would be their manager, tough and incorruptible. Spike would ensure that organized creeps motivated by ideology and the deranged loners who make celebrities' lives dangerous wouldn't inflict so much as a pinprick on any member of the band. Every guest at the wedding reception intuited all that and much more, and they were happy for Benny and Harper even if, in some cases, a little envious.

One thing few at the reception expected was that, during the new band's first rehearsal, Harper would sing along on a number and reveal a spectacular voice, although if you think about it, there were only two ways the marriage could go.

First, as Benny and the boys became ever more successful and were on the road touring, some emotional distance would open between him and Harper; he'd be tempted by adoring women and drugs. Benny was too nice to cheat on Harper; so there was nothing to worry about in that regard. Spike would strongly advise against spiraling into drug use, and it would be difficult to imagine Benny doing cocaine and heroin and that sort of thing. On the other hand, Benny was human; therefore, it could not be ruled out that, like two other losers in the past eighteen hundred years, he might ignore the craggle's advice and engineer his own horrific death.

The second option was that Harper would join the band, husband and wife bonding even tighter because of the respect they had for each other's talent and because of shared experiences. So that was what happened. Nothing other than that could have happened, really, for their story wasn't a soap opera like *A Star Is Born*.

Moreover, considering that Benny witnessed the cold-blooded murder of his father, endured psychological warfare waged by his maternal grandmother, survived both Bugboy and Mrs. Baneberry-Smith, was abandoned by his mother, weathered the destruction of his real-estate career, accepted the smashing of his favorite chair, put up with much mockery regarding his hair, and abided through so many other troubles and offenses, there would be no point to a fantasy adventure that ended with him being hacked to death by a blood-soaked swordsman with an enormous dirty beard or in any other way than happily married to Harper.

Fantasies can become realities. There's no reason that craggles couldn't be as real as trains and cranes and girls named Jane. That is a conclusion to which the discoveries in physics over the past century lead us if we have the imagination and courage to think through the evidence.

As Spike the craggle observed in Llewellyn Urnfield's kitchen, and as he went on at some length yesterday at lunch: On the quantum level, down at the subatomic bottom of everything, there is no such thing as matter. Matter as we know it—everything from rocks to water, bone and blood, flora and fauna, everything, everything—arises out of nothing tangible. The universe appears to be woven from something as immaterial as thought waves. Everything is at base impalpable, discarnate, transmundane. Furthermore, the smallest and most fundamental subatomic particles seem not to exist until they are observed in the process of human inquiry. And so it seems that, as a reader collaborates with an author to envision the story being told in a novel, so all of us collaborate with some author unknown to imagine what occurs in our world as it is and as it will become. In that case, to at least some extent, to a degree we cannot know, we possess the power to weave the lives that will bring us happiness if we're wise enough to be nice, but not so nice that we're foolish, and if we realize that our free will and creativity should be used with humility rather than to acquire power to oppress others.

Not least of all, if bitten and injected with the accumulated knowledge of an extraterrestrial species millennia more advanced than human beings, we must never succumb to the temptation to use it. As Spike noted at breakfast this morning, no knowledge of that kind could bring us greater happiness than the recognition of the truth that, as coauthors of reality, we can revise ourselves so that we are characters who have the courage to endure. Furthermore, we can write a life after this one that is better yet and that is no less real than the current world where matter is both a hard fact and an illusion, where at the bottom of everything we find only something like thought waves forever weaving.

ABOUT THE AUTHOR

International bestselling author Dean Koontz was only a senior in college when he won an *Atlantic Monthly* fiction competition. He has never stopped writing since. Koontz is the author of *After Death*, *The House at the End of the World*, *The Big Dark Sky*, *Quicksilver*, *The Other Emily*, *Elsewhere*, *Devoted*, and seventy-nine *New York Times* bestsellers, fourteen of which were #1, including *One Door Away from Heaven*, *From the Corner of His Eye*, *Midnight*, *Cold Fire*, *The Bad Place*, *Hideaway*, *Dragon Tears*, *Intensity*, *Sole Survivor*, *The Husband*, *Odd Hours*, *Relentless*, *What the Night Knows*, and *77 Shadow Street*. He's been hailed by *Rolling Stone* as "America's most popular suspense novelist," and his books have been published in thirty-eight languages and have sold over five hundred million copies worldwide. Born and raised in Pennsylvania, he now lives in Southern California with his wife, Gerda, their golden retriever, Elsa, and the enduring spirits of their goldens Trixie and Anna. For more information, visit his website at www.deankoontz.com.